BLOOD FOR BLOOD

BOOK TWO OF THE DISC CHRONICLES

MADELEINE MOZLEY

For Mom. Love you more.

PART 1

CAPTIVE

CHAPTER ONE

———

RAT TAIL PUSHED HIS WHEELBARROW OVER THE DRY, cracking earth, the wheel squeaking rhythmically as he avoided cacti and short sand dunes. The sun warmed his leather beanie —which he'd retrofitted into a balaclava with scratch pieces of fabric stitched from ear to ear—but the wind was starting to pick up. There was a sharp chill to the air, a sign that the cold season had arrived. The nights were bitter these days, and he intended to finish his work long before the sun surrendered to the horizon.

His wheelbarrow was already half-full of rebar, bolts, and undamaged cinder blocks. A good haul so far. He reached a pile of rubble. To an untrained eye, it would look like nothing more than a trash heap caked with sand. He set the wheelbarrow down next to it and unslung the square shovel strapped across his back. After a quick adjustment of his worn leather gloves, he gripped the shovel and jabbed it at the base of something that poked out from the pile like an arm jutting from a stack of corpses. He unearthed the long coil of copper and added it to the wheelbarrow with satisfaction.

This was not trash, but that's what they called it—those people cowering in The Disc, sheltered snot wads who'd never been outside its walls. The women he paid for at Screws & Gears called him a dumpster diver. Little Rat Tail, burrowing in ancient garbage. But he, like most other Scavengers, took pride in what he did. Someday, it would make him a rich man.

If he could find something Thallium wanted for his collection, he might be able to make a leap toward retirement. Something shiny or a whole book. The Principal always paid for books in decent condition, extra if they had hard covers. And if Rat Tail found something to add to his majesty's machine collection, he'd get paid for sure. Maybe enough for a permanent room at Screws and the best of the women—Rivet with her brown pigtails and the little mole in the shape of a heart on her chin. For him. Just for him.

"Rat!"

Rat Tail hissed softly and turned—Frederick knelt on a slight rise with a scope pressed against his eye as if he thought himself a grand explorer. Beside him was a Keeper, his striped robe abandoned for more practical travel attire. Thallium had begun requiring his Scavengers to work under protection due to The Disc's current reputation in the Open. The Keeper had a rifle under his tan cloak, the barrel peeking out beneath the hem.

"We need to hurry through this corridor," Frederick continued. He tossed the scope to the Keeper, who caught it and continued surveying. "I have to make a sweep of the grasslands before we cut west for Non. At this rate, we'll be stuck out here for an extra day and night. Onward with haste!"

Rat Tail just grunted in response. He liked working alone, a single man in the wide outlands. It was safer that way, no matter what Thallium thought. He could cast a drop cloth over his wheelbarrow and skitter under the lip of a boulder if

Marauders happened by. Partners were liabilities, and partners that didn't respect him were dead weight. He'd left them in crags and caves before, and once out in the sun with a leg pinned by a steel beam. He'd walked away from that one with regret. That steel would have bought him a month of dinners at the Storehouse.

But the Principal made his Scavengers go out in pairs now. "Increased accountability," he'd said. They'd drawn straws, and he'd ended up with the worst of them all—Frederick, with his stupid fox scarf and that khaki top hat with fur earflaps, both just begging for someone to steal them. Or destroy them. Either would make Rat happy.

Even though he was stuck with Frederick—something he planned to remedy soon for the sake of his own safety and sanity—it was better than being in The Disc right now. People there were starting to get twitchy. Strange how, for as long as Rat had been in the city, very few citizens had wanted to leave the safety of its walls, yet once the option to do so was taken away, everyone started craving the Open. It wasn't the Open itself they wanted, of course. When they could walk through the door, they didn't care to. But now that the door was sealed? They were trapped, and they felt like it. It was the *freedom* to leave that they wanted, even if they would never have the guts to actually go through the front gate.

The city was locked down, trade shut off. The farms had harvested what they could and stored it for winter, but it wouldn't be enough. Without trade in the cold season, people would starve. That was a fact, and it spread through bars and alleys like an icy whisper, breath from the ghosts of people who'd be dead come spring. Already, theft and street violence were picking up. There was talk of going outside and taking chances there, of elaborate plans with rope and pulley systems to get over the wall or slowly digging underneath it after nightfall. They were still fantasies, but they wouldn't be for much longer, and people were going to die as traitors for attempting to violate the Principal's lockdown.

Nobody was allowed in or out, not even Resource Seekers. But that was good for Rat. Thallium still let some Scavengers out, those who had brought him something valuable in the past, and he was one of them, along with Frederick. The Principal even gave them keycards to let them come and go from The Disc through an underground entrance near the Main House, a door that a privileged few knew about. Each Scavenger pair just had one keycard to share and were sworn to keep its existence a secret. Nowadays, people would kill for that card.

He took a break from moving refuse to pat the keycard through his shirt where it hung against his chest. He'd have to take care of Frederick before nightfall when the keycard was supposed to change hands. Too risky to act without the key around his neck. Fully ignoring Frederick's request to hurry up, Rat resumed his work.

Rat believed that it was a shame to waste crises, and he would make good use of this one. The Principal had a weapon —his Keepers-turned-goons had said so when they had too much Yellow Fever at the bar. He was going to use this weapon to become ruler of this whole stinking scab of a desert. Cheers! Rat wanted a piece of that, and if he stayed on Thallium's good side, he just might get it. Little Rat, with his tiny nose and crooked teeth, bald head at thirty—he'd be a king.

He heaved a section of drywall off the pile with his shovel, and it thudded on the ground. After the dust settled, something glittered on its surface. He leaned his shovel against the wheelbarrow and fell to his knees to pick up a delicate silver bangle, thin and remarkably unbent.

Two red-orange stones were set on either side of a larger blue stone in the middle that was veined with gold. He blew on them to remove some of the dust. His breath caught—turquoise *and* coral. Perfect condition. It might not buy him retirement, but it would buy him Rivet's exclusive attention for a week straight.

Frederick's approaching footsteps crunched through the rubble behind Rat. "Time's up! Pack it away. We need to get moving."

Rat kept his back to Frederick and slowly reached for the folding knife in his breast pocket. "I don't take orders from you, de Bourgh."

"Oh come on, friend! I'm running behind. Just need to make up for some lost time, that's all."

As Rat turned to face him, he held the bracelet up high to distract Frederick as he moved the knife down to his hip. The Keeper was still surveying the horizon, distracted, clueless.

Frederick's eyes grew large. He took a loupe from the pocket of his pants and held it up to the bracelet. "Magnificent piece! That turquoise—powder blue with a gold matrix. Rare indeed!"

Rat flipped open his knife, careful to avoid touching the paralytic coating the blade. "Too bad the coral's faded," he said as he raised the knife for a swipe at the exposed flesh of Frederick's hand. But before he could strike, something hit the back of his knees hard. He went down shouting and flipped onto his back to face his assailant.

A woman stood there, holding his shovel aloft, her full, tanned chest taking in the sun. She moved the shovel to one hand and tugged her dusty scarf off her face with the other to reveal teeth like shards of dirty glass and wild, dark hair.

Rat Tail could hear the sounds of a scuffle behind them where the Keeper had been, but he was too terrified of the woman to take his eyes off of her. He expected to hear a rifle shot. But nothing. Only a thud as something heavy hit the dirt, then the whistle of the wind.

"Please," cried Rat Tail. "I'm just a Scavenger. A shit-sifter."

To Rat's surprise, she ignored him and addressed Frederick, "You're late."

"I apologize," Frederick replied. "I've been saddled with the irksome burden sprawled on the ground before you, as well as Thallium's babysitter. Believe me, I did try to reach our meeting point on time."

Rat sat up, outrage driving him to action. "You were going to betray me, de Bourgh? Sell me as a slave? We were partners!"

The woman spat at him with a skillful shot to his cheek. She scooped up his pocketknife from where it had landed on the ground and sniffed at it. "Reaper jasmine. Potent reduction too." She bent down and held the knife close to his neck. "Who'd you hire to coat this for you? Because I know you don't have the balls or brains to do it yourself."

He tried to wet his mouth with enough saliva to speak, but it had gone dry. The sickeningly sweet smell of the paralytic met his nose. "Please, I don't have anything valuable."

"I disagree." She set the shovel down to grip the thin chain around his neck with rock-hard, icy fingers and yanked. The square keycard attached to the chain came out of the top of his shirt. His only way back into the city.

"That's scrap metal. It's worthless!" He couldn't stop from ending his plea with a squeak of panic.

She tucked the card into her bust. "Worthless? I've been watching you and all of your nasty habits out here. I'll tell you what's worthless." She switched her grip on the knife as if to slash his throat.

"Survivor!" called a masculine voice behind Rat Tail. He looked over his shoulder and there, not six feet from him, was a

Marauder. A tall one covered in honor scars. Beyond him, the Keeper lay still, his neck bent sharply to one side, dead eyes open as if to show he should have seen this coming.

"Please God, no!" Rat scrambled in the dirt, kicking up a cloud of dust with his effort until he backed up against the rubble pile in which he'd found the bangle. The bangle! He still clutched it in his hand. "Here!" He held the jewelry up. "Take it and leave! I'm begging you!"

The Marauder's gaze cut straight to Rat's core as he approached. Scars crawled across his brow, down his temple, even under his eyes. They were everywhere. The dirt crunched beneath his skin boots when he squatted across from Rat. He took the bangle from his palm, pinching it between two of his big fingers as if it were a single hair. He tossed it to the woman.

"Do you have to?" Frederick asked tentatively.

Rat Tail didn't understand the question, but then realized it wasn't directed at him.

The woman closed the knife and pocketed it with the bangle. "Yes," she replied as she grabbed the shovel from the ground on her way to the Marauder's side. She wasn't much taller standing than he was squatting in the dirt.

"But you got what you needed. He's going to die out here anyway," protested Frederick.

"Don't be so sure," she replied with a sneer that displayed her horrible teeth. "It's slick little ones like him that always find a way to slither on. We can't risk him reporting us to The Disc, card or no card."

Frederick started, "But I—"

"Go for a walk, Freddy. This won't take long," said the woman.

Frederick looked like he was going to puke but did as she said and headed toward the hill he'd been scouting from earlier.

Once Frederick was gone, the Marauder hesitated to move,

and Rat Tail thought he saw pity in his eyes. Hope started to well up in Rat's chest, urging him to speak. "You wouldn't hurt an unarmed man. It's not honorable, right?" He hesitantly pointed a skinny finger at the Marauder's scars.

That brought a chuckle from the Marauder's chest, and the humanness of the sound eased some of the tension in Rat's muscles. "Haven't had any honor for years now."

"Enough. Back up," said the woman. She hoisted the shovel overhead and positioned it for a downward swing at Rat's face.

Rat Tail braced himself as his bladder let go.

"Wait," said the Marauder. He stood and took the shovel from the woman.

"Yes! Thank you!" squealed Rat.

The Marauder spoke to the woman, "This is beneath you."

Cold wind rustled the scarf wrapped around her neck and sent chills along Rat's exposed skin. "Just because I don't wear the markings doesn't mean I haven't done the killing," she said. "Nothing's beneath me."

"It doesn't have to be that way anymore. I'm here now." He squeezed her elbow.

Rat Tail started to stand. "Thank you, thank you, sir. I'll just go—"

Before he could finish, the Marauder choked up on the shovel, spun gracefully, and with one swift strike against the back of his head, everything went dark for Rat Tail.

The gray fabric of the tent billowed, pulling taut against the tie-downs in the thrashing of the afternoon breeze. It was a frigid wind, and Caster knew that outside the tent, it would make any unshrouded eyes sting. He also knew that the weather would worsen in the coming weeks into a cold that burned bare skin like fire. Snow was possible, but never promised, and there was a good chance that the whole season would be an empty, fruitless freeze that dried out the skin far more mercilessly than the heat of summer. The Disc hadn't seen a truly harsh winter in three years, and it felt different already this year, as if it were planning to make up for those seasons in which it had slept. The extremes of the desert, products of the proper world ending centuries prior, were vengeful things.

Caster's breath turned to hot condensation against the cloth covering his nose and mouth, wetting it and making it stick. He tugged it loose with his gloved hand and continued to wait for the two visitors that were already four minutes late. One more minute, and he'd leave. Late men couldn't be relied upon.

The two intimidating figures standing on either side of him were likewise covered head to toe. They both wore black balaclavas, and while Gavel concealed his eyes with wraparound sunglasses, Six wore antique flight goggles that probably cost more than he made in six months. One of the perks of keeping rich women company in The Disc and across the Open. The Assassin had murdered more hearts than people, and he'd murdered a lot of people.

Caster let his eyes show between the folds of the scarf around his head, but only barely. He wanted the recruits to see his eyes, grasp the seriousness in them. What they were doing here was important enough to kill and die for, and these recruits were likely to do both by the end.

Caster, Gavel, and Six wore thick foil strips around their ID bracelets—Freddy swore it would block the bracelets' signaling capabilities. If Thallium or another bigwig tried to ping one of their locations during private business such as this, they'd get no response. They'd just think they were in a thick-walled building. He'd guaranteed their secrecy. Hard to believe, but none of them had been questioned about their whereabouts yet.

Gavel looked at his watch, then over at Caster. As Caster was nodding for them to leave, he heard two sets of footsteps approach the outside of the tent flap.

"Are you open?" It was a young male voice, and Caster sighed at the way it cracked.

Vee stood from her stool behind a table showcasing her colorful glasswork. She shuffled over to the entrance, and her baby blue robes caught a breeze sneaking under the tent. She shivered and muttered something in Japanese before reaching the flap.

"Closed. Come back later," she said through the fabric.

The men on the other side whispered to one another, and Caster's Scout hearing picked up every anxious word as they argued about whether or not they should just leave. On Caster's right, Six dragged his hand over his goggles and down his face as he shook his head.

"Um," tried the pubescent voice again, loud enough for everyone in the tent to hear this time, "I'm looking for some amber. Do you have any brooches?"

Vee looked over at Caster for a yes or no, and he nodded. She pulled back the tent flap. In walked two young men. The first had the lanky stature of a kid who desperately needed to grow sideways, and he whipped his gaze around the tent until it landed on Caster in the back corner. A goofy smile spread across his face. The other man was a few years older and far more serious, almost skeptical. His gait was tired, that of someone who was training regularly, and his swollen nose said he'd likely lost a fight less than two days ago. They approached Caster.

Six stepped in front of them. "Weapons on the ground," he said, voice muffled by his balaclava.

The older one hesitated, hand hovering over the short, rough-hewn trench club at his belt. He'd probably made it himself. His companion nudged him with his elbow as he tried to peek around Six at Caster, that smile tugging up farther on one side as if pulled by a hook. The older guy unstrapped his weapon and placed it on the ground.

"You too," Six said to the kid.

"I'm not armed," he said.

"Then you're a dumbass," said Six.

The kid's smile deflated. Caster cleared his throat, and Six stood back in his place on Caster's right. The two men approached, and Six held up five fingers. "Five minutes. No more."

For a few seconds, they just stood there, and the only sound was Vee humming a dissonant tune behind her table of glass as she polished a piece of onyx.

"Are you," started the kid, "really Tyr?" He whispered the name as if it were a sacred title.

"Yes. Who are you?" said Caster.

"I'm Trevor. This is my big brother, Javen."

Javen looked Caster up and down, almost making a show of it.

"You got a thing for men?" asked Six. "Because if so, he's only moderately good looking under all those big strips of bedsheets. Hunky enough, but not nearly as pretty as me. And unfortunately for you, both of us are of the hetero persuasion."

Javen snorted, but he stopped staring. "Sorry."

"Why did you come?" asked Caster.

Trevor opened his mouth to speak, but Javen put his hand on his shoulder and said, "My brother feels we should join you. I'm beginning to think he actually believes you're a god. I guess I want to decide for myself."

"I'm not a god. Far from it. If that's all you've come for, then our meeting is over."

"No! That's not why we came," said Trevor, bursting out from under his big brother's grip. "We want to fight for you."

"And why is that?" asked Caster.

Trevor hesitated. He looked as if he were unsure of how to answer, like Caster was testing him and he was afraid he'd get the question wrong. Smart kid.

"Thallium has to go," Trevor finally said. He glanced at his brother, waiting.

Javen shuffled his feet, then slowly nodded. "Everyone's talking about what he did to those people in Hallund. Nothing's keeping him from doing the same thing in The Disc. Or where our parents live in Non."

"And he's losing it up here." Trevor tapped at his temple, clearly emboldened by his older brother's speech. "We're going to die locked behind these walls. Our neighbor already did; she couldn't get medicine to fight an infection in her foot. Doc tried to save her. Didn't work. We used to get herbs from Non—our folks grow them—but we need more."

"And more nopales, hoppers, preserved fruit, beans," Javen added. "My buddy works in agro and said we've already eaten half of our winter stock of local crops, and that's with being at half rations. If we don't trade, we'll all starve. Unless the Keepers get us first."

Caster's ears perked up at that. He'd noticed that many of Thallium's Keepers were far less formal than they used to be, no longer holding their posts at the Main House and government buildings as they were supposed to. Some sauntered down Diameter in their robes and clearly on duty but with no particular destination.

"What have you heard about the Keepers?" Caster asked.

Javen dropped his volume. "They're going after people,

especially from our neighborhood on the north side. They feel like it, they mess with them. And not just women." He choked on the next words, unable to physically get them out.

This rumor was new. And by the scowl on Javen's face, it was more than a rumor.

"Are people reporting these incidents? To Internal Peace-keepers?" asked Caster.

Javen laughed sardonically, and Trevor answered while his brother attempted to compose himself. "If someone reports it, nothing happens. And the IPs are a total joke. I mean, they've always been a joke, but now they're drunk by morning. And those're the ones who *haven't* already pawned their uniforms for gambling credits."

"We want to take Thallium out," Javen cut in. He squared his shoulders. "My question is, what would we be replacing him with?"

"You're right to ask that," said Caster. "The only definite role I will play in the future of our city is removing Thallium. His replacement is a separate issue, one that will go to the people. Therefore, ask yourself how *you* would like to see this place ruled and by who. It will be for you to decide. But our meeting here today is to pick sides: ours or Thallium's. That's your only task right now."

Caster searched their eyes—Trevor's lit up, while Javen's were like the inner workings of a clock.

"We want to fight for you, if you'll have us," said Javen at last.

"You are welcome." Caster took the bowie knife from his belt. "Step forward. Raise your chin." Javen obeyed. Caster held the blade to his throat. "You do not fight for me. You fight for what is better: justice, innocence, and a life not lived in fear. You will honor these things, bleed for these things, and die for these things. You will guard the backs of your brothers and sisters in arms, and if you betray them, you give me full right to end your life with this blade. Is this your vow?"

"It is," said Javen.

"So be it." Caster pulled the knife back and bowed his head to Javen.

Trevor stepped up next; he swallowed against the blade. "It is my vow," he whispered.

"So be it." Caster sheathed his knife.

"I don't need to tell you that secrecy is of the utmost importance, but I'm going to tell you anyway," said Six, reciting the parting info he always gave the new recruits. This time, he added an extra dose of dramatic intimidation to the words. "Keep your mouths shut. I don't care if you know someone who wants to fall on his sword for Tyr or storm the Main House single-handedly in search of Thallium's head. If you know someone who wants to join our cause, you leave a mark at your designated drop point. I will find you, and then I will find the potential recruit. You will check your drop point daily for orders. You will follow those orders in silence. If the time comes when we gather our forces publicly, you will emerge with glorious zeal. Is all of this clear?"

"Yes, sir," the brothers said together.

"Good," said Six. "We're done here, unless you want to buy some glass."

Javen retrieved his club from the ground. As they turned to leave, Six smacked Trevor lightly on the ear. "Get a weapon, kid."

Trevor slouched. "We can't afford one."

"Then make another crappy club like your brother's."

"That's not necessary," said Caster. He reached into his coverings and unclasped the sheath of a short dagger from his belt. He handed it to Trevor. "Learn how to use it."

Trevor took it with both hands. "Thank you, sir."

"Put it on your belt," ordered Javen. He stuck his hand out to Caster. "He *will* learn how to use it." They shook hands, and the brothers left, though Trevor stole one last glance over his shoulder.

Vee stood and marched over to lash the tent shut. "They never buy anything. I don't know why I keep letting you meet people in my tent. Does no good for my business."

Caster unwound his head coverings. Flyaway blond hair fell out of the braid stretching down the nape of his neck, and he shoved it away from his face. He gently patted near the jewelry concealed under his sleeve. "I buy things."

Vee scoffed. "You bought one thing once." She rattled off something in Japanese. As she sat on her stool and set to work polishing a chunk of green glass, she took to humming.

Six removed his goggles and yanked the mouth of the balaclava down. "I don't know about those two. Did you hear that kid? 'Do. You. Have. Any. Brooches?' Like he was asking out a pretty girl and had already decided he'd failed."

"He's young. Like Adonis. Give him a break," said Caster.

Six groaned. "Another pissant that lives to irritate me."

"I would advise you never to have children," Gavel said to Six. He tugged off his gloves and headgear and laid them on the display table closest to him. Vee glared at him, and he retrieved his things with a barely audible sigh. He tucked them into the satchel slung across his body. "They're fine recruits. The younger one has time to train."

Caster felt the weight of the piece of amethyst tied around his wrist. "Not much time."

Gavel stood straighter, bracing for the debate they'd had half a dozen times over the past two weeks. "Right now, all we have is time. We're not ready to go to war."

"We've been recruiting one or two guys every few days for

a month, and we're no closer to getting her out of there." Caster jutted his chin east toward the Main House.

"We *are* closer." Gavel crossed his arms and looked down for a second, giving Caster a good view of the top of his head as he gathered his thoughts into what would unfortunately be a very sound and logical argument. "Son, successful revolutions are not those of messy passion and impulse, but those built slowly over time. You know even more than I do that the instant we rescue Wren, we will be at war. It won't just be our men suffering, it will be civilians."

Six crossed the tent to Vee and wrapped his arms around her shoulders from behind. "Like this beautiful creature here."

She pressed her cheek to his arm. "You! You buy things. I like you."

Six kissed her head. "I've adorned fine women all over this city with your masterpieces, Vee."

"*Fine* women?" She blindly tossed a cloth to him, which he caught before joining in her polishing efforts.

He shrugged. "Well, parts of them are fine."

"You're a good boy. I don't care if you're skanky." She tapped a blemish on the silver setting he was working on. "You missed a spot."

He got close to her face and breathed hot air on the metal dramatically, then rubbed at it.

Gavel shook his head and returned his attention to Caster. "We don't have the numbers we need yet."

"Fuck numbers," said Caster.

"Language, *Tyr*! Geez. There's a lady present, sort of," said Six.

Vee swiped up at his cheek halfheartedly without pausing in her work.

Gavel lowered his voice significantly, a tactic he'd used to make Caster pay attention since his first childhood tantrum.

"There are three thousand civilians in this city. There are twenty Bodies with six men each, and eighty Keepers—that's two hundred fighters. How many do we have on our side?"

"With those two today, we're up to fifty!" Six exclaimed with exaggerated enthusiasm.

Gavel ignored his sarcasm. "This is a numbers game. We have a quarter of the total soldiers in this city on our side, and not even all of them are in fact 'soldiers.' That's enough for an ugly fight, but it will only end one way. The goal is to have *no* fight, if you remember. To avoid one, our numbers need to be extraordinary."

Caster threw up his hands. "Then we need to find a new way to get them. One half-starved citizen with no training at a time will get us nowhere. And that's exactly where we are right now—nowhere."

Six set aside the silver he'd been polishing. "I feel like I'm beginning to sound like I got kicked in the head with how often I say this, but we should start looking outside The Disc. We know for a fact that Gray opposes Thallium, so let's send someone to Dearborn. Get him on our side. With Openers backing us, we—"

"Gray. Doesn't. Trust. Me," Caster said for what must have been the tenth time. "Not after what happened in his town. And near it." He wondered if Gray had been the one to find the Marauders' bodies that next morning. The lights, the noise—there was no way he hadn't known something was happening just outside his borders that night. Was Wren now one of his targets? Perceived as even more of a threat to Gray and the Openers than Thallium? The way those Marauders had died…Gray would fathom the threat Wren posed. He'd gather strength until he felt ready to meet it, and then? Then he'd come.

"We're running out of people to recruit here, and no

Openers will believe Thallium's own people are out to betray him after he's protected them for so long," said Caster. "Our numbers are as extraordinary as they're going to get."

Neither man responded for a moment. Caster was undeniably right, and he hoped they were beginning to accept that.

"Six has a point," said Gavel at last. "We need to consider seeking help from the outside. Will you let me speak to Asha about it at least? Frederick is due back within two days—he'll have a report on what's going on in the Open. Hopefully he was able to contact Survivor as well."

Caster couldn't hold his dark laughter back. "The woman who tried to kill me! Yeah, let's keep putting our hope in her. And don't forget her new sidekick, the Marauder whose abs outnumber his brain cells. While we wait for that duo, Thallium's Keepers are a half-sneeze away from kicking off total anarchy."

"That's a rumor as yet," Gavel said. "Confirm it first. If it's true, then it's something you can take action against right now. Thallium would never expect you to allow your people to be abused—even 'on his side' as he believes you to be, you can put a stop to the illegal activities of your own Keepers. A couple of the department heads would likely even lend their people to help. Ollie, Head of Agua, has some fit men who could sub in as IPs."

Everything Gavel said was correct. Calculated. And more time-consuming than could be imagined. Caster shook his head. "I can't leave her there any longer."

Gavel grabbed hold of Caster's upper arm and squeezed. "I'm thankful you have your mother's heart, but you also have your father's strategic mind. Today, you need to think like him."

Six nodded at that. "We'll get your girl back, man. Now's just not the time."

"She's not my girl; she's an innocent that I'm responsible

for. I brought her here. It's on me to get her out, and I'm failing her!" Caster pulled away from Gavel and removed the rags that covered his black coat. "I have to go." He stuffed them haphazardly into the pack on the ground and shouldered it on his way out of the back of the tent.

Wind rushed through the alley, caught between the backsides of buildings and the plastic-draped chain-link fence on the other side. Caster lifted the collar of his coat against it. He jogged through the alley until he spotted a lone drone lazily passing high above. He stopped to let it pass. While he waited, he held out his hand to peek at the purple stone tied to the leather cord around his wrist. Raw amethyst of a deep purple, round but still jagged at the edges. The drone was gone, and he quickly pulled the sleeve of his coat back into place and resumed jogging.

He emerged onto Diameter where he paused in the middle of the street to stare down its length. In the distance, the Main House shimmered like one of Vee's shards of glass in the glare of the afternoon sun.

When Wren was a child, Alma told her that people had gone to other worlds to drift among the stars. They wore special suits that let them breathe as they swam through space—there wasn't any air there. It was a boundless place, stretching farther in every direction than anybody had gone or could ever go. Heavenly bodies all around, light and beauty and power beyond human understanding. Danger, too, but it was dangerous here, so that hardly deterred Wren from letting her mind wander there.

With closed eyes, she floated among the stars, greeting them by name, and then imagined herself drifting faster and faster. The stars turned to streaks as she sped toward glories unknown, maybe even to find those who went before her into all that grandness. They might be looking for her too. She soared in her mind—weightless, joyful, and absolutely free.

A flash of light against her eyelids and a whoosh from the door of the inner chamber above roused her. She opened her eyes to be assaulted by green. Every shade of green. As the long bulbs high overhead flickered to life, the shades of green turned paler as the darkness dissipated.

She felt cold, though Eydis assured her that she'd kept the fluid at body temperature ever since her initial submersion weeks ago. How many weeks, she didn't know. Three? Four? The beginning of her time here was a blur—pain, rage, and terror clashing over and over. Like being born and then dying on repeat.

Once they'd achieved some semblance of a routine and Wren had come back to herself, Bug would tell her the date every morning. But one day, she just stopped, and Wren was glad. Time was meaningless, and she feared that knowing how much had passed outside the box would only make her more miserable inside it. She shivered and wrapped her arms around herself but was unable to warm or even cover her body, which was barely concealed by bands of tight, white fabric. She closed her eyes and tried to go back to the stars.

Quick footsteps navigated the upper landing and came down the stairs in a rapid one-two pattern, pausing for just a third of a second on every fourth step. Sweet whistling accompanied the ruckus. Bug. Wren relaxed and opened her eyes.

"Good morning! How did you sleep?" Bug asked. The greeting was the same every day—bright and hopeful, yet awkward. And, just like every other day, Wren didn't reply. Bug seemed to expect this as she didn't wait for any kind of response but moved right on to another topic. "I thought maybe we could take a break from chess because, I don't know about you, but it always makes me feel like some sort of wannabe military strategist. As if I'll ever use the 'skewer-and-pin-windmill-whatever-the-heck' maneuver in real life. Too much stress. So…" she trailed off as she pulled a white box from behind her back and shook it excitedly. Something rattled inside. "I thought we could try dominoes!" She opened the box to reveal rows of small rectangles covered in various numbers of dots on each end. With a goofy smile, she took one out and held it close to the glass so Wren could see. "They're even the multi-colored kind!"

Wren gave a halfhearted smile.

"Oh, right." Bug closed her hand around the domino, embarrassed. "All green to you." She pocketed the domino and set the box on the ground before yanking her straight, dark hair into a high ponytail. It was a habit Wren was well acquainted with, a reflex triggered when something in the inner chamber made Bug uncomfortable.

Bug fixed her hair a lot.

In an attempt to revive Bug's excitement, Wren tapped on the glass with her knuckles and pointed at the little square table they used to play their games.

Some of the sparkle came back to Bug's expression. She adjusted her glasses, which were too big and clashed with her high cheekbones and narrow nose. "You're up for it? Wonderful!" She picked up the box and took a couple of enthusiastic steps toward the table. "I grew up with dominoes. My brother and I played a ton when I was a kid before he moved out—we're ten years apart, and he apparently thought he was much too sophisticated to continue living with his bratty little sister. It was just us until it was just me." She chuckled forcefully. "Anyway, we'd play Mexican Train, Muggins, but our favorite was Chickenfoot. Well, my favorite was Chickenfoot because he slaughtered me at everything *but* Chickenfoot for whatever reason. And he was a sore loser—it was fun to watch what he did when I beat him. He even broke a toe when he kicked a chair leg once. Metal chair, one. Bare foot and its infantile owner, zero."

She dumped the little rectangles out on the table, and they clattered against the metal surface like a stone rainstorm. Bug grimaced and closed her eyes as if expecting to get in trouble, then started turning the rectangles face down so that the little dots didn't show. "Don't tell anyone," she said softly, "but I stole these from the Keepers' respite room. Thankfully, none of them have the clearance to get in here, or even ask about what we do in here, so it's the perfect crime."

Wren whisked her hair out of her face. It was a constant struggle—hair swirled around lazily in every direction in the fluid. The same fluid that fed her nutrients and oxygen, that contained her power within the confines of the box, that made her float without ceasing. She wondered if everything would feel heavy when she got out of the tank and gravity finally regained its hold on her. What she wouldn't give to bear the burden of her own weight again.

"Let's try Chickenfoot," Bug said, snapping Wren out of her thoughts. She must have retreated inward again, because Bug stared at her with an edge of pity as she asked, "What do you think?"

Wren couldn't help but nod.

"I know you don't like it, but I wish you'd use the BCI. It's a little weird, but—hey!" With a snap of her fingers, Bug darted over to the computer console near the isolation unit. She thumped down in the chair and did a dramatic spin toward the keyboard. "Maybe we could pick out a voice that you really like," she said with her eyes to the screen. The interface program reflected in her glasses—Wren recognized the little double-sided arrow logo that always popped up when it opened. "One that feels like *you*, know what I mean?"

Wren began to sigh—a habit she'd yet to break—and as she breathed in the fluid, her chest grew heavy and tight. It hurt every time, more than a regular breathing attempt, and she was terrified that her lungs would burst if she took too much fluid in at once.

"Okay, voice number one." Bug dramatically pressed a key with her finger and then looked at Wren expectantly. "Come on, think something."

"Something," thought Wren. It sounded through the computer's speakers in a foreign accent, the "th" in "something" coming out as an "f." The confusion must have shown on her face.

"Not a fan? I like that one. All right, take two."

"How many takes are we going to do?" thought Wren. A masculine voice, so deep it vibrated, spoke her thoughts aloud. She glared at Bug.

Bug snickered into the sleeve of her lab coat. "I had to. Sorry!"

Wren shook her head. "No more."

"Just one more. One more!" She pressed a key over and over, grumbling to herself. "No, no, definitely no, nuh-uh. Wait!" She pressed a different key a couple of times. "Maybe?"

"How much worse could it get?" thought Wren. It came out of the speakers in a melodic, kind voice. A young woman's voice. Innocent and hopeful.

"Hmm. Nice. You think?" Bug crossed her fingers.

"It's fine," Wren replied. "Can we play now?"

"Absolutely!" Bug pushed with her feet and rolled her chair backward toward the game table. She didn't stop fast enough, and the impact sent dominoes crashing to the ground. "Oops. I'll get those."

"Who else would?" thought Wren. She'd already forgotten her thoughts were now audible and cringed when her words came from the speakers.

"True enough," sighed Bug. But her excitement rebounded as she put the last domino back on the table. "This is a double nine set, and since there are just two of us, we'll draw twenty each." She alternated dragging face-down dominoes toward herself and to Wren's side of the table, setting Wren's on their edges so just she could see the different numbered dots. "The goal of the game is to get rid of your dominoes. If you can't make a match, you'll have to draw a new one from the pile—the 'chicken yard.' Oh! And one important thing is you do *not* want to have—"

"—the double blank in your hand at the end," someone interrupted. "It's worth fifty points."

Eydis peered down from the upper landing. Wren's stomach fluttered as it always did when she arrived—a goddess descended from above to see her. To call her "little one" and remind her of how special she was. She had begun telling Wren about the world of her past. Some things had been happy, but mostly, she talked about the things that had caused pain. "Humanity's deficiencies," she'd called them.

Whenever she told Wren about the dark time before The Fall, she'd also shower her with compliments and marvel at her potential. Comparing, contrasting. Then she'd leave. And so the days repeated. Every visit it felt as though she ripped Wren's heart out to examine it and then put it back when that day's work was done, only to reappear and do it again the following morning.

With each "education session" in which Eydis spoke of the shortcomings of mankind, Wren felt darkness seep deeper into her. It was a burden to her heart, but it excited her insides and the terrible power there that was eager for release. For every bit of darkness that entered, there was an exchange—light was replaced with darkness, hope with hopelessness, and joy with bitterness. So much bitterness that she feared she'd taste nothing else ever again.

Bug stood and faced the landing. "Hello, ma'am. Do we have a session? I thought today was an off day."

Eydis started down the stairs. She wore sandals with thin gold straps that crisscrossed up past her ankles. And her white jumpsuit with the billowy sleeves. Her steps were barely audible, and she placed her left hand lightly on the railing while her right hand held her red notebook tucked into the crook of her elbow. "That's not for you to decide, is it, Bug?"

"Of course not, ma'am." Bug started to drag the game table toward the far wall of the chamber without waiting for the order to do so.

Eydis finally reached the chamber floor. She tossed her notebook on the desk on her way to the unit. "Good morning, little one." Her smile was wide and warm. Wren wished she could wrap it around herself. "I'd like to share another story with you. This will be our last lesson of this kind. I would like to try something new next time—a way for you to experience the past for yourself. Would that be all right?"

The excited flutter in Wren's stomach turned to a wave of nausea. "No. Let me out." It came through the speakers as a weak plea, one she repeated daily even though it was pointless. "I want to see my sister and Caster. Please let me go."

Eydis usually brushed past her request, but today, she nodded slowly. "I know this isn't easy. The problem, my daughter, is that I can't take you out of the box until you are in control of your gift rather than it controlling you. After what happened in the desert, I wonder: what if you had killed your sister instead? Or Caster?"

"I didn't hurt them then; I wouldn't now." She believed it,

but the words felt hollow. She hadn't meant to kill those men in the desert, but from the bits of her memories from that night, she knew she had killed them nonetheless.

"You would never *want* to hurt them, but as you are now, you likely would. In order to control this power, you have to accept it as part of you."

Wren struck the door of the box. "It's *not* me! It's something inside me that I never asked for!" Purple danced around her limbs, turning the fluid black momentarily. She fell silent and tried to calm herself in the midst of her shame.

Eydis stepped up to the unit and patted its surface. "That's exactly it. You don't recognize this piece of yourself. I assure you, it's as much a part of you as the color of your hair or the shape of your lips. Once you accept it, you will be able to control it. I want to help you not only do that, but also decide how you'll use it."

"I don't want to use it. But that's what you want from me, isn't it? The reason you made me—I'm your weapon."

Eydis shook her head sadly as if Wren had just reduced the splendor of the universe to a pinprick of light in the void. "I have hopes for you, but none of my intentions are as archaic as that. You're here to learn history and, in its light, choose a path. This is the only safe place for you to do so. These panels of glass and the fluid held within them are the only things buying you time to think and decide for yourself.

"I will not try to control you. Not like Thallium would, nor how the hurting people on this planet would if they realized what you were capable of. So I'll educate you in what the world used to be like, how it ended, and what our options are for its future. Are you willing to listen?"

Wren had heard different versions of this speech before when she'd refused the day's lesson. It didn't matter how she responded, Eydis would go on talking anyway. After pointlessly hesitating, Wren gave a small shrug.

"Thank you. Let's begin." She began to pace around the lab, as was her habit. "The last time we spoke, we were finishing up the era of the Corporation Wars. The death toll before the treaty was signed reached two billion, which was nearly one fifth of the world's population. Over half of those casualties were civilians robbed of crucial resources, often by an opposing Corp, but sometimes by their own Corp's strategies, which demanded self-sacrifice.

"This created a toxic dynamic in the aftermath—not a true peace, but rather a necessary pause in the Corps' contest for geo states. There would be no states left to win with the rate at which we were destroying each other. Of course, this reality wouldn't matter after the gate accident. Sheer panic dissolves reason. But at that time, due to an independent research group's insistence that there was land beyond our own Earth's to claim, six men and women met and signed a treaty in faith, one that—"

Another wave of nausea hit Wren. The power in her chest listened to Eydis as if with wide eyes and an open mouth, relishing every word of the vivid picture of sin she painted. But her mind recoiled, yearning to return to the vastness of space, and she willed herself to the stars. Even as she divided herself, she could feel the pulsing of her hands illuminating the water with a purple light of longing, a need for release.

The Open's harsh beauty both attracted and humbled Survivor, though such humbling hardly had the effect of making her feel small or powerless. On the contrary, she felt the magnitude of the Open as she felt her own innermost self—

gaping, relentless. The Open *was* her and she the Open. And like herself, she both loved and hated it.

Out here nothing cared about who she was or what she'd done. She was a target like everyone else, and her past was irrelevant. The Open's many weapons—cacti, poisonous predators, hunger, the sun, the heat, and the cold—had earned her respect. Currently, the cold was a merciless shrew, and Survivor couldn't help but admire her a little even as she stole the feeling from her toes.

Survivor lay on her side, aware of Beo's slow, deep breaths behind her in the darkness. His big arm rested over her under the thick blanket she'd stolen from Dearborn weeks before. Another blanket was spread underneath them to make a cocoon of fabric. Heat radiated from Beo, and Survivor wondered how he could have any left when she continually took it from him throughout the night. It was as if there were a fire within him, forever burning but not consuming. She wondered if she'd put it there or if The Gentleman had. Or if they were both responsible.

The stars were brilliant tonight, lighting up the darkness along with their mother, the moon. As much as big questions like the origin of life didn't interest Survivor, she believed that the night sky had been designed with intention. Its intricacies urged her black heart to respond to the light that was above, even if she couldn't put a name to what, or who, was there. Someone was definitely behind it all, but whoever it was clearly had no interest in helping her. Never had. The stars' glow was cold.

The sky was Wren's area of expertise, and even though her incessant descriptions of the shapes in the stars had irritated Survivor in the past, she missed them now. There had been excitement verging on childlike wonder in Wren's voice when she described them and told their stories, stories which were of course nothing more than myths. But even Survivor didn't have the heart to tell her that. It had been nice listening to Wren, especially on absolutely clear nights like this when even those stars that were often too far away to see made an appearance. Tonight, they seemed swollen to the point of bursting.

Survivor remembered several of the shapes, and as she saw a familiar one to the north, she imagined Wren breathlessly telling her about it. *That one's the little bear—he used to be a man named Arcas, but he got turned into a bear and put into the sky with his mother, the great bear. She's that one lower and to the west. Her name's Callisto.*

With a sigh, Survivor turned onto her back, pushing Beo with her right shoulder. He grumbled and rewrapped his arm around her abdomen.

She reached into her shirt and touched the keycard where she'd stashed it in her cleavage. The cold air rushed over her arm as she took the card from under the blanket and held it up, blocking out a small square of the sky. Technology like this was going to control the world someday—was already starting to through whatever the hell Thallium and that woman in white had done to Wren.

Out in the quiet of the Open, there had been a lot of time for Survivor to think about that woman in white. Though it wasn't *her* Survivor thought about, but rather what she'd said in that prison cell in The Disc—her claim she knew Survivor's past, that great blank swath of time Survivor had never been particularly curious about. She'd been far more concerned with just getting her next meal, next breath. She was starting to get curious now. That's what too much quiet time resulted in: space to think.

The keycard started to feel heavy, weighed down by the importance of what it meant for her sister's future. She dropped her hand to rest the card on her chest and, as she did so, recognized the shape of the stars directly above—Cygnus, the swan. Wren liked that one best of all, especially now in winter when the bird flew high above everything else.

"What do you plan on doing with that?" Beo asked, his breath warming Survivor's ear as he lifted himself onto his left elbow to get a better glimpse of the keycard. He was careful not to let cold air sneak under the blanket.

Survivor adjusted the musclebound arm wrapped around her as she tucked her own hand holding the card back under the blanket. "Holy shit, you're massive. Hard to believe I used to wrap my arms around *you*."

"Stop dodging. We've been wandering out here for weeks. Why?"

She turned her head toward him. "You have somewhere else you need to be?"

"No," he said, "but I think I deserve to be let in on what you plan to do, considering our history. Don't you?" His scars caught the moonlight more than the rest of his face, and they glowed silver as he shook his head. The only intentional scar on her body—The Gentleman's mark of a circle cut through by two slashes—glowed in much the same way on her hand.

Beo hadn't spoken with scorn, but the reminder of how she'd run and left him with the Marauders long ago—even as enamored of that life and his growing status in it as he had been —stung far more than the cold. She hadn't known how he'd react, so she hadn't taken the gamble of telling him she was leaving. The desperation to get out had been too strong.

"Escaping without giving you the option to come with me was a fuckup," she said. "I can't undo it."

"No, but you can make sure not to repeat it."

With a quiet growl, she rolled onto her right side so that they were facing each other. Her toes were icy, and she angled her legs to tuck her feet in between his thighs. He hissed an expletive at her but let her warm herself on him. "I *won't* repeat it. But what makes you think I have a plan to share?"

He snorted, and the sound brought with it a memory of him as a gawky teenager when he'd made the same noise at her nearly every day. "Fine, 'plan' might have been too optimistic. But tell me what you want to do, even if you don't know how you'll do it yet."

"What I *want* to do? What I *will* do is get Wren out of that city and disappear."

He grabbed one of her ankles and tugged at it playfully. "Then why haven't we done that already?"

She rolled her eyes. "According to the Scavenger, Caster's ranks are pathetic. Too small to go against his father."

"Sounds like excuses," he said through a yawn. "They're probably afraid of Wren after what they saw her do. Not too eager to take responsibility for her. You can't trust Caster to get anything done."

"I don't trust anyone, but Caster throwing a petty little coup at the right time *would* help cover our escape with Wren. Regardless of who wins, we'll need to disappear."

He hesitated, then asked softly, "You believe that's possible?"

A brisk wind snuck under the edge of the blanket. Survivor shivered past it. "I hid with her for years. Yes, it's possible."

"And you know that's what *she* wants? To disappear?"

Survivor stayed quiet. Before The Gentleman ambushed them that night a month ago, Wren had chosen to go back to the Open with Survivor. But Survivor knew now that there was too much about The Disc that attracted Wren, not the least of which was the idiot prince Caster. However, after exchanging messages with him since Wren's return to the city, Survivor was convinced that Caster really did want to keep Wren safe. And if that were so, he would have to see that she would never be safe with him—he'd tell her to leave. "She'll come with me."

"She might not go quietly, if at all," said Beo. "She might not even be the same Wren from before. We already know she's changed in ways we can't understand."

Ten headless Marauders splayed across the floor of the desert had made the changes in her clear. But truly, Survivor didn't think they were all that bad. "I'm her sister. She'll come with me."

"Say she does. What then? What if you can't hide like you did before and Thallium finds us? Or someone else does? She's infamous, reality turned ghost story in only days because of what she did to the clan. It won't just be The Disc coming for her. We need bodies to fight whoever comes after us."

"Pretty smart, kid. Glad you're not just a pretty face." She kissed the tip of his nose.

"You've been alone for too long. Say what you will about the clans, but they created a support system that works. We'll need a similar system after we get Wren out of there if you want to keep her safe."

"Agreed. Now that it's cold, where might we start?" She poked him in the stomach.

He stared at her, and she could see him processing before realization hit and his eyebrows shot up, sending creases along his forehead to wrinkle the scarification there. "The Dig-in. You've been waiting for the Dig-in."

She made a big "O" with her lips and sent her hot breath out in a showy plume that enveloped his face. "Feels about that time of year, doesn't it?"

A shudder ran through him that shook against her toes. "The clans want to kill you, and when it's warm again, they'll hunt us down to try. Going there would save them the trouble. You sure you're up for that?"

"I'm more worried about whether *you're* up for it." Even though he was intimidating to behold now, he hadn't always been that way. Past the scars, she still saw him as a kid. A kid she'd abandoned. "I don't deserve your loyalty, and what I'm asking you to do is treason."

He laughed. "Let's get one thing straight—you're not my superior. I could smother you in your sleep. Had plenty of opportunities to over the past few weeks. From now on, I'm loyal to those I want to be loyal to. You can be confident that's you. If that changes, I'll let you know."

A breath she didn't realize she'd been holding came out in the cold. "Fair enough."

He rubbed at his face, struggling as they both were with exhaustion and a lack of food and water. "We're going to need supplies if we're going after the Dig-in."

"I know where we can find them. And Freddy's Scavenger friend provided us with plenty of currency."

"Great. Now get your stinking, freezing feet off my legs."

She moved them to his abdomen for good measure, and he let out a string of curses before yanking her part of the blanket away and onto him. The shock of the air on her skin made her gasp, and she kneed him in the back until he relinquished her share of the blanket again.

CHAPTER TWO

It was time for Caster's weekly security meeting with Thallium. The Principal was desperate to know both who had released Survivor from her cell against his orders weeks ago as well as the identities of anyone else who would challenge him, and he expected results.

It would be impossible to discover who had released Wren's sister from isolation—that cell was completely without tech. No keycards, no cameras. Just massive dead bolts and darkness. Anyone with the clearance to know where Survivor was could have done it, and that list included all of the Keepers and anyone above them on the food chain. Thallium's response to that revelation had been a rage-filled spiral early in the lockdown—booze, tirades, and minor property destruction. Two things in particular had the tendency to enrage Caster's father: disrespect and disloyalty. Whoever released Survivor had engaged in both.

As for finding threats from within, that was trickier to negotiate. Caster had no intention of turning himself or any of his co-conspirators in, which left nothing to hand over to appease

Thallium. Caster had avoided suspicion thus far by feeding him just enough information—all of which was entirely accurate. There was a man named Tyr, or at least the illusion of the man, that people were following. Furthermore, citizens were getting restless in the marketplace and other public spaces, although that was as likely due to the lockdown as it was to true rebellion. But Caster never shared anything damning to his cause, which meant Thallium's patience, like a fuse before the boom, was rapidly burning up.

What made it all worse was that Thallium used this time as an opportunity to reunite with his son, trying to salvage some semblance of a relationship. For what purpose, Caster had no idea. The notion that Thallium felt guilty for being an asshole when Caster's mom died and was now trying to make amends was laughable. Caster didn't believe his father wanted a son to mentor and train up as a successor—Thallium might claim he wanted Caster to accept his birthright, but that would imply the Principal was considering a future in which he wasn't in power. More likely, Thallium saw that Caster was generally liked and trusted in The Disc and wanted him on his side to boost his own image as threats outside the walls loomed closer because of what he'd done to Hallund. None of that surprised Caster. He knew how his father operated. What alarmed Caster was that part of him enjoyed being around Thallium again. Nostalgia was a powerful force, or at least that's what Caster attributed the sensation to. Nothing else made sense.

Thallium had sent a messenger to tell Caster their meeting that week would take place by the reservoir, where the Principal had been spending an unusually large amount of time lately. Maybe it was because water was the one resource they would be sure to have all winter, assuming they didn't overdraw from the aquifer and the equipment which recycled their wastewater continued to function as usual. It was one thing the Principal had control over.

The Water Treatment Plant was near the Bodies' training area, but most of it was underground. This helped to keep the water cool in the hot season, warm in the cold season, and, above all, secure. It was more valuable than money—it was life itself.

After reporting to three separate guard stations within the plant on his way through the halls and down the initial flight of stairs, Caster was allowed to proceed on his own. As he descended the last set of stairs, the sound of rushing water reached him. He came out of the stairwell to step on a balcony of hard-packed earth moistened by the air. He headed for the platform positioned above the reservoir, walking next to a waist-high wall on his left that allowed him to overlook the water below. He could see into the depths of the reservoir, at the four different pools twenty feet beneath. The primary clarifier held still water, the next was a moving bed full of rushing water, then the aeration basin with its gentle current, and then the final clarifier like a bookend of still water on the far side. After these pools, the water would rush on to more disinfection before it was distributed throughout The Disc.

Workers in bright red jumpsuits prowled the walkways suspended above and between the pools, checking the color and odor, taking samples, and doing whatever else Eydis had instructed their predecessors to do decades ago when Caster's grandfather founded The Disc.

Caster had enjoyed walking the bridges at the water level when he was a kid—felt like a fantasy land. It was loud right next to the moving bed as if the reservoir were a living behemoth, a monster centuries old crying for release. Somehow it had soothed him knowing that his family had tamed the beast and made the water flow forever, giving people life when they couldn't guarantee it for themselves. The power of a kid's imagination was fearsome to behold.

Over the rushing of the water, Caster heard Thallium's voice. "Here!"

The Principal stood on the large rectangular platform that jutted out from the edge of the balcony over the center pools like a serving tray holding a snack offering to the behemoth groaning below. A man in a red jumpsuit stood next to Thallium. They both held glasses of ice water, and Thallium toasted Caster from afar and waved him over.

As Caster mounted the platform, he noted a significant change in its construction—it now had a glass floor. He hesitated to step farther. His instincts shouted in revolt at the sight of the water directly beneath him, promising to swallow him if the glass didn't hold. Like the vast majority of everyone else in The Disc, he couldn't swim; there was never enough water for that. Absently, he wondered if his body was still capable of drowning. After the way it had healed when he should have been dead—absolutely, unequivocally dead—he wasn't sure. But he'd rather not find out.

"It's safe, I assure you," said Thallium, drawing Caster's gaze from the floor to his smug expression. "I had it installed when you were living on your own. Better view. Gets walked all over every day and hasn't even faltered. Isn't that right, Ollie?"

"Absolutely, sir," answered Oliver, head of the water plant. He was known officially as the "Head of Agua" around The Disc.

Not only did Oliver's facility recycle wastewater to make it safe for consumption, but it also pumped water up from the aquifer, simultaneously contributing power to the pumped storage hydropower facility that stored energy from all other sources in the city. To say his work was important didn't quite cover it.

The knot of a dark yellow necktie poked out of Ollie's jumpsuit, distinguishing him from the other red suits walking around. He was a powerful man, paid better than nearly anyone else in government work, including Tess who maintained the solar fields and Mr. and Mrs. Indigo, who were in charge of agriculture. Ollie had managed to stay humble about his position—he was a hard worker, good to his men. He was older than Thallium by more than a decade, but still strong, with moisture like dewdrops always along his widow's peak.

Caster had childhood memories of Ollie stomping around down here in his rubber boots. When he'd been in a good mood, he'd let young Caster push buttons or lift levers for him as he carried him around on his hip like he weighed nothing at all. He'd smelled of chlorine from the water and menthol from the salve used to treat outbreaks of heat rash that were common among the reservoir workers. He probably still smelled the same.

Thallium grinned, barely covering a snicker, and held out a glass of water toward Caster. "I'll catch you if you fall. I promise." Oliver smiled politely at his joke.

Caster finally moved but stuck to the outer edge. If the platform broke, he could at least grab the railing. He hoped it looked as if he was simply picking the most scenic path rather than the safest. He reached past Oliver's shoulder to grab the ice water from Thallium.

"Good to see you again, Caster," said Oliver. He bowed his head.

"You too, Ollie." Caster raised his glass to him before retreating back to the railing and leaning on it casually.

Thallium nodded once and sipped from his own glass. Condensation dripped onto the silk sleeve of his shirt, though he didn't seem to notice. He turned to look out over the reservoir and the busy workers reaching across its surface, links in the chain that made the water safe for consumption.

"I was just commending Ollie here for his continued fine work," Thallium said. "We live in extraordinary times, and he's truly risen to the occasion and kept this place running when we need it more than ever."

"My pleasure, sir," said Ollie.

"Strange, isn't it?" Thallium said. "That we're drinking our own piss, I mean. And it tastes so refreshing. Mind-blowing, really."

Caster swallowed his sip quickly and set the glass on the railing.

"It's far more sophisticated than that, Principal. I assure you." Oliver finished his last gulp of water and placed his empty glass by the pitcher sitting near the outer edge of the platform. He stomped about in his heavy boots, confident of his domain even up here on the glass. "Regarding your offer," he called over to Thallium as he pulled out a clear set of safety goggles from his hip pocket, "I'll consider it. Thank you."

"As you should. Nearly fifty years of service is a long time, my friend." Thallium walked over and smacked him on the back.

There was a flash of annoyance in the way Ollie rolled his shoulders, but he only replied, "Yes. It is. Sir." He put on his goggles, bowed his head to Thallium, then to Caster.

Before Ollie could leave, Caster said, "I actually need to speak with you, if you have just a second."

Ollie stood at attention. "Of course."

"Do you have people you could spare for occasional IP shifts? There's been more unrest in the streets. I'm concerned it's going to catch."

"Like a sickness." Ollie nodded. "Most of my crew is

already overworked, but I'll find a few to help. Task them along Diameter?"

"North of it, actually. There are rumors of people being attacked in their homes."

Ollie hung his head mournfully. "I'll get at least two patrolling by tonight."

Caster put his hand out. "Thank you." Ollie took his hand. Caster shook it firmly as he said, "Maybe I could come by again tomorrow when you have some time? Would like to see if there's anything I can do to help *you*." Caster tried to keep his tone relaxed, hoping that the set of his brow and the strength of his handshake made it clear that something deeper was on his mind.

"Certainly. Come by my office around teatime tomorrow." Ollie nodded and released his hand. "Hopefully, we see you around here more often. I'm shorthanded. Could use an assistant—you used to be a good one."

Caster saluted him with two fingers. "Button pushing is my specialty."

Ollie laughed. "I've heard." With a final wave, he departed the platform and took a sharp left toward the restricted access door, which led deeper into the plant.

Thallium stretched his neck from side to side and sighed. "Attacks in homes. Are you certain?"

"No. That's why I asked for Ollie's men. I've heard rumors that our Keepers are growing restless. Taking advantage of our citizens. I'd like to lead an internal investigation into the matter and punish those doing so."

"No need. You must be misinformed. I'm extremely selective about my men—they wouldn't do something so reckless."

Caster closed his eyes and shook his head. "Respectfully, I believe the reports more than your feelings, sir."

Thallium chuckled. "Ah, feelings. Pesky little demons,

aren't they? Regardless, I'd say a potential rebellion takes precedence over rumors of bullying in the low slum." He looked sidelong at Caster. "You disagree?"

"No. I don't disagree. But if these rumors prove to be true, then it means people—your most trusted men—are indeed going against your authority. I don't view these threats as separate but connected. Even if they were to be isolated incidents, breakdowns in the structure of society begin with hairline fractures just like this. We have no choice but to investigate."

Thallium grinned, ran his hand back through his loose, blond hair. "Damn. Look at you, kid. There's genuine wisdom behind those deepening crow's feet." He sighed. "Look, I won't sanction suspicion of my best men. They wouldn't dare take risks like this when I give them everything, and I believe you'd be wasting your time trying to prove otherwise. But do what you have to. As long as it doesn't detract from your efforts to ensure we don't have enemies within our walls. Keep those efforts connected, as you said. Deal?"

"Deal."

Thallium finished his water and gave Caster a once-over. "You look terrible."

"Always a self-esteem boost when I talk to you, Principal."

"Have you been sleeping? Last time I saw you like this, you were sixteen and conditioning through the night so you could get strong enough to beat me in a grappling match."

Caster recalled those nights spent in the cool air of summer evenings, hauling bags of sand between sprints from one side of the private training yard of the Main House to the other. Thallium would occasionally come watch, up at three in the morning for heaven knows why, cheering him on as if he *wanted* to lose to his son the next day. He'd sit in a folding chair with a cigarette between his lips, clapping like a maniac.

The intimacy of the memory made Caster uncomfortable,

even though it was nothing more than that—a memory of a relationship lost, one that never really existed in the first place. Just a naïve fantasy from Caster's stupid adolescent brain of a father who would in reality turn out to be a great drinking buddy at best.

"I had a good reason to skip sleep back then," said Caster. "You promised you'd let me train with the Keepers if I beat you."

"Yes, I did. Too bad that dream died, eh? You never beat me."

"Not for lack of trying."

"You have it easy. One of my dad's favorite things was this little baton," he held his hand out, waving it back and forth as if the baton were in it, "that shocked you. It didn't leave a mark, but it burned. He held it to my gut once—I thought it was burning a hole straight through to my spine. He used it when I interrupted his work or when he thought I was being annoying." He rubbed absently at his stomach, then said, almost bragging, "I must have been annoying often."

The way Thallium had just detailed vicious abuse as if discussing the arrival of the cold season held Caster's response captive. "I hadn't heard that," he finally said. He knew other things Valcin Sr. had done to Thallium, like locking him in a hot box and scarring his arm, the latter of which was a practice he evidently picked up from the Marauders. Although the scars up and down Thallium's left arm weren't rewards for his accomplishments; they were meant to shame him for his mistakes. Caster wondered if they ever had.

Thallium shrugged. "I didn't tell you. Anyway, be thankful I'm your father and he wasn't. Could be worse."

"You left your mark well enough."

"That I did." He drew his finger near his left eye, then along his right cheek and jaw. "Though I regret giving them to you, they're reminders that you started a fight you couldn't finish. A potentially life-saving lesson."

"My mom had just died. I was pissed at you. What do you expect a kid to do?"

"You weren't a kid, you were eighteen. I expected you to be smart enough to not attack the man who taught you how to fight, your mourning be damned. I also know firsthand that those scars have caught plenty of women's eyes—can't deny that you've capitalized on them."

Caster kept his mouth shut and looked out over the ledge of the platform.

"All of that's in the past," Thallium continued. "Now you're the head of my task force! Back at home. It all worked out for the best." He set his empty glass on the railing with a clang of glass on metal. "Tell me, what news of the rebels within our walls?"

Caster checked his tone before he spoke, keeping it as objective and emotionally disconnected as possible, emulating his father's ability to do the same. "Very little. Rumors in smoky bar corners from bored old men and whispers of wanting to leave The Disc from people who don't know any better. Nothing concrete."

"More rumors. Seems all we have right now are rumors. You're certain you're doing all you can? Do you need more men?"

"It's not a manpower problem." It was exactly a manpower problem—one that was keeping Caster from launching an outward assault on the Main House. He continually tried to ignore Thallium's rehashing of the good memories they shared, how he was trying to reconnect, as if there were anything to reconnect to. And it was a manpower problem, nothing more, keeping Caster from killing his father right there on the platform, from drawing his knife and driving it into his chest until his blood covered the ridiculous glass floor.

"Then how do you suggest we proceed?" asked the Principal. "We can't keep doing the same things and expecting different results. Only an insane man does that."

"I suggest we do exactly the same thing for now: keep listening, keep looking, as subtly as possible. If there are rebels—"

"If? My son, there's no question that there are. Someone let Wren's sister out of her cage. That is no rumor, that is fact, and we haven't yet felt the full ramifications of what was done to the Marauders as a result."

"Even so, short of a confession, we can't know who it was. Unless you want to execute all of your higher-ups with access to her cell, there's nothing we can do."

Thallium pursed his lips and lost himself in thought.

"Oh, come on! You're considering whether it's worth killing dozens of people to get one rat?" said Caster.

"Of course not, son. Not seriously, anyway." But he pondered for another minute all the same. Then he shook his head. "Those who want to overthrow me in The Disc would love it if I murdered citizens—give them plenty of political excuses to come at me with pitchforks publicly."

"Whoever they are, they've remained peaceful thus far. Gossip is just gossip, fear just fear unless we give them reason to act on it. We haven't seen what these people are capable of yet, and changing our tactics to more overt methods of eradication could make them lash out."

"Hmm." Thallium mulled. "Very well, son. I trust your judgment. Let's keep in mind though," he picked up his water glass from the railing and overturned it, pouring the few remaining drops into the center pool immediately below, "that they haven't seen what I'm capable of either." The glass clattered back onto the metal surface, making Caster jump slightly. "Did you ever read *King Lear?*"

"I haven't had much time for Shakespeare lately."

The Principal's eyes stared far off, seeing people that weren't there as he turned to the middle of the platform and tucked his hand behind his back, orating to the invisible audience. "'I will do such things—what they are, yet I know not: but they shall be the terrors of the earth.'" His jaw turned hard, the expression of a man experiencing the tightness of extreme pleasure or pain. "Anyway, thank you son."

"I'd like to help more. Do you have any other initiatives going to counter the threats in our walls and outside? I could negotiate with nearby towns that are wrongfully informed about you and settle our disagreements so that those here at home will see the truth and wise up. We could reopen trade before winter hits too hard." He hesitated, but then said the most dangerous thing on his mind. "Maybe it will help to show other towns you don't intend to use a mythical weapon against them, show them that rumor's a lie."

Thallium fought back a grin, looking at Caster as if he were a toddler trying to form words again. "Thank you for the offer. I'm working on a few things, so not to worry. I want you focused on the inside threat. That's the best way you can help me. For now. Don't miss dinner tonight—I requested lamb and mashed potatoes. And after, chess and Sangre like last week? We never did finish our game."

Their conversation officially over, Thallium clapped his son on the shoulder as he passed.

"What about Wren?" Caster called out before he could stop himself. The more he pushed, the more Thallium might shut him out of whatever was being done with her. But he had to try.

Thallium spun gracefully on his heel and strode back to his son. "What about her?"

"I mean, how is she?"

Thallium smiled warmly. "She's well. But as we've discussed, she'll remain in isolation for now."

"For weeks, I've been doing your footwork. I'm with you in this. Doesn't seem unreasonable to ask for one small thing in return—let me see her." He couldn't keep the desperation from his voice at the end.

Thallium's jubilant energy faltered as he regarded his son. A glimpse of the man under the mania flashed across his face, a man who had known pain, who had suffered from it no matter how flippantly he talked about it. "I'll speak with Eydis. No promises, son."

The Principal bowed his head, then left the platform to stroll along the edge of the reservoir. He reached a ladder stretching to the nearest bridge, started down it, and disappeared from sight.

It hadn't been the reaction Caster was expecting. But he refused to let himself feel hopeful, and the way Thallium had looked left him unsettled. He drank the rest of his water. The ice clinked in the glass as he set it beside the pitcher. He stomped across the center of the platform toward the exit, sick of putting caution before action, even if doing so was all that was keeping him alive.

Eydis hadn't seen a courtroom this empty in years. Truth be told, she hadn't attended a trial in person in years, preferring to monitor those of interest from the comfort of her bedroom or the lab. But today she'd felt a need to visit someone here in person, and now that she saw how empty it was, she knew she wouldn't struggle for a seat as she'd feared.

There were only ten or so people in the stands, staring with the dull eyes of those passing time by distraction. It was freezing in the courtroom, and she knew that if they were willing to turn the rationed heat on in here, the stands would fill within the afternoon. But heat was for the Main House and the industrial section, where it was used to keep food growing and water flowing, not for criminals and their spectators here. The limited power used in the courtroom and its adjoining facilities went to maintain basic functions, such as lighting and surveillance.

The ten or so people in the courtroom sat far apart, foolishly choosing personal space over the heat huddling together would create. In her layers of fabric, hood, and tall boots, Eydis could afford to sit alone. She chose a seat at the front within the line of sight of Judge Gamma behind the security net, who was currently questioning a young man accused of theft.

"You refuse to admit that you and two accomplices stole four sacks of oats from the Storehouse yesterday between the hours of two and five in the morning?" The android sat ramrod straight, long arms stretched over the arms of the chair like spider legs, all frame and little flesh.

Across from him, in a chair set lower in the floor with hands bound in clasps at the arms, sat the accused—a young man with dirt crusted in his hair, whose violent teeth chattering was audible throughout the room. "No. But it...was-s-sn't a c-crime."

"It was a crime. Theft is against the law."

"I was feeding my family. B-but starving your own people? That's n-n-not a crime?"

"There is no law against rationing."

"Sc-scr-screw your laws." His repeated attempts to say

"screw" amidst his chattering rendered it a spit-fueled epithet when it finally emerged as a full word.

"They are not my laws," said Gamma, almost to himself. After a moment of quiet, his dexterous pointer finger alighted on the white button on the arm of his chair. "Trial 983-C-K complete. Accused to face two weeks in confinement and a fine of one hundred coins—"

"I don't have money," the man cut in, half-choking and half-laughing at the thought.

Gamma still held down the button and continued with his sentence. "A fine of one hundred coins or the equivalent time spent working in the agricultural sector until the debt is repaid." Gamma released the button, and the clasps on the prisoner's chair receded. The prisoner stood as two Keepers came in from a side door. While they bound his hands, he shouted at Gamma.

"Tyr's Army will bring judgment on this city and the Principal hiding in his castle like a—"

"Like a what?" the Principal's voice came from behind Eydis.

She and everyone else in the courtroom turned to see him leaning against the wall at the top of the auditorium, hands in the pockets of his cream wool overcoat, clove cigarette in his mouth.

The man on trial lost a bit of his fire but cleared his throat and replied, "A coward."

"Come on, you can do better than that," Thallium said. He left the wall and started down the stairs, puffing thoughtfully. "Washed-up dictator? Deluded maniac? Ooh!" He threw his hands up in triumph. "A heartless fiend! That has a certain poetry to it, don't you think? Like I'm a pirate king or something likewise romantic." With a flourish, he gestured to those in the audience. "Let's take a vote. I want to hear from my people. Do you agree? Heartless fiend?"

Everyone sank lower into their seats.

The Principal sighed. "You're no fun at all." He stopped at Eydis' chair near the net and addressed the man on trial. "You truly believe this Tyr has your best interests in mind?"

"He...he says he can help us."

"Mark my words, young man, the only one he wants to help is himself. All people are the same. The difference is that I admit I enjoy my position. However, I also value my citizens." He swept his arm across the expanse of the room. "I know things are difficult right now. But there are people on our doorstep demanding my head—*our* heads. Don't delude yourself into thinking there's an easy solution here, a wise figure come to make you all enlightened gods. Satan had success with the same ruse ages ago. There's nothing new under the sun." He tilted his face to the ceiling as if basking in the sun's light.

In the ensuing quiet, the prisoner gave in to the Keepers' grip and nodded silently.

Thallium dropped his cigarette and crushed it with his heel. "Waive the fee please, Judge Gamma. Two weeks in confinement should be sufficient for Mr.... "

"Balas," the man replied.

"For Mr. Balas to reconsider his life choices."

Gamma pressed the white button on his chair again. "Revision to sentence for Trial 983-C-K. Two weeks confinement for thievery to be paid immediately. Take the prisoner out."

"Thank you, Principal," Balas said softly before the Keepers marched him through the side door and to his new cell, likely to be double occupancy due to the rapid increase of internal lawbreakers. Hopefully, he'd be paired with just another petty criminal. If not, he likely wouldn't see the family he'd stolen for again.

"Trials are convened for the day," Gamma's voice boomed. "Please file out in an orderly fashion."

With the few spectators there, it would have been a challenge to be disorderly. People roused themselves and bowed clumsily to the Principal as if still waking from sleep before stumbling toward the door in fits of shivers. After the last one left, Eydis stood from her chair.

Thallium wrapped his coat around her from behind. "If you needed a break from the lab, there are plenty of better options than the courtroom. More private locations," he said, making little circles with his hands against her stomach under the coat. His drive for physical intimacy had hit a new high, and she suspected it was from necessity rather than desire. He wasn't sleeping. The only thing that occasionally eased him into it was being with her.

"While it's tempting," said Eydis, "I came to speak with Judge Gamma."

"Oh?" He rested his chin on her shoulder. "And what do two androids chat about? The plight of us poor, mortal humans? Doomed to get wrinkly in all sorts of unfortunate places?"

She reached back to stroke his cheek. "Occasionally. But not today. I'm here to talk to him about Wren."

His chin turned rigid against her shoulder, sharper. "It seems like all we've been doing is gathering data, talking. Which I find strange, as the continued existence of my city depends on her ability to defend it. You've been speaking with her for so long now. Does she wield the power we thought she did, or will she have to defend The Disc with a stern tone of voice?"

"She'll be ready when the time comes, Principal."

His grip around her waist tightened. "She's already proved the damage she can do. Practice time is over. She needs to be ready to fight this war that she's helped cause—The Gentleman's people will seek retribution for his death. Just as the towns around us want my head for what happened in Hallund."

"First, we need to get her to accept what she's capable of. Power without ownership is more risk than resource."

"And hiding her away and conditioning her mind is how we achieve that, eh? And I thought my daddy was cruel."

"We're not conditioning her; we're teaching her. Brainwashing is not reliable. It could break down at any moment, and when she came to her senses again, we'd be the first two people she'd turn her power on. She needs to accept your assignment as this city's defender of her own volition, and until she does, it's too dangerous to let her out of the isolation unit." She turned to face him. "You recall what happened for the first two weeks of her containment? Unfettered, inconsistent outbursts. Provoked and unprovoked. This city you're so intent on protecting would have a large crater where the Main House used to be were it not for my methods you're so quick to criticize."

His lips twisted up, either fighting a chuckle of amusement or an angry tirade sparked by her attitude. And why shouldn't he be angry with her? He believed her to be an object, a servant to command—which was what she needed him to believe.

She tried to backtrack, compensate for her asperity by taking hold of his hips and giving a little squeeze as she said, "Please, sir. Have I let you down before?"

His irritation faded, and he threaded his fingers together to rest against the small of her back. "No, you haven't. As for this issue, like always, you've made your point efficiently. I retract my criticism. For now." With a light kiss on the side of her head, he continued, "I confess I've sought you out not to argue, but because I have a request. Could we let someone into the inner chamber for a visit? We've done so before to lift her spirits, grease the wheels." There was something in his plea that caught her off guard—a trace of humility.

"You mean Caster."

He shrugged. "He cares about her, keeps insisting on seeing her. I think he's earned it."

"He does care about her; of that I have no doubt. My concern is how Caster would view our methods of her confinement, and how that could negatively impact your relationship with him. Your goal is to reconcile, is it not, sir?"

She saw genuine surprise in his expression then. He hadn't considered how Caster would view their treatment of Wren because that would be akin to worrying about how a prince would care for the living conditions of a piece of technology. She wanted to slap him—for his ego, mostly, but also for being a leftover image of everything she resented about the world past.

"While you and I understand that she's an instrument to be put to good use," Thallium said after a long minute, "to him, she's not a tool. She's his hope." He paused and shifted his weight as if bumping up against an uncomfortable memory. "It's cruel to keep hope from a man for too long."

"Sir," she whispered, allowing sympathy to soften her words, "you will lose him if he sees her as she is now."

He didn't respond, but that was enough to show he agreed.

"I'm making progress with Wren. In fact, I'm here to speak with Gamma about how to expedite it. For now, perhaps it would be best if you simply blame me for denying Caster's request," she continued. "I am still in charge of this initiative. Aren't I, sir?" She briefly stroked the inside of his thigh with her fingertips.

He groaned and pressed himself to her. "I know how you like to take charge."

Her own body responded to the rasp in his voice, felt a

need that she'd soon have to fulfill. But not at this moment. She pushed him away gently with her hands on his shoulders. "Perhaps you're right—I should come by your room soon for that break you suggested."

The heat in his smile showed that he'd forgotten all about his concerns regarding Wren and the work Eydis was doing with her. He bent to her ear and said, "I'll be waiting. Don't take long here." He smelled her hair as he stood straight again, looked her over, and growled once. As he turned and sprinted up the stairs, he called over his shoulder, "Give the lady what she wants, Gamma! It's better that way. Trust me."

Eydis steadied her breathing and waited for her heart to stop thumping—Gamma was a perceptive android, and the desire her weak body felt would be hard to pass off as anything but human unless she gained control of it. Once she'd calmed herself, she headed down the stairs toward the judge's chambers.

Gamma stood patiently waiting for her on the other side of the net. As she approached, his ink-black eyes grew larger as he took her in. "Mistress Eydis. Would you like to come around and have a seat?"

"I won't be here long, thank you." She joined him close to the net and craned her neck to stare up at him. He dropped to his knees so she was able to look straight at him instead. "I need your help with Wren."

"Has she committed a crime?"

"No. Nothing of the sort. I recall she trusts you. That you two have had...conversations."

"She has sought me out in the past, yes."

"When she's feeling lost and needing counsel?"

"Counsel related to matters of the law. Regarding her sister's crimes, her own past offenses, and the like."

Eydis nodded. "Then she's been more open with you than

with me. I'm trying to reach her, help her find purpose. Do you have any insight into how I might help her find it?"

"I do not think she requires help finding a purpose," he responded without hesitation. "Her purpose is her family."

Eydis had been the same once. But it was easier to remember the pain that purpose had brought than the joy. Wren had experienced similar loss. Perhaps she needed to be shown that she and Eydis had more in common than their genetics.

"Thank you." She turned to leave, then stopped. "Do you remember anything from your past? The time before I found you?"

Gamma replied, his voice a deep echo answering back from a well. "I have bits of recorded sound, fractured images. The clearest is of a pair of children, a boy and girl. We were in a closet, hiding. They clung to me. There was an explosion. The closet was gone, and I was staring up at the sky. It was snowing, but it was summer."

Eydis sighed. "One of countless tragedies that should never have happened." She had similar disjointed memories more than two hundred years old, still as vibrant and fresh as if they were happening anew. The flutter of a million leaflets dropping from the sky, early morning coffee in bed, blood in an arching spray. "Human history is riddled with the pain of those who didn't write it."

"*Your* history, you mean."

Her skin turned cool and mottled at his words, beyond the chill of the room. "Excuse me?"

"Human history is your own."

She shuddered from head to toe.

The judge's eyes twisted and turned, growing bigger, the faintest clicking revealing the deeper inner workings of his machinery. "Your vitals tell me you're uncomfortable with my knowledge of your composition."

She thought she'd been so careful, but clearly not careful enough. She stripped emotion from her voice before she asked, "How do you know I'm human?"

"You made me so I could know. You awoke me from the dust and repaired my systems. I'm a judge—I read all things in all people. Including their physiology. Yours is human. Mostly."

She waited for Gamma to continue, but he simply stared at her, unblinking. "Have you told anyone else of what I am?"

"It is not my concern. You are my superior. You found and restored me. I care not about your composition."

"The Principal would not share your disinterest in that information. He would be too keen on seeing me examined, wanting to understand how I don't age. Please keep it to yourself."

"I have and will continue to do so, mistress. You are my creator—I answer to you."

"Thank you." She hated that she had to struggle to keep her voice steady.

"Is she in danger?" There was something strange in his inflection, something akin to worry.

"You're concerned for her? Are you no longer objective in your role?"

The judge fell quiet and still. One walking into the room would have thought he and Eydis were temporarily shut down, recharging their power supplies—two androids taking refreshment together. Finally, Gamma held his head high. "I am programmed to be objective, mistress. I do not have the ability to be anything else. Not as you do."

She chuckled. "I think you just may, in fact. Don't worry, my friend. It's not my intention to cause Wren pain, but to free her from it. Thank you, Judge."

He reached out a hand through the net and enveloped her warm fingers in his icy flesh.

———

Adonis preferred the Ragged Squirrel to other locations for reconnaissance missions. It was outside and freezing, but everywhere was freezing at night, including inside. The Squirrel at least had fires at each table, and Nita, the owner, had added a trough stretching through the center of the seating area filled with long-burning coal to add warmth.

Being outside didn't keep the smells at bay, however. Tobacco smoke mingled with the occasional whiff of the salvia that most pretended not to smell. Dried-over vomit hastily covered by a kick of dirt, backwashed remnants of Yellow Fever in the bottoms of glasses, body odor from workers stopping by before resigning themselves to the cold confines of their homes, all mixed with Nita's barley stew and dense rye bread—the only things on the menu these days.

It was 8:30, which meant that most patrons fresh off work had powered through about three drinks and were well on their way through a fourth. Voices grew louder, volume awareness a social tool to be disregarded until tomorrow morning when the pounding of one's head made it a requirement. Conversations blew between tables, gusts of personal stories, problems, and fears passing between friends with all secrecy abandoned. A perfect place to listen for rumors and dissent among the common man, if you were skilled enough to pick them up.

Unfortunately, Adonis wasn't.

"Focus," said Sans, breaking through the din to get Adonis' attention. The Thief sat across from him, expression nondescript, brown eyes the kind you could look right through, body motionless. Even Adonis could forget he was there, which was the whole goal of a Thief in the first place. Blend in, get the job done, fade out before anyone noticed you, and if they did, they couldn't even remember what color your hair was. Adonis cursed how his hair made him stand out—big brown curls like shining chocolate. He'd taken to tying it back when he was out on missions with Sans to blend in, but he doubted it helped much.

"There's just noise," grumbled Adonis, poking his finger to make a tenth hole in the dry half-loaf of rye on his plate.

"It's information."

"It's noise!" Adonis said again, refusing to admit it was his lack of skill that was making him frustrated and not Sans' teaching.

Sans made something between a sigh and a grunt in his throat. With one finger, he pushed his half-full glass of Yellow Fever toward Adonis. "Drink. Relax."

"But this stuff kicks my ass. You know that."

Sans' eyes lit up in mild amusement. He was undoubtedly remembering the last time Adonis drank Yellow, after which he'd tried to proposition a prostitute and then forcefully vomited down her front from her neck to her navel. "Finish what's there. Then listen."

Adonis screwed up his nose, sloshed the sickly yellow liquid in the glass, and then upturned it. The alcohol hit his tongue and filled his mouth like water thrown onto hot rocks. It tasted as if bleach had been mixed with a touch of overripe radish—it probably had been to make this batch. The heat filled Adonis' face only to immediately fade and leave his mouth and throat feeling sterile and tasteless. That's how people could drink it. There was a kind of pain amnesia after each sip. He set the empty glass down and waited for the inevitable swimming feeling in his limbs.

"Thieves don't only steal property," said Sans as he

adjusted his kanabō where it rested against his knee beneath the tall table. "We steal information. Since you insist on becoming one, you need to understand the art."

"You're so poetic, old buddy."

"Hush."

Adonis leaned over the table and put his weight on his elbows, settling in to listen. He started with those sitting closest, hoping he'd hear enough to give his confidence a good boost before he tried to stretch his ears further. A man, young and big by the sound of him, immediately behind Adonis was complaining about the quality of the coal he purchased last week. He suspected it was more lava rock than anything else, the seller rationing his coal stock while charging more for it. The woman with him, probably his wife, murmured her sympathy. A table closer to the bar was surrounded by three women, one pregnant, who were discussing baby names with too much enthusiasm; it was as if they were trying too hard to encourage the new mom, whose baby would see a life worse than she if The Disc continued down this path to self-destruction. Beyond them, an old man was singing "Down to the River to Pray" into his newly refilled glass of Yellow.

"Nothing useful," said Adonis finally, louder than he'd intended. He cleared his throat and tried to rein in the effects of the booze.

"Be patient," said Sans, dropping his chin to feign a nap and avoid filling the empty space between them with conversation to convince others they weren't eavesdropping.

From this angle, chin to chest, muscles hardly anything to brag about, Sans sure didn't look very threatening. Definitely not like a Harbinger. But a Harbinger he was, and a scary one at that. Nobody knew when the original Harbinger had come along, when the mutation had formed. Adonis asked Asha about it once, and she had theorized that it probably happened sometime after The Fall, when nuclear fallout and disease covered the earth, morphing things into different things, things with tails or lymphoma. It was a mutation passed on to kids from their fathers, and it was most often seen in men rather than women. Or maybe women were just better at hiding and controlling it—Asha liked that theory.

Part of Adonis envied that power, being able to flip a switch and go apocalyptic berserker on someone who pissed you off. But then there was the downside—the whole inability to control it fully thing—that made him content to be plain old human.

"Do you like being a Harbinger?" Adonis blurted. Six had warned him never to ask Sans about his condition. It was "inappropriate." He'd said that with a straight face, which was so rare with Six that it got Adonis' attention. The booze must have loosened his tongue too much, and now it was too late to pull the question back in. He watched it float between them, flapping wildly like a bat in daylight, unable to be taken back to the dark where it belonged.

Sans opened his eyes but didn't change position.

"I'm sorry," sputtered Adonis. "I shouldn't have—"

"I live with it. That's all."

"Right. I guess that's all you can do. Like, I don't like being short, but I live with it. Not that it's the same thing. Because it's not. I mean, being short doesn't cause me to rip out people's—"

"You know what's ironic?" Six declared around a mouthful of greasy corn chips as he returned to the table from who-knows-where. "That you guys are the Thieves, or wannabe Thieves, and I'm the one stealing snacks." He dropped a plastic tray of chips in the middle of them and straddled a chair backward. It was the first time Adonis had been genuinely happy for him to appear and interrupt—rambling stupidly to Sans had been more painful than rolling through cacti.

"We're working. Silence," Sans said softly.

"Doesn't look like work to me," said Six, going for a double fistful of chips.

"Then we're doing well," said Sans. He looked to Adonis. "Try again."

Adonis sighed and closed his eyes. Six crunched chips incessantly, and Adonis kicked his shin under the table. "Knock it off."

Six chewed louder. "Oh, is my masticating distracting? Think of it as a training aid. Stress yourself, Donnie. Only way you'll grow."

"Enough," said Sans, almost at normal speaking volume. Six chewed more quietly.

After another minute of failing to hear anything beyond Six's disgusting mouth sounds, Adonis opened his eyes but kept his gaze downward. He poked holes in his bread, wondering if he was cut out to be a Thief in the first place. A couple of months ago, he'd told Gavel he was interested in Thief training. Gavel was fine with it, simply warning him that it would take a minimum three years of training before he even got the Thief modification, and that was if he was a natural. He'd remain a Grunt during those years while also shadowing Sans in his spare time. Adonis wondered what Sans thought about having a kid shadow him for the foreseeable future, but if he'd complained, he'd never done so to Adonis. But then, he didn't say much to anyone anyway.

Considering it only took two years to become a Soldier— and Gavel's Body had a vacancy that had yet to be filled since Mainstay's death—it had been tempting to go that route. But Adonis would never be a Soldier. Not a good one, anyway. He was small for his age, and even though he worked out at the same rate as the others, he wasn't getting any bigger. If he had to fight, sure, he could. But he wasn't big enough to be a real

threat, likely still wouldn't be two years from now, and he definitely didn't have much hope of becoming a great marksman
like Mainstay had been.

But he was quick. Quick and quiet.

And apparently a terrible listener. He crossed his arms on
the table and put his head down, failing to distinguish white
noise from anything of value. After a couple of minutes, Sans'
whisper made him start.

"By the bar. Look carefully."

Casually—at least he hoped it was casually—Adonis did as
Sans said. At the far end of the bar, tucked in the half-dark of
the tarps tied up as wind blockers, were two Keepers. One
stood with his face fully visible to Adonis, and what a face. Dal.
More livestock than man, whose nose had been broken
multiple times, mostly by Caster. His white and gray striped
robes were disheveled as if they had been hastily put back on
after he'd enjoyed having them off. The color in his face and
the mess of his hair were more evidence to that likelihood. Dirt
and small red-brown splatters stained the hem of his robe. He
leaned heavily on the bar and ordered two drinks.

Across from him stood another man, taller, darker, and
leaner than Dal. Straight and rigid profile, like he had a
constant toothache. His hair was hidden under head coverings.

"Who's the guy with Dal?" Adonis asked Sans, passing him
the bread as a pretense to make conversation.

Sans picked a corner off the bread and chewed it. "Amsel.
A hunter. Not from here. See the tattoo on his wrist?"

Adonis glanced back at the man, catching a glimpse of the
tattoo as his sleeve slid to his elbow when he threw back a shot
of something black. Two diamonds joined by a dot in between.
"I see it."

"He ran with a group of hunters for hire in Ranlock."

"The Second Facet, right?" said Six.

Sans nodded. "Until he killed them all. Tired of the competition. Thallium tracked him down and offered him a job after news spread."

Slowly, the bits of gossip Adonis had heard from Keepers and fellow military men came back to him. A man who hunted not for a job or even the money, but for the feeling of it. He liked hunting women best. Not young girls, but women. Level-headed women who were smarter than the men who often accompanied them, men who usually felt an obligation to stand their ground and fight their pursuer rather than play the game. Amsel the lady-killer, though Adonis was fairly sure looking at him that he'd kill man, woman, or child if it suited his mood. And here this monster was locked inside The Disc with everyone else. Hopefully he didn't get bored.

Amsel threw back a second shot of thick liquor and then wiped away a drop that escaped from his lower lip—Adonis noticed there was a piece of missing flesh there, an old wound that had healed poorly. He hoped it was an injury from one of his quarries.

Another pair of Keepers entered, shoving through tables and people to reach Dal and Amsel at the bar. Younger Keepers —their robes were too clean. They looked like they were itching for something to do.

"Can you hear them?" asked Sans.

"From here?" Adonis blew a raspberry. "Course not."

"You're an embarrassment." Six picked up the empty chip tray and tapped the crumbs from it into his mouth.

Before Adonis could knock the tray from his hand, Sans stopped him. "Read their lips. You've been practicing as I told you, I assume."

He had, but it wasn't as easy as he thought it would be. Everyone spoke differently and at different paces. Reading lips was like trying to count the flickers of a candle in the breeze.

He rested his head in his palms, covering up a good deal of his face and masking the rest in an expression of boredom in case any of the men caught his stare.

Dal and the taller of the two Keepers who'd just arrived were doing the majority of the talking, so Adonis focused his attention there. The new Keeper was probably early twenties, with a smooth face that hadn't seen hard sun or work and eyes that hummed in their sockets as if there were something eager and unpredictable behind them trying to get out. "—guys hear about Dearborn?" he said.

"Hear what, Oran?" said Dal, as if annoyed by a little brother approaching him at school.

"Their leader's forming an army, a bunch of dumbasses signing up to fight against The Disc," said Oran.

"So?"

"So, aren't you curious? I mean, if Thallium does have a—" Weather? Warrant? No, weapon. "—then he'd better be ready to use it."

"*If* he has a weapon." The skin around Dal's wrecked nose pulled up as he chuckled to Amsel, whose only reply was a slight shake of his head.

"He does have one then?" asked Oran. "The girl? Come on, Dal, we've heard bits and pieces. Just tell us the whole story. What can she really do?"

"Doesn't matter what she can do if we take down Thallium before he gets a chance to use her."

Damn. Bold words for a night at the bar, especially coming from one of Thallium's personal Keepers. They all fell quiet, and Adonis took the opportunity to rest his poor eyes for a few seconds.

Oran took in the sight of Dal's disheveled robes. "Looks like you had fun without us."

Dal replied, "Since when do I give a shift—" No wait, shit. "—shit about you getting some?"

"I just thought we were going out together tonight."

Dal finished his drink and shook the empty glass at Oran. "If you're gonna complain, go get yourself taken care of. Lenka in the low slum, house with the broken window and blue curtains. Nice body, keeps pretty quiet."

Adonis' face burned with indignation, and he realized again that it was a good thing he wasn't a Harbinger. If he were, he'd be yanking Dal's arms off and smacking his face with them right now, shoulder sockets bleeding all over his light-colored robes. The image filled him with joy.

"You know that's not my type," replied Oran.

"You're sick, man. I ain't helping you find boys." Dal turned back to Amsel, and with a nod, they left the bar and strode off into the street.

The newbie looked at his friend as if for empathy, but the guy—older with a bulging paunch—just shrugged and took a seat at the bar. Oran glanced around the tables, only now taking an interest in the patrons, and his gaze landed on Adonis. Those eyes hummed faster, almost seeming to vibrate with excitement, and a smile crawled across his face. He waved.

Adonis ripped his gaze away, back to Sans.

"Wave back," Six singsonged.

"What? Hell no!"

"This is an opportunity," said Six. "Learn to recognize them. Right, Sans?"

Sans hesitated, cracked his neck, then nodded.

Adonis crossed his arms. "Nuh-uh. Nope. And I seriously doubt that guy knows anything of value."

"Even if he doesn't, he needs to be put in his place," said Six. "I heard what he said. We'll tell Caster—he needs to see for himself that the rumors about the Keepers are true."

Adonis' heart dropped. "*You* could hear him?"

"Assassins have good hearing too, you sad little student. Now wave."

"I hate my life." Adonis threw up three fingers, the most he could muster without grimacing.

Oran's eyes shimmered, and he slid in between the half dozen tables that separated them.

"Set up a meeting for tomorrow night. Alley behind Screws," said Six as Oran came closer.

The situation combined with the Yellow in his stomach sent Adonis' head swimming. "I'm gonna puke."

"Don't you puke, Donnie. Courage up, vomit down," hissed Six. He and Sans stood and went to the bar, freeing the table for Oran to make a private introduction. Sans shoved his chair under the table with more force than usual, and as he walked off, his back heaved with the effort of keeping his anger under control.

Adonis tried not to lose his crappy dinner as the Keeper sat.

CHAPTER THREE

OLLIE AND CASTER SAT IN HIS PRIVATE OFFICE, A WONKY
little square of space tucked under a low ceiling of pipes
running in all directions. It was warm and moist—the armpit,
Ollie used to call it when Caster was a kid. Across from Caster,
next to Ollie's desk, was a wall of gauges and a large touchscreen covered in red text denoting the various stages of water
treatment in the facility. There was a constant whirring noise
even here in the depths of the facility, and Caster raised his
voice just enough to be heard above it.

"I have to say, when you said teatime, I didn't think we'd
actually be having tea."

A fat, round teapot sat on the desk; Caster recognized its
blue china pattern from its use in the Main House. Except this
teapot was chipped around the spout, and the two cups likewise showed their use. The floral smell of chamomile came
from the pot when Ollie lifted the lid to examine its steeping
progress. He removed a little muslin sack full of tea and set it
on a matching saucer near a plate of rustic scones.

Ollie chuckled. "You didn't think I wouldn't offer you a

drink after you came all this way, braving the depths of my domain, did you?"

"Of course you would. But I'd have guessed vodka—you used to crack open your flask around this time back in the day."

Ollie poured tea for both of them. "At my age, tea is the better choice. My wife insists I drink at least three cups a day. However, I still keep that flask in the desk drawer for emergencies, if you'd like. Would have thought you'd smelled it when we sat down."

Caster shook his head. "Your cousin's mods are great, Ollie, but a closed flask is a bit too much even for my sharp nose. Tea is great anyway. I'm staying away from the stronger stuff."

With a proud smile, Ollie pushed a precious jar of honey toward Caster.

"Thank you for meeting with me," Caster said as he drizzled honey into his cup with a small spoon. "And for sparing your men. I think it will really help keep things civil."

Ollie allowed himself a testing sip before he responded. "Of course. I have family in the high sector—just want them safe. Any idea who's instigating these crimes?"

Caster shrugged, hoped it was convincingly casual. "I'm working on it."

"Probably just cabin fever. It really will do a number if you let it. I would know." He jerked his thumb toward the cluttered ceiling. "Anyway, I'm glad to have your ear. As someone who has known Thallium a long time, I'm concerned about your father."

After a drink, Caster said, "When I interrupted the other day, it seemed as if he was making you an offer?"

"Hmm. Yes. A generous one. Retirement."

Caster whistled. "Not many people are offered that luxury. Are you considering it?"

Ollie drummed his knuckles on the desk. "I am. He's wise

to look toward training a replacement before I get too old to lumber and creak through these passages and up and down skinny metal stairwells. Although I'm not sure what I'd do with myself if I were to suddenly have so much free time. Especially now during a lockdown."

"Understandable. It's got us all on edge."

Ollie um-hummed and took an overly long drink of tea.

Caster narrowed his eyes. "What is it?"

"It's just…I really am concerned about your father. I've known Thallium a long time. Something's…off in his temperament."

"Something's been 'off' there forever, Ollie. Got anything specific worrying you?"

"He's restless. Spends more time down here than in the past, kind of like he's looking for something to do. He asked me if there was any work he could help me with."

"And you said, 'Thank you, but I'd rather you not lose your fingers and blame me for it.' Am I right?"

Ollie added more tea to his cup. "Something more politically neutral than that, but yes, pretty much. It's ironic because I really do need help. Several men have taken sick leave for themselves or to care for a loved one. Others quit."

"Quit?" Of all the higher-ups, Ollie would be the most tolerable with which to work.

"Had to put my foot down about my policies down here. Didn't sit well with some. Maybe Thallium's irritability is catching, eh?"

"He does seem more irritable than normal. I believe the situation with the Open has him on pins, feeling more like a captive than a warden. I've been wondering what his next move might be for The Disc." He leaned forward and rested his elbows on his knees. The little cup warmed his hands. "What would end this lockdown, do you think?" he said into his tea.

"Honestly?" Ollie lowered his voice, though it was unnecessary down here. "War."

Caster looked up, and Ollie was already watching him with the concern of an old friend. The warmth in it rivaled that of the tea.

"My workers talk over their meager lunches about how we're already at war," Ollie continued. "Bone-pickers returning from the Open have said as much."

Caster sipped his tea, then sat up straighter. "My father is eager to fight that war. Once he feels ready."

"You mean the girl."

Caster eyed him but said nothing.

Ollie shrugged one tired shoulder. "People are talking about her out there. More'n they are about Thallium, probably. Dearborn spilled the details about the red-headed girl who glows, who can explode with a force that used to be limited to fairy tales. Some think that those deaths outside Dearborn were the doing of Marauders. Only problem with that is that it was Marauders who were killed, and they haven't had a civil war in years. I'm more likely to believe the fairy tales, but then, I am old-fashioned."

For as cooped up in this facility as Ollie had been, he was perceptive of the broader world. Caster hedged, still unsure how much to share with him at this point. "I was there."

"I know, kid. I figure if you wanted to tell me what happened, you would've by now in the conversation. She's special, that much is clear. And she's special to *you*—that's even clearer. See it in your eyes. Am I right?"

Caster just smiled politely.

Ollie waited for a few more seconds for Caster to answer. When Caster didn't, Ollie gave him a teasing slap on his knee. "Anyway, let's focus on why you came to me—to see what help you could offer in return for my men keeping an eye on the citizens."

"Well, that and the tea." He finished his cup and held it out for Ollie to refill.

Ollie spoke as he poured, "What you could do in return for my help, silly as it sounds, is listen to the ramblings of an old man for a few minutes. Seem fair?"

Unsure of where this was going, Caster simply gestured for Ollie to continue.

"You're in charge of finding Tyr," said Ollie. He wasn't asking, and yet he made it sound like a question. There was an undertone of suspicion in his words.

"I am."

"See, the problem with that is I'm not so sure what Tyr's saying is all bad," Ollie said boldly.

Caster tried to keep his tone light and wear his best indifferent face as he checked the room for the red light that would indicate the presence of a camera. "You don't think so?"

Ollie shook his head. "There are no cameras in here. We can speak plainly. I want what's best for this city. Lately, I wonder if things need to change. I don't know if Tyr is the answer to that, but I've been around long enough to see what's coming—total chaos."

"You agree with Tyr's proposed changes then?" It was strange asking a man, without asking him outright, if he wanted to see Thallium unseated. It felt juvenile.

"I do. Although I don't know that trusting The Disc to this stranger is wise."

Gavel wouldn't be happy about what Caster was about to do, but damn it, having Ollie on their side could be the advantage they were missing in the struggle that was coming. He had to risk it. "What if Tyr weren't a stranger?"

Ollie leaned back against the headrest of his chair, rocked a little. "No?"

"My mom, Reina, she loved Norse mythology." He smiled at the memory. "In particular, the myth about Tyr. Do you know it?"

"Afraid not."

"Tyr was a god who volunteered to placate Fenrir by putting his hand inside the giant wolf's mouth while the other gods bound him to prevent him devouring the world."

"Brave god. Stupid too."

"It cost Tyr his hand, but the world was saved."

Ollie adjusted in his seat until he was at its edge. He looked down as he thought for a minute, then said, "Are you prepared to lose your hand, son? Or more?"

"If it means ending this insanity, I'll give everything I have."

Ollie took his gaze from the floor and studied Caster's eyes. "That include your loved ones? You ready to lose them? Because innocent people will die if you go down this path. If not you, someone else who doesn't deserve it. Cost of saving the world."

"I'm trying to prevent the loss of more life, not cause it."

"Definitely a noble path. But a naïve one. You're a good kid, better than your father by far. Heck, better than this city deserves. Which is why I wish you'd just walk away from your cause."

Caster pushed his cup back and stood. "I hope you can understand why I can't. Is my cause one you're willing to support? Your resources and, most of all, your endorsement could keep things from turning deadly in the city."

Ollie stood and faced the touchscreen, put his hands in his red jumpsuit pockets. His back looked curved, weary. He was a good man, and Caster wished he hadn't been gone so long while Ollie stayed here aging amidst the water tanks. "It's been my responsibility to keep this city alive since I took this position. Without water, there is no life." He turned to face Caster again. "I'll not abandon The Disc, even at the end of my duty within her walls. I'm with you."

Wren's limbs were cold and weightless, gently bobbing up and down. Her vision was dark until all at once she was somewhere else. The feeling of weight and direction came back to her as she walked through a doorway into a large room.

A professor wrote on a big whiteboard on her right as she entered. To her left were two rows of desks in a semicircle. It occurred to Wren that she shouldn't know what these things were—professors, whiteboards, desks—as she'd never seen them until now. But that thought slipped away as quietly as it had snuck in, and the familiarity of everything was nothing but comfortable.

She grabbed the desk in the back row at the far end of the semicircle, unshouldering her pack and sliding into the seat. She'd done this before. So often that it was routine. She took a heavy green book out of her bag and opened it. She could understand the words, all of them, even the long ones. On page eighty-seven, she found a Punnett square describing a cross breed of two different types of bees.

The professor finished writing the day's notes on the board, and Wren took out her notebook and balanced it on her textbook. The professor started to talk, lecturing about the probability of trait inheritance.

"A print text *and* pen-and-ink notes. What century are you from?" someone asked. She jumped at the interruption.

The guy in the desk on her right snickered under his breath. He had brown hair swept back in a messy pompadour.

"You forget your sphere?" he asked. Hovering over the corner of his desk was an intel sphere—the new, even smaller model. Similar little spheres hovered over the desks of the other students, their lenses pointed at the professor so their AIs could take pertinent notes as the students used their retinal links to peruse the textbook and look up whatever they wanted online.

"I like paper," she whispered in response. "Reading the text, writing my notes. Helps me remember everything."

With a thoughtful nod, he nabbed his sphere and tucked it in his pants pocket. "Worth a shot. Got extra pen and paper?" He waggled his eyebrows, and his dimples went on full display.

She nodded. As she pretended to rummage through her bag, she checked her reflection in the camera of her watch—creamy skin, shining red-blond hair, and bright green eyes. She wiped away a stray bit of liner from the corner of her eye before coming back up with a pen and ripping a new piece of paper from her notebook. When she handed them to the guy, he whispered that his name was Liam. She stuck her hand out —Charlotte.

Then she was wearing a white, form-fitting dress that flared at the bottom with a strap over her right shoulder. Green grass was under her bare feet, and a draped ceiling of white fabric stretched over her and the hundred or so people sitting in folding chairs on her right. Liam stood across from her, their hands joined between them. The pastor on her left pronounced them husband and wife, and Liam howled with delight. The guests laughed and clapped, and her cheeks were sore from smiling all day. Liam rushed forward and tipped her backward, kissing her hard.

In a flash, they were sitting at their thrift store kitchen table in their one-bedroom apartment. She cut off the end of her sausage and egg burrito smothered in green chile. The table wobbled each time she sliced, and she reached down to stuff another wadded-up paper towel under the leg. The perfume of coffee filled the open living area as Liam brewed a second pot behind her. She put on her G-specs, blue light pulsing from them as they came to life, and started scrolling through the day's headlines with the motion of her eyes. The news channels were saturated with the same topic, and she began greedily devouring barely different versions of the same story.

"Stop looking at that trash," Liam said as he set her favorite mug in front of her. He'd given it to her as a gag gift for her last birthday, but she'd ended up treasuring it. On the side in flowing script among dashes suggesting a flight pattern, it said "Let it bee." The flight path led to the handle, where a chubby porcelain bumblebee sat atop the curve.

She took a sip from her mug and tried to keep her excitement to herself as she continued reading.

He sighed. "Or just keep filling your head with infantile politics that are bound to make you cranky for the entire day. Then you can take it out on me when I ask you something innocent like what you want for lunch—my suggestion of turkey melts will be met with apocalyptic rage. That works too."

She closed her eyes for a couple of seconds, and the specs went dark. "Cranky?" she said as she took off the glasses and put them on the table. "Really?"

He slurped a strip of tortilla smothered in red sauce into his mouth. "Well, rightfully cranky. Just don't take it out on me or the fine Burque Turkey from The Yellow Sub." He flicked the G-specs with his finger. "Any new developments?"

The smile she'd been keeping in broke through.

At her expression, he set down his fork and swallowed a giant bite of food. "They signed it?"

"They signed it!"

He jumped up, banging his knee against the table and

sending two glugs of coffee out of their mugs to spread amongst their plates. "You're serious?"

"Signed. Done. We're on."

He stretched to where a towel hung from the handle of a cabinet drawer in the kitchen and yanked it from its spot to giddily clean up the mess he'd made. "Damn Corps actually agreed. I owe Davis fifty Ultirian. Kepler, here we come!"

"Once we can actually survive it."

"But we're close, baby. I know it." He scratched lovingly at the little bee on her coffee mug with his pointer finger. "Just a matter of time."

She nodded absently and focused on cleaning up the spots he'd missed on the table. As she ran the damp towel along the bottom of her mug, she thought of the obstacles before them, the weight that was now on their shoulders. And, for the first time, she felt the targets on their backs and the gravity of what would happen if they failed.

"Hey," Liam's voice broke through her focus, "do I have something on my face?"

Red chile was smeared all over his mouth. He asked for a kiss. She giggled and said no, which gave way to a chase over the couch and back into the kitchen with him accusing her of not loving him.

Then it was evening, and a dozen candles sat on tables and bookcases to dimly light their living room. His dress shirt and her bra lay strewn on the floor where they'd shed them immediately upon coming home from their anniversary dinner. Champagne and chocolate-dipped strawberries sat on the coffee table, half drunk and half eaten.

Charlotte finished off her glass, letting the bubbles wash away the sticky sweetness from her tongue, and then settled back on the couch. Liam rested behind her. He put his arm around her waist and pulled her to him. The alcohol and his body heat eased her deeper into his embrace. She reached down and grabbed his hand, lacing her fingers with his. Their wedding rings rested side by side, and she watched their silver surfaces shimmer in the low light.

Before she could slip into sleep, he started kissing the back of her neck. She sighed, feeling her stress go out through her feet. He moved their interlaced hands to her chest, and together they unbuttoned her blouse. He slid out from behind her and got on top of her. She pulled his T-shirt off over his head, then reached up and ran her thumb over his lips.

"I love you," he said under her touch.

She pushed herself up and kissed him—

Wren's eyes shot open, casting the inner chamber of the Main House in the usual sickly green. Her heart raced, and when she squeezed her eyes shut, she saw the fading image of Liam's face over hers, as bright and receding as if she'd looked at the sun. She suddenly became aware of her body, her private areas covered only by thin strips of white cloth. She wanted desperately to cover herself.

Long cables, skinny as spiderweb, wound around her limbs, pointed out of each fingertip and toe, and stretched down to the bottom of the booth where they disappeared into its base. There were more she couldn't see, but she could feel them tingling out of her eyes, her lips, her neck. All were silvery and alive with light.

Eydis had her back to Wren, facing the console several yards away; her hair was tied back and flowed between her shoulders in a river of strawberry blond. The glow of the thin cables attached to Wren dimmed. Bug watched with concern from nearby.

Wren closed her eyes and tried to calm her breathing, only to remember what Liam's lips had felt like against hers.

"That last memory went further than I intended, but I

guess I got caught up in it. I must be feeling a little sentimental today." Eydis' voice made Wren open her eyes. Eydis now faced the isolation unit, still standing next to the console with its various monitors and gauges. "Based on your vitals, I'm guessing you've never experienced that last part yourself. Sorry to shock you."

Wren tried to clear her head. Finally, her thoughts came through the sound system: "What was that? Why are you showing me these things?" She stared down at her feet as they drifted lazily from side to side in the delicate forest of cables.

"Alma raised you, not me. But I'm still your mother, and I've lived a long life from which you can learn." She hesitated to continue, then added, "I've had to pretend I'm something I'm not for lifetimes while I search for a way to make things right again. My hope, if I dare to call it that, is that you will help me. If you're willing, I believe you'll not only help me, but everyone on this planet."

Wren met her eyes then, and they were soft, as if the two of them were sharing their hearts in the quiet of the night even as Wren couldn't say a word.

"But before I can make such a grand request of you, you need to see the way this world was before it ended. To understand the solution, you'll first need to understand the problem."

Fix this world? Who was capable of such a feat? What would it even look like? Yet when Eydis talked about it, Wren found it difficult not to believe her capable of almost anything. She was damned to float forever as a prisoner or accept her inhumanity because of Eydis, who had locked the glass door of the isolation unit behind Wren after leading her in by the hand.

"I don't trust you. Why should I believe anything you say?" Wren asked.

Eydis nodded slowly. "Why indeed. I did this." She gestured at the lab in a sweeping turn. "I'm keeping you here.

As difficult as it may be for you to believe, I love you. I made you out of love. I know family is as important to you as it is to me."

"You're not my family!" The booming voice made the speakers crackle.

Eydis winced at Wren's words. She crossed her arms, and the swishing of her silver skirt around her calves as she walked toward the isolation unit made it seem as if she were floating. "Fine, but you're *my* family. The only family I have anymore." She moved her hand to her heart. "I care about the people you care about. I was the one who broke Survivor out of her cell. I'm the one who saved Caster as he was dying in the med ward from Survivor's poison. I did—"

"What?" Wren's brain sputtered. She shook her head, trying to think as anger started to cloud everything. "How...What exactly did you do to Caster?"

Eydis sighed quietly, as if the answer to Wren's question was obvious but she was trying to be patient. "I changed him to be like me." She stepped right up to the isolation unit. "If you're willing, I'd like to show you exactly what that means. After you've rested. You're agitated."

Wren pressed herself against the front of the box as if she could will herself out of it. "No, tell me now. I've done nothing but rest in this box. Tell me what you did to him!"

"Next time," she replied with a benevolent smile. "I promise."

A switch inside Wren turned over, and she lost it. Sometimes, when she felt the power within her stirring, she tried to shut it out like she was refusing to open her eyes in the dark. She'd feel the hot breath of a beast on her face, hear it panting. But she'd keep her eyes shut tight as if doing so made the thing inside her shrink in size and took away its control. It never did shrink. Instead, it got mad. Then she'd lose herself when the power took over. After it faded, Eydis and Bug always stared as if they'd just seen something otherworldly.

But this time, there was no warning. No time to resist. Before she realized what was happening, she came face to face with the beast, and the hair on her arms stood on end.

Energy uncurled from her core, and she sent it out through her limbs. It seeped through the liquid gradually, darkening it to nearly black. Purple light went out from her fingertips and toes, slow at first, just little pulses like purple petals. The light came faster, turning to jagged ribbons, and it coursed along the inside edges of the box. The box confined both her and her energy, and the challenge of breaking past it was too enticing to ignore.

"I have much more to show you," said Eydis. Her tone was that of someone approaching a big, hungry animal. "Please calm yourself."

Wren didn't hear her after that. She became absorbed in the stretching of her limbs, the power flowing through them in pulses like ripples of water; it soothed her muscles and took her mind from the box. She let it flow faster, breathing deeper, somehow feeling she was inhaling fresh air and sun. It was as if her body left the lab and soared above it.

She had a vision of Survivor standing impatiently next to Alma. They were waiting for Wren at the front gate of The Disc. Alma held her arms open to Wren. When Wren reached out in response, she felt herself pulled toward something behind her and stopped short—a warm presence like a morning sunbeam was at her back, and she turned around. Caster stood there, black coat dusted with dirt and golden hair bright in the daylight. He seemed unsure of himself. He didn't reach out to her, but neither did he turn away. He looked on, as if waiting for her to make a choice.

Then, suddenly, everything turned a hot, white-purple. A

flash. Caster turned to ash, and a following boom that shook the ground scattered him in the air. Wren turned—Survivor and Alma were likewise destroyed. The last few trails of their ashes rolled along the ground. The wave of Wren's making washed over The Disc so fast that the people in their homes didn't have enough time to scream.

"Stop!" shouted Eydis.

Wren grew embarrassed like a corrected child and felt her power begin to recede. Her mind came back to the lab, and she watched as Bug banged her hand against the monitor that currently showed broken, flashing lines rather than data. The liquid in the box turned back to green, and the last ribbon of purple fizzled out. She was exhausted; these were the times when she was thankful for the weightlessness of her environment. Her limbs went slack, and she hung her head.

"You haven't been meditating as I asked you to, have you? I believe it will help with your ability to control yourself," said Eydis. She felt far away, her voice fading in and out, and Wren knew that sleep would take over soon. "I'll come check on you later this evening, little one. Please be patient for answers." Her heels clicked against the floor, loud at first, then fading to nothing.

Wren tried to open her eyes.

"It's okay," said Bug, her voice gentle and quiet. "Get some rest."

With her last bit of energy, Wren pulled her knees up under her chin and wrapped her arms around her legs. She imagined the warmth of someone else against her back, her mind returning to the memory that wasn't hers, the emotions she'd been forced to feel. As she fell asleep, the only embrace was that of the liquid holding her aloft.

"This seems like a hell of a risk," said Beo, not for the first time that afternoon.

"Ranlock's on the way," replied Survivor gruffly. Her back right molar was throbbing, and it set her on edge. She scanned the desert scrub as they headed toward the sunset, aware that darkness would soon fall and that the opportunity to spot the tiny white flowers of wild yarrow would be past. "With their leader gone, the clan will head for familiar territory for the Dig-in. Where did we go most often?"

A sigh came from his chest. "The High Cave."

She stepped farther away from him in her search and spoke over her shoulder. "Just a couple hours' walk away. And where else would you suggest we trade? No humble village is going to let us in, not with your beauty marks." A cluster of white off to her right caught her eye, but it was just desert holly. "Damn it," she groaned.

Beo came up beside her and nudged her with his elbow—he held a bundle of yarrow in his fist, its bunches of white flowers greeting her like a macabre bouquet. "And you're so innocent and non-threatening."

Survivor grinned up at him. She moved her hands from under the warmth of her outer cloak to pick the feathery yarrow leaves. As she chewed them down to a paste, she replied, "Hardly. But I am a woman. Even The Gentleman knew how to leverage that in people's minds." She moved the clump of paste to the back of her mouth and packed it around her aching tooth with her tongue.

He folded the remaining yarrow into a strip of cloth and tucked it into the top of his pack. "People are idiots." He watched as she pressed the outside of her cheek to get the yarrow tighter to her tooth. "Any better?"

She nodded. The sweet-bitter flavor of the yarrow dripped

down her throat, but it was a small price to pay for the relief it had already started to give.

They trekked across the worn footpath leading to Ranlock through semi-flat scrub lands—the depraved town was so eager to entertain guests that it even maintained a clear path to its door. Before Survivor and Beo, the sun set in a brilliant spray of yellows, oranges, and pinks across the swath of sky. Streaks of cloud wisps stood out from the colors like the warm whispers of a lover, urging them to Ranlock.

The footpath veered south, and more people started emerging from between the yuccas and junipers onto it, clearly eager for the easier way after hiking through the brush. With a man in front of them and a trio of women behind, Survivor's shoulders tightened. Her breathing turned shallow and fast.

"Don't tell me you're already feeling claustrophobic," Beo whispered.

Survivor growled at him. "Small spaces are fine. People? They're the torture. They stink."

"So do we."

She lifted her arm and got a whiff of salty cheese. "I'm used to our stink."

"Try sleeping next to you."

She replied to that with a swift kick to his shin, which he took far too happily.

Spots of orange light waved at them from up ahead in the growing dusk as the colors of the sky faded. Across the distance to the lights, voices resounded. Laughs and shouts from up ahead, as clear as if their owners were beside Survivor. They came to the end of the footpath where the ground sloped steeply down into an ancient auditorium. Arced benches of mortared stones, worn smooth by the backsides and fumbling shoes of Ranlock's visitors, ran down the slope in two separate sections like seating for an archaic wedding. Here, in the summertime, tourists watched the thousands of bats that called Ranlock home fly out in a whirling stream to hunt at night. For such a mass exodus, they were nearly silent in flight, except for the light flutter of their rubbery wings.

At the base of the auditorium stood representatives of Ranlock's establishments, all ready to lure incoming visitors into their traps with free drink vouchers, promises of filtered water, and strategic arm brushing and winks from private dancers.

Survivor looked behind them to see the women closest to their heels staring with wide eyes at Beo, whispering to each other. "Put up your hood," said Survivor.

He frowned down at her. "I thought we came to this place because it doesn't matter what I look like here."

"It matters less, but it still matters. If these people don't trust us, they'll toss us out. Subtlety wouldn't hurt."

"You. Subtle." Beo rolled his eyes, but he did as she said. He didn't really have a "hood," but the blanket she'd taken from Dearborn was large enough to cover his head and fall below his knees. He draped it so that only the tip of his scarred nose poked out into the dim light of the evening. The blade of the shovel they'd gotten from the Scavenger days ago showed at Beo's right hip from where the tool sat across his back, as did the barrel of the rifle slung over his left shoulder.

They avoided the salesmen at the base of the auditorium and hurried as fast as the man ahead of them would allow toward the narrow path that headed farther down into the entrance of the cavern. The nearness of warm bodies made Survivor shiver as the cold started leaving her bones.

Across from their current position sat the top of the entrance—a vertical rock wall stretched above it, and at the top were desert scrub and the bare remnants of prickly pear cacti that had been replanted in a half-assed conservation effort.

Survivor had noticed it when she'd been here a decade ago—they hadn't grown as much as she'd expected. A big metal contraption sat on the top of the wall where it stretched out along the surface of a giant hill. Around the contraption atop the hill, four men like points on a compass stood armed with bows and blades. She didn't know what the contraption did other than somehow make the lights stay on, taking energy from a sun farm a ways to the north. That farm was so important to the functioning of Ranlock that people who visited often would volunteer for shifts to guard it, which showed how much its visitors really valued the place if they were willing to stand in the blinding sun to protect its future. It was the most orderly, and the most self-sacrificing, anyone would be in Ranlock.

Survivor let her gaze trace along the massive rock face stretching down from the desert floor to the open mouth of the cave—a yawning dark spot far below, with the path disappearing into its depths. Survivor and Beo started along the steep trail of switchbacks that went down, down, down. The chatting of those descending with them was replaced by heavy, rhythmic breathing. Kerosene torches stood at the end of each switchback, sending their fumes into the sky. As Survivor and Beo reached the end of another switchback, the stinking fumes of a torch sent Survivor's mind back to the first time she'd made this trek. It had been the last trip she'd made with The Gentleman, right after Beo had been promoted from slave to clan member. The Gentleman had taken Survivor as his valet in an attempt to smooth things over with her.

That time, they'd descended into Ranlock long after nightfall. The Gentleman's steps had been slow and plodding but strong for his age. She'd carried his satchel, canteen, and coat as she walked behind him on his left and said nothing as he prattled on.

"We're going down around eight hundred vertical feet on

this path that's over a mile long, and that's just to get inside. Can you believe it? Just wait until you see the cavern. The depth and breadth of it almost makes a man feel humble."

She'd remained silent, her gaze on the path and the way its smooth black surface grazed against her leather slippers as the frayed edges of her linen dress kicked up.

"You need a rest?" he'd asked, his voice clearer as if he'd turned to look at her.

She shook her head once. But when they reached the next switchback, he pinched her elbow with his surprisingly powerful fingers and pulled her aside from the main path. The two other Marauders following them, Reskin and Fen, stopped too. A young couple making the descent—who had not so subtly attempted to keep distance between themselves and the group of Marauders—came up short and froze, unsure of what to do.

The Gentleman took off his white brimmed hat and waved it at them. "No need to wait on our account. Please, go on ahead."

The couple looked terrified but wisely decided to obey and sped past them around the bend. A slow stream of people followed after them while Survivor and The Gentleman huddled by the wall near a kerosene torch. Survivor's nostrils and eyes burned in the smoke.

"Daughter," The Gentleman said as he replaced his hat, his tone that of a wise, patient father, "I know you're unhappy with me. But you need to understand that Beo made his own choice. Didya see me twist his arm?" He still had his grip on her elbow.

She just stared at the torch light, watched the thick smoke drift about.

"I invited you here hoping that we could reconcile. Don't you think there's a way we can make things right between us?"

At that, she finally turned to meet his gaze, which made

him smile. Those damn perfect teeth of his caught the light of the lantern. He reached into the pocket of his khaki slacks and pulled out a round peppermint dotted with a tiny tuft of lint and held it out to her on his wrinkled palm.

She imagined yanking his hand back until his wrist snapped, shoving the candy down his throat, and shattering his smile with her fist. "Yes. There's a way."

He sucked in air through his teeth and moaned contentedly. "That's all I wanted to hear. Take it. Don't be shy." He grabbed her hand and held it open so he could dump the peppermint onto it. He waited.

She hesitated. Reskin cleared his throat nearby. She glanced at him out of the corner of her eye, the emotion under his half-mask of scars readable only to her. Concern. Finally, she plopped the peppermint into her mouth. The lint caught in her throat as she crunched on the candy, and she had to swallow hard to get it down.

"There's my girl. Better get going. Rat races will be startin' soon!" He turned to continue their descent as the mint and kerosene mingled in Survivor's mouth and nose.

"You all right?" Beo asked, snapping her out of the memory.

She realized they'd made good progress down the path as the remnants of the sunset faded from view and the dark grew thicker. Beo's scars, shimmering under the edges his hood, made her gut twist.

"I'm fine."

He looked skeptical but didn't push it further.

The darkness near the entrance was nothing compared to that inside. In the main chamber and along the trails leading up to it were round spotlights fed by sun power—kerosene fumes wouldn't do inside the cave with no means of escape. But the lights had been known to go out on occasion. It had happened when Survivor visited years ago, and when it did, the cave had been overtaken by darkness that gripped her spine through her chest and demanded respect for its power. Awesome to behold.

As they crossed under the overhang of rock where the stink of the torches was behind them, the air felt thicker on Survivor's skin. There was a heaviness to it that made it almost sticky to breathe, but the increasing warmth of the cave entrance made the effort worthwhile. The temperature stayed more or less constant here year-round, which made it warm in the cold season and cool in the hot season. If it weren't for the shortage of food due to overhunting and foraging in the area, and the constant threat of being attacked by the scum that comprised the fluctuating population here, it would be a paradise.

They leaned back as the descent grew even sharper before they reached the bottom of the entrance trail and the path leveled off into what The Gentleman had called "The Devil's Pit." Tired metal railings kept them on a trail, which led deeper into the caverns, and the last bit of twilight from the entrance faded. The lights around them were the only things holding back the growing darkness.

The atmosphere on the trail began to change as they passed through the half-light, signaling a shift from the concerns of the surface to something else entirely. Entering another world with more pleasures and even fewer rules than the one above. Those who were clearly returning regulars whooped and chatted with each other excitedly. Their voices sent echoes bounding through the corridor to meld together into an indecipherable mess that hurt Survivor's ears.

The corridor opened up into a high chamber. Whatever was beyond the trail was in total darkness, but Survivor could feel the enormity of the space, and the echoes of the eager visitors went farther than she could see. They passed tall rock formations—skinny and gnarled. An old sign declared them the

"Witch's Fingers." Thicker formations, big domed columns of ancient stone, loomed near the edge of the trail along with thin sheets of rock draped like fabric. Everything was damp, and though it was far warmer in here than it was in the Open, it was still cool. The Gentleman's trivia about how it stayed near exactly fifty-six degrees Fahrenheit came to Survivor's mind again, and she hated him for still not shutting up despite being dead.

Footlights near the edges of the path spilled their yellow light onto it. They reached Big Rock, an obstacle weighing tens of thousands of tons, around which the path forked. If they went straight, they'd go through the exclusive recreation rooms, the prize of which was The King's Room—the premier gambling parlor with games featuring cards, dice, and living creatures all eager to take your money. Instead, Survivor and Beo veered left.

They approached a pillar of stone engraved with "Assembly" in violent, overlapping slashes halfway up its length. A man in a black cloak with ragged edges sat above the sign, atop the pillar of stone, as if he'd flown up there himself. Black makeup was smudged all around his eyes, and on a cord around his neck hung an ancient, preserved bat with its wings frozen around its body and an open mouth full of teeth. The man sat hunched forward on his elbows, chin in his hands, and spoke with a lilting voice to the crowd as they passed by below.

"Welcome, weary travelers. Seekers of fortune and pleasure. Luck may be a fickle queen, but she's brought you here alive tonight. Perhaps trust her for a while longer. Ranlock is her body. The Assembly is her heart, and she's already proved generous by allowing us to join in its beating. Enjoy, fellow enduring spirits of bone and flesh. Enjoy!"

The Assembly, as the demented man at the entrance had proclaimed, was the center of activity in Ranlock. A chamber filled with round booths manned by barkeeps, muscle for hire, questionable cooks, and merchants who sold everything from custom weapons to bat guano. Big ring lights were suspended above each booth, casting the wares in a halo of attractive yellow.

A short, bent man stood behind the guano booth. A woman with torn-up farmer's hands approached, and the old man stepped up onto something behind the counter to reach her height. She quickly put down a coin with an uneasy glance around as if she expected someone to jump her at any second, and the bat-shit salesman took it. He reached below the counter and came up with a large glass jar of tiny, dark pellets, which his "Guano y Guano" sign proclaimed to be miracle fertilizer for dead soil.

Off to Beo and Survivor's left sat the main bar, called JW's, in one of the biggest booths, where food and booze were available to those who could somehow afford them and didn't care what exactly they were made from. Tables and chairs were set out near the bar, and most customers sitting there looked as if they'd been partying all day. After all, in this universe there was no day or night, no sun to tell you the hour or make demands on your time. There *was* no time.

Beo passed the bar and raised his nose when a pale waitress walked past carrying a tray with three glasses of what looked like bourbon.

Survivor elbowed him. "We're here for supplies."

"You drag me down here and I don't even get one drink?"

"We don't have money for booze."

"Didn't plan on paying for it, but whatever," he answered, sounding just a bit like the boy she'd raised. He looked over the tops of people's heads, then took her hand and moved it to the blanket on his back. "Supplies are that way."

She gripped his blanket, and he pulled her behind him,

using his big body to shove past the bungling people. A sickly young man stepped right in front of Beo, the immovable object, then promptly bounced off of him and splayed on the ground. Droplets of the man's sweat jumped into the air with the impact.

"Hey!" he said as he stood, clearly on an end-of-life party crusade. He held his arms out, welcoming a fight, but when he caught sight of Beo's face staring down into his, he shrank in on himself and dashed away like a spider that had been poked.

As he watched the man's retreat, Beo grumbled, "Humanity is doomed."

"Would've thought you'd realized that a long time ago," Survivor replied.

They finally reached a general supply booth. A couple of people waited to be served by the bald merchant who was busy chatting with someone over the counter, a man who seemed to be selling rather than buying. Survivor squinted at the visitor—he was familiar, but she could only see the side of his face from her current vantage point. Sharp jawline, average build, black hair. He laughed heartily at something the merchant said, lips pulled back to reveal his teeth. His sharp canines—like those of a cat—jogged Survivor's memory.

"Son of a bitch," Survivor muttered. She pulled a knife out from the depths of her cloak and tried to charge around Beo, but he caught her in what would look like a big hug from behind to any bystander.

"What are you doing?" he whispered.

She jutted her chin toward the cat man. "He had his people hold weapons on Wren in Dearborn. Before The Gentleman found us in the desert."

"Did he use those weapons on her?"

"No. But only because she would have blown him away if he'd tried."

"He's laughing like old friends with the merchant we need to do business with. Killing him would probably stop us from getting supplies, wouldn't you say?"

She watched as the man gripped the back of the merchant's head playfully before waving goodbye. He popped a thin piece of wood into his mouth like a cigarette and headed lazily in the direction of the bar. His hands rested in his pockets as if he had nothing to fear here in the depths of the earth, surrounded by depraved underdwellers and killers who made the former look tame.

"Let's at least get what we need first," said Beo. His grip loosened on her. "Then we can kill him if it will make you happy."

"Fine."

They waited in line, and Survivor grew more impatient by the second. She couldn't see the cat man anymore and feared she was too tired to track him down in these dark tunnels. Not that she wouldn't try anyway. Finally, they stepped up to the booth.

"What can I help you find today?" said the bald guy to Survivor. Beo stood behind her, gaze low, blanket obscuring his face.

"Looking for pill capsules," she replied.

"Making medicine, eh?" The man took two quick steps to his right and opened a deep drawer from which he pulled out a square box of tiny white capsules. "You know, I just got some echinacea from up north. Good stuff. I also have a little of my own batch of powdered garlic left. Either would work perfectly in these." He shook the box of capsules. "They come in dozens. How many would you like?"

"Not those. Nothing that will dissolve—I need something sturdy. Steel, if you have it. Just one."

The man's polite smile faded, and out came the no-bullshit

expression Survivor expected countless sinister buyers had been met with. "Won't be cheap. Exact size?"

"As small as it can go and still fit six hundred milligrams."

"Depends on how densely you pack it," he replied. Her hand was flat on the counter, and he studied it for a second. Then he gently tapped her overgrown pinkie nail. "But that's as small as I can go if you want it to screw open and closed."

She held out her hand—from base to end, her nail was over an inch long, maybe a quarter of an inch wide. "I'll make it work."

He nodded. "I can have that ready by tomorrow morning, assuming you can pay now."

She held out her hand toward Beo, who grabbed the silver bracelet from where he'd stashed it in a pocket inside his shirt. It was warm from his body heat. She set it down on the counter between them.

A magnifying glass on a standing metal arm sat near the merchant on the counter, and he ran the bracelet under it. "Turquoise and coral. This'll be more than enough."

"Good, because I need something else. Apricot kernels."

The merchant took the time to really study her and Beo then. He bent down to get a better angle of Beo's face. "No kernels for Marauders. You all might have jurisdiction up there, but down here I don't have to deal with you if I don't want to. I won't sell you that."

Survivor kept the anger from her face, covering it with a different kind of intensity. She pulled the edges of her cloak farther back from her chest as if she were getting more comfortable, then leaned forward on the counter. "If you only knew how much I empathize with you and what I plan to do with those kernels, you'd give them to me for free." She tilted her head at him. "You'd thank me."

He threw the bracelet at her face, and it caught her in the eye. "Hyena scum!"

Survivor squeezed her eyes shut as the one he'd hit began to sting. A commotion took over—cursing, a thump on the counter, the clatter of a hundred pill capsules spilling to the floor.

Someone grabbed her arms and pulled them behind her back. Beo cursed somewhere in front of her, but when she tried to look for him, her eye wouldn't open. With her good eye, she caught a glimpse of a barefoot woman wearing thick black eyeliner before she hit Survivor in the gut. Air rushed out of her chest, and she fought for a breath as she dipped down to one knee for just a second before getting yanked back up from behind.

Survivor looked down to see that whoever was holding her arms behind her was barefoot like the woman who'd struck her. These were big, hairy feet that looked as though they'd never seen the sun, and they framed Survivor's own snakeskin moccasins, whose dried-out scales had begun to stand on end. She lifted her leg and slammed her heel down on the delicate bones in the top of her captor's foot—his scream carried through the chamber as he released her.

Free but still half-blind, Survivor shouted toward where the woman who had hit her had been standing earlier. "Don't stop now that it's a fair fight! Come on!"

An approaching voice shouted, "Knock it off!"

Survivor saw the vague outline of a man. He got close to her face. She went to strike in the general direction of his nose, but the pain in her gut slowed her down and he deflected her hand.

"Down, woman. I'm not after you. Let me look." His fingertips inspected around her eye, and she was so shocked by his gentleness that she let him. Expensive bourbon was on his breath—an edge of pecan and vanilla. "Can you try opening it?"

She caught sight of him when she did. "Cat man," she said through her teeth.

He chuckled. "Gray, actually." His mirth faded as something clicked in his head. "I know you."

Beo was pressing the merchant's face into the surface of the booth. He released him and silently came up behind Gray, the dead look of a killer on his face. Survivor shot him a glance and he stopped.

"You know her?" the bald merchant asked wetly through the flow of blood pouring from his nose. "Want to say why you stopped me from defending myself against her and her hyena mutt, Gray?"

Beo stepped nearer the counter and pinned the merchant in place with a look threatening another punch. The blanket had fallen to his shoulders, leaving his scars on full display.

"Words have power, Ishmael. To build up or to kill," said Gray. He took his hands from Survivor's face but stayed close, watching her as if she would swipe at him any second. It really was tempting. For a brief moment, he gave Ishmael a side-eyed glance. "Say 'hyena' again and I'll have to buy a bar of Emmeline's soap from two stands down to wash it right out of your vocabulary."

Gray refocused on her. The way he wouldn't back down even when she radiated fury toward him was unnerving. Nobody stood their ground against her. Nobody sane, anyway. He raised his voice loud enough that all of the witnesses to the scuffle could hear him. "If we Openers keep dividing ourselves with our hatred for each other, we'll make it a lot easier for Thallium and others like him to take us over. Besides, all are welcome here, isn't that right? It's one of Ranlock's tenets, if Ranlock actually has any."

"Maybe," said Ishmael, "but I also got a right to refuse service to whatever surface-walker I don't like."

"True enough," said Gray. "But throwing something at that surface-walker's face? Starting a brawl? Kinda immature, Ish. Seems you started something you couldn't finish. Right, big guy?" Gray finally turned from Survivor and spun around to shake Beo's elbow through the blanket draped over him. With a gentle rub at the fabric, he said, "Beautiful craftsmanship. I remember our best weaver, Mirabel, made it—she was sad when it got stolen." He grabbed the corner of the blanket where there was a strange marking of a circle surrounded by rays. "She embroiders this little symbol on her pieces—something unique to this area in the pre-Corp days. She keeps it alive. Always does it in red."

"Wait. They stole from you?" Ishmael sputtered. "And you're defending them?"

"Irrelevant to our current situation here." Gray bent down and picked up the silver bracelet from the stone floor. He held it out to Survivor. "She's got money. Do some business and be done with it, Ish."

"Gray, I know you're 'the man' down here when you stumble in from the overworld once a quarter," he spat on the ground in his booth, "but you ain't *my* boss."

Gray pressed his hands together in front of his chest and gave Ishmael a small bow of his head. "True enough. But perhaps we could discuss my worth later? Right now," he held his arms open to Survivor and Beo, "I think I'll treat these two to a drink—show them Ranlockian hospitality, since you seem incapable of it. Shall we?"

Survivor didn't move. "I need what this man has. If he won't sell it to me, I'm going to take it."

Gray got closer to her, his expression cheerful. "It's murderous habits such as that one that get dainty yet sharp bracelets thrown in your face and make people not want to serve you. Come with me now, or you'll never have the joy of burning in the oppressive sun again." He subtly swept his eyes around them, and she did the same—the bustling traffic in their area of the Assembly had died down. There weren't many who could really call Ranlock "home," but their faces that had never seen the daylight were easy to spot amongst a sea of sun-leathered skin. Residents stood still with hands on weapons beneath their coats, bodies angled toward them, shoulders high and tensed like the tops of bat wings.

"How about that drink?" she said loudly. The residents relaxed and went about their business. Gray turned and waved a hand above his shoulder, telling her to follow.

Beo came up to her side. "You sure?" he whispered.

"No choice," she muttered back. "Not after you broke that guy's nose. Idiot." She started following Gray, and Beo shortened his stride to keep in step with her.

"You're welcome."

"For what?" she spat. "Destroying our chances of getting what we need?"

"We'll get it somewhere else."

"We don't have time to find somewhere else, and I don't want to. They specialize in this stuff here—if I'm going to do this, I'd like to trust the tools I'm using."

"I don't trust anything that bigot was selling."

"He's a man refusing to make deals with demons. Can hardly blame him."

Beo stopped walking and shook his head. "That's not me anymore."

Survivor stopped with him, and they stood in the midst of passersby who now gave them an extra wide berth. She took his big hand, one that used to feel scrawny in hers, and squeezed it once. "I know that."

A whistle came from the bar they'd passed earlier—Gray stood at a corner table and waved them over.

Survivor searched Beo's expression. "You good?"

He dragged his forearm under his nose quickly and blinked away the moisture in his eyes. "I'm good."

She let go of his hand and led them toward Gray. The table by which he stood was roped off. Gray unhooked the rope from the wall, sat at one of the cushioned chairs there, and gestured for them to do the same.

"What's the plan here?" Beo whispered as they approached the table. "Kill the cat?"

"Don't know yet. Keep your fists to yourself. If you can manage that, you might even get a free drink out of this."

Survivor sat across from Gray while Beo removed the blanket and hung it on the back of his chair on Survivor's right. Gray eyed the rifle and shovel as Beo removed them from his back and leaned them against the table before he sat.

"You had those on you and didn't use them?" Gray jerked his thumb in the direction of the booth where the fight had broken out.

Beo's brow furrowed. "For that back there? Not worth the bullets or the risk of breaking the shovel's shaft."

"Touché," said Gray. He raised a hand, and a young man in black with ragged bare feet came over to their table. "A bottle of Yellow I think, Trent."

"Bourbon. Aged," said Beo flatly.

Survivor glared at him.

Gray snorted. "Well, I'll be damned. A Marauder with taste. A bottle of Incendio instead then. Thanks, Trent."

"Deep pockets?" Survivor said.

Gray slid down in his chair to rest his shoulders against the back. "I don't like to brag."

"I doubt that."

Trent returned with a bottle of honey-colored liquid and three glasses. He set the glasses in front of them and then proceeded to pick at the red wax covering the top of the bottle like it was a scab he was afraid of making bleed.

"Just leave it, friend," said Gray with pity as he held out his hand.

Trent set the bottle in his hand and sighed his relief as he turned to leave.

Gray propped the bottle on his knee with his palm wrapped around the top. After a while of just sitting there, Survivor felt the tension growing in Beo as he shifted in his seat.

"We going to drink that?" Survivor asked. "Or are you just going to cuddle it?"

Gray sighed. "Impatience is unbecoming."

"Yeah, otherwise I'm a real classy lady."

Gray shook his head. "If you don't warm the wax first, it breaks apart. Can flake into the bottle when you remove the cork. I'd like to drink bourbon, not wax." He rolled the top of the bottle between his hands, nodded, and then pulled a tiny folding knife from his pocket, which was curved as if it had been made solely to open bottles of expensive alcohol. A rich man's knife. He deftly sliced through the wax with one twist around the mouth of the bottle and then pulled the wax and cork off together. The sweet kiss of the cork as it popped out had Beo shifting in his seat again.

"They age this in an oak barrel that was charred for exactly —*exactly*—one minute," Gray said as he poured two fingers into each glass. "That's five seconds more than is typical for high-level charring. But I think it makes a difference. Plus, that extra carbon in the barrel means better filtration. Helps get rid of that sulfur flavor the water has around here. When you sip it, notice it tastes like warm sugar."

Beo cradled his glass and took a long, purposeful sip, but Survivor just threw it to the back of her throat and gulped it down. It burned. All booze was the same—fire. She shuddered as she fought back a gag. Never did understand the appeal of alcohol.

Gray shook his head again but poured her another two fingers. "What I love about this bourbon is the effort that went into producing it, the attention to detail, almost as if this isn't a product but a child. It's the same care that my people put into their craft. Mirabel put that kind of care into that blanket—the one you stole from my village." Anger flashed in his eyes, but he just sipped more Incendio. "I'm sure you're sorry."

"Does the wolf apologize to the rabbit when it rips into its throat?" asked Survivor.

"Bedtime fable told to you by your Marauder family?"

"Reality taught by life," she said. "I needed something; I took it. Just like I'll take what I need from that seller over there."

"Something so important that it's worth the risk of being overrun by pale undergrounders, most of whom only emerge into daylight to find the next life they were hired to take?"

She shrugged. "Yes."

He ran his hand over his mouth and squeezed his eyes shut. "Stop screwing around. I saved you over there because I believe in giving people a chance to repent. Gave the same chance to my uncles years ago—they didn't take it. Took a long time to die, but even then, no remorse." The alcohol in his glass was only half-gone, but he pushed it aside. "Don't get me wrong, I like the fight in you. A lot." He smirked to himself, and the mass of lines that formed around his eyes when he did so revealed that he was older than he looked, or maybe that, rich as he was, life had prematurely aged him. A darkness crept into his voice. "Tell me what you're doing here, or I'll give you both to these undergrounders who enjoy tossing outsiders into dark holes to find out how deep they are by the length of the screams."

He wasn't bluffing. They would bury them down here if they caused enough of a stir—it was a common custom above ground, and here below, it was even easier. She pushed her glass over to Beo. "I'm not sorry for what I took from you—I needed it. I would do it again. You probably don't understand that. But I'm not in Ranlock to make trouble. I'm here because of my sister."

"Wren, right?" Gray asked. "Sweet girl." He clicked his tongue. "Well, incredibly scary girl, but sweet."

"Too sweet for her own good." Survivor scraped at a blemish on the table with her fingernail. "Thallium has her locked up just like he had me."

"Ah, he's added kidnapping and unlawful imprisonment to his list of crimes. You think you know someone, but then they find new ways to disappoint you." He retrieved his glass and went in for a sip.

"Wouldn't know. Never met the guy."

The bourbon nearly came out of his nose. "Wait. He has your sister locked up, had *you* in prison, and he never even introduced himself?" He took a more careful drink. "Actually, that sounds about right. He wouldn't lower himself to that. Trust me, you're not missing much. Looks like Caster but older. More nauseating machismo though."

"Good to know. I'm sure I'll enjoy killing him when I get my sister back."

His brow knit together as he studied her, canines flashing briefly. "And what you need here will help you do that?"

"Yes."

Gray fell quiet. There was something intriguing about him. It had been a while since anyone had dared to call Survivor a hyena to her face, and although Marauders had embraced the slur as a compliment, it had gotten under Gray's skin. Taking offense at the term put him in the minority in the Open. Most Openers thought that by defending Marauders, you were no better than them and deserved a death as horrible as they did. To say what he had in front of all those people, he had to possess more influence and have stockpiled more goodwill than could fit in this whole damn cavern.

"Rumor is," said Gray, "Thallium has a new weapon. Most people don't know that weapon's a person, but I got to see the rehearsal of that horror show. Even got to see the Marauders' bodies, or what was left of them, outside my town a couple days after you all had gone. That was Wren's doing, wasn't it?"

"I helped," said Survivor. "Not all of them lost their heads."

"All that I saw did. Made a mess and a half."

Her heart hammered. Once her mind caught up to her body's fear response to his words, she asked, "Wait—you didn't see an old man? Neck cut deep?"

"Didn't see any necks at all. None that were attached, anyway. That worry you?"

She took a minute to decide if it should, and her heart rate began to slow. Survivor had made sure The Gentleman was dead. After Wren did her damage, Survivor had taken that moment of shock and stillness in the air to double-check that he'd bled out. For her own sanity, for her sister, she'd had to confirm she'd killed him. But if The Gentleman's body was missing, it meant someone else knew what she'd done now too.

"No," she finally replied to Gray. "Not worried."

Gray stretched his arms high over his head, then leaned across the table. "Look, if you're going after Thallium, you're in good company. The main reason I'm here is to recruit a militia."

All at once, Survivor understood Gray for who he really was. This wasn't an easygoing salesman—he was a fighter. A leader, based on the way he talked up the public down here. She leaned forward on the table, drawn in by a new revelation. "You're trying to unify the Open."

"Psh, it's already unified," he replied. "Thallium did that hard bit himself. Kept people out of his thriving domain with a thirty-foot wall, put them on trial if he deemed them trouble-makers, infected them with a virus that's left a slow and steady trail of bodies through the southeast. Now he's scrounged up lost tech to subdue them completely. The Open's together; they just need to know when and how to take their shot."

An angry rabble eager to strike out against Thallium would only help Survivor. She needed to keep him pinned down, distract him with a struggle more urgent than his need to pursue her and Wren once they were back in the Open again. If they could actually do damage to The Disc in the process? All the better. Gray would be useful. "How many fighters do you have?"

He sat back and said, "Whoa now, we're not buddies yet. There's enough of us to make a mighty mess. That's all you need to know."

"Any Marauders under your flag?"

He coughed out a laugh. "Afraid not. Haven't gotten around to asking—they're not the friendliest bunch. But you already know that."

"Seems like that would be a nice group to have on your side —fighters rather than farmers."

"Don't underestimate the motivation of a farmer under threat. Though I'll admit that you're not wrong—people with more training who don't scare easily could help our cause. Openers would take some convincing to work with them, but the damage Marauders could do for our side would be worth the politicking I'd have to do."

"Help me get my supplies then."

He pointed at her with a finger wrapped around his now empty glass. "Your supplies would somehow add Marauders to my militia?"

She nodded.

He pondered that, studying her as he did. "You got that shiny little bangle?"

She took it from her pocket and reached across the table to put it in his hand. He took hold of her fingers briefly and ran his thumb across her knuckles. "Rough." The way he said it made it sound like a good thing. She yanked her hand back.

He didn't bother to examine the bracelet, just tucked it away in his jacket. "Seems we can help each other. I'll do your trading for you. What do you need?"

"That's it? You trust me?"

He put his glass on the table and leaned in toward her again. "I'm a pretty perceptive guy, and I've played every card game in this hole countless times over the past fifteen years. I can see when a bet's worth the risk. But there's one more caveat —I'd like my property back." He held out his hand to Beo and snapped his fingers near the blanket. Beo glanced at Survivor, then leaned forward to grab the blanket from behind him and hand it over. Gray sniffed it and grimaced before tucking it under the table. "Your shopping list?"

"You have a pencil?" Survivor quipped.

"Always." He pulled one from the inside breast pocket of his coat and slid it across the table to her along with a little pad of paper. The pad was filled with receipts and order totals for Dearborn's textiles. Survivor flipped to the first blank page. As she wrote the items she needed, Gray said, "I also want you to get a message to Caster for me. When you go back for your sister, tell him I'll see him soon—I owe him for nearly destroying my town."

She flipped the pad closed and set it on the table between

them with the pencil inside. "You believe that the prince does the king's dirty work?"

"Holed up as he is in the holy city with daddy himself, he hasn't given me a reason to think otherwise. I'll be sure to ask him when we bust through the wall someday soon."

"Too bad. I was there when you two had your lover's spat—lots of affection there. Makes it sting more, I'm sure. Miss him being the big spoon?"

"No, *I* prefer to be the big spoon." He looked her up and down when he said it. She cleared her throat and tried to ignore her weak body's response to his attention. He stood and draped the blanket over his arm. "Will you be heading back into the Open this evening?"

"Can't afford to stay here."

"I figured not. You're welcome to use my room." A grunt came from Beo at that. Gray turned to him. "Both of you."

"Won't you need it?" Survivor asked.

He shook his head and popped the splinter of wood from his pocket into the corner of his mouth. "I don't sleep much when I come here. Just use the room to stay clean and stash my stuff. There's a rock shower you'd be welcome to. Looks like you could use it."

Survivor glared at him, but then cleared her throat. "Thank you." When Beo said nothing, she kicked his shin with her heel.

Gray dug around in his pocket and pulled out a small black key. "Room 6. Just off the main trail. Help yourself." He tossed the key to her and left without looking back. As he walked away, his gait smooth and confident, she tried to ignore the ache in her gut that betrayed a hunger she'd long suppressed.

PART 2

GHOSTS

CHAPTER FOUR

"Smells like crap back here," said Adonis. He shoved the contents of an overturned trash bin—one that had certainly been overfilled to begin with—against the back wall of Screws & Gears with the side of his boot. When a tissue, sopping wet with who knows what, fell apart in sticky smears under his shoe, he decided he was making it worse by spreading it around. The smell hung heavier in the air now too, as if the mounded trash had been a creature with a stinking defense mechanism. People all over The Disc were finding their occupations less and less appealing as the feeling of being trapped grew stronger, and that apparently included the sanitation workers.

"This seems like the ideal romantic setting for your date," said Six.

Adonis shoved him. "That's not funny."

Six tucked the throwing knife he'd been toying with into his belt with several others, freeing his hands to tug his hair back and tie it off. "I'm just saying, Caster isn't here yet. If your date—"

"Stop calling him that!"

"So sorry. If your boo gets here before Caster does, you might have to stall for time is all. A little light chitchat, maybe more." He smacked Adonis' butt hard on the right cheek as he passed, heading into the shadow of the alcove surrounding the back door of Screws.

"I said that's not funny!"

"Come on, you don't want to take that anger into a first date do you? Try to—"

"Quiet, Six," Sans said over his shoulder from farther down the alley where he was watching for Caster and their guest. His voice carried along the stone with suppressed rage. He'd been on edge ever since last night, nearly as much as Adonis.

Another man entered the alley, and even though Adonis knew it had to be Caster by how Sans greeted him with a salute, his heart still flip-flopped. Caster stepped out of the shadows into the pool of red-orange light coming from the giant neon screw mounted on top of the roof. In the light and the ominous nature of the situation, Adonis couldn't help but see him as the badass Tyr persona he'd spent weeks creating. His blond beard was lit up in neon, facial muscles tense with pent-up rage, weirdly speckled eyes ready to release the frustration behind them. If something did go wrong here, he'd at least avenge Adonis' honor, a wrathful god bent on justice.

"When's our guest arriving?" asked Caster.

Adonis remembered to salute and did so, rushing through it. "Any minute."

"You think he has useful intel about Wren?"

Adonis hesitated. Six answered for him. "We don't know for sure, boss. Dal's really the one who might know something about her, but he's too high up to grab without drawing attention. This guy Oran is at least clearly involved in the rumored Keeper shenanigans around town."

"He knows things that make him worth this effort," said Adonis, trying to convince himself. "Was mouthing off in the pub to Dal and a couple other ghost robes about towns joining up against us. Starting with Dearborn."

"Gray. Making good on his word. Not too surprising. Hopefully this Oran knows more about the Keepers' illicit activities." Caster's sigh showed he was unimpressed, bored even, like tracking down a lead wasn't as rewarding as he'd thought it would be. Adonis had a feeling he knew why, and he wanted Caster to be proud of him.

"It did seem like he knew more, or had at least heard more, about Wren," Adonis said with the surest tone he could muster.

Six pushed Adonis back a step with a hand to his face. "Stop trying to convince him, kid. We gotta take this guy into custody regardless—he's a sick, sad bastard. He's got a thing for boys."

A sudden foul taste filled Adonis' mouth.

"I noticed," said Caster with a concerned look at Adonis. "Let's show him how we feel about that."

Six nodded. "Will do, boss. We'll follow your lead."

Sans suddenly appeared next to Adonis, manifesting silently as an apparition, as he often did. "He's coming."

"Then let's get this over with," said Caster. He squeezed Adonis' shoulder. "Just distract him for a minute, then we'll jump in."

"Yeah, a *long* minute," said Six.

Adonis swiped at him, but Six dodged it easily and faded deeper into the shadow of the alcove while Caster ducked behind a dense row of trash bins a dozen feet off. Sans hesitated. Adonis nodded at him, and the Harbinger finally joined Caster in hiding. After a deep breath, Adonis turned to face the entrance of the alley.

Oran ambled around the corner. He was whistling. Not a

familiar, popular song, just the wandering notes of someone in a great mood. He emerged from the shadows between the buildings. When he spotted Adonis, he waved and walked faster. Adonis' stomach turned.

Oran walked into the light of the neon sign and took a look around. "Kind of dirty, isn't it? Strange choice for someone so pretty." He sidled so close that Adonis could smell him over the garbage, then took one of Adonis' curls in between his fingers and tugged at it like a spring.

Adonis said nothing, just waited for the guys to jump Oran and pummel him for information. But they didn't.

"Nervous?" said Oran. His expression brightened, absorbing the red light washing over it. "Don't be. I'll go easy on you." He reached for Adonis' belt and Adonis jumped back, bumping up against the closest trash bin. Oran's gaze turned impatient. "You asked me here—stop teasing. It's better when we're both into it, but I'll take it either way."

He lunged at Adonis, but his fingertips just touched his shirt front before a knife flitted through the darkness and grazed Oran's arm. Oran cursed and looked for his unseen assailant.

"About time!" shouted Adonis.

Six emerged from the shadowy alcove. "It stopped being funny." His tone was light and joking, but Adonis knew that look—darkness creeping in around the edges of his eyes like ink into paper, cool fury that looked all too natural in his typically smart-ass expression. Adonis realized that was probably the last sight of Six's targets, and his stomach knotted.

"It won't be funny when Thallium hangs you—I'm a Keeper," said Oran.

"Yeah, the striped robe was my first clue," said Six. He withdrew another throwing knife from his belt and held it poised, ready if Oran tried to run for it. "That was a warning

throw. You move, the next one will hit something painful.
Squishy."

"This is a private meeting between two men," said Oran.

"*Men*, you sick, entitled ghost robe? He's thirteen."

Oran snickered. "A moral Assassin?" He nodded at Six's
black ID bracelet, which bore the cursive A of the trade. "So
what if I like them young and unblemished?"

"What poetry. You don't like blemishes, Robert Frost?
Maybe you just don't have enough to appreciate them." Six
lunged in his direction, but Oran turned to run. He only made
it two steps before thumping into the Harbinger standing
behind him—Sans, red eyes boring through the darkness, chest
heaving with ragged breath as he held his kanabō out at
shoulder height, ready to swing the mighty club at Oran's
head.

Oran squealed.

"He won't hurt you unless I tell him to." Caster walked into
the light to stand within an arm's length of Oran.

Oran blinked several times. "The Bastard? Since when do
you police your father's men?"

"I'm tasked with protecting The Disc from traitors. I think
someone raping qualifies. And underage victims at that."

"You see this?" Oran tugged at the chest of his robe. "This
is my 'do whatever I want' outfit. I don't take orders from
you."

Caster pointed at Oran. "You know, you might be right. If
Thallium gave you permission to screw around with citizens,
he'd have mercy on you, just box your ears and put you on
probation to put on a show for me. That is, until I tell him
you're part of a rebellion."

Oran looked him up and down, narrowed his gaze and said
carefully, "What rebellion?"

"Bet Thallium would let me do whatever I want with you if

I told him you're a part of Tyr's Army. Hell, he'll insist I make an example of you."

Oran released his breath as if he'd been holding it and gave a giddy, high-pitched chuckle, like Caster was the butt of the joke. "Oh, that cute little rumor? Pretty sure that some bored old man in a pub came up with it because nobody would listen to his same three stories over and over anymore. I'm not a part of that."

"I know you're not. You know how I know?" He stepped closer, getting right in Oran's face. "Because I'm leading it." He took the throwing knife from Six, then yanked Oran's hand out by his middle three fingers. In a flash, he held the Keeper's arm taut and ran the stiletto through the back of his palm, eliciting a scream which Sans quickly stifled with a hand over Oran's mouth.

"Uh, boss man?" whispered Six. "What are you doing?"

Caster ignored him. He pulled harder on Oran's fingers and gave the knife a good twist. Oran shrieked against Sans' flesh. "Wren, the girl Thallium's keeping locked up," Caster said after Oran's screams had quieted to soft groaning. "You called her a weapon at the pub yesterday. What do you know?"

Sans waited until Oran went quiet, then took his hand away from his mouth. "Nothing," he whined. "You picked the wrong Keeper to torture."

Caster twisted more and down came Sans' hand again. Caster got close to Oran's ear. "That's where you're wrong. You're expendable—a scum-licking bottom-feeder. Nobody would notice if you disappeared. They'll think one of your victims got the better of you, buried you out in the sand. Please understand—I picked you with intention." He yanked the knife from Oran's hand. The Keeper whimpered and swayed but managed to stay on his feet. Caster reached into his coat to retrieve a small snuff box. He opened it, took a big pinch of the powder inside, and put the box away. "I will get what I want. What was it you said? 'It's better when we're both into it, but I'll take it either way?' My thoughts exactly." Oran tried to cradle his hand against his chest, but Caster grabbed it and rubbed the powder into his wound. Oran's eyes rolled up, and he finally went limp, making Sans catch his dead weight before he could hit the ground.

"Wake him up," ordered Caster. Sans nodded and took out his canteen.

"Boss," said Six, "what are you doing? We're not here to get information about Wren, we're here to stop Keepers from hurting innocent people. Besides, you must know way more than he does about what's going on with her."

"Donnie, Oran mentioned Wren at the pub, didn't he?" replied Caster.

Adonis just nodded dumbly.

Caster nodded in return and spotted Six's scarf. "Give me that."

Six slowly untied the strip of black cotton from around his neck and handed it to Caster, clearly accepting an order that surprised him, but one he understood.

Adonis finally found his voice. "But what if he tells Thallium about Tyr? We can't let him go now."

Caster's gaze met Adonis', and for an instant, there was guilt there—pale and fearful—and Adonis saw a man willing to shred his soul by doing whatever was necessary to save someone he loved. "No, we can't." He knelt next to Oran on the ground as Sans poured water onto his face, causing him to sputter awake.

Adonis blurted, "Wait, we can't just—" Six's grip on his elbow pulling him back cut him short.

"Stay back here with me, Donnie."

"But I—"

"Quiet."

Adonis fell silent. He watched Caster—a comrade he admired, who had encouraged him and protected him from bullies like Mainstay over the years, his friend—prepare to murder a man.

"What's Thallium doing to Wren?" Caster asked, and if Adonis had closed his eyes, he would have sworn it was the Principal talking.

Oran shook the water from his face. "I don't know."

Caster took the scarf and held it taut over Oran's nose and mouth before nodding to Sans. Sans drizzled water onto the fabric and Oran flailed, a fish caught under the spear that was Sans' right arm across his chest.

Caster lifted the scarf from his face. "He's keeping her in the lab, isn't he? Does he ever let her out?"

Oran's eyes bugged from their sockets as he coughed. "I don't know, damn you!"

"But you've heard rumors. What are they?"

"You're just going to kill me. Why tell you anything?"

"No. If you tell me, I'll let you live."

Oran stared at him, then at Sans' red eyes, then back to Caster. "You swear?"

"No."

Oran swallowed. "The guys on duty near the lab say she never comes out. Thallium's so paranoid that he's making those other genius people work in the dining hall of the Main House, and even that staff's cut to essential personnel. Only the android, Thallium, and the lab assistant—that Bug girl—go in or out of the lab."

"You have no idea what they're doing to her?" asked Caster. "You mentioned a weapon."

"That's the rumor—they're trying to make her into something. She turned on the lights in the city, right? Maybe the Principal wants her to power more than just streetlamps."

"Maybe? You don't know?"

"Like you said—I'm a bottom-feeder. I don't *know* anything."

Caster nodded.

"That's all I've heard," Oran squealed, still remarkably indignant despite his perilous position. "Torture Dal or that tracker Amsel if you want something more."

"I'll consider that." Caster met Sans' gaze. Something passed between them—an order without words. Caster stood and walked away.

"Now let me g—" Oran's words were cut off by Sans' forearm coming down on his throat. Oran flailed like a fish again, more desperately this time, and Adonis turned and vomited near Six's feet.

"Caster, stop!" came a plea from the end of the alley.

Adonis turned to see a pale shape limping toward them, accompanied by the *tap-tap* of a staff hitting the ground.

Prady stepped into the light. His broad shoulders and furrowed expression were stern, but the old man looked tired. Exhaustion was settling in to rest in his wrinkles with the wisdom. Sweat gleamed along his gray hairline, and his Keeper robe was covered with big streaks of dust, as if he'd run here, kicking up dirt with the awkwardness of his gait. "Cold murder, Caster? I see your father's methods aren't as far from you as I once thought."

A flash of shame disturbed Caster's calm, but it passed quickly. "I can't let him go."

"Oh, sure you can. Into my custody. But I won't take a dead body." Prady pointed at Sans and the now motionless Oran with his staff.

"Let up," said Caster to Sans, who did as he was told.

Adonis was sure Oran was already dead until he saw the shallow, labored rise and fall of his abdomen.

Prady walked over and tossed Sans a pair of e-binds. Sans put them on Oran's wrists; they hummed to life with blue electricity.

Caster got closer to the old man. "You suddenly care about punishing Thallium's thugs? They've been running wild, and you've done nothing."

Prady sighed. Adonis always thought he'd have made a better priest or healer—ruffling his feathers was almost impossible, as was keeping him down for long. Wren's psycho sister had fractured the kneecap of his bum leg over a month ago, but here he was on his feet. The man had more strength than Adonis probably ever would, and at over sixty, Prady still intimidated him.

"You're Thallium's new number two, and you think to lecture me, son? First, remove the plank from your own eye," said Prady. He leaned against his staff. "What I've been doing until recently is lying in bed with a cast. When I wasn't doing that, I was struggling to get up to use the bathroom or hobbling outside of my apartment for fresh air. I've been listening to the Keepers in my building for weeks, and I don't believe things are as simple as Thallium encouraging them to indulge themselves."

"What do you mean?" Caster asked in a daze, like he was waking up.

"I don't know enough to say anything for certain, but the Keepers who have been terrorizing citizens and ignoring their duties all started acting out around the same time. I believe there's something going on here that even you aren't privy to."

"Why wouldn't Thallium just tell me he gave them permission to do whatever they wanted?"

"Are you so sure he did?"

"Wouldn't he do anything to keep their loyalty at a time when it's at a premium?"

"If you have no proof, best to withhold judgment for now," said Prady. "I'll continue to look into it. Trust that not all Keepers are acting out. Don't lump good men in with the garbage making this noise. It's too easy to only hear the loud ones and disregard those doing their jobs quietly and with honor." Prady turned to Adonis. "Help an old man out." He retrieved a roll of bandage from his robe and tossed it to Adonis. "Don't want this prisoner fainting of blood loss once he comes to."

"What do you want with this pervert, Prady?" Six kicked Oran's foot.

"To make a difference again, Assassin," Prady replied plainly. "I've been demoted from commander to glorified mannequin at the Main House because of my leg. It seems I'm ancient and broken, only fit for holding up a wall now. I had to beg to keep my robe so that I can discover what's turning my men into beasts. This boy is one step toward that." He bent down to check Adonis' bandage on Oran's hand. "A little tighter, son."

"You're stationed at the Main House?" Caster asked. "Why haven't I seen you?"

Prady grunted as he pushed off his knee to stand again. "I'm stationed close to our little outlier lady."

It was as if the air had been sucked out of the alley for a second before Caster asked quietly, "You've seen Wren?"

Prady chuckled kindly. "No, I've not seen her, but I managed to get on a lab guard duty rotation. They want men they can trust on that detail more than young fighters, thankfully."

"You always preferred active posts. I'm surprised you accepted a stationary job," said Caster.

"Sir, I made that young woman a promise to protect her—the same promise I made you years ago." He bowed his head. "I intend to keep it."

Caster took that in, and he relaxed his stance. "We need to get her out of there. Will you help us?"

Prady raised his gaze. "Who exactly is 'we'?"

"Tyr's Army!" Adonis announced proudly from the ground where he tied off the bandage around Oran's hand.

Six kicked him lightly. "*Secret* army, putz. Can't take you anywhere."

"Not as secret as you might think, Assassin," said Prady. "Tyr's name's being whispered in alleys just like this one all over the city."

"We're putting together enough manpower to get Wren out of there," said Caster. "Us and Wren's sister—we've kept in touch through Freddy. She has a way into the city, but we're waiting to send word for her to use it when the time's right."

"Ah, the sister," he tested the weight on his leg, "would not be my first choice for an ally."

"Wren's well-being is a common concern of ours. She won't betray me while her sister's in danger here. She wouldn't risk it."

Prady didn't look convinced. "In answer to your question, yes, I can help you."

"This is bigger than Wren, Prady," said Six. "Getting her out is only the first step—"

Prady put a hand up. "I don't need to know everything. Probably better I don't, for now. But know that your foot soldiers are getting eager. I feel it in the pubs, in the streets, the eyes of young men and women boring into my striped back with hatred like fiery vinegar. Things with these rogue Keepers will only get worse. Eventually, on a particularly bad day, one of you young folks is going to snap and act out, fueled by the luster of rebellion and righteousness. When that happens, The Disc will dissolve into total anarchy. Best to plan out our mayhem, wouldn't you agree?"

"What do you advise?" asked Six.

"Get Wren out soon. If your rebellion starts before you do, I'm afraid the Main House will put up defenses you won't be able to break past."

"I agree," said Caster. "We'll need your help."

"I know. I'll contact you. You have a drop point in the market, yes? A certain jeweler's tent?"

"You're a frightening man, Prady," said Six.

"No need to contact us," said Caster. "We'll be meeting soon to discuss strategy. If I send word, will you attend?"

The Keeper nodded. He looked down at Oran with annoyance. "Going to need him awake, I'm afraid."

"I've got it," said Six. He squatted next to Oran, then fiddled with a ring on his right middle finger. It opened like a tiny silver flower. Before he brought it under Oran's nose, he slapped him across the face for good measure. When Oran smelled the salts in the ring, he sputtered awake, disoriented and in enough pain that he just lay there helpless for a minute.

Prady tugged Oran's binds to drag him to his feet.

"What are you going to do with him?" asked Caster.

"Something the elderly are always good at—disciplining the youth. See if I can find out why he and his associates are boldly indulging the sin in their hearts. I'll tell the Principal he needs to be in solitary for a couple of weeks. Should buy you some time." He kicked Oran's heels, and the prisoner stumbled forward. "Walk and keep your mouth shut."

After they left the alley, Caster turned to Sans. "Find that tracker you saw Oran with last night. I want to know where he hangs out."

"To join up for a drink?" joked Six.

Caster didn't even give him a pity chuckle, just kept his gaze on Sans.

"We'll find him," Sans said.

Adonis stepped up. "Yep, we've got it, boss. Thieves are on the job."

Caster raised an eyebrow.

Sans nodded, then mouthed silently, "It's fine."

"I want you listening to Sans," said Caster. "Follow his orders, Donnie. Understand?"

Adonis saluted him. It somehow felt more official now, shadowing Sans, and that almost took the sting out of this horrific night. Almost.

Six spoke up again, "When we find him, boss, what do you plan to do?"

Caster didn't reply, just broke off from the group and headed in the direction of the Main House.

"No plan. I assumed as much," said Six. The Assassin watched Caster's back, and that cold killer expression came back to his face.

Adonis had long thought of Six and Caster as his bickering older brothers. Always up to throw down, sure, but always there to pick each other up afterward too. Caster had been less and less apt to do the latter lately. It wasn't only Six he was shutting out; it was everyone. Six just refused to be okay with it. If it continued, the next time the two threw down, one of them wouldn't get back up.

"Let's get out of here," Sans said.

"Drink at Screws first?" asked Six.

"No!" said Adonis, startling the two of them. He cleared his throat. "No Screws. Never again for me."

Six threw his arm around Adonis' shoulders. "Fair enough, kid."

The three left the alley and its stink behind and turned

away from Screws and the boisterous line of people waiting to get in, bodies bumping together like moths after the neon light.

———

Asha stood inside the primary med ward near the entrance and watched the clock on the wall above the door tick past 5:30. The sun had already gone down behind the wall, and the fluorescent lights inside the med ward took on the burden of keeping out the dark, which was beginning to seep in thickly through the front windows.

He was late. Again. "Unreliable, bone-picking schmuck."

Asha forced her attention away from the med ward door and back to the mitered corner she'd already refolded three times on the bed nearest the entrance, one of only two empty beds in the whole building. She folded and tucked one more time and decided it was good enough. She then grabbed a wool blanket from the pile on the rolling table behind her and draped it across the foot of the bed. Apparently, the med ward wasn't crucial enough in the eyes of their fearless leader—or Tess in solar or whoever decided what to do with power in this time of rationing—to deserve adequate heating.

Every day, Asha's number of patients increased. A half dozen suffering from either the flu or pneumonia were quarantined in the beds along the wall opposite from where she stood. Cordoned off with plastic curtains, they shivered beneath scratchy blankets, and the heat of their breath gradually caused the curtains to fog up. At least a third of them wouldn't leave their beds; they'd shiver there until their end.

"Doctor! A little help?" Yvette called from halfway down the ward.

Asha took a breath before turning to start down the aisle. The sick season always arrived with the cold, but this year the med shortage made it far more challenging. Medicines were going out faster than they were coming in, and if a patient needed medicine that was out of stock, they were out of luck.

Freddy better hurry his ass up.

As she reached Yvette's patient, she saw the nurse holding an IV catheter as if it were about to sting her.

Asha pinched the bridge of her nose. "Nurse North, do we really need to have this conversation again? You can do this. You did two others this morning."

"What's going on?" asked her patient, an older man who'd come in suffering from minor hypothermia and dehydration. He made periodic appearances in the med ward; he lived alone and couldn't take care of himself well, which was only compounded by the lockdown. Sweet guy with tufts of white hair in a ring around his otherwise bald head.

"Nothing's wrong, Eamon," said Asha. "We're just a little overworked. That's all." She pulled the blanket that had slipped from his head back up.

"But yesterday when I did one wrong," Yvette said to Asha in a rush, "it filled up Mrs. Rincon's arm like a balloon. What if I do it again?"

"What's going on?" Eamon said again, louder this time. His wiry eyebrows pulled together in uncertainty.

"Not a thing, Eamon," said Asha. She put her hand on Yvette's back. "Excuse us for just a minute. Can I get you another cup of tea?"

He brightened at that and held his nearly empty cup out shakily. "Mint? With about that much agave?" He held his pointer finger and thumb apart a half an inch as if that were the universal standard for measuring sweetener.

"You got it. Be right back." Asha steered Yvette away toward the sustenance station at the back of the ward. As Asha filled the cup from the hot water dispenser, she said, "Nurse

North, I recognize that you haven't finished your formal training yet, and I do appreciate you volunteering to help here when we're short-staffed. However, do you really think that what your patient needed to hear just now was how you messed up yesterday?"

"Ma'am?"

"Skip the 'ma'am.' 'Doctor' or 'Doctor Keating,' please." Asha cursed under her breath—she'd forgotten to leave some room in Eamon's cup since his hands tended to bobble and spill whatever drink they held. She sidestepped to the sink and poured a third of it out. "Do you think your lack of confidence makes you a more approachable medical professional?"

"Um, no? But—"

"But nothing." She set the cup on the counter and finally turned toward Yvette. "You're fully capable of being an excellent nurse—your patients need to see that you believe that. If you *don't* believe that, then you need to find a new profession. Understand?"

Yvette nodded rapidly. "Yes, doctor."

"The peppermint tea is in the cabinet to your right, behind the rosemary. Eamon likes it strong."

Nurse North hustled to the cabinet. "And the agave?"

Asha blew a raspberry. "I wish. We haven't had agave for days. But he shouldn't notice—can't taste much." Asha got closer to her, lowered her voice. "You will not reveal confidential information about another patient again. Is that clear? Go place that IV properly. If anyone's arm ever balloons up like Mrs. Rincon's did, what should you do?"

Nurse North ticked items off on her fingers. "Stop and remove the IV, elevate their arm, assure them it will be fine, and 'get it fucking right next time.'"

"Excellent."

The door of the ward opened with a whoosh. Cold wind

rushed down the aisle toward Asha and Yvette, rustling the bed curtains as it went. Freddy stepped in with a satchel hanging from his shoulder. He bowed dramatically to her and patted the satchel.

She speed-walked down the aisle toward him, and he tried to hide how he shrank in on himself at the look on her face.

"You motherfu—"

"And a majestic afternoon to you, Doctor. Yes, I'd love to come in out of the bitter wind and have a seat, thank you." He took the satchel off and put it on the check-in desk before plopping in the chair there and putting his feet up.

"Where have you been, de Bourgh?"

"You act as though coming back from the Open is as simple as returning home after a quick trip to the apothecary. Not so, my darling doctor. You didn't expect me to meet you without first washing the filth of travel from my intrepid self, did you?" The maroon coat he wore was fringed with fur—from what animal, Asha couldn't tell.

As she opened the satchel, she eyed his scarf. "Still wearing that horrifying thing?"

He angled his chin down so he could admire his scarf made from a fox pelt with the animal's skull still attached. When he pinched the back of the skull, the mouth opened so the teeth could clamp down on the tail. "Petunia? Of course I'm wearing her. It's called fashion." He opened and closed Petunia's mouth at her and made the chirping noise of a fox.

"I'll take your word for it." As she withdrew the contents of the satchel and set them on the desk, she mentally checked off what she found from the supply list she'd given Freddy. "There's no butterfly weed. What the hell, de Bourgh? That was top priority."

"It's also a hot commodity—the cold's upon us."

"Yes, hence why I need butterfly weed."

"I got wild licorice." He waved his hand around lazily. "Same thing."

"Same thing? I had no idea you were a doctor. You hide it well beneath your façade of incompetence." She shoved the empty satchel at his chest.

"Well," he tossed his hair back and placed the satchel on the floor, "that's just rude."

"Wild licorice won't treat the lung. Help with coughing? Sure. But it won't get to the root of the issue." She lowered her voice. "I have people dying in here, Freddy. Did you really do everything you could to get it?"

"Short of selling my body, yes. I mean, I offered, but they weren't interested." He shrugged as if it was their loss.

"They? You mean you *were* able to find butterfly weed?"

He slipped his feet off the desk and rubbed at his temples, eyes closed. "Look, people aren't trading with us. Not the apothecaries in Non, not even the gatherers who kept the excess from the summer and fall herb harvests for themselves. The things I *did* get I finagled from old contacts that owed me favors. Nobody wants to help The Disc right now."

Relying on others came naturally to Asha as a doctor—everyone relied on her, and she relied on those she trusted, like Gavel and Ark, to help her. But this, people forsaking an entire community because of one man's actions, it was going to make her beg for help. And begging? She was terrible at it.

Asha sighed as she walked around the desk. She felt Freddy's neck, palpating all over his lymph nodes. "How are you feeling?"

"Just fine, Doc. Wore a mask when it was time to trade and all that, just like you told me. Didn't drink the local water, blah, blah, blah."

"Open your mouth," she ordered.

He dramatically stuck his tongue out and "aaahed."

Asha sniffed. "Tarragon?"

"Treated myself to my favorite fresh herbs. Very sensitive about how I smell to others, you know."

"You're definitely keeping it fresh, Freddy. If you start to feel ill, you come find me immediately. Rubedo is out there, and we don't know how far it's spread. The one good thing about this lockdown is that it should keep it out."

"From what I heard, people are still dying. After what we saw in Hallund..." He searched for the right words. "Even if there was a cure, once symptoms show up, the sick die fast."

Asha had been so caught up in her need for meds that she hadn't asked the main question she was supposed to when Freddy got back. "What's the situation out there?"

"Well, goodness gracious, Doc, the fine desert people are thoroughly exasperated with our esteemed ruler. Shocking, I know."

"People are gathering then?"

Freddy wobbled his open hand back and forth. "Rubedo has slowed those efforts. People have to be cautious. However, one particular name was mentioned frequently—our favorite textile merchant."

"Gray," she said softly, careful to keep her voice low just in case Theo the Operator happened to be listening. "It's what we feared."

"Fear is a powerful motivator, naturally, and it has the Open ready for a battle they would never have considered fighting without it. All those dainty communities that prefer to keep to themselves banding together? Serious business."

Asha slapped the desk. "Damn it. If I could get out there, I could help. Go to Dearborn, meet with Gray, heal his sick people. If I got to speak with him face to face, he'd listen."

"You'd like to go to the man who happily spread the word

to his fellow Openers about Thallium's treachery and promised us a war? And you called *me* incompetent."

"Have a little faith in people, Freddy."

"Other than the skill of my own two hands and yours, dear doctor, I have faith in very little. Grace is something your God gives. The people of the Open aren't so generous."

Helplessness made her feel heavy, and she leaned onto the desk as she tried to work through her frustration without causing a scene. But before she could stop herself, she tossed a pile of paperwork onto the floor and shouted, "Fuck!"

The quiet conversations of nearby patients faltered at her expletive but then kept right on going. Most of them were used to her occasional outbursts by now.

Freddy stood and smushed her in a dramatic hug, which she would tolerate from less than a handful of people. Since they'd returned from the Open with Wren and the others, Freddy had morphed in Asha's estimation from ostentatious man-baby to tolerably annoying friend and—dare she admit it—a confidant.

"We're on our own, my darling," said Freddy. "As are the sick outside our walls."

Frigid air accosted Asha's back as the ward door opened, and she shivered against Freddy.

"Ah, Mr. Keating!" Freddy called out over her shoulder. "Perfect timing. I need to attend to other matters, but I believe if I release your wife here, she'll start breaking things and scaring the invalids."

Asha thumped him on either side of his ribcage, and he spun her around to face her husband.

Gavel was an intimidating man, at least to those who didn't know him. Asha occasionally found herself in that mindset, seeing him from the perspective of her patients—this quiet force walking into a place of healing. Tall, broad, and stoic. He pulled the balaclava from his mouth and removed a wool beanie she'd made him for one of their anniversaries. He'd let his hair grow out as he did every cold season—his dark head no longer shone but was instead covered with short black and gray hair. A similarly colored beard adorned his face. She liked that the most—the beard. When they'd met, he'd had that beard, minus the gray.

Gavel bent down and kissed her cheek. "Have you eaten?"

"Actually," said Freddy, "I'm starved. Let's go." He started tightening his outer layers. "Your treat?"

"Goodbye, Frederick," Gavel said.

"You're no fun at all." Freddy started to lean in to kiss Asha's other cheek.

She stopped his kiss with a shove toward the door. "Those lips have been places I don't want to touch. Get out of here. Bring me some damn butterfly weed next time."

As he walked backward toward the door, he pulled a pencil from his breast pocket. "Abraca alacazam!" He flicked the pencil high in the air. "Tragedy. Still haven't manifested magical powers. I'll discount my body to rock bottom prices during my next scheduled outing. Promise."

"Smile pretty!" she called.

He blew Asha a kiss, tugged Petunia closer around his neck, and headed out into the cold.

Asha spoke to Gavel as she snatched up the satchel and started repacking it. "No, I haven't eaten. I thought I'd just see what's left in my pantry stash here."

"You need to get out for a while. Come home with me. Eat. Get more than a couple hours of sleep. Maybe even next to me in our bed."

"Whoa, that's a little too ambitious."

"Please, baby?"

She stopped packing the bag and eyed him. "Seems like

there's something more going on here than you worrying about me. What happened?"

After a long pause, he said, "Let's go to dinner and talk."

"We're talking now. What happened, Gav?"

He leaned against the desk and folded his arms. "I'm concerned about Caster." She opened her mouth to speak, but he said quickly, "Before you ask, no, he's not hurt."

"Not in body, I'm sure." Nothing could injure him, after all. "You're concerned how?"

"He's losing perspective. Growing impatient."

She pushed his knees apart so she could step between his legs. "What are you afraid of?"

He put his arms around her and rested his hands at the small of her back. "Somebody dying. Him killing someone, maybe getting himself killed. He's growing unbalanced."

"You're his Head. Surely he still has respect for that."

"I'm only his Head in the Body. Not in our other venture. Can you come eat with me and chat? Tomorrow night, we could even go out—share a *smoke*."

Asha hated speaking in code, mostly because Gavel was terrible at it. But if they were in the med ward, all wired up to the Main House operating system, they couldn't be frank. It went against her core to be anything but frank. "Smoke" meant it was time for those leading the rebellion to meet at Pip's. "Share a smoke? Mr. Keating, how mischievous of you."

He sighed quietly. "How about dinner for now? Overdue time together at home?"

She went in for a kiss. He kissed her back gently, but she turned the kiss deep before he could pull away. She ended it and backed up. "Absolutely." He glared at her, but even a public tongue kiss couldn't get him to break his composure. "I just need to—"

There was a crash on the other side of the ward, then a shrill, "Sorry, sorry, sorry!" from Nurse North.

"Ah, shit," Asha muttered.

Gavel kissed her on the cheek and pushed off of the desk. "I'll meet you at home when you're free."

"Might be a while."

She watched him leave—caught up in naughty thoughts only appropriate for the man's wife—before jogging down the aisle toward Nurse North's most recent catastrophe.

Cool water trickled down Survivor's back. The rock faces surrounding her in the tight space trapped the moisture and made it seem as if she were in a dreamworld. A bar of soap was wedged in a small hole in the wall. She yanked it out and sniffed it—some kind of milk and rosemary, both the green leaves and its little blue flowers. She rubbed it all over and watched the dirt and grime come off, leaving her skin an altogether different shade underneath. Her hair was the most challenging part of the whole ordeal, but the moisture in the milk bar loosened it up enough for her to work through the worst of the tangles with her fingers. When she tipped her head back under the stream and let it hit her square in the face, she tried to remember the last time she'd fully bathed. Not since her time with Wren in their cave. Not with soap since long before that when she'd had access to perfumes and creams whose smells were lodged in her brain, eager to yank her back to the past.

This soap was simple and effective. She considered stealing it but found herself tucking it back in the alcove. She finished up and shifted a heavy metal lever down to stop the flow of water from the pool embanked above. She realized she hadn't thought to bring a towel inside the shower. After squeezing as much of the water as she could from her hair, she headed back into the main room in nothing but her skin.

The stone room was dark and warm, not large but plenty big for sleeping and getting clean. Two spotlights high in the ceiling put out a warm, red glow that touched the bulk of the small space, at the center of which was a generously sized bed with what Survivor had come to recognize as Dearborn bedding—thick and soft, likely white but cast pink in the light from above. Beo sprawled out on the bed with his hands and feet dangling off, but the sloppy smile on his face said he didn't mind.

"Where would a rich guy keep his towels?" she asked him, dripping onto the stone floor.

He glanced at her and rolled his eyes. "Still no shame."

She looked down at her chest, let her gaze follow along her legs to her callused feet. "Shame?"

He got up—reluctantly, by the exaggeration of his sigh—and walked around her to a basket near the entrance to the shower. He took the woven top off and pulled out a towel, which he tossed to her in a huff before taking big strides to the bed and jumping back onto it with a heavy thump.

She rubbed at her hair with the towel before wrapping it around her body. It stretched from her shoulders to skim the floor. The plush texture was unreal. "Rich people," she muttered.

"I'm not complaining."

"You did nothing but complain earlier when he made this offer."

"That was before I saw the bed." He put his hands behind his head and spread his legs out in a wide V. "All is forgiven. Seems like a nice guy."

No longer dripping, she dropped the towel to the floor and went to where she'd laid her clothes on the trunk at the foot of the bed. "There are no nice guys. He wants to screw me."

"That's awfully conceited. If he wants to screw you, where is he? Doesn't he have to be here to accomplish that?"

Her clothes were missing. "Where's all my stuff?"

"Someone—sweet little old lady—came in and took them to wash. Said she works with Gray."

Survivor dragged her hands down her face. "You just let her take them? What if she's sold it by now?"

"Didn't strike me as the pawning type. No shifty eyes. Gave her most of my stuff too."

She remembered she'd left the keycard on top of her pile of clothes. "Where's the key, idiot?" She dropped to the floor to look under the bed and scrambled around like she'd dropped something in the dark.

"Relax," Beo said, watching her with amusement from the edge of the bed, lying on his stomach. "Despite appearances, I'm not a complete jackass." He pulled the key out from under his shirt and brandished it.

She leapt up and snatched it, yanking the chain over his head with no attempt at gentleness. "Give me that." Feeling it cold against her skin took the edge of panic away and returned her focus to her mission—why she was in this dank hole in the first place. "You didn't think to keep anything out for me to wear?"

He waved a hand toward his bag on the other side of the bed on the floor. "Left you a tunic of mine. Yours all stank, so I told her to take everything."

"Smartass." She lunged for the bag and yanked out the tunic, then threw the white thing over her head. The billowing excess fabric fell just below her knees, and the sleeves went to her elbows. "Perfect." The chill of the damp on her skin finally got to her, and she started shivering. Right when she'd dived under the covers next to Beo, there was a knock toward the bottom of the door as if the person on the other side had used their foot.

"Get it," she said between her chattering teeth.

"No way. You were just up."

"I hate you." She slid out from under the blanket, took four quick steps to the rickety door, and opened it.

Gray stood there, balancing three covered plates of food on top of a wooden shipping crate. His gaze started at her damp hair and then traced the lines of her body down to her bare legs and feet. "How was the shower?"

"It had running water, so fucking great."

"Excellent." He pushed past her, and she found herself letting him. As he brushed against her side, a whiff of red chile came from the plates he carried. Her stomach growled, and he heard. "Good, you're hungry. Brought you both a tamale. Hope you like your red sauce hot. Only way they make it here."

Beo sat on the edge of the bed and jutted his chin at the plates. "How much did those cost?"

Gray slid them off the top of the crate onto a low table near a pile of hot stones that kept the room comfortably warm. "Too much. But luckily, the cook here needed a gift for his wife, who loves my town's scarves. Worked out fine. The filling's just beans—you don't want the meat they have here."

Survivor thought of Mainstay. "I'm not picky."

He set the crate down by the table, and its contents clattered with the twinkling of the glass and gear inside. "Got everything on your list, but the capsule won't be ready until tomorrow. There's no way you can afford the metal shards you wanted from the smiths here, and I didn't bring enough cash to spot you any more than I already have. Afraid you'll just have to forget about that purchase. If I knew what you wanted them for, I might be able to help you think of a substitute. Mind telling me what all this is?"

Survivor ignored him, but Beo replied, "That's a family matter." Beo shoved the top off of the crate, which clattered loudly against the stone floor. He then plucked the machete from the midst of the supplies and gave it a couple of tight swings to test the weight. It was half-rusted, chipped along the edge of the blade as if its previous owner hadn't known how to wield it properly. Even so, the way it stirred the air brought ghosts into the room that Survivor had spent years pretending weren't there. "This is garbage," Beo said.

"It'll do," said Survivor.

"You want to fight with a long piece of garbage?"

"I'll find a replacement. Just need this to get started."

He shook his head and slid the machete back into the box.

Survivor sorted through the other supplies: apricot kernels, bundle of dried juniper wood, bottle of Yellow Fever, small tin of pine pitch, sulfur crystals from the nearby mine to the north, six large glass jars, needle-nose pliers, a ball of cotton string, sugar, and the biggest sack of bat guano they sold.

Survivor looked up at Beo. "We good?"

He grunted and turned away from the supplies toward one of the tamale plates. Red sauce dripped all over his thumb and pointer finger as he ate it in two bites. A water basin stood next to the shower, and he headed to it to wash the sticky masa and staining red chile from his hand.

Survivor felt Gray's gaze on her as she opened and closed the set of pliers. "Something on my face, cat man?"

He didn't answer, and she glanced up and over at him through her wet hair. He gave her a toothy grin. "Wasn't looking at your face."

She turned and quickly pressed the flat side of the pliers

hard against his cheek, right under his eye. "That'll cost you a lot more than a couple of tamales," she hissed.

"Good thing I'm not looking to buy." He pushed the pliers down calmly but firmly. "But I am looking."

Color warmed her cheeks. She looked away fast toward the supplies. The fact that a man could elicit this kind of juvenile response from her body wasn't just humiliating, it was disturbing.

"Glad you're happy with the gear," said Gray. "Hope it shows that I'm serious about our arrangement. Remember your part of it. If you bring enough Marauders to the Open militia, we can make the march to The Disc."

Who knew how long that mobilization would take. Gray needed to start it now if they'd be ready to confront Thallium when Survivor needed them to. "Go ahead and send the word out—I *will* deliver."

Gray shifted his weight toward her, and instead of anger, she felt horrifying excitement. "I believe you."

"Have any booze?" Beo asked as he stomped over, wiping his hands on one of Gray's fluffy towels.

Gray didn't look away from Survivor as he spoke. "Brought that bottle of Yellow you asked for. That's not enough?"

"That's not for me," said Beo simply.

Gray sighed as if that made no sense but then took a small metal token that looked vaguely like a bat with open wings from his pocket and tossed it up. Beo caught it. "There's a private bar near the hub. That'll get you in."

"I don't have any money." Beo raised his hand as if he intended to toss the key back.

"Put it on my tab."

Beo shoved the token in his pocket straightaway. "Well then. I'll be going." He tugged on his boots next to the door and then poked Survivor in the back excitedly. "You coming?"

Gray raised an eyebrow at her, toyed with the cuff of her sleeve.

She turned toward Beo. "No. You go. Drink up."

He eyed Gray behind her, then sighed. "Really? You're gonna let him?"

She squeezed his big hand. "Have fun." Her nails dug into his palm for good measure.

He sighed again but left.

Gray came up behind her and moved her hair over to one shoulder, sniffed lightly near her neck. "Rosemary. You used my soap."

She turned around and got close to his face. "Almost stole it too."

"Nice of you not to." He put a hand on her hip, and she shoved him back with a firm push against his chest.

"I'm not nice."

He smirked. "I've noticed." He paced around her slowly, keeping his distance but holding her attention. "If you like rosemary, I can get you fresh cuttings. Flowering year-round."

"That's bullshit."

"Is it? Easier to assume a man's lying, I guess. You do that a lot?"

"What's it to you?"

He eyed her up and down. "Just a question. That's what people do to get to know each other—ask questions." Something in his easy gait, the way his shoulders curved toward her as he circled closer, made it hard to focus.

"Got no answers for you."

He stopped circling when he spotted the card peeking out from the low collar of the tunic. "Which means you won't tell me what *that* is, either."

"No."

With a shrug, he said, "Happy to wait for answers until

you're ready to give them. I'm patient." He tucked a long strand of hair behind her ear, and the tender gesture caught Survivor off guard.

"I don't need this," she said quietly, unable to find the volume she wanted in her voice, unsure if she was trying to convince him or herself.

"Would you like me to leave?" he whispered back.

"It's your room."

"Then you want me to stay?"

She hesitated. "I *want* a lot of things," she finally said.

He reached out to run the back of his hand down her arm slowly. "Tell me."

"My family whole again. Revenge. Power."

"Damn." He snapped his fingers. "Seems I'm not on that list."

After a few seconds, she growled, "Didn't say I was finished."

She pushed him again, and he fell back on the bed. He propped himself up on his elbows and grinned at her hungrily with those dangerous canines. She strode over and leapt on top of him, straddling his hips.

"This means nothing," she said.

He put his hands on her knees and slowly moved them underneath the tunic and up her thighs. "For you, maybe." His eyes danced all over her face. With a swift motion, he yanked the tunic over her head, and her damp hair fell over her chest and back. The chilly air hit her skin again, but when Gray started kissing everywhere, she forgot all about the cold.

CHAPTER FIVE

———

There were a few benefits to living in the Main House. The first, and perhaps the most obvious, was heating and cooling. But close behind that was access to Thallium's private library. Even though Caster didn't have the headspace to read—hadn't for a while—that didn't stop him from trying. Just the habit of getting settled in his bed, propping up with an arm behind his head as his eyes scanned the pages was comforting. He might only get through a few paragraphs, but nonetheless, the sound and motion of turning the page brought peace. Temporary peace, anyway.

His mind was a hive, buzzing, buzzing, never stopping. The urgency to jump into action crippled by the inability to show his hand. Not yet. Always not yet. Thallium had said Eydis wasn't allowing Wren visitors. Something about how it would distract her when she couldn't afford to be distracted. Total bullshit, which he had to continue tolerating in order to keep his cover as the loyal son.

It was driving him mad.

The purple stone attached to the cord around his wrist

poked out from his sleeve as he adjusted the book in his hand. An idiotic gift he'd bought for a girl who probably wouldn't even remember seeing it in Vee's booth weeks ago. Surely whatever she was going through now had made that memory seem inconsequential. A nightmare overshadowing a daydream, a nightmare he'd brought her into. His frustration overflowed as a rough exhale through his nose.

As he readjusted his arm under his pillow, his fingers found his bowie knife concealed there. He retrieved the knife, craving the comfort of its familiar weight in his hand. There had been no time to dwell on what had happened in the desert, when he'd been killed in front of those he loved only to stand up afterward. Ever since then, he had been solely focused on what needed to be done to get Wren out of the inner chamber, get her away from The Disc. He'd ordered everyone around him to do the same. Even Asha had stopped asking questions about how he was feeling and what his body was up to. After the past few weeks, he had a lot to tell her. If he ever made the time to do so.

It had become his habit when his thoughts buzzed incessantly, when he lay with his wings clipped in bed because there was nothing else productive to be done at that moment, to take out his knife to investigate his newfound invulnerability in a manner that Asha definitely wouldn't approve of.

He started at the fleshy part of his palm, right under his thumb, and made a one-inch cut. Watching it close was mildly terrifying but fascinating. Some force he couldn't see—tiny, mystical things knitting his flesh—pushed the cut together, leaving no trace of its presence. That was the only way his mind could attempt to explain something so beyond his understanding. Others had felt this way before in history. People on the field the day the first man flew. Witnesses to that first atomic explosion in the desert just over one hundred miles from

The Disc, at least according to the maps in Thallium's collection. They'd all been naïve humans trying to fathom something so powerful that it shook the world, and that was precisely how he felt every time his body healed itself.

He stood up, letting his book flop gently onto the bed. He set his left hand on the bedside table, next to the oil lamp by which he was reading and his half-empty glass of water. He paused there, considering which digit to target. Not the thumb, nor the three middle fingers—he'd need those for combat, and this could go horribly wrong. Couldn't take the risk. The pinkie, then.

With his fingers spread apart, pinkie out as far as it would go, he took his knife and lay it atop the first small joint there, knowing full well what a terrible idea this was. But it was also something he could control, an outlet, a test. With two big breaths forced between his lips, he put his weight behind a firm push down with the blade. He managed to swallow most of his cry of pain.

There was a powerful urge to grip his hand to his chest, put pressure on the wound, but he fought it and kept his hand where it was. Blood spread along the table more slowly than he would have expected. The tip of his pinkie rocked gently from side to side an inch away from the rest of his finger, then fell still as he forced himself to wait. Somehow, the bleeding stopped as if there were pressure against the wound that Caster couldn't feel. But then nothing happened, and he tried to think of an explanation for Asha since it looked like he'd have to wake her up in the middle of the night to reattach the damn thing.

He moved his finger closer to the separated end, just touching them together, and then things started happening. Tiny strings of muscle, bits of bone, grew out from his finger toward the severed joint, attaching to it, the magical sewing on full and brilliant display as the complex inner workings of his finger were reconstructed as if from a pattern. When it stopped, he wet the end of his sleeve with water from his glass and wiped away the blood from his skin. No pain, no scar. He made a fist. Perfect.

This was further proof that his waiting around until they hit a certain number of recruits was asinine. He could get Wren out of the Main House himself right now. Even if his father sent all of his Keepers after him, they couldn't put him down. He'd just heal and keep going. Taking her would effectively remove the threat Thallium posed. With no supernatural weapon on his side, he was limited to human forces—Keepers and Body members loyal to him, a number that continued to dwindle as things got worse in the city. There was no reason to wait.

Caster dashed to the door and left his room. The hallway was dark, save for the dim glow of oil lamps with low wicks along the walls. It was warm here, far warmer than it had been when he'd come home that evening down the streets of The Disc where people hunched around bin fires and drank Yellow, spiced cider, and just about any other beverage that would allow their bodies to feel warm, even if that warmth was a lie. When winter set in fully and fuel for fires was gone, maybe half of those people would make it through to see spring.

He reached his father's artifact collection in the foyer and blew through it toward the stairwell on the far side. He paused with his hand on the railing, considering going up instead of down, seeing if his father happened to be sleeping in his room. He could end it if he were, silently, easily, even mercifully, which was a luxury Thallium hadn't offered to many. Yet, he didn't take that first step upward. Caster held foolish hope for Thallium upon which he'd based his decision to overthrow rather than execute him. The man was a monster, but tonight at least, Caster wouldn't let himself become the same breed of monster. Instead, he went down.

The stairwell was dark and quiet with an air of death, feeling similar to how Caster had imagined the barrows in *The Fellowship of the Ring*. It seemed an age ago that he and Wren had sat at the Ragged Squirrel chatting about *The Hobbit*. It had only been, what, less than two months ago? He'd thought about a lot of things in the intervening month since their separation, but his mind continued to return to that night they'd gotten to spend together in one another's company. He wished he hadn't taken it for granted. And as he picked up his pace down the last flight of stairs, he made a note to tell her the next part of the hobbits' story when they were finally reunited.

He came out of the stairwell, his footsteps incredibly loud as he headed for the main door of the lab. If the Operator were sleeping already rather than manning the cameras, which would be lucky enough alone, he might be awoken by the slapping of Caster's bare feet against the tile. Bare feet—he really hadn't thought this through. Even if the opportunity to escape tonight did arise, he'd already shot it to hell by not preparing. But he was just so damn sick of preparing.

"Sir, is there something I can do for you?" a voice called politely in the dim. There, in the low lighting of the hallway, propped against the wall as if he were part of the architecture, was Prady. His gray hair and striped robe took on the blue of the lights down here.

Caster knew they were likely being watched by the Operator, as did Prady. He shifted his walk from desperate to official, even proud, and approached the Keeper. "I didn't realize you were on the overnight shift now."

"I've been doing split shifts, sir. Not much else I can do to be useful around here. I'm just happy to help. Do you need anything?" Prady lowered his voice. "I thought you were going to wait for me to contact you. This isn't the place for this."

"Unable to sleep, I'm afraid. I thought a walk might help." Caster kept his back to the cameras and spoke softly. "Let me in. I have to see her."

"Excellent idea, sir. I find it's more productive to make the body move rather than lie in misery." Prady said more quietly, "I have no access to this room."

"Has Bug left for the night?"

"No. And she may not at all. She often sleeps here." He raised his voice. "Wonderful to have you home, sir. How is your father doing? Have you spoken with the Principal about how we might make your time here more comfortable?"

"Yes. He's too busy with more important things. I'm on my own."

Prady nodded. "I wish there were more I could do, sir. But everything happens in its own time, I believe." He whispered once more, "There's nothing you can do tonight. When it is time to act, trust me—I will be right by your side."

Caster tried to control his angry breathing. He felt like a total fool standing there on the threshold of Wren's prison without shoes or two ideas to rub together. "Do you mind if I rest here, Prady? Just for a moment?"

"Not at all, sir."

Caster went to the other wall bordering the door, put his back against it, and slid to the floor. He closed his eyes and put a hand to the floor—the same hand he'd just butchered upstairs. She was down there. Just one story below, but she might as well have been across the Open in a hole somewhere for his ability to get to her, to get her out. The Open was frightening, to be sure, but there was something far more frightening about being crippled in his own home. About being a captive trying to rescue another captive. Biding his time, drinking, eating, and sleeping but not really living. He couldn't until she was out and far away from here.

Far from him.

When she'd met him was when her life had been stolen. He had to get it back for her.

The tile was cold under his hand, but it warmed as he continued to sit and nod off to sleep with his chin to his chest.

In her mind, Wren was a child, the smallest she remembered being. Her earliest memory was the feeling of sunlight—completely new, strange. Warm but painful. Alma had warned her not to look directly at the sun, to keep her face from it whenever she could. But in her memory now, Alma was nowhere around.

Wren stood in the middle of a swath of desert, strange plants all around that she knew instinctively not to touch. She closed her eyes and bathed in the light of the sun, reveled in it. This was a miracle from a new world. She giggled at the feeling until something crawled across her foot. She looked down at a rattlesnake slithering between her ankles and leapt back. The snake didn't like that. The shake of its rattle like dry rain sent her hair on end. The snake lunged with an open mouth at her heel, but she lifted her foot and brought it down on the snake's head. The cracking of its skull cut off the sound of the rattle and sent a thrill up her young body. She picked up the snake, now slack and quiet, and started running.

Then she was at Alma's back, tugging at her bright white coat. She came up just to Alma's chest. Alma turned around slowly and looked down at her with the joyful familiarity of a loving mother, and Wren wondered at how being looked at in such a way could feel even more warm than the sun. Wren took the snake from behind her back and held it out to her with both hands. Alma recoiled, so slowly that Wren didn't realize it at first. She tilted her head, realized Alma's steps backward were growing longer, and her heart sank.

She dropped the snake, thinking she'd simply scared Alma with it, but Alma's expression didn't change. Shame and disgust came out in the high-pitched scream Alma released, and Wren knew both were directed at her, not at the once dangerous animal. But that couldn't be. The snake had tried to bite her, kill her—she was right to strike back. It had tried to take her life, so she had to take its life. *Had* to. And what's more, she'd wanted to. As she wanted to take her next breath or sleep in Alma's arms. It was natural, satisfying.

Why didn't Alma understand that?

Wren walked over the snake, misshaping its long body further with the weight of her footsteps. No longer did she rise just to Alma's chest—she towered over her. She absolutely still loved her, even pitied her as she brought up her foot and brought it down on top of Alma. Crushing her skull was far more satisfying than crushing the snake's.

Wren woke screaming with no sound. For the first few seconds of wakefulness, she thought she was drowning until she remembered that she already had. She remembered the booth, the lab, Eydis. The rush of purple light in the green fluid. She screamed again, desperate for the release it would bring in the open air, settling for the pressure of the effort on her vocal cords as they vibrated silently in her throat.

She'd once been a daughter, a sister. After Caster, she'd also been able to call herself a friend. She was someone, she had someone. Now, she felt all the recognizable parts of her being overtaken. Being torn from herself was a kind of torture she'd never fathomed. Physical pain, hunger, fear. These she knew. But this? It was true agony.

The things that had driven her before—family and the hope for a simple life—were only vague impressions, history written down in plain text. Death lured her, seduced her with its power. Every passing day, the temptation to let death pull her firmly over to its side and embrace her grew. Because here, stuck in the middle with her arms being pulled in opposite directions of human and other, here was nothingness. Here was hell.

She struck out weakly at the glass of the box, then made a proper fist and hit it harder. Needles of pain shot through her hand and up her forearm. She hit it again and again with both fists, fighting the resistance of the fluid. Panic took hold, would have taken her breath if she'd had any to take, and she flailed and spun, churning the fluid when she beat at the glass, shredding her vocal cords noiselessly all the while.

With a dull sense of surprise, she realized she wasn't alone in the lab as she'd thought. Bug stood by watching. Wren tilted her head at her as she had at Alma in her dream.

"What am I?" she mouthed.

Tears ran down Bug's cheeks. She opened her mouth to speak, closed it again as if she were the one trapped in fluid, likewise voiceless.

Then something pulled at Wren's mind, her whole body, breaking the powerful grip of her terror—a familiar presence like that warm sun from her memory. It was...energy. A unique melody of notes and vibrations that her whole body recognized. Close by. Upstairs? Just outside the lab, not moving, still, and humming at a unique frequency.

She wrapped her arms around her shoulders and pulled her legs up, allowing herself to feel the damage done to her hands and the pain in her arms from lashing out. But the pain was secondary to the comfort of the energy coming from upstairs.

"Caster," she whispered.

Crankshaft stood with her feet spread wide, one far forward and one behind, in the doorway to Screws & Gears. It was only midafternoon, but by the look of her, any passerby would think she was prepared for a weekend evening rush. Or perhaps a war. The 20-gauge shotgun on the sling over her shoulder was a new accompaniment to the baton on her hip—she carried both boldly and openly. The buckshot in the wall and floor nearby, as well as the dark remnants of a hastily-mopped-up bloodstain, suggested she'd used the gun at least once recently. Thallium had gifted her a vest of body armor a couple of years ago to help her protect his favorite recreation spot, but she'd never worn it until now.

"Stop," she said. "Where's your invitation?"

Thallium pulled back his hood to show his face. "My apologies, Crank. I wasn't aware an invitation was needed."

Her stance loosened and she bowed. "Principal Thallium. You don't need an invitation, of course. We've had to change our procedures after an incident last week."

"Incident?"

"Yes, sir. Someone tried to come in with his weapons. I refused him service, but he tried to come in anyway. I didn't like that."

"Ah, that explains the new paint job in your entryway here."

She nodded.

"What did this man look like?"

"I didn't recognize him, except..." Her stern face had never been adept at showing emotion, but it was as close to expressive as Thallium had ever seen it now. She chewed the inside of her cheek.

"Except what, Crank?"

"He wore a Keeper robe, sir."

Thallium sighed deeply. He was too tired for this. Caster was onto something after all, and these men were causing problems at one of his favorite places. "On behalf of that Keeper, I apologize. Was he alive when he left your establishment?"

"Limping but alive, yes. I only got a piece of him." She looked away as if ashamed but recovered quickly. "Should I arrange for your normal table?"

"Actually, would you please keep it quiet that I'm here? I'd like to have a little downtime to myself."

"Of course, sir. Please come in." She stood aside, and Thallium raised his hood again as he passed her.

An aroma cocktail of vodka, rust, and sweat met him. Normally, Thallium made a grand entrance, but not today. He'd even donned a traveling cloak he hadn't worn in ages instead of his usual showy attire—deep colors and hammered tin buttons and rare animal products. He wasn't there to be seen, but to do the seeing. To listen and get a reading on his people's state of mind. He knew what he was asking of them was difficult, infuriating even. Didn't change the need for it, but it did complicate things. People liked to do that—complicate things.

He preferred to simplify, which is what he'd done when addressing them at the start of the lockdown. Before the paper notices went up around town, he'd made the announcement over the Operator's system: "We have enemies who would love to see you all dead—I will not let them harm you. Until we know the threat is passed, I'm ordering The Disc locked down. No entrance or exit. We keep to ourselves. Watch over our own, as we've always done. We will get through this together."

There were minor protests—mostly boys with too much testosterone, but also nongovernment workers here and there. Traders and Scavengers in particular had been furious, but they protested privately to the Principal himself; they were smart enough to know who paid them best for their finds from the Open. Under the new rules and restrictions, he'd allowed his favored few to go out to appease them. He benefited from their eyes on the outside, anyway. And as precious as the first carrier was, he couldn't help but hope that more pieces of lost tech were out there waiting to be plucked. Now that he'd gotten a real taste of it, he couldn't help himself.

Everyone who had been initially displeased had since stayed in line. Except, apparently, his Keepers. They would be a genuine threat, assuming Caster's hunch proved to be correct. But how could it be correct? Thallium had given his men everything. The best housing, meat, extra water. Bonuses based on performance. Yet, the ludicrous idea of a sect of them acting out had nagged at him since Caster had brought it up. Termites of possibility gnawed away inside his head, and though he'd been battling insomnia ever since the beginning of the lockdown, this new potential threat had robbed him of the little rest he'd been grabbing in two-hour stints in the dark, early mornings. Answers would help. He had to see for himself what things were like in the city. No better place to get a feel for it than by running his hand along its sticky underside, in a social spot where he'd spent countless evenings. Until he'd locked down The Disc, at least. He'd told himself he wasn't afraid of this "Tyr" and his would-be rebellion, but he'd concealed his favorite double-edged knife under his old traveling cloak all the same.

Screws was busy for an afternoon, but there was still a stool open in the middle of the bar, and he headed to it with his head lowered, a slight limp in his step to put off anyone who might recognize his bearing.

Linchpin slid off her own stool where she was reading a tattered mystery novel Thallium had gifted her from his own collection. The thick black bathrobe she wore with lilac heels, about three inches too high to be safe for a woman her age, concealed her increasingly bony curves. He had to give her credit though—she still knew how to hold her own against any disrespectful patrons. Those patrons didn't stay patrons for long.

"Get you something?" she asked, her tone different from the overly perky one she always adopted when she spoke to Thallium. She knew who sponsored her business activities. "A new cloak, maybe? That one's seen better days."

He kept his gaze down, hood low over his forehead, and shoved the bit of pine sap gum in his mouth over to one side to change his speech. He also raised his register. "Just a Yellow, miss."

"'Miss.' Ooh, I like you. Let me know if you see anything *you* like." Her curves found life again under her robe when she shifted about enough to make the shoulder slip down.

"Just the Yellow tonight, thank you."

"Sure thing."

She shrugged back into her robe as if he had no idea what he'd just missed out on and fetched his drink from under the counter. The tin cup was bent but clean, and the liquor was even more astringent than Thallium remembered as he took a tentative sip. The last time he'd had Yellow was when he'd been too young and tasteless to care. It was the one alcohol he didn't drink anymore.

Linchpin eyed him another few seconds, long fingernails tapping out a rhythm. "I know you?"

"Friend of Crank's."

"Huh. Didn't know she had friends." With that, she shrugged, mounted her perch, and licked her thumb to find her place in the paperback.

He forced himself to sip the Yellow again before turning to

his side and engaging the young man seated next to him, who was likewise drinking Yellow. Kid couldn't be more than twenty and had a decent tunic. A trade apprentice, maybe. Or a low-level street vendor.

"Excuse me, friend. Seen any Keepers around this part of town?"

The young man looked sidelong at him but then moved his gaze forward, his voice quiet as if he were hiding. "Yeah. They're always down here." He shifted his body away from Thallium, leaning toward the far side of his stool.

"Sorry if I'm bothering you," said Thallium. "Just don't want to run into any of 'em, that's all. You hear things."

The kid glanced at him again, and his expression turned less guarded. He cleared his throat. "Don't worry about it. You're not really their preferred target. But they're hard to spot —a bunch of them don't wear their robes anymore."

"Then how do you know if someone's a Keeper?"

He touched his nose. "Soap, for one thing. You can smell it on them if they're close enough. Besides, when trouble starts, they're quick to announce their titles to get what they want. Not much mystery about it."

Thallium nodded and dared another sip of his drink. "Don't you think—"

An arm looping around the young man's neck in a mock choke hold cut off Thallium's question and, it would seem, the rest of their conversation. A tall man with a muscle shirt on despite the cold finished embracing his friend and sat at the stool on his other side.

"Good to see you, man. How you been?" The new arrival looked around. "You didn't bring Trevor?"

"To this cesspool?" the young man whispered. "You insane, Murph? No, he's at home."

"Too bad. That kid's got spunk. Fun to hang with."

"Yeah? Try hanging with him 24/7."

Murph tried to order a drink, but Linchpin held up a skinny finger, commanding him to wait as she continued reading. He cursed quietly. "So," Murph lowered his voice further, "did you find him? Tyr?"

"Yeah, man. Yeah," he replied, as if he'd seen a holy man.

"Well?" Murph asked eagerly as he tried to steal a sip from his friend's drink. "You gonna tell me what he's like, Jav?"

Jav smacked Murph's hand away from his glass. "Unless you're going to join, can't talk about it."

Linchpin finally got off of her stool and, without asking what Murph wanted, expertly poured a glass of Yellow and slid it to him before going back to her book. Murph raised the drink to her, then downed half of it. Once his lips had unpuckered, he said, "Then he accepted you, huh? Low threshold for entry, then."

Jav punched him in the arm. "Too high for you. Not that you're ballsy enough to sign up."

Murph rolled his eyes. "I told you I can't risk it. Got my siblings to think about," he said seriously. "If I die in a civil war, they're dead too."

"Yeah." Jav nudged him in the arm gently with his elbow. "Yeah, I know."

Murph trailed his finger around the rim of his glass, then said with enthusiasm, "Bet Trevor's psyched. You?"

"I don't know," replied Jav. "I think I'm more resigned to what I've chosen. When Tyr calls us to fight, hopefully I'll be psyched. If not, he'll kill me, so there's that."

"What do you mean?"

"Not sure. Well, not sure if he'd actually kill me if I changed my mind. But if I betray him or the cause, he swore he would. Swore the same to Trevor. Put a huge blade against my neck to make that point stick too."

Murph's eyes got big. "Like a sword? Damn."

"No, no. Like a combat knife maybe? I don't know. Haven't seen one before." He held his hands a foot apart. "Big, shiny, curved a little bit just at the end. Sharp enough to shave with. Even nicked me a bit."

"Bowie," Thallium said softly as the rage and hurt inside him bloomed. "That would be a bowie knife."

Murph looked past Jav over the bar and spat, "Private conversation man. Back off."

"Did you see his face?" Thallium asked Jav with his gaze on his drink. The tin cup between the Principal's hands threatened to collapse the rest of the way with the pressure he was applying.

"What?" asked Jav.

"Tyr!" Thallium bit out. "Did. You see. His face?"

"No," Jav said nervously with a tight shake of his head. "No, it was covered. All of them had their faces covered."

Silence fell as the two younger men braced for what could easily have turned into a fight. It would hardly be the first brawl at Screws. Thallium simply cleared his throat and hunched forward over the cup as he made himself relax his hold on it.

The two slowly pushed their stools back and retreated across the room toward the sunken fire pit.

"It's him," said a rich voice flitting around between his ears. It was both beautiful and chilling, still capable of arresting his entire being, though its owner was long dead. His chest turned tight near his heart.

"Reina?" he whispered.

"You've suspected something was off since he returned from the Open and you saw him anxiously hovering over that poor unconscious girl. Take comfort that your intuition was right, I suppose. It usually isn't."

Out of the corner of his eye, he could see her sitting there on the stool next to him, the one Jav had just vacated. He tried to look at her straight on, but when he did, she faded away. Part of him was disappointed, the other relieved.

When he turned his gaze forward, she appeared again as a hazy silhouette with long brown hair. She was just out of reach, as she had been to him until the end. "He's finally chosen what's better. Wish I was there to see it."

"But you're not." His chest felt tight all over now. "You're dead."

"Well, yes. And you weren't there to watch me go, T. Caster was, though. Good Lord, it was hard for him. Fairly certain he was in even more pain than I was."

He had to fight to draw a deep breath. "Stop it. You're dead."

"Your mistakes never really die though, do they?"

"You're dead!" Once the words left his mouth, he realized he was standing. Both his stool and the one next to it were on the floor, and there was no sign of Reina anywhere. He'd knocked his hood back when he'd stood.

Linchpin squinted at him, braced to call Crank over, until recognition changed her expression and she swallowed her words.

A hand gripped his shoulder gently from behind, and he spun around.

Crank stood there. "Sir? Are you all right?"

He brushed past her and strode swiftly through the entryway before the entire establishment could realize that the Principal had been hiding amongst them. Yelling at a ghost.

CHAPTER SIX

CASTER OPENED THE DOOR TO PIP'S PUFFS AND PASSED
through the curtain of clay beads inside. He'd been going to
Pip's since the tender age of thirteen, and it smelled exactly the
same now as it had then—brush fire mixed with artificial pine.
Although Pip's business was supported by Thallium and had
the option of electric lighting, he preferred a different aesthetic.
The shop was dim but cozy, lit by skinny pillar candles on
mosaic plates. The shelves that normally held blends of various
herbs were nearly empty. From the back room behind another
curtain of beads, Pip called out, "Just about out of everything,
but if you're here for incense, I have a couple of varieties left. I
recommend our famous Evergreen Euphoria!"

Pip's arm shot through the curtain and swept it back. When
he saw Caster, his salesmanship took a sharp downturn. The
cheer in his voice was replaced with tiredness, and rather than
covering up the bit of natural wheeze his voice carried, he let it
out plainly. "Ah, great. Another moocher." He laughed at his
own cleverness and paid for it—his wheeze turned to a wet

cough, and he had to grab the edge of the sales counter to steady himself as he pushed through the fit.

Caster walked over and took Pip's hand in his, thumping him on the back. "Hey, old buddy. Not sounding great."

"Not much older than you, my friend. Behold your future." Pip opened his arms, then reached into the chest pocket of his collared shirt for the cigarette there. He placed it between the first two fingers of his artificial hand. Metal and unskinned, not nearly as subtle as the prosthetics issued to military and other service employees. Functioned well enough for Pip, though. If it could hold a cigarette, it suited him fine. He lit the cigarette with a match and took a long drag, holding it in his lungs for just a couple of seconds before letting it out. The smoke was light, almost odorless.

Caster looked behind at the empty display jars. "Thought you were out of mullein."

"For the public, you bet I'm out. *You* need any?"

Caster shook his head. "Lungs feel fine."

Pip spit out a second drag with force. "Asha, man. She was all over me the second she got here. Wants me to donate my reserves to the med ward."

"So you stood your ground and told her tough luck?"

"Exactly! In my head, anyway. When you got here, I was in the middle of boxing up most of what I have left for her to take after the meeting."

"Wuss."

"Hypocrite."

Pip jerked his hand back toward the doorway behind the counter. "You're one of the last ones. Better hurry up." He raised his chin to Caster in what was apparently Tyr's Army's salute. It was fairly inconspicuous, which Caster appreciated, but it still felt strange to have people exposing their throats to him, despite the oath he'd made them swear under his knife.

He returned the gesture to Pip before heading through the curtained doorway.

It had been dark in the front room, but it was even more so back here. And colder. Caster passed the storeroom, which was nearly empty save for the small crate Pip had been packing when he arrived. Down the hallway, the door to the bathroom was propped open with a rock. Caster walked inside, went to the only stall, and opened the door hanging off-kilter from its hinges. He knocked above the toilet once, twice, twice again. A scraping, then the groaning of metal as the wall opened at a seam to the right of the toilet, creating enough space for him to pass through.

One of the old black-market rooms. There were a handful of them behind businesses in this sector, all connected via a tunnel system, all made of concrete inlaid with wire mesh to block the signaling capability of ID bracelets. The existence of these market rooms wasn't a well-guarded secret so much as a promise of privacy to those intending to do dealings. Since The Disc's lockdown, Pip had closed his black-market room. With no outside trade, there was little dealing to be done.

When Caster had approached his friend, needing the room to host a group intent on ending the lockdown, Pip had welcomed him on the condition that he make three things happen—find peace with the Open, reinitiate trade, and save Pip's Puffs from going under. As loyal as Caster believed Pip to be, he was also a shrewd businessman with simple motivations. Anybody who did something entirely for free in this city would have been far more suspicious anyway.

Six closed the door behind Caster, and the two walked together down the dim passageway toward the quiet chattering coming from the market room ahead. The candlelight within glowed a weak yellow-orange at the end of the passage.

Six absently spun a stiletto between his fingers. "You're late."

"Good thing I'm the boss."

"Is it?" He folded the blade and tucked it into the pocket of his pants. "Leaders are supposed to be the first ones in, last ones out. You've inverted that dynamic, buddy."

"Yeah, I'm a terrible leader. Didn't want the job. No idea why anyone is surprised." He tried to step through the doorway, but Six stepped in front of him.

After a quick glance back at the market room, Six got eye to eye with Caster and said in a low voice, "Gavel and the others won't be upfront with you because they're worried it'll send you into a downward spiral. Or they're just plain scared of you. I'm neither." He looked older in the half-light, as serious as Caster had ever seen him. "Your impatience has become a hazard. If you can't settle into the idea of biding your time, someone will end up dead. Might be you, might be me, might be someone you love. Might be all three." He jerked his thumb toward the market room. "Those people in there—your friends —need you to listen to them, not bully them into doing what you want."

Caster passed his tongue over his teeth and sighed deeply before he responded. "Look, I didn't ask to be put in this position, but now that I have it, understand something." He waved his finger in a circle. "This isn't our Body. I'm your leader, not your Scout."

"I had more respect for you when you were. You inherited more than your daddy's hair. You're wearing his disposition now." Six made a point of straightening the collar of Caster's black coat. "And it fits too well."

Caster shoved him hard, then pinned him against the wall of the passage with his forearm across his chest. "You really do talk too much."

Six looked wholly unalarmed. He sighed with disappointment. "Sorry, sir."

Caster held on a minute longer, then released him. "Did you find the tracker?"

Six pulled his leather vest back into place. "Yeah, we found him. Living in the high quarter near the Main House. Thallium put him up in a Keeper apartment."

"You think he's still loyal to Thallium? Despite his buddies at the bar?"

"Only way to find out is to ask him. Less risky than grabbing Dal at this point. Sans and I can pay him a visit."

"Fine. I'll go with you." Caster started to turn toward the market room, but Six stopped him with an unsure hiss.

"I'd rather you didn't come." Six hooked his thumbs into his belt loops and stared straight into Caster's eyes.

"Did I ask what you would rather?" Caster said cuttingly.

"After our last hostage, I'm not sure you're in the right headspace to question another. You're hardly acting human anymore."

Caster got nose to nose with the Assassin. "Is that right?"

"Pretty much. Hey, tell me something," Six continued, unbothered by Caster's stance. "If I were to punch you in the mouth right now, would you even bleed?"

"Not sure, but *you* would."

"Boys!" came a voice at the end of the hall. Asha stood at the threshold of the market room, half in shadow, exuding three times the presence of her physical form. "You done? Group's waiting." She turned and disappeared within.

Six stepped sideways out of Caster's reach and held his arm out toward the market room. "After you."

Caster suppressed the urge to dismiss him entirely and hated the superiority he felt over the Assassin even as he leveraged it. Six would follow orders, and if he was incapable of doing so, he would be relieved of his position. He and the others had shown that if anything was going to get done around here, Caster had to make it happen. Nobody else would.

Five people stood waiting in a messy circle. Beeswax candles burned nearly down to nothing lit the room along the floor and atop empty shipping crates. Sans and Adonis stood closest to the doorway—the kid started to wave at Caster but then stopped himself and stood at attention. Freddy held a candle in his hand, letting the wax drip onto his fingers and clearly wishing he were somewhere else. Gavel walked through the group toward Caster with Asha by his side—she rarely attended these meetings, and even though she'd just called him out on his crap, he was glad to see her. He kissed her cheek.

Gavel raised his chin to Caster. These elite members of his rebellion followed suit and saluted. Only then did Caster realize their chattering had stopped during his confrontation with Six, that it hadn't just been Asha who had heard every-thing. He brushed past it and saluted them in return.

Caster looked to Adonis first. "No Prady?"

"Said he'd be here, sir," replied the kid.

"We'll get started without him," said Caster.

"Perhaps we can start with the topic you and Six were going over outside?" suggested Asha. She nearly managed to keep the mothering tone out of her words.

"Six said we've located Amsel, the hunter from the bar the other night," said Caster. "I'd like to question him."

"If this man is as terrifying as the rumors around him suggest," said Gavel, "we might do best with a less forceful approach. Diplomacy seems prudent."

"It might help to have a woman present too," said Asha.

"I don't think you're as disarming as you might hope, Ash," said Caster.

"No. But I'm levelheaded. The testosterone in here is so

thick it stinks. I would like to be there when we meet with this hunter. The tension between you two," she pointed at him and Six, "tells me that neither of you should be there."

"Hey!" snapped Six. "Don't project Caster's lack of control on me. I'm not the one—"

"Quiet! I didn't ask for anyone's opinion," Caster barked. Nobody offered theirs again, and Asha seemed taken aback. "Gavel, Asha, and I will meet with Amsel at his home. Six and Sans will scout it out before and serve as lookouts during. I don't want us interrupted."

After a moment, Adonis asked in a small voice, "What about me?" He'd somehow managed to blend into the background of the trading room.

"Two outside is plenty, Donnie," said Caster. He'd never seen Adonis' face fall so far and so fast. The kid had ambition, but in times like this, it was a liability.

Sans spoke. The rare sound caught Caster off guard and made him start. "I'd like him to be involved. It will help with his training."

Caster rolled his head from side to side to crack his neck. "Okay, fine. Just stay out of sight."

He'd expected Adonis to be excited, grateful, or something other than pissed, but the kid glared at him and crossed his arms. If he'd been bigger, Caster would be expecting him to throw a punch or two with those eyes. Teenagers were exhausting.

The others nodded their acceptance of Caster's order except for Six.

"How are you planning on getting inside the apartment building?" asked the Assassin. "Probably don't want to shove your ID bracelet around and get in on your good name. This is a stealth mission, after all, in a building populated by soldiers who may or may not be traitors."

In the distance, Caster heard the tapping of Prady's staff. The way he shifted his weight as he walked down the hallway toward the market room was distinct. The Keeper entered the room and nodded to Caster. "Pip let me in. I apologize for my lateness. I'm still not used to how long it takes me to get places these days."

"Have a seat, please," said Asha. She smacked Freddy off the crate he sat on, and he picked it up with a huff and carried it to where Prady stood.

"Normally, I'd turn down that offer. But not today, thank you. Too little sleep last night." Prady settled onto the crate.

"We were just discussing something you could help us with," said Caster.

"Oh? My timing is better than I thought then," replied Prady.

"Do you still live in the high quarter?"

"As long as the Principal continues to pay for my apartment, yes."

"We need the code to a Keeper building. Hoping to follow up on a lead there that might help us with Wren."

"Is it a lead I can follow up on *for* you?" asked Prady, still winded.

Caster shrugged. "Not this one."

Prady nodded. "All right. The codes change weekly, and they're due to turn over tomorrow. Once I have it, I'll get it to you."

"Thank you. What about your lead? Were you able to find out anything from Oran?" asked Caster.

"Not as much as I wanted—no details about how many people are involved in the illicit activities, no idea of scope or names to offer. But what he did know, he didn't hold back. Dal is the one who untied his hands. Seems he's been encouraging

Keepers to stir things up in The Disc and make Thallium look bad."

Caster's mind whirred. "Why would he do that?"

"Recruit men and women to his side for the purpose of removing Thallium from his seat? Yes, who could fathom the idea." Prady lazily waved a hand at the lot of them. "What these Keepers are doing makes the Principal look bad, and that means your father is more than likely not endorsing their actions. I believe Dal wants to take out Thallium, same as you, but with one key difference: he doesn't care who has to die to get it done, including the Principal."

"So my father wasn't lying. He didn't give those men a free pass to cause trouble," said Caster.

Prady shook his head. "From what I can see, Thallium's not doing much of anything these days. Only follows Eydis around almost as though their roles are reversed. That's just my observation as a fly on the wall outside the lab, mind you."

Thallium was listless—Caster had observed that for himself. Poetic, really, since he was the one who had slammed down the door to this oversized cage.

"Ollie's seen the same thing—Thallium is restless, taskless," said Caster. "It's driving him up the wall. Ollie seems unnerved by what the Principal might do once he's ready to use Wren. He's eager to help our cause."

"Oliver, Head of Agua?" Gavel asked.

Caster nodded, preparing for the onslaught of outrage from Gavel. Subdued as it would come across, it would cut deeper than a shouting match.

"When I suggested you ask Ollie for IPs volunteers," said Gavel, an edge of irritation in his voice, "I wasn't suggesting you bring him into the fold. He's a good man, but he is far too high up to risk our exposure. If he betrays you to Thallium..."

"He won't. We were going to have to bring in one of the administrators eventually. We'll need their support for a change of leadership, and Ollie carries more clout than any of the rest of them. He *is* the water in this city. Best of all, he comes with about fifty strong men who are loyal to him—with his help, we should have the numbers we need to assault the Main House. Now all we need is the opportunity. Bringing him in was my call; it was the right one."

"More and more ruler than leader every day," Asha said softly, and she sounded almost wounded. She grabbed his gaze and added, "Keep an eye on that, kiddo. Or you'll end up on the throne you despise."

"Ooh, Asha darling. Scathing, you are!" Freddy made a hissing noise and chuckled too heartily for Caster's liking.

"Therefore," Caster said, louder now to put Asha's comment to bed, "we need to get Wren out as soon as possible. We can't wait any longer."

Everyone fell quiet and still, as if they all had the same thing to say but shared their reluctance to say it. The candlelight flickered against the dark walls. Six put his hands on his hips and stretched his back dramatically, as if this entire meeting was a waste of time.

Freddy broke the awkwardness. "Well, thanks for letting us in on that particular plan, Caster dear! I for one feel incredibly included in this insanity! Far too included, in fact."

"What Freddy is trying to express here," Gavel said through tight lips, "is that your plan may be shortsighted. Say we assault the Main House and it goes well and you assume power and we get Wren somewhere safe—then what?"

Caster threw his hands up. "What do you mean, then what?"

Asha took a couple of steps forward. She exchanged her normally straightforward speech for something sweeter and slower, and Caster couldn't help but feel condescended to.

"After you take over The Disc, what will you do? Just end the lockdown and invite people into our walls who won't care if it's you or Thallium on that throne, who feel only their need for vengeance?"

Caster ran his hands down his face, exasperated. "We'll have time to figure that out. But we won't have that time if Thallium uses Wren first."

Asha rubbed at her forehead, and the sweetness in her voice disappeared. "Fine. But I would like to go to Dearborn to speak with Gray. He needs to hear from us, learn our side of things. I could offer my help as a healer, and he might lend us help in return. Supplies, support that the other Openers can see. We could avoid a war entirely."

"Even *if* that was a good idea," said Caster, "which I'm not convinced it is, we don't know where he is. We're assuming he's in Dearborn, but he's more likely traveling, gathering allies. I know I would be. If we did manage to convince him that our motives align and he agreed to negotiate with the Openers bent on killing us, we still have the immediate issue of Thallium taking Wren to war any day now. Can we all agree on that, at least?"

After a short stretch of silence, heads started to bob around the room.

"Okay, you want to get her out first, but don't act as though there isn't danger in that option," said Asha. "All sides of this struggle would love to use her. We would have to hide her until all of this is over. Not here, but deep in the Open. Your place would be here, not hiding like the guilty party. You couldn't go with her."

Even though Caster had already come to the same conclusion himself, it still bothered him. The thought of Wren in the outlands terrified him nearly as much as the thought of his father keeping her captive indefinitely. "Agreed. Her sister will take her into the Open. Freddy, I'll need you to tell Survivor. Time for her to join us."

Freddy gave him two overly enthusiastic thumbs up. "Oh, sure, let me just give her a ringaling on my imaginary com device." He spoke into his hand. "Yes, Survivor darling, we'll be storming the castle in a few days' time when the weather's fair. We do hope you can come!" He put his hand down and clucked his tongue. "I haven't heard from her since we gave her my keycard. After she used it to let me into the back gate, I asked her where she was going. She said, 'South.'"

Caster shook his head. "Damn her!" He kicked a hole in a storage crate nearby. That had not been the arrangement. Survivor was supposed to get the card and stay near The Disc until Caster told her it was time to get Wren out. Then she could enter and help with the plan, whatever the plan happened to be at that point. Of course she'd betrayed them. Who knew why or to what end. Everything about that woman made Caster's skin crawl, but Wren loved her. Needed her. And as much as Caster hated to admit it, without Survivor, they were at a disadvantage. She was worth twenty soldiers, and they couldn't get enough of those currently.

"Did she say she would be back?" asked Caster after he'd composed himself.

"She didn't say much of anything," replied Freddy, "nor did her lump of a Marauder sidekick. Seems to me that she has bigger plans than an attempted snatch and grab of her sister. Shockingly, I don't believe working with others is her strong point."

Caster really hated that woman. "We're on our own. We'll find another option then. When we have Wren, two of you can take her out of The Disc. Sans, you know the Open. Ash, you have contacts in towns nearby. We'll make it—"

"Jumping too far ahead of things, aren't you, Tyr?" interrupted Six. "How do we get her out?"

Once again, Caster turned to Prady. If Caster were ever willing to take his father's place, he'd set the man up with a retirement unlike any seen before. "Could we break into the Main House's surveillance room?"

Prady cleared his throat and raised a hand respectfully. "The only place that's more of a fortress than the lab is the surveillance room. You'll make a spectacle of yourself trying to get in there, and I believe secrecy offers you the best chance of success. I can distract the Operator while you're let into the lab. You will still need someone with access to the lab, which is currently only Thallium, Eydis, and the assistant, Bug."

"Seems obvious—we kidnap the assistant and get her to open the door," said Six.

"Bit rash, don't you think?" replied Caster.

"Oh, *I'm* the rash one." Six put his hand to his lips and closed his eyes. "Sweet lady irony, kiss me again." After a deep breath, he said, "Fine." He ran his hand through his dark hair. "I'll seduce her and take the key."

A gravelly chortle burst from Prady, which made everyone jump. He rubbed at his knee absently, then cleared his throat again. "Apologies. If you only knew her," he said to Six, "you'd know how ridiculous your idea is. Have you considered we could simply *ask* Bug to help us?"

Six walked over to rest an elbow on Prady's shoulder. "She's got a pretty sweet gig in there, P-man. Working with the Principal's robot queen, getting her belly filled every day, sleeping in comfort. Doubt she'd want to throw that away, but even if she were willing to, she'd be taking a dangerous gamble —executed if Thallium finds out, imprisoned at best. No way will she play that hand."

Prady brushed Six's elbow away as if he were a mosquito.

"I've seen Bug more than about anyone else in this city during my short stint guarding that lab. Son, trust that I have a better understanding of her than you do. She's hurting for Wren. More every day. I believe if she has to choose between her comfort and her humanity, she'll choose the latter."

"Can you arrange a meeting with her?" Caster asked Prady. "Would she be willing to talk?"

"I believe so."

"Still think I should just throw a bag over her head and demand the key," muttered Six. "She's a shut-in who never sees the sun, probably doesn't ever see scary guys like me. Telling you, this could be taken care of in less than a minute with a few stern words."

"No," said Caster. "You'll meet her. Listen to her rather than *bullying* her into doing what you want."

Six snorted. "Fair enough, *boss*. I'll meet the lab rat. Set it up, Keeper." He spun and headed for the door, half-heartedly calling over his shoulder, "We done?"

"Yeah," Caster said to those remaining. "We're done."

"Well, this is all very exciting, and I thank you for that. I do get bored, you know." Freddy took a deep bow, and when he came up with his arms out to his sides as though he might rise and float above the rest of them, blood flowed from his nostrils and down over his lips in thin rivers. He put his hand to his face and examined the mess on his palm.

"Oh dear. Asha, darling? Help?" He collapsed on the floor.

As Asha rushed to his side, she pulled her scarf over her nose and mouth and tied it behind her head. "Everyone, back up!"

They all retreated to the walls.

She stretched Freddy out on his side, then opened his eyes and shone her penlight into them. Checked his pulse. Her hands were shaking when she sat back on her heels.

"God help us, it's here." She turned to Caster. "Rubedo is here."

The name of the sickness stuck in Caster's gut and made him feel sick. The way his mom had looked when she passed—struggling for air with bloodstains on her beautiful face—came to him afresh. Now, thanks to his father, rubedo was back.

"What do we do, Ash?" Caster asked quietly.

"Let's get him to the med ward," Six said, covering his own face before coming to help carry Freddy.

"No!" said Asha. "We can't move him. He's started bleeding—anyone who comes into physical contact with him now could spread the virus."

"How do we know he hasn't already been spreading it?" Six said. "Before symptoms showed up?"

She thought about it, then shook her head. "From what Caster told us, Thallium engineered the virus to have a longer incubation period. Because of that, it can travel farther before people start showing symptoms. But as for it being contagious during that time, before symptoms show up? No, rubedo hasn't worked that way before. Let's pray it hasn't changed now. Everyone get out of here before I change my mind. Except for Caster and Prady. Hang back."

Everyone filed out, hugging the walls and giving Freddy mournful glances as they passed. Finally, it was just Caster, Prady, Asha, and an unconscious Freddy in the old market room.

"Caster, Thallium told you he made a treatment for the virus," stated Asha.

Caster tried to ignore the weight that had settled in his belly. "He did. No way he'd risk dying from it himself. There's a cure."

"I'd bet my ass it's in the lab and that Bug has access to it, even if she doesn't realize it." Asha looked to Prady. "She has an opportunity here to reveal her character. Hopefully she's as eager to help as you think she is."

Prady nodded. "I'll see her during my next shift tomorrow. Any sooner would arouse suspicion. Can he hold on that long?"

"During the outbreak in which we lost Reina, old rubedo took patients within a week," said Asha. "This new strain? I'm guessing forty-eight hours, maybe seventy-two. Caster, I'm going to make a list of supplies I'll need—ask Gav to help you gather them, then bring them back here. Tell Pip he's going to need to keep this room closed off until Freddy recovers or..."

"He'll recover," said Caster with as much confidence as he could muster.

"*If* he does," Asha said, "I *will* take treatment into the Open." Her mom voice took full effect. "I'm not asking permission, honey."

Caster smiled fondly at her. "When do you ever?"

With that, he left. The walk back to the storefront felt impossibly long. Death was creeping into the city. Fear in the citizens, unrest among the Keepers, Thallium's erratic behavior, and now rubedo.

The time for patience had passed.

Thallium and Eydis were speaking together in the observation booth. Bug tried hard not to stare up at them, these two beautiful people with more power at their disposal than anybody Bug had ever heard of, and she lived her life in books. Biology texts above all, but also botany, computer science, old Army survival manuals in case she ended up stuck in the outside world she studiously avoided. And, oftentimes, history.

Fragmented history, admittedly, but the books in Thallium's library did go as far back as the twentieth century. Wars that resulted in the loss of millions upon millions of lives, the creation of the atomic bomb back when there was still a United States before the dissolution of nations during the global restructuring. Then there was the use of antimatter explosives in the Corp Wars, which was short-lived due to the hazards of storing them. After that, bioweapons emerged that were genetically specific to particular targets—infect a whole water supply, kill one important person. All terrifying, absolutely awe-inspiring, and deadly.

After what she'd seen here in the lab—the data she'd personally gathered—all of those weapons throughout history were footnotes by comparison. The Principal and his android chatting above her in the lab would be starring figures in the books that would be written about today, about this very minute.

Of course, that was assuming someone would be left to write them. That someone would have to be her, and she wasn't sure she could stomach the task.

Lately, whenever she spoke to Wren or dared to look at her, she was forced to question her own role. How would she appear in the accounts of these events? As a modern Doctor Mengele? Like Ursa, the traitorous second to the Master Vera Lou? A ruthless mind like Markus of the Northeast Corp, who was responsible for the sensible solution of starving his own people to root out traitors?

Since she'd been a kid—a weird kid tucked away in her room creating new green chile cultivars that would have even greater drought tolerance—she'd wanted to help. To discover and propel humanity forward. Even if being around people made her anxious, she could still help them. But it didn't feel like she was helping anyone anymore.

As she finished entering information into Wren's chart from that morning, she forced herself to take her eyes from the screen and glance over at her. Wren had taken to sleeping whenever she wasn't in session with Eydis, and now she slept, her face hidden behind her slow-moving mane of hair. The slackness of her limbs, especially her arms as they floated at strange angles, sent a shiver down Bug's back—more disturbing to Bug than anything else, even as a kid, had been dolls and puppets. Things that looked like people on the outside but were tools, fakes, only made alive when someone started pulling the strings.

A doll in a case. That's what they'd turned her into. A doll whose only chance of escape was playing however they wanted her to.

It felt as though the walls of the lab pulled closer in, a strange sensation for someone who was frightened of open spaces but had no issue spending every day in an underground room. Bug realized she was sweating nearly through the armpits of her lab coat. She looked at the time on the screen— close enough to her midday break.

After clearing her throat, she stood and waved at the booth. Eydis caught sight of her and pressed the intercom button. "Yes?"

"I'm going to step out. My break," Bug managed to say and keep her composure.

"Certainly," said Eydis pleasantly.

The Principal nodded at Bug and gave her a wink, and she could barely keep herself from running up the stairs. She entered her code on the keypad clumsily, nearly locking herself out of the system, but managing to enter it correctly on her third try. She walked through the main lab past the half-finished projects of other researchers that had been abandoned when Wren came along. More footnotes. They'd entered a new age.

Bug punched a different code into the exterior door's

keypad and slid through before it had opened all the way. She spilled into the hallway and tried to slow her breathing.

Someone close by cleared their throat, and she turned to see Prady standing by the door, staff propped against the wall, a white mug in each hand. "About that time, isn't it?" He handed her a cup of tea.

She remembered to smile, took it, and sniffed the steam. "Where on Earth did you find lemon balm?"

"Oh, I have my sources, young lady."

"You're a saint." The warmth of the mug made her realize how cold her hands were. She cupped it more tightly, hoping it would calm her nerves. For once, her thoughts ran amok rather than her mouth, and even small talk proved difficult.

After an awkward minute, Prady spoke. "You're quiet today. I'm not used to carrying the conversation."

"Sorry. I'm distracted."

He nodded as if he understood, even though there was no way he possibly could. Prady was the only Keeper who treated her as if she were a real person rather than a quirky feature of the Main House. He actually spoke to her, brought her snacks. It had been forever since, well, anyone had cared about her like that. Or at all.

"How's she doing?" he asked.

She tried to think of how to phrase it. How were you supposed to describe someone being disassembled and reassembled? If she could find the words, how would he view her? Probably wouldn't bring her tea anymore, and that was the best case. "Something...changed recently. Shifted."

"You're concerned?"

"More and more." She leaned her head back against the wall. "I don't know how to move forward with all of this. I don't know that I can."

"Hmm," he said, and Bug wondered if he was now required

to report her for insubordination. She realized he likely hadn't been the only one listening, either—there was always a chance the Operator had heard.

"The Principal and Eydis, they're wonderful," she babbled. "I mean, they've been wonderful to *me*. I don't want to sound ungrateful. I am. I just…I can be grateful *and* questioning what we're doing, can't I? Is that allowed? I don't think they *want* to hurt Wren. Not really." He said nothing. "Prady, please, I'm sorry I said anything. I know my duty. I have a place here. I guess I just…I just wish Wren's place was different. That's all." She watched and waited for him to respond.

Prady sipped his tea thoughtfully. At last, he spoke. "Years ago, I had a daughter."

Bug finally breathed out and took a deep drink. "You've never mentioned her before."

"Afraid I'm not strong enough to talk about her often. There came a point in her illness when she was still alive but gone at the same time. I lost her before I lost her. I'm still not sure which death was harder. If I could have stopped things, I would have—whatever the price, I would have paid it."

She nodded and finished off her tea to hide the guilt she felt.

Prady reached out to take her empty cup and lingered there with his hand on hers. He caught her eye. "I don't know exactly what's going on in there, but I know that young lady behind those impressive doors is very special to me and others. Not for what it's rumored she can do but for who she is. I guess you have to decide if you're willing to pay the price to keep from losing her."

Bug put her other hand on top of his and whispered, "I wouldn't know where to start."

He took her empty cup, stacked it inside his own, and set them on the floor near the door of the lab. "You already did.

With a cup of tea." He stood again, taking a scratch pad and short pencil from under his striped Keeper robe. "I thought I might write down the address of the tea shop I frequent, if you're interested."

"Yes, please! Who knows, I might even find the time to get out of here for a break. I've needed a change in scenery lately, for the first time in years."

He held his staff under his arm as he wrote on the paper. "If you do choose to go out, be careful. The Disc isn't the best place to be right now. The Open isn't much better, from what I hear."

"Oh? What have you heard?"

"Rubedo is taking its toll, spreading slowly but steadily. Everywhere it touches, people become angrier. Even here in The Disc, people I know, people I care about, are becoming ill."

The way he looked at her then cut past pretense in a way words never could. He knew about the virus. Not that it existed, but where it had come from—this very lab. From the concern in his eyes, he'd seen the terrible effects of the virus himself. While she hadn't worked on that project personally, she knew those who had, Eydis among them. At the time, Eydis had said they were studying it so they could cure it. She'd even shown Bug the treatment. It was good work, and so Bug hadn't thought any more of it. She wasn't as smart as she thought she was, that was clear now.

Prady peered straight into her heart, which already ached over another experiment that had become twisted, perverted. As he did, everything Bug had done in that lab with the best of intentions was called into question in her mind. Her life's work, all the innovations she'd come up with—synthetic protein, increased crop sustainability, the bare beginnings of her forays into genetic engineering with reptiles in order to regrow limbs

—were stripped of any goodness. Turned out, it didn't take much sin at all to taint the whole of a person.

"I wish we had a way to help people here at home and to demonstrate to those outside that we don't want more death," Prady continued. "Something we could do to show them that they aren't alone." He ripped the sheet from the pad of paper and put it in her hand. "You, my dear, aren't alone, either. If you don't want to be." He took up his staff. "Same time tomorrow?"

"Absolutely."

He bowed, then reassumed his watchful position near the door.

She entered her code and slipped into the main lab. After the door sealed behind her, she stood there dumbly, truly not wanting to be there for the first time. Absentmindedly, she opened the paper he'd given her. On it was not the address of a tea shop, but a plea: "Caster needs your urgent help. For Wren, for others. The Market, stall 21. Tonight, 6pm. Bring rubedo treatment."

The inner chamber door opened at the far side of the room, and out stepped Principal Thallium. "Ah, Bug, excellent," he called. "Do you have a moment?"

Bug crushed the paper in her hand and tucked it into the pocket of her lab coat. "Of course, Principal."

He strode over and placed a familiar hand on her shoulder. "I just wanted to say thank you. Not only for assisting Eydis, but for making Wren feel at home here. I'm sure without you she'd feel overwhelmed by everything."

"It's my pleasure, sir. But with all due respect, I believe she feels pretty overwhelmed regardless."

He nodded, giving her shoulder a squeeze. The skin under his eyes was darker than usual, and he was generally disheveled. A slight glistening of sweat dotted around his nose and down his neck. He looked over his shoulder like he'd heard something but quickly wiped the surprise from his expression and began studying her as if he'd lost his train of thought.

"Perhaps if your son were to visit," she continued, "that might raise Wren's spirits? And maybe even his too? Although it's not my business, I believe she misses him."

His lack of focus left him in a burst of energy, and he clapped her on the back. "I've had thoughts along the same line. Someday soon, I hope. I'll discuss it with Eydis." He stepped around her, a bounce to his steps, and she caught the first few notes of a whistled nursery rhyme before it was cut off by the lab door. Bug tried to shake off the usual nerves she felt whenever she spoke with the Principal.

Eydis would still be in the inner chamber. Nobody else was working in the main lab right now. A clock near the ceiling said it had just ticked over to noon. If Theo the Operator was still a creature of habit, he was breaking right now for lunch like most of the other Main House staff. He'd be distracted. Besides, he didn't know what they were working on anyway. To him, it wouldn't look strange for Bug to access any particular cabinet in the lab.

The rubedo treatment, a combination of antibodies in vials, was in the fridge near where they kept the virus. There couldn't be more than twenty vials, but just a handful of those could help hundreds of people. They would need to stay cold until the meeting tonight. She could move them to her own refrigeration unit now, behind her private research samples of artificial poultry and beef, and grab them on her way to the meeting. A meeting that could easily get her killed if Eydis or the Principal discovered it. She could say she wanted dinner out or needed fresh air? Ugh, fresh air—nobody would believe that.

She had to stop analyzing. She was always thinking too

much. After a deep breath and a quick push of her glasses back up her nose, she walked as casually as she could manage toward the fridge with the ominous pink vials, behind which were clear vials of hope.

Caster wasn't looking for a fight. Hoped against one, in fact. Six didn't seem convinced of that at all as they neared the high quarter and tall multilevel buildings swallowed them up in an unnatural forest of vertical slit windows. By the way the Assassin eyed Caster, any bystanders would think *he* was the target tonight. Caster didn't dignify his self-righteous glare with a response. He didn't deserve it.

The Keeper apartment buildings were situated near the Main House, which wasn't merely a decision made for the convenience of a short work commute. It was for defense. The Main House was at the end of the city, close to the east wall. The Keeper district sat between it and the rest of The Disc and was in fact a death trap in the event of an attempted breach. Caster had the privilege of knowing that the apartment buildings housed weapons that could be unleashed by any high-ranking Keeper in the event of an attack. Shock tablets were loaded in the exterior walls, smoke grenades were kept in a storage room, and physical barriers could come out of the ground with a button push in front of entrances. The buildings formed a circle with a "kill zone" in their center, which, during normal times, served as a recreation area with tables and children's play equipment like seesaws and slides. An innocent face painted on top of something sinister—the design style of Caster's grandfather neatly encapsulated.

No little kids were playing outside under the noon sun, but a group of teenagers sat at one of the tables throwing dice. They glanced over at the sound of someone approaching as if expecting to be told to go home. When they saw Caster's group was masked and uninterested in their activities, they went back to their business, their excited chatting taking over the quiet outdoor space.

"He's in building one, top floor, apartment 303," said Six. "Sans has been watching the rear exit. Donnie's inside on the third floor keeping an eye on Amsel's door from cover at the top of the stairs."

Caster scanned the thin windows—303 should be toward the middle at the top. Seemed quiet enough up there. "Wait here. Watch the main entrance," he said to Six.

"Was planning to." Six leaned against a picnic table. "Scream if you need me."

Before Caster could quip in response, Asha nudged him in the back toward building one. He started walking with her and Gavel, hoping that they looked as though they belonged. The building was a tan stucco box, but its humble outside belied the security measures within. A keypad was installed next to the ultra-thick glass door. Caster entered the code Prady had given them; the door latch clicked. Gavel went in first, then Asha, and Caster checked once more over his shoulder before following.

People weren't often home at this time of day—a few Keepers on their lunch break, but most ate with each other closer to their designated posts. A baby cried somewhere on the first floor as they walked through the hall of doors toward the stairs at the back. Younger kids should be at school now. The quiet made sense, and it was usually a good thing on these types of missions, but for some reason, it didn't feel right.

They reached the third floor where Adonis was supposed to be waiting at the top of the stairs. He wasn't there.

"Where's Donnie?" Asha asked, about to lope right into the

hall to look for him. Gavel put an arm in front of her and peered cautiously around the wall.

This floor was even quieter than the other two. No babies cried, no dishes clattered, and nobody argued behind the closed doors. Caster strained his adept ears and still got nothing in return for his effort. Then he caught a whiff of something—Adonis had been here recently. His scent trail led into the hall toward room 303.

"He's in Amsel's room," he said quietly.

"I thought Amsel was home," said Asha.

"He is," said Gavel finally.

The three shared a heart-sinking moment, then Gavel snapped into action. Through hand signals, he told Caster to watch his back—Gavel was going to breach the door. His closed fist told Asha to stay put, but she used a more colorful hand signal to show him that wasn't happening. He didn't waste time arguing, and the three of them ran toward 303.

Gavel prepared to put his full weight against the door, but Caster put his hand on his elbow—it stood an inch open already.

Caster pushed ahead of them both into the apartment.

It was nice as far as apartments in The Disc went. An open design centered around a small kiva fireplace. A two-person dining table separated the living area from the small kitchen, and seated there was Adonis. Amsel stood behind him, hand clasped on his neck.

"No, no, no," whispered Asha.

A small smile pulled at Amsel's scarred lower lip. He was a big guy, probably close to Gavel's age, with dark skin and short black hair.

"Looks like you've been expecting us. Sorry we're late," said Caster as calmly as he could manage.

"Not at all," Amsel replied. "As a hunter, I not only pursue, but detect when I'm being pursued. This young man," he moved Adonis from side to side, "smells like stress sweat. Not regular sweat, but stress-induced perspiration. It has its own tang, entirely unique. Each man's—or almost-a-man's—is different." He bent closer to Adonis' ear. "Your sweat has a nutty note like almond cake. I picked it up at the bar the other night on that nasty little man, Oran, when he came back from having a chat with you."

"Screw you, creep!" Adonis said against the force of Amsel's grip, his voice wavering even as he tried to act as if he wasn't terrified. This hunter had a reputation, and Adonis was nothing to him. As eloquently as he spoke, this was a life-or-death scenario. Adonis wouldn't walk away if he tried something stupid.

"Don't be embarrassed, young man. Everyone smells, as your Scout friend knows." He eyed Caster. "You, god of war, smell of things likely beyond your fathoming—wood and rich earth. But the most captivating of all," he breathed deeply and straightened his posture, "is the sage in your hair, madam. I confess I could drown in that smell. Happily." He put his fingers to his temple and then out to her. "Good to see you again, Asha."

Caster waited for Asha's usual tough front, her don't-screw-with-me bravado, but it didn't come. He turned to see her remove the scarf from her face as if it would give her a better view and reveal all this to be a hallucination.

"You left...Why..." Asha stuttered.

"A new name, Quin?" Gavel had already pulled down his balaclava and moved in front of Asha. His overt protectiveness was such an unusual sight that Caster had trouble processing it, but Asha's fear was even harder to reconcile. She looked horrified.

"A new *life*, Gavel," the hunter replied. "One I've been living for a long time now."

"Lady-killer, if the rumors are accurate. That part's not changed, at least." Gavel studied him, then announced, "You look terrible."

Quin waved his free hand over his head. "Did you lose a little height? Or maybe it's the gray in your beard that's throwing me. Time betrays us all, Gavel. But then," his joking tone fell away, replaced by a cold anger that sent a chill up Caster's spine, "betrayal is something you're already familiar with."

Caster took a step toward Gavel. "You know this man?"

Without taking his eyes from Quin, Gavel replied, "He's from Kino. He was my Alpha."

"Let's not forget I was also Asha's fiancé," said Quin.

"Bullshit," spat Asha. Her eyes welled up with angry tears, and the sight so unnerved Caster that he stepped toward Amsel—apparently Quin—hand on his bowie at his hip, adrenaline pumping. But before he could close the distance between them, Adonis was already taking a chance to escape. He shoved the chair out from under him and dropped with his full weight to the floor. A decent move, using his smaller size as an advantage, but Quin stopped it easily. He grabbed Adonis in a one-armed hug to yank him to his feet, then put one hand to Adonis' forehead and the other around his chin. Ready to snap his neck. The hunter tsked, an odd fleshy sound around his scar.

The front of Adonis' pants grew wet.

"Let him go," Caster said.

"I never did enjoy killing children. It sometimes has to be done, but I don't like it. Please don't come any closer and force my hand."

"What do you want, Quin?" Gavel asked.

"Only your full attention for the time being."

"You already have it," said Gavel. "Release the boy."

Quin thought about it, as if deciding what he'd like to eat for dinner, before unhanding Adonis. The boy stumbled, and when he rose to his feet, he could barely bring his gaze from the floor. His cheeks flushed red. Asha waved Donnie over, and he didn't stop her from wrapping her arms around him.

"You think I'm your enemy, but hear me—I am your ally," said Quin. He sat in the chair he'd kept Adonis in and stretched his back against it. "The Principal? The evil mastermind he's built up to be? It's overblown nonsense. He's a neutered male waiting to be supplanted. There are people in The Disc working to do just that."

"Tyr's Army?" Caster said. "You're looking at it, freakshow. But thanks for the revelation."

"No. There are others. The Principal doesn't have all of the men he thinks he does. The longer he keeps his people trapped here, the faster they'll embrace this new leader who's siphoning off the Principal's Keepers and recruiting men like me."

"What do you know about our politics?" asked Gavel.

"Politics are the same everywhere," said Quin. "They're the same here as they were in Kino."

"We haven't murdered anyone in the street yet," Asha said, the barest of trembles in her voice. "I'd say we're plenty different."

"Who is trying to recruit you?" Caster asked. If someone other than Thallium wanted to hire Quin, it had to be someone with money and a need for muscle that rivaled Caster's own.

"I don't know any names. But I believe you know Dal? He knows you, regardless. Has endless trash to talk about Caster, the Bastard of the Desert. Dal's been treating me to a good time on his employer's behalf. I confess I'm enjoying being wooed. Little else to do here."

"Will you accept their offer?" Caster said. "Fight Thallium?"

Quin groaned as if all of this scheming and secrecy was beneath him. "I don't care about this city, but I am stuck in it—Openers won't respect me anymore. Thallium's hired me too often for their taste, and they'll try to kill me for it. I prefer to be the hunter rather than the hunted. Until there's something worth leaving for, I'll stay put and favor a side in this town when one of them shows it's the winning one." He stood and headed for the kitchen, clearly confident that they couldn't take him even if his back was turned. "Unless you're going to woo me toward Tyr's Army with trinkets and sweet words, get out of my home." He began rummaging through the cabinets casually.

Asha held Adonis to her side and left quickly, as if she would puke if she stayed in the room a second longer.

"Will you tell my father what I'm doing?" Caster asked.

Quin scooped coffee from a tin into a cloth filter over a glass decanter. "As I said, I don't care about this city. I don't want to be here; I certainly don't want to get any more embroiled in its fate or your family problems. Leave in peace, Tyr." He closed the lid of the coffee tin. "Stay for coffee, Gavel?"

Gavel spoke from someplace deep in his soul that Caster didn't know existed. "When the opportunity to leave The Disc comes, I suggest you take it. The risk out there might be great, but I promise you: it's greater here."

"I'll keep that in mind," said Quin. He waved them out.

The fact that Six still hadn't said anything about Quin basically holding Adonis under his fat leather boot like a bug several hours after it had happened showed just how relentlessly embarrassing the whole thing was. If there was an opportunity to give Adonis a hard time, Six took it. Adonis dislocated his finger when he'd gotten it caught in a pack strap? Six referred to him as "knuckle boy" for a week. Puked all over himself talking to a pretty girl? Six had pretended to dry heave multiple times a day, every day, garnering laughter from any Body within hearing distance. Crapped his pants from food poisoning in the Open? Well, that one was simple—uncontrollable laughter for forty-eight hours straight.

But after what happened today? Nothing. Zip. Silence.

Somehow, it was the most humiliating reaction possible. If it was bad enough that even Six didn't find it funny, it was bad. Adonis felt the shame in his gut. Deep, aching. Horrible.

Sans hadn't said anything either, but that was less surprising. Sans rarely said anything, and ironically, he was the one person Adonis was desperate to hear from. Adonis wanted Caster's respect, sure. Even his friendship, something like brotherhood. But Sans and Adonis shared history that had built a bond thicker than most.

Sans had delved into his deepest personal hell to rescue Adonis from his own. He'd risked his life and gone against the MO of the Bodies to pluck Adonis from the Open when he was waiting to die. A runt kid nobody wanted, not even as a slave, about to be killed for being useless—that's where Sans had found him. There was real love there, at least on Adonis' part. Letting himself be humiliated by Quin in front of Sans? Yeah, that hurt.

"How do you even talk to a lab rat anyway? Think she has basic social skills?" Six asked nobody in particular as he dealt another hand of plunder. He and Sans had hefty piles of tricks in front of them; Adonis was yet to score. They sat around Six's kitchen table, the remnants of a quarter order of potato cakes in their midst. Quarter orders were more expensive than full orders had been before the lockdown, but Six had insisted on picking up the tab. The green chile sauce was watered down, but so was just about every other food product capable of being thinned out these days.

"I've met a lot, dare I speak my pride and say *all*, of the eligible women in this city. Bug? Never heard of her. That should tell you something." Six finished dealing the hand. "This is the girl Caster thinks holds the keys to Wren's free-dom. I'm telling you: something has fried Caster's brain at the genetic level. He's changed. Don't you feel it?"

"Just play," Sans said as he arranged his new hand.

Adonis fanned out his cards. Part of him realized this was a fairly decent hand despite not being able to focus on the suits. Just a jumble of colors and symbols. He dragged his thumb down the edge of his outermost card, garnering an impressive papercut. He felt Quin's grip on his neck again and swallowed hard.

"Donnie?" Six's voice grabbed Adonis' attention. "You with us, man?"

Adonis examined the burning cut on his thumb, then looked at Sans stupidly.

"Bid's to you," Sans said gently.

"Oh. Sorry." Adonis tried to make sense of his cards, calcu-late probability in his head. Might as well have been trying to turn the cards to stone with his mind. His struggle must have shown on his face.

"Argh, didn't realize what time it was," said Six. He tossed his cards faceup as he stood. "Off to meet the lab rat. I hope P-man's right about her. Otherwise, this is a massive waste of relaxation time. I get fussy without it." He reached for the last potato cake in the folded-down bag, then paused with his greasy fingertips outstretched. "Here, kid," he said, and he nudged the bag toward Adonis.

As Six moved around the table toward the front door, Adonis said under his breath, "Don't give me your pity." They both heard him, of course—Assassin and Thief with skilled hearing that was yet one more way in which they were superior to Adonis.

Six shrugged, reached with his long arm across the table, and yanked the potato cake out of the bag. He shoved it into his mouth. With a smack to the back of Adonis' head, he was out the door. It was about the nicest gesture he'd ever made.

With Six gone, the room fell quiet. Painfully quiet. Even though Sans simply continued to study his cards, Adonis imagined he was judging him from where he sat. The quiet got heavier and heavier until Adonis had to break it, and he did so with the truth that had been weighing on his chest since he'd thought he was going to die earlier.

He dropped his cards and said, "When I was a kid and you found me in that shipping container, I was stinking, weak, and pathetic. Today, I felt like I'd never left it."

Sans pushed his cards into one neat stack and set it on the table. "You did leave it. You were strong then. You're stronger now."

"No, I'm not! I'm a dumb kid, a freaking liability. You saw me with Amsel—I wriggled like a worm between a kid's dirty fingers. I can't improve my body no matter how much I try. I hate it!"

Sans' eye contact and his wry smile caught Adonis off guard—it was a rare sight, to not only be truly seen by Sans, but to also see emotion in him. "I know what it is to hate your body. The drive to change it. I changed mine as much as possible, but I still live within its limitations. I've accepted them. If you don't, you'll trap yourself in that container in your mind and never emerge."

Adonis shoved his chair back from the table and threw his hands up as he stood. "Limitations? *You* don't have limits. I mean, you have to keep your body from excelling!"

Sans remained seated. "It doesn't excel. It kills without thought if I let it take over. Trust me—none of us are without weakness. We all fall to our knees at the mercy of our own limitations."

"I *live* on my knees, Sans!" Adonis shook with frustration. "Shorter than everyone, younger than everyone, dumber than everyone. My own family sold me for a garden hoe. Did I ever tell you that? I was in that container, then up on a rock like a piece of meat at auction, because a metal stick was more valuable to my family than me. And now? Now I'm so useless I can't control my bladder. What am I even doing here?" He hurled his chair halfway across the room. "I'm worthless!"

Just like everything else, he couldn't stop his tears from coming. Anger dripped down his cheeks, and he closed his eyes just so he couldn't see the shame in Sans'. But then he felt the Thief's arms wrap around him, one across his back and the other around his neck.

"You have worth to me."

Adonis returned the embrace, holding onto the back of Sans' baggy coat to steady himself as he felt his legs go soft. Sans took his weight and let him cry.

PART 3

NO MERCY

CHAPTER SEVEN

This was going to be a complete waste of time.
Which was ironic since Caster was so fixated on how they were
running out of that commodity.

Shoppers went up and down the market aisle. They
brushed past Six as he pretended to examine a set of clay mugs
at a vendor's table two booths down from Vee's tent. It wasn't
the number of shoppers there used to be. Something was
shifting among the masses, and he had a feeling it had more to
do with the uptick in violent incidents in The Disc rather than
with how cold it was in the open marketplace. Fewer people
socialized. Those that had dared to come here clearly came for
a specific purpose, stuck to lines on an invisible map with trea-
sures like bits of soap and used coats at their ends. A father
with his toddler asleep against his shoulder made a beeline to a
fruit vendor and her meager stock. An elderly woman pushed
her tired body as fast as it would go toward an herbalist's booth.
Young men grabbed cones of roast hoppers and took them to-go
rather than lingering to talk to one another. Tension wound
through the booths.

One booth, owned by an ex-Scavenger named Mal, was guarded particularly heavily on the opposite side of the aisle, across from where Six stood. Mal still had good relationships with Scavengers who were privileged enough to be allowed out of the walls and had found a new career in the form of selling the desert and pre-Fall waste they foraged as firewood. All of it could be burned to keep people warm—splintered pieces of houses long leveled and dried desert scrub. Mal had three guards holding blunt implements surrounding the booth. This was what Thallium's lockdown order had done to his people—deprived them of basic needs to the point that they were guarding garbage with their lives.

Strange how he'd decided to attack the Openers upon whom The Disc relied for trade, how he'd thought his people could stay inside all winter with only a handful of Scavengers bent on their own profit released to provide for them. No, strange wasn't the word. It was asinine. An action driven by insanity. Or was it pride? Greed? They all blended together nowadays.

Caster was proof of that. He'd never been much for the elegant touch, but now, he was a couple of rash decisions away from a move as genius as his father's. The same ambition ran in both their veins, the kind that got people killed.

Thallium hadn't prepared for an emergency like this. There were no stockpiles of food, no surpluses of medicine or fuel in case The Disc ever shut its walls. Since the dawn of its existence, those in The Disc hadn't feared the Open so much as Openers, especially outliers like Wren, had feared The Disc. Its reach, its eyes on them, its sheer numbers. Once that fear started to wear off, Thallium must have thought he could keep Openers in line by killing them in secret and then swooping in to win their affections with his generous offer of help. So much for that brilliant plan. Now here they all were, soon to be in a full-on Trojan War situation. Siege warfare should have been left in ancient times.

A figure in a square white coat trimmed in green, hood up, turned a corner at the far side of the market and headed in Six's direction. The white coat was so clean that it was nearly blinding. Underneath the bulky clothes, the wearer's figure was feminine, at least to an eye as keen as Six's. Round metal eyeglass frames poked out from the depths of the hood, and the woman's gait was awkward. Anytime she came near another person, she quickstepped the other way. Not fearful, exactly. More uncomfortable.

The woman wore a satchel across her chest. She clutched at it protectively with one hand, and Six marveled at how she'd managed to get all the way to the market without being robbed when she showed such obvious fear of her bag being touched. It simply screamed, "Steal me!" Didn't take a Thief to notice.

The woman turned toward Vee's tent, but when she was just outside the tent flap, she turned on her heel and headed instead for the firewood booth, bumbling like a fly trapped in a jar. If this was the lab rat he was meant to meet, then he shouldn't be staring at her. Hardly inconspicuous to do so. But it was always hard to turn away from a spectacle when entertainment was scarce.

The hooded figure perused the bundles of fire scrap at the booth, clearly unaware that she'd just cut in line. A dirt-dusted man with a sleepy little girl on his hip elbowed her out of the way.

"Privilege won't get you special treatment down here!" the man shouted at her. "Not anymore."

A pair of sanitation workers nearby—still in their telltale gray jumpsuits—tried to take advantage of the distraction and run off with one of the bundles toward the outside edge of the booth. The guard nearest them reached out and landed a blow to the back of the woman sharing the burden with her male coworker. She went down, and so did the bundle. The scuffle invited others to watch as more desperately cold citizens rushed the booth. In all the tumult, no Keepers came. But high above the scene, a drone's orange eyes watched it all. It hovered there lazily as if it were bored and had nothing better to do. Thus embodied was Thallium's authority and devotion to his citizens—presence but inaction.

As the situation devolved further and citizens absconded with bundles of kindling that would last them maybe one evening, Six caught a glimpse of a white hood bobbing along near the ground. Crawling. She was crawling away.

"Not just a shut-in, but a hazard to society," Six muttered to himself as he tugged his balaclava up just beneath his eyes and slipped across the path. "Being right is such a burden."

He knocked people back with swift jabs and body checks on his way toward that white hood. Once he finally reached the girl, he yanked her up by the back of her coat like a sack of grain to get her out of harm's way. As soon as they were clear of the mob, he set her on her feet. She started to lower her hood, but he stopped her.

"Face down," he barked. "Follow me."

Thankfully, she did. Right into Vee's tent.

"No protection for you here!" Vee snapped, her eyes fixed on a magnifying glass set up on a table. She slipped a piece of amber into a silver setting. "If you're not here to shop, get—" She looked up from her work when Six lowered his face covering. She waved him off like a pest and promptly went back to work as the sound of the fight nearby subsided.

Six walked toward the hooded figure until her back was against the far tent wall. He got well within her personal space and said, "Tell me your name."

"Me? Who are you?" a feminine voice hissed. The woman

shoved the hood back. Sleek black hair slipped down past her shoulders. Her glasses were askew; she reached up to fix them and glared through their big lenses at Six.

He tsked. "That's just the kind of question a spy would ask."

"I am a spy. Your spy. My name's Bug." She slid over in an attempt to put more space between them. "Prady set this up."

"Who? Never heard of him."

Bug groaned. "This is pointless. His note said that Caster needs my help and to meet here, but if you're the kind of people Caster's associating with, then we don't have a chance." She pushed her fingers under her glasses to pinch the bridge of her nose. He noticed how striking her profile was underneath the glasses.

"No, we don't have a chance if you keep making scenes like the one you made out there," said Six. "For all citizens and drones to see. Espionage doesn't suit you."

"I thought it would be better to pretend I was shopping a little before coming here! It made sense to avoid suspicion!" She yanked her hair into an angry ponytail. "You know what? No, you're right. This was a bad idea. I should just go, should not have agreed to meet. Eydis will find out, because of course she will; how could she not when she knows the exact times I take my bathroom breaks?" She shook her head nervously. "Take this." She withdrew a silver cylinder from the satchel and held it out to him. With a hissing twist, it opened to reveal four vials inside. "This is the treatment for rubedo. The antibodies must be administered intravenously—I've included instructions on the label inside the canister. Keep the vials in the canister until you're ready to administer the treatment. Temperature control is important." The cylinder hissed shut, then she handed it to him. "Now I need to get out of here."

"Wait! Thank you for this, really. I have an annoying friend who will also be thankful once he's feeling better. But I need something else from you." He tossed the cylinder up and caught it before tucking it away in the interior pocket of his coat.

Her hand shot to her chest. "For the love of all things, please don't throw that."

He ignored her and continued, "Caster would very much appreciate your help with Wren."

Something in her panicked expression turned soft. "Help with her how?"

"I thought that was obvious—break her out of the inner chamber."

Bug looked around Six at Vee, mouth gaping at Six's boldness.

"What, her?" he said with a jerk of his thumb. "She's a friend. Besides, she's so antique she can't hear us."

"Oh, I hear you. Like I hear water dripping from my roof all night long." Vee made dripping sounds by popping her lips. "Never shuts up."

Bug relaxed. "Okay, clearly she knows you well. But Wren, what, you want to just take her? Bust in, break her chains, and leave the way you came? You can't be serious!" She dug a streak into the dirt with her pacing and spoke rapidly. "This is why I don't leave the lab. This, right here. People are morons. Yet here I am trying to do the right thing. I *do* want to help Wren—my friend, I might add—but this is ridiculous. Maybe I should just sneak her out in the trash bins like I was going to originally. Why didn't I listen to myself? Stupid overanalyzing genius brain! What's wrong with—"

"Wrong with you? Currently, how you won't stop talking."

She folded her arms and tried to lean confidently against the wall of the tent, but before she did, she realized it wouldn't hold her weight and swallowed a squeal as she caught her balance. After straightening up, she proclaimed, "I have a lot to say."

"Obviously, lab rat."

She cleared her throat. "I prefer Bug."

"Okay, Bug. I'm Six. Assassin. Friend of Caster's."

"Well, Six Assassin, friend of Caster—I'm a friend of Wren's. What you're asking is impossible without getting caught, imprisoned, and probably hanged."

Silence hung between them. He'd been too blunt, clearly. He'd have to put in more effort to gain her trust. She was lovely enough, and gawky enough, that he figured he might as well take the flirtatious approach—two birds.

"I apologize, Bug. You're right. I shouldn't talk so casually about all this. It would put you at great risk." He held his hand to his heart. "I'm sorry. Can we start again?" He put on a warm grin for good measure.

And got nothing in return. She didn't even give that reflexive little smile he was used to women giving him. Just crickets. "Start again?" she said. "Pretty sure that's also impossible."

"In my experience, not much is truly impossible." He grinned wider.

She blinked at him a couple of times, probably in much the same way as she did at a specimen under a microscope. "Look, I don't have much time, so let's skip to the important part. How are you going to break her out?"

Six's grin fell away, knocked back by a shot of humility to his chest. This woman really didn't find him attractive at all. "We don't want to *break* her out," he said at last, trying to stand taller than he felt. "We want to *let* her out. Quietly, cleanly. Nobody caught in the cross fire. We just need someone to open the door."

"He says as though that's a simple thing." She began

mumbling to herself, almost arguing, wrestling with options. After an uncomfortable minute of that, she took her hair down only to put it up again, her fingertips punishing her scalp as she attempted to smooth out the bumps that refused to settle. Once she had it squarely back, she exhaled. "I can do it."

"That's a bold statement."

"It's a true one. I wouldn't have said it if it weren't. Do you want to hear how or are you going to keep wasting both of our time with patronizing one-liners?" She dug around in her coat pocket and took out a round silver watch. "I have about three minutes left to relay the essential details of the lab to you or else I'll fall under suspicion. Can you shut up for three minutes?"

"You obviously can't," he scoffed.

She paused, then finally asked, "You done?"

He cleared his throat and waved his arm, motioning for her to go on. Something about her made him feel small. It was infuriating.

"The best time to go in will be at night when Wren's alone," she said. "She'll be in something called an isolation unit. The unit's a box about six feet high and four feet wide filled with biosynthetic fluid."

"You put Wren inside a box?"

"Eydis did, yes. She keeps Wren in the unit."

"Wait, wait, wait." He waved his arms around. "Wren's been in a box of liquid for *weeks*?" His voice went up an octave on his last word.

She winced, then whispered, "Yes."

Six pressed his lips together as he exhaled through his nose. "Well, Caster's going to freak right out at that."

"As he should."

"I see it didn't bother *you* until now."

Her jawline went rigid. "You don't *see* anything at all," she said slowly, articulating every syllable like she was teaching him to speak. "You don't know me, assassin man."

He held up his hands in deference and took a step back. "You're right. It's your neck if they find out you helped us."

"Of course they'll know it was me. Every time one of us enters the lab, a record is made of who and when." She held up her ID bracelet, similar to Six's own.

"You aren't afraid of what Thallium will do to you when he finds out?"

She swallowed hard. "I don't plan to be there when he does." She ran her hands up and down her arms as if trying to warm herself against a sudden chill in the tent. "I'll be...somewhere else. Not sure where yet."

At that moment, what she was sacrificing became clear to Six. Her livelihood was tied up in that lab—her job, her home, her daily meals. By helping them, she was forfeiting all of it. She was more remarkable than she'd seemed.

"You're brave to be doing this. Really," he said. "We'll find a place for you, either in The Disc or outside of it."

A wave of fear came off of her, so thick Six could smell it. "Inside, please. Leaving the Main House is bad enough."

He shrugged. "The Open can be nice. Better views. Less mob mentality."

His joke didn't break the tension as he'd hoped. She just stared at him flatly.

"*In* The Disc," he said. "No problem. Caster wants to move fast. Is that possible?"

"Not much is impossible, right?" She looked at the pocket watch again. "Out of time. Talk with your people." She lifted her hood. "When you're ready to move, send Prady to the Main House with a gift for Wren—a book. Caster is a big reader, I believe. He'll have one. Once I get that signal, I'll meet you here again the next day at dawn. We'll plan the details."

Panic struck him at seeing her leave. He wanted her to stay, to understand her better. "Why are you doing this?" he asked in a rush.

She paused by the tent flap, spoke over her shoulder. "Because my work has no meaning. Not anymore." With that, she left.

Six wondered why his stomach was tied in knots at seeing her go.

"You better buy something, murder boy," Vee said. "Or else get to work polishing."

He felt the weight of the canister in his coat. "Not today. I've got an annoying Scavenger to save." He kissed her on the head on his way out the back of the booth and into the alley.

There was a strange sense of power and promise as the canister hissed open under Asha's careful touch. Caster watched her withdraw a vial of antibodies and invert it slowly, purposefully. He stood far back as she worked. He was lucky Asha had even allowed him to stay; she'd shooed Six away after thanking him quickly for the canister, but Caster had insisted on being here. He had to see for himself if this would work.

He and Asha wore masks. Long ago, Gavel and the others had avoided infection in Hallund while trapped in a building full of sick citizens all intent on their demise. Theoretically, an unconscious Frederick Hawthorn de Bourgh was less of a threat. But in the end, this virus—and nature in general—would find a way of doing whatever it wanted to humanity. The Open always did.

Asha sat next to an unconscious Freddy, who she'd hooked up to an IV and made comfortable on a bedroll with his back propped against the wall. Maybe "comfortable" wasn't the appropriate word, but it was the best they could do down here, and they couldn't risk moving him elsewhere. Asha's face covering was more advanced than Caster's simple bandana—three layers of cloth around her nose and mouth, tied behind her head with sturdy strings, along with a plastic face shield.

Freddy had looked better. Sweat slicked back Freddy's dark hair, glistened on his bare chest. Blood still came from his nose, drop by drop. More dripped from the left corner of his mouth, the direction his head was tilted, watered down and runnier because of his saliva. It was a promise of more to come. When it started pouring from the eyes and ears, that was when death wasn't far off. As much as Caster often wished he would shut up and be still, getting it like this just wasn't what he'd had in mind.

Hopefully, they'd gotten the cure to him in time to make a difference. And, still more hopefully, Bug was truly on their side and what she'd put in those vials was indeed the cure. As highly as Caster thought of Bug, he still wasn't sure he could trust her. The list of people he could was fairly short.

Asha prepared to inject the antibodies into his IV and went perfectly still with the syringe in hand. Her other hand she held open facing Freddy. Caster wondered if something was wrong until he saw her eyes were closed. Praying. Over Freddy, for him. Caster closed his own eyes and attempted to join her in his own silent, clumsy way. When he looked again, Asha had stuck the needle into his IV. When she finished, she turned her attention back to comfort care, wiping under his nose with a gloved hand.

As if appearing out of nowhere, Sans was at Caster's side, wearing a bandana across his mouth and looking on at Asha and her patient like he'd been standing there the whole time.

"Geez, man. Didn't hear you coming," Caster said softly, not wanting to wake Freddy.

"Sorry," Sans replied.

"You really shouldn't be here. The fewer exposed, the better."

The Thief nodded. "I understand. I won't be long—can we step into the corridor?"

Sans rarely came to Caster alone. Whatever he had to say, it was important to him. "Sure."

They retreated to the dim light of the corridor leading back toward Pip's and stood across from each other, masks pulled down to their necks. Didn't matter that Sans was his friend, nor that he was the most gentle and soft-spoken man Caster had ever known—standing across from the Harbinger under the full power of his attention was more than intimidating. It felt like looking into the eyes of a predator that could choose to devour him at any second.

"What's on your mind?" Caster asked.

Sans sighed quietly as if he were still debating how to say what he needed to. "I'm concerned for Adonis."

"Asha checked him out after we left the apartment. A little bruised, mostly a bruised ego, but he'll be fine." Thinking they were done, Caster started to put his mask back in place.

"This time, yes," Sans said seriously. "Next time is less certain."

Caster lowered his mask and folded his arms. "Next time?"

"Despite appearances, we're at war. Adonis isn't ready for that."

"He's come a long way. Do you think you're maybe underestimating him?"

"I don't underestimate his drive. I question his mindset. His focus has slipped." Sans tapped himself on the forehead lightly. "Fights large and small are won in the mind—he's distracted."

"We all are," Caster scoffed.

"But we're not so young. With our Body, if we continue down this path, he'll get hurt."

Caster couldn't argue that—the kid already had. Which meant he had something to prove next time around. No telling what he'd do to show them that he could handle himself. "I understand your concern, but I won't kick him out of the Body. He's earned his place there."

"I'm not asking you to release him, but to retask him. Something safer that gives him space to clear his head."

Retask him to what? Sharpening knives and holding their coats? Then Caster thought about Ollie, how he'd said he was spread thin at the treatment plant. "How do you think he'd feel about becoming our liaison with Ollie in water? Might be nice to have one of our own among his men, listening."

"You don't trust Oliver?" asked Sans dubiously.

"I do. But his men? Perhaps less. They'd make a tough enemy if they decided to subvert Ollie and side with Thallium—sounded like several disagreed with him enough to quit recently. People make stupid decisions in tense environments, and I'd say The Disc is pretty damn tense lately."

Sans scratched the back of his neck. "Water worker? Doesn't sound like Adonis."

"It might once he finds out that Ollie's cousin heads up the division that installs mods for new Body recruits. Not a bad guy to get to know when your heart is set on going under his knife someday."

Sans thought about it, then smiled. He nodded slowly.

"I'll talk to Ollie," Caster said. "If he's amenable, then you can tell Adonis about his new assignment. Sound good, brother?"

Caster could tell from the way Sans' shoulders pulled up that this had been a true weight on his mind. Adonis had always had a bond with Sans, but now, Caster saw that Sans cared for the kid in much the same way. It was just harder to tell.

"Thank you," said Sans. He raised his chin in respect.

Caster returned the gesture.

Around the corner, Freddy whispered to Asha, "You look terrible, darling. Did someone disrespect you? I'll remove their manhood."

Caster and Sans yanked their masks back up and returned to the black-market room. Freddy wasn't only awake, he was *standing*. Half out of his mind with fever and brandishing an imaginary sword, but standing. Caster said another prayer, this one of thanks for Freddy's apparent improvement and the fact that he was at least wearing underwear.

Asha pushed down on his shoulders before he could rip out his IV, and he sank back to the bedroll. Freddy smacked his lips loudly and wetly. "Copper, copper. Give me a coin, I'll give you a whopper. Copper, copper!"

"Seems like a good sign, huh Ash?" Caster said.

Asha's unseen smile lit up her eyes. "It is. Not just for him, but for everyone in the Open."

With this test, she had proof enough that the antibodies worked. Which meant she'd be out of The Disc as soon as possible to use it to help others. If the Openers hesitated to kill her long enough to accept her help, that is. Gavel would have his work cut out for him in keeping her safe.

***

Survivor lay on her back with her head on the folded bedroll Gray had given her as some sort of bizarre romantic parting gesture. The canyon in which the High Cave was hidden was long and wide with towering walls. Most annoying of all, it was incredibly rocky. Which was why Survivor had taken the bedroll.

The west wall of the canyon stretched up above them at an incline that started gradually but grew suddenly steep about a third of the way up. They'd set up camp in a sheltered branch of the canyon, southwest of Ranlock by a couple of miles but still north of the cave that was their final destination.

Close by, Beo dropped another piece of the juniper wood they'd gotten in Ranlock into the fire pit he'd dug nearly a foot into the ground. Pure, glorious heat and only the barest wisp of smoke poured out of the pit against Survivor's side when Beo exhaled into the smaller ventilation hole he'd dug. Their wood would be soft ash soon—juniper was notoriously fast-burning. Beo would have to work quickly tonight.

"Do it already," grumbled Survivor. When she gritted her teeth against the pain in her head, the resulting throbbing forced her to relax.

A layer of rocks crunched under his heavy feet as he moved to squat behind her head and unpack supplies from his bag. "Sit up until I'm ready to start. I know it hurts more when you're lying down."

She'd never told him about when it hurt more, but he had noticed on his own. He was right—sleeping, or trying to, was the worst. Their two nights in Ranlock had been her best sleep in days due to her continual access to a bottle of Incendio Gray had left next to the bed. Swishing it when the pain woke her got her back to sleep for a couple hours at a time. She convinced herself that was the only reason she felt rested. It had nothing to do with how Gray had pulled her to his chest whenever she settled back under the obscenely soft blanket or the way his stubble-covered neck smelled like warm rosemary.

Beo reached for a bottle of Yellow sitting open on the ground. "Drink."

The Yellow was hot and tasted of salty phlegm, a different kind of burning from the Incendio. After three large gulps of the devil's piss, she held a mouthful around the tooth. She nearly choked at the initial pain but kept her wits and held the alcohol there until her gums lost most of their feeling.

Beo took the bottle back and poured it all over the needle-nose pliers Gray had provided with their other supplies. "Ready. Lie back."

She spat the Yellow toward a nearby agave plant, unable to stomach any more, and then put her head back. Her lower jaw on her right side with the rotten tooth throbbed with the motion, sending shooting pain into her ear and up the back of her skull. She felt like her head was about to explode—partially wanted it to—and was thankful that Beo didn't hesitate to do what needed to be done as soon as she was in position.

He tucked the keycard hanging from his neck into his shirt so it wouldn't get in the way. He then held the top of her head firmly with one of his meaty hands as he clamped down onto the dead back molar with the pliers. It sounded like a creaking door as he gave a couple of experimental tugs, and Survivor couldn't stop her legs from kicking out. Even with her flailing, Beo kept her head still and continued his work. They were a mile out from the High Cave, but she couldn't scream. Sound carried in the canyon. The tooth started to separate from her gums, lightning shot up the side of her head, and she moaned as loudly as she dared until the pain blacked out her vision.

She woke on her side. Her new bedroll stretched underneath her, and Beo's wadded, scratchy, spare shirt propped up her head. The smell of something rotten had woken her. Familiar, yet accosting. Cold drool pressed against her cheek from where it had soaked into the fabric of Beo's shirt. She listened closely and, from the northeast, carried through the rocks and crevices of the desert, came the commotion of new visitors making the dusk descent into Ranlock—whoops and the pitches of salesmen giddily accepting money for preorders before the descent. She thought about Gray, where he might be tonight. She got as far as picturing the way he could keep that toothpick in the corner of his mouth even when he was laughing before she shook the thought away. Shook hard enough that she got dizzy.

"It's done," said Beo from behind her.

As she rolled onto her other side to face him, she felt around the right side of her mouth with her tongue. It was so packed with cloth, there was little to feel. And she was swollen. Very swollen.

"You should wait to go in for a couple of extra days," he said. His long legs straddled either side of a big rock while he skillfully ground sulfur crystals into a powder in a depression in the rock with a smaller round stone. The mystery of the foul smell that had woken her was now solved. "Need time for that swelling to be totally gone—they'll be suspicious otherwise."

She started to shake her head again but thought better of it. "Done waiting," she mumbled around the mass of cloth packed into her cheek.

He sighed. "Fine. I guess there will be enough damage all over you in the end that your jaw won't stand out any more than the rest."

She snickered and nearly choked on the spit trickling down the back of her throat. The right side of her mouth and face felt tight, itchy, and still throbbed. But the pain down her neck and up her head was gone. Relief by degrees.

"This is too risky," Beo muttered.

She tried to respond, but the damn cloth was still in her way. She removed the bit of it closest to the front of her mouth and tossed it aside. "We already agreed on this plan. You've been in a weird mood since we left Ranlock. What's really bothering you?"

He separated the fine powder from the remaining larger pieces of crystals with a sweep of his fingers, attention glued to his task. "I don't like how you let him use you. Gray."

"Use me? If anything, I used him."

He failed to keep his smirk concealed and glanced down at her out of the corner of his eye. "How many times?"

"Shut up." If she'd had the energy, she would have hit him. Preferably somewhere he would have felt it the next day.

"You really liked him."

"You don't have to like each other to do what we did."

"Some people don't, but most people do. You do."

"What makes you think that, smartass?"

"You never had feelings for Reskin in all those years?"

Reskin had been bigger than Beo, his half-mask of scars denser and more intricate. If Beo could have been called her protégé, she could have been called Reskin's. He'd been her shadow, demon, and protector rolled into one. "I had feelings for him. None of them simple."

"Well, love's not usually simple, is it?"

The way he'd asked it stopped the jab she was about to make at his virtue—the man had done some astonishing deeds since they'd been apart, but in one of the cold evenings in the desert when they'd talked idly to pass the time, he admitted he had still not been with a woman. His naïve tone and the genuine curiosity in it took her insult and tossed it up into the icy breeze on which the stink of sulfur flew. "No. Guess not."

"You can like whoever you want," he said, mask of toughness back in place. "This whole thing's just brought ancient shit up. I'm dealing with it. Don't worry."

He stopped his work when she reached up and pulled at his elbow. "I *am* worried. I need your head level for this.

There's just me and you to get this done. Without you, it won't get done. I'll die. Wren will probably die without us to come for her." As Beo could easily have done after she left him. But that wiry teenager, all limbs and suppressed trauma? He'd fought to stay alive. Now he was about to help her do the same. "You here?"

He set down the grinding stone, delicately spread out the powder again to check for any large crystals he'd missed. "I'm here."

"Will we be ready in time?"

He met her gaze, a heavy seriousness in his tone as he said, "I'll be ready."

"Good. And all that past shit that got dragged up? The monsters that won't stay asleep? Point them at what we're about to do."

He nodded.

Survivor relaxed against the bedroll, and the rhythmic grinding of stone against stone eased her back to sleep.

Asha's hands shook as she filled the kettle for the sixth and last time, watching the water level fall past more lines on the tank built into a tall cabinet in the kitchen. Thankfully, they'd just been issued their water the previous day. They could only carry so much with them in the Open, and by the time they returned, another ration would be due. They could afford this little indulgence. Hell, even if they couldn't, she needed it. She had no taste for booze or drugs that could relieve the incessant trembling of her hands. A bath would be good medicine. She hoped.

Probably a quarter of each kettle-full had splattered onto the floor in a trail as she walked from the kitchen across the tiny living space to pour the water into the metal basin she'd set up in the bedroom. She never got the shakes like this. Wholly embarrassing, especially for a doctor.

With two hands and a thick towel, she moved the kettle back to the hearth, hung it on the pot crane, and swung the metal arm back over the fire. The arm creaked with the motion, overworked as it was, and the sound took Asha back to the memory of a cramped metal cage with a damp floor and a door that groaned every time it opened.

TWENTY-NINE YEARS EARLIER

Asha's butt and legs were itchy and wet like the earth on which she sat, and the back of her head hurt all over from resting it against the frame of the cage. Gavel had brought a starchy soup that smelled of onions. He wasn't supposed to, not after how she'd acted that morning. His hand waited inside the bars, holding a spoonful of soup.

"You have to eat," he said.

"I don't want it. You know what I want." There was only one thing she needed—for him to open the cage and kill her already.

He took the spoon back. "And you know I won't give it."

"Then leave!" she yelled, straining her throat. She kicked the door of the cage with her heel. The force would bruise her bare foot, but the satisfaction of the clanging metal made it worth it.

Unlike her cage, Gavel was far from rattled. He never got angry with her. In fact, none of her behavior had irked him, as much as she'd wished it would. Ever patient and—despite the stern face he wore around his subordinates—kind. Far kinder than any of the rest of them. But then, she'd watched a mob of them murder her parents. Not too hard to look decent compared to that. She lied to herself as she sat in that cage that her positive regard for Gavel must be due to the evil that was around him, not anything exceptional within him. But despite her best efforts, she was starting to see that he was a good man, would be considered so even outside of Kino.

Quin came in then. He often interrupted them, sidling into the small earthen dome full of cages—empty, except for Asha's—and walking toward her as if he were posturing for a crowd of hundreds. Confident, sure, sociopathic.

Gavel stood and turned to put himself between Quin and Asha's cage, resting his hands behind his back out of respect. Gavel was big, but Quin was bigger by inches.

"Nala says rain is coming. Last monsoon," said Quin.

Gavel's hand tightened on his own wrist as if to restrain it from delivering a right hook to Quin's temple. "The end of the rainy season." The way he'd said it went beyond weather commentary—it sounded like a writ of execution. "Then you will go through with your plan?"

"Aidan won't live to see many more years. We need a new healer, but she must be Kinoan. Or made to be."

"I understand, Alpha, but she won't accept me."

"Not you. Me. She will accept me or leave this world as her parents did." Quin didn't wait for a response from Gavel, which had probably been a good thing. Asha had known Gavel for all of a week and only had a view of his back, but even so, she could sense his anger. Incredible how Quin didn't, but he'd been too busy moving to kneel in front of the cage.

The way he looked at her made her feel like merchandise, even less than an animal. Then he attempted to smile, and it was horrifying—a lifeless expression from a man who had thrown the first stone at her father's head.

PRESENT DAY

The screaming of the kettle made Asha start. She yanked the crane arm, and the pot swung out from over the fire too fast, splashing boiling water on top of her foot.

"Unbelievable," she grumbled as she rushed to peel her sock off before the water could scald her skin too severely.

The bolt in the front door slid open, and Gavel pushed into the house with his shoulder, his hands full of new travel gear they really couldn't afford, especially considering what it was going to cost to get a keycard from one of Freddy's Scavenger associates. All of their savings, plus the majority of Asha's ethanol stock that she'd worked hard to distill and build up, and the last of Freddy's own vehicles that he'd restored. Her decision to leave The Disc to help others was costing them their future livelihood. Of course, this venture could easily end up killing them anyway. What did it matter at that point how many, or how few, possessions they left behind?

Gavel took in the sight of Asha's mess across the room before closing the door behind him and sliding the bolt back home, shutting the darkness outside. The cold air he'd let in sent her hands shaking again.

"Everything all right?" he asked as he joined her in the kitchen and set the gear—a new bag to replace her med pack that had been vomited on in the ward, an extra-large canteen, spare socks—on the table.

"What a stupid question, Gav," she snapped. "No, it's not all right." She tried to hide her hands by tucking them into the sleeves of her bathrobe, but she wasn't fooling him. He wrapped an arm around her shoulder and pulled her close as he took the kettle from the fireplace.

"Making tea?"

"No, a bath. Audacious of me, isn't it? I figure it'll be a long time before I get to feel clean again. Might as well enjoy it tonight."

He gripped her more tightly and walked to the bedroom. They reached the basin, and he topped off the now cool tub with the fresh kettle. The steam rose up to battle the cold air. Before long, the cold would win.

Their bed was within reach, and he removed and threw his duster onto it. He pushed his white sleeves up past his elbows and then stuck his hand in the water. "That's as perfect as it's going to get. Don't waste it." He pulled her robe off her shoulders, caressing her curves as it fell down. The shaking of her body stopped when he took her into his arms for just a moment before guiding her into the tub.

The water barely came up past her belly button. Even so, it was enough to make her body sigh. She closed her eyes and rested her head against the edge of the basin but was reminded again of the cage and sat up quickly. Gavel noticed.

He skirted their bed and sought the dresser on the far side of the room. Asha watched him paw through three drawers.

"Might be easier if you told me what you're looking for," she said.

He chuckled. "Lavender oil, please."

"Bottom drawer on the left. In the back." She lifted an arm out of the tub and watched the water drip down her dark skin in meandering trails. The drops fell back into the water with little plinks, a sound that brought her a sense of freedom unlike anything else. In a torrent of those drops, she and Gavel had begun their life together away from Kino.

When he returned, he emptied a full dropper's worth of oil into the tub, then stoppered it.

She breathed deep. "That stuff isn't cheap, you know."

"Probably why you hide it with your emergency coins and secret honey stash. Never would have found it on my own."

"Oh, my love, it could have been on top of the dresser, and you would have looked right past it."

"Good thing I have you." He settled onto his knees on the floor. He took a washrag from where it waited for use on a dish next to the basin with a thin sliver of soap.

"Yeah. You're no good on your own," she said. As he washed her back, she could all but hear his mind aching for the right words to say. Amidst a firm stroke down her spine, she whispered, "I'll be fine, Gav. Don't worry. Seeing him today just threw me."

He rubbed more soap into the rag. "It threw me too."

"Didn't know anything could do that to you anymore."

"Likewise." He moved down to the end of the basin. "Foot up." She complied, and he set to scrubbing. Hesitantly, he said, "We never talk about them. Why not?"

With no effort at all, her parents' images came to her. Nothing from a specific memory, but rather embodiments of who they were. Her rosy-cheeked father laughing with his whole body and putting his arm around her mother's slender shoulders. Her mother, not laughing, but quietly reveling in the sound of her father's joy as she reached out to Asha to come join their embrace.

"Honestly," Asha said after a sniff, "I can't talk about them without the tears coming. After decades, I can still cry like that," she snapped her fingers, "when I think about them. Easier not to bring them up. Besides, I think you and I said everything we needed to say back then in that cave. As the rain poured."

He paused with the washrag cupped around the arch of her foot. "Did we?" he asked softly.

Her foot slipped back into the tub with a squeak against the metal. She slid through the water, splashing it over the sides in her haste to be closer to him. "You have to know I don't hold you responsible. Never did. *I* pushed them to help in Kino." She squeezed his forearm.

As if revering a sacred object, he kissed her forehead. "Because of my request."

She patted his cheek, sending a little splash of water into the air. "No. Because it was my family's calling." A calling to heal that she'd been trying to fulfill here in The Disc for years. Healing people's bodies, she was good at. Ministering to their spirits though? Her parents had always been better at that.

He shook his head. She recognized that they were both getting older, but seeing him like this, the guilt he'd apparently been keeping in his body for nearly thirty years of marriage now tightening his features, she felt ancient. And she knew he had to feel the same.

"You should have blamed me," he said. "Instead, you blamed yourself. And God."

Her heart sank again at what he thought he'd cost her. "You think I had a crisis of faith?"

He rung out the rag before taking it to her skin again, this time at the tops of her arms. "You were angry with God."

"Absolutely true. I was pissed but not disbelieving. Please, hear me." She tugged the rag away from him and let it fall to the bottom of the tub. She wrapped his strong hand in both of hers. "I don't blame you for any of it."

He kissed her hand. "You should."

"No." She shook her head emphatically. "He promises us pain. Even with that promise, understanding it from a young age—accepting it, actually—I just felt betrayed when it was kept." Instead of joyful and beckoning to her, she saw her parents as they had been in her last moment with them—faces cut and swollen, no longer their faces, with her father's body wrapped around her mother on the ground in a vain attempt to protect her.

She cleared her throat and tried to speak but found she couldn't yet.

He ran his free hand along her cheek. "I still don't understand how you're comfortable with the reality of a God who allows bad people to do evil things."

She swallowed hard and found her voice again. "What's comfort?"

He chuckled.

She shrugged. "God gave us free will out of love. That's what it comes down to for me—trust in his love. When I lost Mom and Dad, it was like my body no longer had bones. I was so furious that I thought my teeth would break from how hard I clenched them. But all that time, I felt his hands on either side of my face as I walked a beam across an abyss. Heard his voice."

"What did he say?" he asked gently.

"The same thing over and over: Look at *me*."

He kissed her hand again.

"I really did make peace, Gav. With all of it, as much as I could. But seeing Quin, hearing him speak—it shot me straight back into the head of a twenty-year-old girl who felt utterly helpless."

"But you're not helpless."

"No. I'm not. Plus, I've got you." She put her forehead to his. They stayed still for a minute, close enough to breathe each other's breath. "I better get out. Leaving predawn tomorrow is going to kick this middle-aged ass of mine." She pointed to the chair behind Gavel where she'd draped her towel earlier. "Do you mind?" She stood.

He hesitated to get the towel, instead just reveling in the sight of her.

"Come on! It's cold!" she laughed.

Finally, he wrapped her up, and she stretched to kiss him. When they separated, he said with all the fierceness from his youth, "I will not let him hurt you."

She ran her fingers over his beard. "I never assumed otherwise."

CHAPTER EIGHT

SHE HADN'T MADE THE CLIMB IN YEARS, BUT STILL,
Survivor remembered the rises and falls, the gentle curves, the
growing expanse of the wide canyon opening up the higher she
rose. Grays, browns, and greens as far as she could see. Rock
and scrub turning to swaths of vague color. In the warm season,
heat waves would turn those swaths hazy and lure her toward
them, tempt her to step off the edge of the path and let the
warmth swallow her as she fell.

The familiar ache of her thighs took her back to the years
when the effort of the ascent had been greater with a toddler or
two strapped to her body, carrying packs, supplies. Water.
Water was the worst with its shifting weight, harder to bear
than the burden of the children, because they didn't try to
wriggle and escape. As much as she'd wished they could have.

Some of the trail had washed out since she'd last been
there, bad enough in areas to force her to scale the canyon wall
for short stretches. The sentries toward the end of the trail
would see her any second now. She'd waited until the sun was
high, but it wasn't quite the hottest it would get all day. By late

afternoon, they'd be dozing against their own will, finally warm all the way through, missing the oppressive sun of the prior season like someone looking back fondly on childbirth—forgetting the pain, remembering the joy.

Survivor was sheltered from the wind until the trail took a turn and exposed her back to a dry breeze. It tossed her skirt and hair around and blew her scent ahead. They'd be on her soon. Anticipating this, she raised her hands in a gesture of surrender. As she did so, she caught sight of two turkey vultures soaring overhead, the undersides of their great V-shaped wingspans a cool silver. The red dots of their heads were focused below.

A wide juniper spread from the edge of the trail above, curving downward onto the rocky slope like an open fan. From behind it, a familiar high-pitched voice hailed her.

"Looky what I found. Someone wanting to die."

Survivor stopped, raised her hands higher. "Fen? You made it back home, you parasite?" He came out from behind the bush with his machete resting on his shoulder. From the yellow of his skin and the way his belly sagged out, she knew he didn't have long left. "Of the two of us," she said, "I'm not sure who is closer to dying."

"You. Only come home *after* Father died—prodigal daughter returns too late. That demon sister of yours took him!"

"Well, she made an impressive dent in his forces. But him? No. *I* killed him."

Rage turned his yellow sheen a disgusting pink, and he shook so hard his bony features rattled. "He gave you a family! How? How could you?"

"Depends on what you're asking. I did it gladly. As to exactly how, I cut his throat," she showed her jagged teeth, "just like I was taught."

He swung at her with his machete, but she sidestepped the

strike easily. His shoulder had been holding up the weight of a weapon he didn't have the strength to wield anymore.

She raised her skirt and pulled the rusted machete from its strap across her thigh. "Looks like the family has written you off, eh, brother? That's why they stuck you out here on a rocky slope. Waiting for you to fall asleep and not wake up, same as the vultures circling above us." She swung the machete across her body and welcomed him to step forward. The blade really was trash.

Fen narrowed his yellow eyes and hefted his weapon. She started to mirror him, thought better of it, and tossed her machete down the rock slope. The motion caught Fen by surprise mid-swing. She grabbed his wrist and shook it; he dropped his machete and all but collapsed into her embrace.

Hatred filled the cracking features of his face as she lowered him to the ground, teeth in a hard grind of determination, his hands groping for her throat. With little effort, she brushed his hands away and held them together against his chest.

"Tell me, Fen—is your voice as tired as the rest of you? Or can you give me a big scream?"

"You'd like to see me wail. Cry. You'd be satisfied with that."

"Don't need that kind of satisfaction. Just need the noise. Yell whatever you'd like, just yell."

He closed his mouth, clearly unwilling to do what she wanted, even if it did mean help would come.

She sighed, then set her elbow against his swollen gut, putting her weight on it. A scream came from him then, one that was surely loud enough for those at the entrance of the High Cave to hear.

"Thank you," she said as she took the Rat Scavenger's

poisoned blade from her dress pocket. "The birds have been patient enough, don't you think?"

His crazed eyes traced their flight pattern above, and he spat out a "No!" before she slashed him down the cheek. Not too deep, but deep enough for the paralytic to penetrate and act fast.

Small rocks tumbled down from above as more sentries ran down the trail. She left Fen there, writhing but unable to speak or stand, and picked up his blade. It was shining and sharp, practically unused. Before the sentries had line of sight on Fen, she'd concealed herself behind the juniper bush.

She let the first one pass, and the Marauder dropped to one knee next to Fen. Stupid. Clearly a whipping boy stuck with guard duty to prove he possessed skills he didn't have. His companion wasn't far behind, a woman not much bigger than Survivor. As she passed close by the juniper, Survivor could make out the sharp smell of yucca soap on her hands—still pulling laundry duty in addition to trying to work her way up the food chain. Couldn't blame her for that, so Survivor was gentler than she would normally be when she sprang at her back and pushed hard to the left, knocking her down the slope. Rivers of rock spilled after her as she slid down. She'd have bruises and cuts, but she'd live if she had enough sense to run once she hit the lower ridge.

The man heard the commotion and turned in time to see the last bits of his partner's hair slipping out of sight. He took a blowgun from his belt, a weapon that would have served him well if he'd stayed at his upper post and remained hidden. But here, it was useless. As Survivor rushed at him, he clumsily loaded it with a dart, likely coated in a paralytic similar to the one on her knife, and started raising it to his lips to fire. Not fast enough. She ducked and blew into the other end, and the dart lodged in his throat. He could only claw at his neck before he fell to his side, smashing up his face on a small boulder.

"Damn it. Too quiet." She took the blowgun. Taking his belt lined with darts was harder—she had to roll him around to get it out from under him—but she secured it to her own waist at the tightest belt hole.

Then she was running. There would be at least three more sentries on the trail before she reached the guards at the cave entrance, and this was getting tedious. She held the machete in her right hand, down by her leg, like an extra limb moving in time with her quick strides. In her left, she held the blowgun, a dart loaded and held in place at the end by the pressure of her thumb. As she ascended the next stretch of the trail, a sentry armed with a bow rose from behind a rock face. Survivor dropped to a slide, and an arrow passed over her as she fired the blowgun with a powerful breath that emptied her lungs. The shot hit the sentry in the chest.

Rocks had gotten under her dress and sliced up her legs, but she had no time to dwell on it since someone jumped down from above and landed next to her, machete aimed at her back. Survivor dropped the blowgun and rolled away, and her attacker's blade collided with the stony ground, but he rebounded quickly and ran toward her before she could get fully to her feet. He managed to catch the outside of her left bicep. She roared in frustration and kicked hard at her attacker's shin from her position close to the ground, throwing him off-balance.

She struck him so deeply in the shoulder with her machete that the blade got stuck; she let go of it. Her attacker bellowed in pain. His body had to be screaming at him to let shock settle in, but he fought to stay conscious, stay alive. When he swiped at her again, she stepped to the right and yanked on the stuck machete with all of the power in her uninjured arm. He managed to get half a scream out before he collapsed.

"At least someone's making noise," she said to herself. "Finally."

A hard yank on the hilt of the machete finally removed it from his shoulder. The bit of his shirt that looked the least dirty Survivor ripped away and tied around her bicep. The muscle was severely separated, but she managed to join it back together with a firm tug of her teeth on the fabric. The high of battle kept her moving, stirred her to laugh.

The quality of the sentries went up as the terrain did. One got the drop on her near the last bend where the path turned to solid rock with deep overhangs. He tackled Survivor and took her to the ground where he got in a hit square on her nose before she brought her knee up into his groin once, twice, three times. Her vision went dark for what felt like forever as she sputtered on the blood flowing freely down her face. But he didn't attack again and coughed up blood of his own, which landed on her chest. She heaved him off and elbowed him in the head with her good arm. He stayed down.

She stopped only long enough to wipe her mouth with the hem of her dress before climbing the final rise and coming face-to-face with the four mid-ranks guarding the cave's entrance. The heavy metal gate, rusted with age, was locked in place across the opening. The Gentleman's symbol in white paint—paint that she'd put there years ago—adorned the rock above the gate, a territory marker warning shelter-seekers that this cave was spoken for.

The guards were familiar, although their names escaped her. She'd never gone out of her way to put names to Marauders—made them feel too human. These four—three men, one woman—seemed anything but. There was no fear here, just the annoyance of being inconvenienced. That is, until they recognized Survivor. She saw the realization flash in their eyes at her presence, as if they were seeing a ghost they deeply hated. Survivor still had Fen's machete, a fact that didn't escape the attention of the guards. They hesitated, looking at each other. They knew the risk of engaging this ghost.

Survivor spat to clear the mess from her lips before she declared, "Your father is dead. I killed him. I'm here to reunite you."

The three tenets of Marauder culture were chanted in unison after great victories—loyalty, unity, no mercy. To the three should have been added fury—the necessary fuel for and response to the life they lived. It was fury that filled the bodies of the entrance guards, morphed their faces into twisted shadows of humans with little else to cling to. But before they could attack, a shout from inside the cave snapped them to attention.

"Hold!"

Genevieve. Her head rose to the top of the ladder on the other side of the gate. Survivor could tell it was her rather than her twin sister by the resentment in her expression as she stared at Survivor through a gap between the bottom bars, by the way she bit her lower lip. She had less hair now, and more scars. A lot more scars. She and her sister had been beautiful children. High cheeks, round faces, bright eyes that were one size too big. A lot like their father who had died trying to protect them, who hadn't trusted Survivor as his companions had. Smart man. Gone before he could see what The Gentleman would turn his daughters into.

One of the guards opened the gate. It swung outward with an aged groan, and Genevieve finished mounting the ladder to emerge from the cave. Her long-sleeved wrap, dipped in deep dyes of red, orange, and yellow, caught the breeze and billowed behind her like wings as she stood. "It *is* you. I can't believe it."

Survivor looked her up and down. "Little Genny all grown up. Where's Mel?"

Genevieve started removing layers of clothing, starting with the billowing wrap, and handed them to the closest guard. "The mouse is inside. I'd be more worried about the cat in front of you, though." She'd stripped down to tight leggings and a wrap across her bust. The last to go were her shoes, and her callused feet gripped the bare rock with ease.

Survivor's dress was shredded along the bottom, the sleeve lashed to her injured arm with the bandage. She settled for ripping off the skirt to increase her mobility, revealing the cropped pants beneath. "You hear what I said a minute ago?" she asked Genevieve as she kicked off her shoes.

"That you killed my Master? Yeah, I heard. Not that I needed to. I already knew it was you. But the others with their heads turned to pulp from the inside out, you didn't kill. Your demon sister did that. Fen couldn't shut up about her when he crawled back into camp. But Father, how he died...I found his body, knew it was you. There were so many darkling beetles covering him that I couldn't see his face until I scattered them. All along the slash in his neck, sparkling like a necklace of black beads."

Survivor stretched her calves. "Sorry I missed that."

"If he'd just let me come with him, he'd still be here."

"From the way it looks, you're the new Master. Supreme matriarch." Survivor lifted her machete up and spun it once. "Could it hurt to say 'thank you'?"

Genevieve charged her then, no weapon, probably expecting Survivor to honor their ways and put her blade down. Survivor did disarm herself—by throwing the machete at Genevieve's chest. It swept through the air, completing two revolutions before she dodged it. But Survivor's throw had been so powerful that it found another mark in the guard toward the front of the line, who dropped Genevieve's clothes when the blade lodged in his gut. Her colorful wrap fluttered away, flying over the canyon lip with a snap of fabric in the wind.

Energy sparked between Survivor and Genevieve. This was unlike Survivor's other confrontations along the ascent to the High Cave; Genevieve's movements were urgent like she had been *waiting* for this, tensed to spring for years. There was a cleanness to her strikes that showed she'd imagined every move of this fight. The way Survivor cried out when Genevieve scratched her face elicited a groan of satisfaction from Genevieve that rivaled the sounds Survivor had made with Gray the night before.

With as thoroughly as Genevieve had thought out this fight, Survivor had to find a way to use that confidence against her. When Genevieve went for an uppercut into Survivor's core, Survivor tensed and let it hit, pulling her in closer. Survivor jumped onto Genevieve's front, wrapped her legs around her waist, and dug her teeth into the side of her neck until she tasted wet copper.

"You bitch!" squealed Genevieve. She punched at Survivor's back and sides, even the back of her head, but she held fast and sank her teeth in deeper.

Panicked, Genevieve managed to hook two fingers inside the corner of Survivor's mouth. Before she could yank hard enough to rip through Survivor's cheek, Survivor stopped biting her neck and turned her attention on Genny's fingers. The skin tore near the corner of Survivor's mouth as Genny pulled her hand out before Survivor could clamp down, and that combined with Survivor's still sore jaw made her give up her grip everywhere. Genevieve threw her weight forward and landed on top of Survivor, who fell off the rest of the way.

Survivor let the ground take her weight, surrendering, which disgusted her more than Genevieve's foul taste. Poised above her on hands and knees, Genevieve reached for her throat and squeezed it hard, but clearly not as hard as she would like to.

Genevieve released a rageful scream loud enough to make Survivor's ears ring, then jumped off of her and stood fast. The effort cost her, and she stumbled from losing the blood which now made her left side slick down to her navel.

"I've heard new mothers are often tired. Could someone get the Master a chair?" Survivor cackled from the ground.

A guard came over and handed Genevieve a scarf, which she wadded up and held tightly to her own neck. The guard stood next to her, not touching so as to prove that his Master was strong and undefeated, but present in case she lost consciousness.

Genevieve launched mucus from her throat and made a show of stretching her neck. The fury she'd shown in their fight returned to her eyes as she spoke to Survivor. "You left us, but you're still held to our law—you'll stand the trial of the Masters. The Gentleman would have liked that."

"You always did know what he liked." Survivor licked her lips.

Genevieve kicked her in the head.

Survivor woke to the semidarkness inside the cave and the faraway plinks of water against stone. Genny was barking orders for a messenger to write copies of a summons and hailing the fastest runners they had. Tons of feet thumped against the moist ground as paper rustled.

Two Marauders held Survivor's slack body between them as they mounted an incline of flowstone with the aid of ropes. After they'd reached the top and moved farther into the cave, Survivor raised her head enough to see the Great Marauder—a giant stalagmite covered in a shroud of pale flowstone, like a skull wearing a hood over its eye sockets. An image of a corpse in a dark tomb, a recurring figure in Survivor's nightmares. In her nightmares, he was even larger than the formation before her now—he blotted out the sky.

Near the Great Marauder's base, a circle of candles burned to nearly nothing made the flowstone shimmer. An impeccably clean skull sat in their center, with perfect teeth and topped with a stiff-brimmed, white hat. When Survivor had last seen that hat, it had been sullied with dirt after she'd tossed it aside and watched its owner's life seep out through his neck.

At a snap, the Marauders dropped Survivor in front of the shrine. She swore The Gentleman's scent was still on the hat, that those teeth would start chatting at her, and felt herself start to sweat under her arms even though she'd killed him.

"You'll join him soon. But unlike him, no one will mourn you," Genny whispered just behind Survivor, a quiet noise that carried like a proclamation in the closeness of the cave. "You'll be a stain on the earth."

She kneed Survivor in the back, knocking her head toward the flame of the candles. The stink of singed hair joined The Gentleman's scent. Genny called out impatiently for Amelie as the guards grabbed Survivor again and dragged her through a narrow corridor. She knew they were taking her up to the Holy Tree where they would put her in chains.

⸺

250 YEARS EARLIER

Charlotte's black pumps struck staccato clicks against the tile as she speed-walked down the hall. She held a folder full of files tight under one arm and a coffee in her other hand. The ID badge around her neck thwacked into her chest with every step. She passed door after door, some of which posted warning signs of radiation or other hazards for any potential entrant to beware.

On her left just up ahead, a door opened, and a man stepped out. He wore a white dress shirt with his sleeves rolled up and a green checkered tie with the knot loosened. He spotted her and threw up a wave in greeting. She nodded in his direction, stopping for a chat as she reached him. If she didn't, he'd find her later anyway.

"Morning!" he said, far too cheerfully for an early day greeting.

"Morning. Weren't you wearing that tie yesterday, Davis?"

He looked down and tightened his tie. "Been burning the midnight oil. You know how it is."

She just nodded, eager to continue on her way but not wanting to appear rude.

"Big progress with cryo." He leaned against the doorframe with a satisfied sigh. "I've managed to fix the thawing problem. Your Corp seems quite grateful. I think the words 'significant bonus' were used. Straight from Magnate Miles himself. Just hung up the phone." He paused, eyes bright like he'd been imagining her reaction to his accomplishment since it had happened hours before. When she didn't congratulate him, his chubby, stubbled cheeks fell in disappointment. He shrugged it off quickly with a renewed smile. "I hear you all are making progress of your own. Rumor has it that our fearless bosses have their eyes on you. Eager to pour credits into *your* personal account. Exciting stuff. Care to share details?" He leaned in closer, doing a poor job of hiding a glance at her legs where they emerged from her pencil skirt.

"Not really." She made to take a step, but he spoke again before she could.

"You hear about Kepler? Boots on the ground! They sent the first transmission last night—got to hear it when it came in at 3am. Can you believe it? The gateway's connected. Our very own superhighway to a new heaven and a new earth. If God could do it, so can we, eh?"

She shifted her weight to her other leg. "Humans thinking we're God has never led anywhere good, Davis."

The spit from his raspberry hit her cheek. "Sure it has! Drought-resistant crops, the birth of AI, selective gene manipulation."

She wiped at her face with the back of her hand. "The famine of the Northeast Corp? The death of Vera Lou? Ambrose's Eugenic Revival? Those ring any bells?"

He shrugged. "Cost of doing business."

She furrowed her brow. Really, she was too tired for this, but she couldn't help herself. "Or we could look even further back at Galton's brainchild. The forced sterilization of tens of thousands of mentally ill in the former United States? The Final Solution implemented by Hitler shortly thereafter? Millions murdered."

The dumb expression on his face was slap-worthy. "What history book have you been reading?" he asked dubiously.

Her furrow deepened. "One featuring reality, and reality is painful. As is the origin of the gene manipulation you referred to with such admiration."

"You mean the gene manipulation *you* practice?" he teased.

"The very same. Let's not pretend like playing God doesn't have a cost. It's a steep one. Sometimes more than we can pay."

He shrugged one shoulder. "Then you'll just have to get us to Kepler before the collection man comes calling."

"Not if you continue to keep me from my work."

He put his arms up in surrender, and she stepped around him finally, heading toward the lab at the end of the hall. She

felt him watching her backside and fought the urge to shoot
him the triple finger gesture of her native Northwest Corp.

At the lab door, she swiped her badge in the reader—Charlotte Lambeau, her face in the picture smiling, a neat bun of
red-blond on top of her head. Corp Collective Department of
Development.

Suddenly, Charlotte was looking through a microscope at
yellow and black hair, almost fur—a bumblebee. Wings like
stained glass waiting for its color, black oblong eyes shining.
The bee was still, save for its mandibles and the occasional
poking out of its tongue. With extreme care, Charlotte held the
bee's abdomen down with a pair of tweezers. She moved a
second pair of tweezers close to the bee's thorax, this pair
holding a silver pill the size of a sesame seed. She just barely
touched the pill—Biorg, she corrected herself—to the bee, right
where yellow and black met. The tiny Biorg turned from a solid
seed to a moving creature, looking something like a silverfish
with little paddle legs and two antennae at one end, a narrower
point at the other. It entered the bumblebee antennae first,
poised gracefully as it dove into the black and yellow sea.

Charlotte took away the now empty pair of tweezers and
held her breath. This was the worst part, the waiting.

The bee's mandibles stopped fluttering, and its tongue
retreated from the air it had been tasting. It curled its legs up
toward its body, feeling pain perhaps, or maybe it was just its
nervous system's natural response—it bothered her not knowing, but she tried not to dwell on it. Its delicate wings grew soft
and fell slack against its back, never to carry it through the air
again.

"Shit," said Charlotte. She backed off of the microscope
and shook her head at Liam standing next to her. He groaned
deep in his throat, took a red marker out of his shirt pocket, and
headed over to the white board next to the table on which their

research—binders of documents, schematics of the little silver-fish Biorg, crumpled DNA mappings—sat, splayed out in controlled chaos. Liam wrote a few notes in a column titled "Series 6, Generation C." He then took a small, plastic baggie from his jeans pocket as he walked back to Charlotte. He held it open for her.

She took the bee from beneath the microscope, hesitating just a second to take in its dark eyes one more time, before dropping it into the baggie. Liam slid the tackle box on the table closer and opened it, revealing identical baggies of curled up bees in little compartments, their tiny plastic coffins. He placed the new victim in its coffin labeled "S6, GC" and closed the lid.

It was later. Days? Weeks? Hard to say. But the overflowing trash, fast-food bags, dirty coffee mugs, and Liam's budding beard, suggested the latter. Liam was adding "Series 10, Generation K" to the white board. Charlotte removed the top from a deep terracotta pot coming up to her knee. It was dark inside, and she very carefully shone a dim light toward the bottom—the bumblebees were at work as always, tending to their clumpy interconnected pots and fluffing the dry grass and other nesting material. The queen was easy to spot, nearly three times the size of the workers.

Charlotte carefully stuck in her gloved hand holding an open glass jar. She scooped up a bee fiddling with a tuft of cotton near the top of the nest, separated from the others. She quickly draped a tissue over the top of the jar, closed the nest, and then headed for the microscope.

Liam was waiting, a spark of excitement in his eyes despite the shadows beneath them. He held up a tiny glass vial containing a single Biorg and winked at her. She smiled, forgetting for just a moment how much she missed her bed, missed waking up late on Saturdays in Liam's arms. Even more, she forgot for that instant the gravity of this trial series. This was really it. Their funding, their jobs, most likely their lives if the Collective took their failure personally. Certainly, the Collective's offer to pay for not only early retirement but anything they could ever need or want played a factor in their motivation too. God, they needed a breakthrough.

Just as before, she gently put the bee under the microscope. The Biorg activated upon contact, looking much like the others that had come before, save for its gold antennae. It dove into the bee's thorax, and Charlotte looked into the insect's black eyes as if it could be encouraged to accept the Biorg if she stared at it with enough hope.

Nothing happened for several minutes, but then everything happened all at once. The bee's legs went motionless, its wings tensed as if frozen in mid-flight. Its eyes turned from cold black to smooth gold—like perfect droplets of the precious metal. The bee started moving again, sticking its tongue in and out to taste the air as if it had simply woken up.

Liam whooped, shoving a stack of documents from the table to the floor in a flutter of paper. He grabbed the back of Charlotte's neck and kissed her hard, laughing against her lips. She laughed too and pulled herself away to tuck the precious bee into the jar and cover it with the tissue. The moment she'd finished, she leapt into Liam's arms, wrapping her legs around his waist as he spun her around the lab.

Time accelerated again, and Charlotte was ripped from Liam's warm embrace, the smell of his neck, and the strength of his grip. They hovered over a guinea pig on an exam table —*Cavia porcellus* 25, as the tiny ID tag on his ear read. White with a half-mask of brown and little bulging black eyes that reminded Charlotte so much of her bumblebees. Cp 25 chattered his teeth together softly.

"Ready?" Liam asked.

Charlotte slowly exhaled.

"Hey, we're almost there," he said with more energy than Charlotte felt in her entire body. "Completing our first round of mammal testing is huge. And with no fatalities! I talked with Brianne last night, and she said the Collective is thrilled with our progress." The way he rubbed her back with the tips of his fingers made her shoulders unwind.

"Right. Proceed then," she finally said.

He tipped out a Biorg from its vial near Cp 25's front foot. It slipped lithely through the skin between two toes, and Cp 25 twitched that leg just for a second. His chattering teeth picked up in volume. Nothing happened for several long seconds, then Cp 25 squealed—a high-pitched shriek that made Charlotte jump. It seized and flailed. A spurt of blood came out of his nostrils and mouth, turning his big teeth red. Then it just stopped. Everything stopped.

Charlotte felt cold and sick. As she ran from the lab, Liam called after her, something about acceptable margins.

Charlotte lay on a cold metal table in a hospital gown— mint green, thin. The gown's ties were bunched up under her, and she tugged at them until they were smooth against her back. The spotlight above the table turned on; she closed her eyes against the shock of the brightness.

Liam's hand grabbed hers from where it rested on her abdomen, and she opened her eyes at his touch. He looked better, clean-shaven and overall less haggard, but stress was impossible to wash away. The dark circles under his eyes had been replaced by deep lines of worry, making caverns at their edges and at his brow. As he squeezed her hand, she realized he was shaking. Her teeth knocking together betrayed the confidence she tried hard to exude and reminded her of Cp 25.

"Cold?" Liam asked.

"That must be it," she said.

He disappeared, then returned with a thick, cotton blanket. He draped it over her and rubbed her limbs through it.

"Better?"

Her teeth still clashed together. She bit down hard and nodded.

"That makes one of us," he said softly.

"Really?" she said with a glare. "You've talked of little else the past two months except for what the Collective wants. How their offer is time sensitive. You should be giddy for today."

"You think I'm giddy to see my wife laying where we tested Cp 25? It should be me on the table."

"We already discussed this—females have a higher chance of success with the integration."

"Then we get a female volunteer."

"I *am* the volunteer. I'll not test my work on someone else. If someone's going to die today because of my failure, it will be me."

He smacked the spotlight, knocking its beams toward the ceiling. "You're too valuable."

She reached up to adjust the light. "You know the work. You wouldn't need me to continue."

"I mean you're too valuable to me." He leaned down to kiss her and pick up her hand. "We need to do more testing," he said as he backed away. "Other species, a new series."

"Agreed. If we had time, that's exactly what we'd do. But the Collective is clear—objective achieved by tomorrow or the deal's off. None of the other research teams are anywhere close to where we are. It's our necks on the line. The admission lists for the first shuttles are almost finished. We're out of time."

"Then they can go to hell."

"That's where they'll send us tomorrow if I don't do this now. So if I die, what's the difference?" She took her hand from him and rested it by her side. "Let's get this over with."

He reached over to the surgical tray on his left near the table. The tray held an array of emergency medical implements—scalpel, epinephrine primed and ready to go, an AED—that gave them a false sense of security more than anything. They couldn't prepare for this. Not really.

Liam picked up the vial holding the tiny silver Biorg, still a solid seed waiting to be activated. He unscrewed it and picked it up with tweezers, then shifted back over to Charlotte on the table. Carefully, he moved it toward her wrist, the application site they'd decided had the best chance of success—not too close to the heart. But before it touched her skin, Liam jumped back like something had bitten him.

"I can't!" he shouted. "Switch with me—I'm bigger, my mass will help me take the change."

"Honey, you're babbling."

"No! I'm right. Dammit, I'm right!"

Before he could continue, she grabbed his hand with the tweezers and brought the Biorg in contact with the inside of her wrist. It awoke, a little silverfish unfurling, and dove into her skin, gold antennae first.

"Shit, no! No. Damn it!" said Liam, flitting between shouting and mumbling.

Charlotte sat up and grabbed his chin. "I love you." She kissed him gently.

He held her, and for a long ten seconds, nothing happened.

Then her insides rebelled.

She convulsed with such force that Liam had to lower her to the floor so she wouldn't fall from the table. She saw flashes of the lab, the bright light above her, the cold tile beneath. Liam's expression morphed into calm focus, panic shoved to the back of his mind so that he could function.

"Breathe, Charlotte. I need you to take a breath."

She sucked air through her mouth in a hard, ragged pull. It

burned her chest.

"Good. Again."

She obeyed.

"Hold still." He took the syringe of epinephrine and stuck it in her arm. Everything hurt, although that was too tame a word. Her muscles felt as if they were being peeled back fiber by fiber, her organs squeezed like playthings, all while her lungs fought for her next breath. She threw her head back, feeling near the end.

In the beam of the spotlight above, a shadow floated toward her. A silhouette of a bee gracefully sailing downward as if it intended to land on her nose. Then everything went black.

PRESENT DAY

Wren started awake, limbs stiffening into ropes of muscle pulled taut as her spine arched and she stared at the top of the isolation unit.

"Bug, adjust the sedative! Now!" Eydis' voice, somewhere far off.

"Ma'am," replied Bug, "she needs to come out. I know the Principal is eager, but she might not—"

"Thallium isn't ordering you, I am. Do it, or I'll find a new assistant." A pause—silence, broken only by a throbbing pulse in Wren's ears—until Eydis demanded, "Now, Bug!"

"Yes, ma'am." Weak—were those tears in her voice?

Then, warmth. Wren's muscles released, the ropes slackening at last until she felt weightless once more. The darkness returned.

250 YEARS EARLIER

Wren awoke under a blanket on the table in Charlotte's lab, wearing Charlotte's body again. As she stirred, she felt Liam's touch as he kissed her forehead. She breathed him in and opened her eyes.

He gave her a dashing, crooked grin. "I didn't think it was possible for you to become any more beautiful. Why do you always have to prove me wrong?" He held out a hand mirror.

She sat up and took it, holding it in front of her face. Her eyes—if she could call them that anymore—were speckled gold. Their once flush, green irises were now dotted all over as if sprinkled with gold dust.

"It worked?" she breathed.

"It worked, baby," Liam said. "Holy hell, did it work."

Then it was Liam on the table. He was in only his boxers as he laid back.

"Commence male testing," he said in a robot voice.

Charlotte smiled. "You know I don't want to do this. Stop trying to make me laugh." She got the Biorg ready, plucking it out of the glass tube with tweezers.

"But I'm usually so good at it. Hmm. Regardless, we'll both have dreamy eyes now."

She coughed dryly. "Priorities." She looked around the lab, this box they'd made a home for over a year now. The potential for progress in every page of research, the death in tackle boxes. The potential for more death. No, not just potential—it was guaranteed. "Four percent," she whispered.

"Ninety-six percent," he whispered back with a poke at her stomach.

"Four colonists out of every one hundred will die. And those who live will continue to indefinitely. The Corp leaders will take the integration, too—warmongers with endless life."

She stared at the Biorg in her tweezers. "Who are we to give life like this?"

He sat up on his elbows. "We're helping humanity."

"No, we're helping the Corps get rich. Helping them send people across the galaxy to somewhere we never needed to go in the first place. For kicks. Just because we can! We can't fathom the cost of what we're doing here." She put the Biorg back in the vial, capped it, and dropped it in her lab coat pocket.

Liam sat all the way up. He took her face in his hands. "We have to do this. Char, please. Let me do this. I don't want to lose you."

"As though I want to lose *you*? Why do you think I'm hesitating here?"

"If you don't do this to me, we'll both be killed anyway. I'm having déjà vu of our debate when you were the one on this table. And if we don't do this now, you'll have to watch me grow old. Hair gone, sagging skin, fake teeth," he pulled his lips around his teeth dramatically, "old. Then I'll die." He flopped his head over to the side until she laughed. He straightened up and put his arms around her. "Now, I don't mind staying with a vibrant, youthful woman for the rest of my life regardless of how old I get, but I'd prefer to stay young and virile *with* you. Let's skip the burying each other thing, huh?"

He pulled her to him and kissed her fiercely, their breath hot and mingling. Desire mingled with fear and excitement. Finally, he pulled back to separate them. "It's time." He reached into her coat pocket for the vial and placed it in her hand. "I'd like to join you in eternity now, please." With one last peck on her cheek, he lay back on the table and tapped the inside of his wrist as if it were his watch.

She set the Biorg on his skin where he'd tapped. It unfurled and came to life, digging in.

"Be gentle. This is my first time," he whispered seductively to the little thing.

"Shut up."

For a moment, nothing happened. Then just like with her, the convulsions started. Liam seized, but this time she was ready for it, the epinephrine already in her hand.

"Try to breathe honey, remember? Just—"

He screamed. A chilling, dark pit of a scream that rose up from the soles of his feet. Charlotte jabbed him with the epinephrine, but before she could even remove the needle from his arm, he coughed and sputtered, blood coming from his mouth in a brilliant spray. It soaked her face and chest, streaked across Liam's notes on the whiteboard, and splattered the bee pot like a surrealist painting. In mere seconds, his lips turned blue, and his eyes clouded over in a milky pink haze.

She started CPR. Time became meaningless, and there was no telling how long she worked over him. Finally, she resorted to pounding on his chest over and over, trying to get a reaction from his heart. With each blow, she released her anger at him, her anger at herself, and the terror that as soon as she stopped trying to bring him back, his being gone would become reality. Her efforts slowed when she realized he was already stiff, as if he'd been gone for hours. Maybe he had. His arms and legs stuck in strange contortions, and she remembered the trial bees —little legs curled up against their bodies, creatures shriveled in on themselves.

After one last strike to his chest, silence rang in her ears.

She slumped to her knees, then onto her side as if the chilly tile might turn to liquid and swallow her so that she could drown. The silence relented enough for her to hear the low humming of the bees in their pot close to her head. Endless humming.

Memories came in flashes after that, just one snippet after

another, as if a coherent string of events was either too painful or simply impossible to put together.

Charlotte running, covered in Liam's blood, to Davis' lab. Demanding a cryo chamber. Passing out. Waking up in a Northwest Corp hospital with Davis in a chair next to her. Liam was gone, his body confiscated by the Collective. Colonists were being integrated with Biorgs already. Acceptable margins. Incredible achievement.

A barely overcast afternoon, the sun shining even as tiny raindrops hit Charlotte's face when she looked up, catching a shimmering glimpse of the space gate high above—round and hungry-looking. She blinked at the intensity of its presence, attention lazily coming back to the dozen or so people gathered in the far corner of the cemetery. Liam's mother wept, smearing navy mascara over her temples as people kindly ignored her sobs of anguish. Davis was there—the only coworker in attendance—still wearing that sickly green tie. Sniffing around Liam's widow like a dog waiting for a scrap to fall.

Then she was back at the research facility, sitting at a long table. Made of mahogany, she realized. Magnate Miles of the Northwest Corp, recently voted Magnate Superior of the Corp Collective after his scientist had been the first to complete the Genetic Protection Initiative, spoke at the head of the table. A box of a man with disproportionately narrow hips. Could have been a gymnast as easily as the supreme leader of Earth.

"We have fourteen weeks before we send the shuttles through the gate." He clicked a button on his command bracelet to flip through holo-blueprints of the gate and the schematics of the shuttles and their capacities above the table. "Which brings us to the matter at hand—ensuring the success of our colonists."

Charlotte didn't have to look around to know the eyes of the most powerful people on the planet had shot to her; she felt the weight of them—their admiration, their eagerness, perhaps even their pity—like beams of light. Together, they burned her skin.

When she said nothing, Miles continued. "Doctor Lambeau has given us enough Biorg implants for the colonists, which are being administered as we speak. We understand that a small minority of those will have an adverse reaction to the implant. But frankly, we're out of time." He addressed her directly. "I'm sorry for your loss." He tacked the last part on.

"Well, if you're sorry, then," she said under her breath.

"What was that, Doctor?" Miles said in such a way that it was clear he did in fact hear what she'd said.

"My husband is dead."

"A loss that can never—"

"Stop talking!" she shouted, and those closest to her nearly jumped out of their seats. "All you ever do is talk." She stood slowly, muscles tensed with fury unlike any she'd ever known. "The rest of us move mountains, change humanity at its very core, and we hope that we do it fast enough to avoid being lined up against the back of this building and shot, or worse, robbed of our minds through cerebral reclaim—another process developed by a researcher under duress, which was later used on its own creator when she showed remorse for those robbed of their personhood through her work."

"Doctor, you're out of line," the Eastern Corp head to her left proclaimed.

"You disgust me. Every one of you at this table." She looked around at them pointedly. "You're less than human. You're despots. Children each trying to build a bigger sandpile. Shoveling, shoveling, shoveling, people getting buried with every stroke. Faces disappearing under the sand. That gate, it isn't the future; it's our end."

"Get her out of here," ordered Miles to the two guards near the main door of the conference room.

She lunged at the Magnate Superior, hurling herself across the table with nothing but her bare hands with which to take his life. The two guards shouted something, and the other Magnates of the Collective hit the floor. After she'd barely scratched Miles' collarbone with her fingernails, a guard hit her with a sonic blast. Her vision blurred and her ears rang out in pain. Vertigo sent her to her knees, where she vomited on the mahogany.

Sometime later, she awoke. Slowly at first, eyelids too heavy to move. There was a heat source behind her—warmth that was fast becoming uncomfortable spread over the top of her head. She finally gained enough of her bearings to hear someone speaking.

"—said this was the only way to be sure since she's a synth," said a woman.

A man replied, "Don't know why we're bothering to obey the Magnate Superior at this point. The Northeast is about to make all of this meaningless, anyway. Not that we'll be here to see it."

The heat grew, and Charlotte smelled burning hair. She leapt up only to fall off of a conveyor belt onto a concrete floor in the midst of what looked to be a large repurposing room belonging to her Corp's research facility. While many of the materials that came through here would be recycled, many would not. That was what the incinerators were for.

"Strong sedative, my ass!" said the woman, a soldier with neck muscles bulging out the top of her collared uniform. She opened fire with a white beam rifle, filling Charlotte's core with perfect round holes. Charlotte rolled onto her back and gasped.

"Not so invincible, I guess," said the woman. "Get her back on the belt."

The man grabbed Charlotte's arm and slung her weight over his shoulder. Before he could drop her back on the conveyor belt, her breath returned, and the pain left. She kicked toward his groin and hit it hard enough to make him double over. She threw her weight over his shoulder to knock him onto the belt and then used the nearby control console to accelerate it to full speed. He all but flew into the violet light incinerator and turned to dust before he could scream.

The woman started firing again, but Charlotte ducked under the belt, grabbed the woman's ankles, and yanked her feet out from under her. The woman fell on her back hard enough to make her drop her rifle. Charlotte scrambled across the concrete, grabbed it, and turned it on her before she could stand. Dripping in sweat and blood from wounds that had already closed, naked, with the smell of burnt hair still in the air, Charlotte powered the weapon to full with the toggle near the trigger.

"You work for the Northeast? What are they doing?" Charlotte asked. The woman remained silent. Charlotte studied her uniform—a First Quarter moon emblem on the left side of the chest. "Why are you in a Northwest Corp uniform? You just said you're a Northeast member."

The woman sucked air through her teeth. "You weren't supposed to hear that."

Charlotte counted the stars on the woman's uniform and lost count when her vision started to blur. She blinked hard. "Why'd they send such an elite member to do their disposal work?"

"You're a high-profile associate," the soldier said mockingly. "This couldn't fail."

"Yet here we are. Now tell me what the Northeast has planned!" Charlotte shouted. Her finger shook against the trigger, and she realized her whole body had started shaking. The scientist in her postulated it was an unintended aftereffect of the Biorg's nanotech deposits' healing and began pondering ways to fix the problem even as she fought for her life in the violet glow of the incinerator. Then her finger slipped, and she shot the woman through the delicate bones of her hand.

Through heavy breaths as she clutched her hand, the soldier said, "After the Corp Collective's ship goes through, followed by the Northeast Corp transports, the gate will close."

Charlotte blinked past her confusion. "You mean it will be held in stasis for the second wave."

"No, it will close. And it won't open again."

Charlotte shook her head harder than it was already shaking, nearly losing her grip on the gun. She held onto it with all she had left and raised it higher. "They can't. They can't do that. The exotic matter can't support that kind of cutoff. People will die."

"They will. Then the Northeast will rule Kepler the way it was intended to rule Earth before Miles betrayed his brother Markus and murdered his way to supremacy. Supremacy you also helped him obtain."

Charlotte sank to rest on her heels, holding onto the rifle with the last of her strength.

"You can't even stand. You won't make it out of here," said the soldier as she took a step toward her. "The incinerator is painless. At least, that's what they tell us."

"Back off." Charlotte gripped the rifle's stock tighter against her shoulder.

"Come on, let's get this over with." The soldier darted forward.

Charlotte opened fire. The shots went wild, and the woman turned her momentum and ran. Still, Charlotte kept pulling the trigger until the soldier had left the repurposing room.

Time passed, and it wasn't clear just how much. Water sloshed in jugs on a pallet jack as Charlotte pulled it off of a freight elevator and into a square room with a low ceiling dotted with red lights. She pulled the jack over to the wall lined with supplies—more water, stacks upon stacks of emergency rations, canned food, and medical supplies. Nearby, a raised bed of vegetable sprouts flourished underneath a grow light. The full bed from her apartment was against the far wall, adorned with the blue flannel duvet she and Liam had been given when they got married. Boxes of packed clothes sat near it, as did a stand holding a radiation suit and other survival gear. Save for a treadmill, a small library of books, and a cushy armchair, the rest of the space was taken up by equipment from the lab she'd shared with Liam—things she'd stolen from the Collective with Davis' assistance. Most precious of all was her research, including the Biorg. Research she would continue. Whoever survived this—if anyone did—would need it.

An alarm chirped from her G-specs. Five until noon. It was almost time. She went to sit on the armchair, closing her eyes and resting her head. But it was no good—she had to see it.

She ran to the freight elevator and hit the button. The door closed and the pulleys creaked as they worked, taking her up, up, up. She opened the live news report on her specs where a reporter in town stood with the mass of spectators looking to the sky. The crowd waved flags covered in all of the Corps' emblems and held signs aloft that read, "Victory for the Collective!" and "United, we reach new heights!" The cameraman panned out for a wide shot of the gate above, a ring on the world's finger, promising it a happy ending.

The elevator hiccupped to a stop. She pulled the lever to release the lock and threw the door open. The desert scrub, green and gold and brown—beautiful in its own way—greeted her. She covered her brow with her hand to cut the glare as she looked to the gate. On her specs, the reporter said that the last of the Northeastern shuttles had just gone through. The crow's cheers rose into the clear blue above to join the ships in flight.

And then, the flash. In the already bright, clear sky, the flash outshone the sun. The gate collapsed, sparkling chunks of metal flying apart like a firework. The wave of energy that came off of it was purple and blue, palpable in its intensity—felt in the bones. The hushed shock and horror of the reporter and the people in the street was soon followed by one single wail in the crowd. The wail sent a ripple of others through the people, the reporter scrambled for something to say, and then the feed went black.

One last look at the gate, the now broken ring, and Charlotte turned on her heel and entered the elevator. She closed the door and hit the button.

———

PRESENT DAY

Wren opened her eyes. The thin cables going into her body swayed gently back and forth with the motion of her waking. An echo of that first wail in the crowd from Eydis' memory replayed in her mind.

Eydis sat in a folding chair across from the isolation unit with her feet crossed at the ankles. It struck Wren how tired she looked there. She was the same age as the woman in the memories but worn all over. A song being forever sung from a tired throat. There was no white in the strawberry hair hanging loosely in front her shoulders, as if it had been too tight during today's lesson and she'd removed the pins keeping it up. No wrinkles in her milky face. But there was age there, nonetheless. Although she was undeniably more than human, she'd never looked as human to Wren as she did now.

"I've improved the Biorg since then. There's still a chance of rejection, but it's slim. If we'd had more time, we could have avoided most of those fatalities, at least." She fell into thought, then said, almost to herself, "They took Liam's body through the gate. A specimen to learn from, dissect—we both signed a contract that included an agreement to donate our bodies to science. I had to let them take him. I buried an empty box."

"I'm sorry," Wren thought before she could stop herself. Her words came through the BCI.

"It wasn't my intention to make you sad. However, I had to teach you my history. It will help you understand why I'm doing all of this." Eydis waved her hand around as if she'd been putting on a show up until now but had finally grown tired of her role.

"Why are you doing this?" Wren asked.

"We have to show them," Eydis said simply.

Another evasion. "Show who what?" Wren asked, her volume rising through the speakers as her patience started to fade.

"The Corporations—the self-proclaimed elite. The women and men that damned Earth out of desperation to tag the next achievement first. Show them we not only made it, but we're also more than they could ever be. *You're* more than they could ever be. They thought they'd reached the pinnacle of power, brushed their lips against immortality. They hadn't even touched it yet." She stood and pushed her chair back with her foot. When she got nose to nose with Wren, separated by only glass, the gold of her eyes gave credence to the memories she'd shown Wren, what she'd become. "Look at what I've accomplished—what *we* have—with nearly none of the resources they carried with them through the gate. They left us to burn, but here we are, thriving in the sun."

Wren couldn't stand it anymore—this box, this room. Eydis' beautiful voice dripping with sadness and heavy-handed morality. She tried to rip the thin cables from her face and hands, but before she could, Bug entered a command at the console for them to retract. Wren shouted, "Enough 'we' and 'our!' I'm not *with* you, I'm your prisoner. No more riddles! No more lessons, no more dreams where I relive your pain. You keep saying you need my help. Tell me now—what do you want me to do?"

"I want you to show them the cost of their mistake." The bitterness in Eydis' voice stood out like the answer to a secret. Everything slipped into place.

Wren hung her head back and closed her eyes. "That's what you want. Revenge."

Eydis didn't respond at first. "It's not that simple."

"It's exactly that simple, isn't it? You're just like the rest of them. Like every other monster I've met, including the one inside me—out for blood."

Eydis slammed both hands against the box, making Wren jump. "They took him from me!" she bellowed in the vast space. Her rosy lips tightened to a white line, and her gold eyes were unblinking.

Wren let the pounding of her heart quiet. "I'm just a weapon to you after all."

Eydis shook out her head and hands as if embarrassed. She searched Wren's face. "Your true design is far more elegant than that." She returned to her chair and collapsed into it, suddenly spent. "You aren't merely weapon, at least not by design. You're meant for more." By the way she spoke, it was as if she were holding something precious in her hands. "You're a key, little one."

"Key? To what?"

"Have you ever felt like you weren't made for this world? Like you're meant to be somewhere brighter, more beautiful and complex than this place?"

Wren pictured the stars and the glorious space between them but said nothing.

"You've seen the door to that other world your whole life." Eydis raised her hands above her head, palms up.

Wren knew it before Eydis had the chance to say it. "The gate."

That alluring ring in the sky had called to her along with the stars since she was young. Alma's stories, Wren's daydreams —both simple sketches of something nearing the divine. After what Wren had been through, what she'd become, she felt even closer to the gate because like it, she too was broken.

Eydis' shoulders rose as she took a deep breath. "So that's the answer to the riddles," she said in one great exhale. "Why I've been showing you my memories. I created you and your siblings for the purpose of opening the gate so that we can confront our betrayers and save Earth from herself."

Wren and Bug both fell still at the enormity of Eydis' goal.

"Then I want to take us all there," Eydis continued. "You, your family, Caster—those who are the best of this place through the gate to join the brighter future on the other side. We'll send back resources to help those remaining here find a life worth living. Oh little one, I want to show you the stars!" She looked up toward the ceiling, then back at Wren, now with a deep furrow in her brow. "I don't know how long it will take for you to be able to control what's within you, but I do know that you're capable of doing so. If you accept it, things will get better. My question for you is—will you try?"

Something clicked inside Wren. In that moment with Eydis looking more vulnerable than Wren thought possible, looking as lost as Wren had felt since losing her family so long ago, something slid into place. The disconnect, the conflict, the sensation of being adrift in an ocean she'd only heard stories about, began to fade away. She longed for the stars, because this world? It wasn't her home. Not really. She wasn't made for it.

Resisting Eydis was resisting herself. The power within her was part of her. There was no denying it just because it was hard to look at, alarming in its potential to kill and destroy. If there was no way to get rid of it, she'd have to learn to control it. Drown herself in its embrace. Because she'd already been drowning long enough here.

"Yes. I'll try." Wren said, and as she did, she felt the last of her hope in who she'd been before leave her body.

"Good. When you feel you're ready to get out of that box, I'll open it. It's up to you now, little one." Eydis went to the control console, and Bug rolled her chair to the side to give her space to work. Eydis tapped at the keys. The screen changed color, and Eydis continued to type commands in green letters. She then looked back to Wren. "I mean it—you just tell me when and I'll open the door." Her hands hovered over the keyboard as if she were waiting for Wren to ask for her freedom.

Excitement at the thought of release filled Wren's chest. Release from this prison, from this world. And she longed to finally release the force inside and give it room to stretch its aching legs. But in response, fear wracked her body. Stole her non-breath. Her earlier vision of Caster and her family turning to ashes, a city full of people doing the same, told her that this box she was in would likely be her grave. Because if she left it, she could unintentionally send everyone she loved to theirs.

Wren's temporary voice came through the BCI. "I'm not ready."

Eydis continued to type, and the screen went back to displaying its usual readings. "Before long, you will be."

Eydis' hair slid through Thallium's fingers. She slept on her stomach, and her hair cascaded down her back and onto the bed around her. It occurred to Thallium how he didn't truly feel her hair even as he watched it slide over his skin. It was as though he were watching someone else move his hand, touch her; he was floating near the ceiling, leaving his body an empty, moving corpse. But soon he came back to himself and dropped her hair, wondering how its golden fire hadn't burned him.

How strange that an android would have a preferred sleeping position, that an android would sleep at all. But she did. He took peace from watching her. Living vicariously through her restfulness that continued to elude him. Always after they were together, she fell asleep quickly and efficiently on her stomach. Perhaps it drained her power source to be athletic as they were, doing the things he wanted to do—although she took charge in the bedroom at least as often as he, and usually with more fervor.

Or did she want to be somewhere else entirely? Pretend that she'd just been with someone else? Did she have memories of her past years of service to other humans that she revisited in a dream state? Assuming she dreamed.

He considered waking her, going again, but, unlike his mind, his body felt suddenly spent. They'd started their evening together when he'd requested an update on Wren. The longer they waited to utilize her, the more time there was for people to second guess him. Caster, his Keepers, men and women too scared and hungry to think straight. He'd shared all of this with Eydis.

She'd nodded and said...something. What was it? Something about how she was doing her best, but people weren't machines. They couldn't rush this just as they hadn't been able to rush Wren's restoration. Then she'd removed her shirt and the conversation petered off. The way it always did.

He was beginning to feel like a cuckold, pretending he had control over his reality rather than admitting he was gradually giving it away. Something had changed in Eydis since Wren's return. A disconnect from him. Not an obvious one, but he saw it in the way she didn't smile quite as brightly, in the way she engaged in conversation with him with a subtle tension that implied that every second he spoke was a second wasted. In how her head was no longer bowed but raised and focused elsewhere as if her program to serve him had run its course. He wondered if, somehow, it had.

As he brushed her hair behind her ear, he saw Reina's face instead of hers. He'd been seeing Reina ever since the bar. After his initial panic at the hallucinations, now he almost looked forward to them. Manifested them, even. He didn't want to lose her again, much less when he felt those closest to him slipping away. As much pain as his visions of Reina caused him, he had loved her. Poorly and often against her wishes, but he'd loved her. And no other.

The first time he and Reina slept together, she'd insisted on covering herself with the sheet after. He'd brushed her hair back, brown and rich like molasses, and then teased her by tugging the sheet down. He'd gotten caught up in just looking at her until her giggle finally roused his attention. When she rolled onto her back and pulled him on top of her, her warmth had been the deep breath he didn't know his lungs were missing. A memory older than he'd been when he met her, and still it hadn't aged a day.

"Children. We were just children," he said aloud.

Eydis stirred to hug her pillow more tightly. He tossed his blanket aside and set his feet on the floor. His black pants lay in a heap, and he tugged them on as he walked to the door of his study. Reina's laugh came again from behind him on the bed where he'd left Eydis. He fought the urge to look over his shoulder. Instead, in his periphery he watched Reina's silhouette rise from the bed, a sheet trailing behind her as she wrapped it around her shoulders. Thallium had long suspected he was slightly mad—yet another inheritance from his father—but these increasing hallucinations confirmed it well enough. They threatened to take what was left of his sanity. Part of him wanted them to.

He nudged his study door open with his bare foot and slid inside. Heat from the dying fire near the desk found his chest and, at the same moment, so did Reina's caress from behind, reaching around his ribs. Mid-reach for her hand, he stopped himself and headed toward what he'd come for—his half-finished glass of Sangre del Sol that had been interrupted by his antics with Eydis, which had started on the desk. When the last sip hit his throat, he heard his father: *"Filthy habit. Weak. Just weak."*

Thallium smirked, poured himself another two fingers, and waltzed around the desk to plop down and put up his feet. He leaned into the memory, remembering the way the desktop used to look—clean, practically unused except for when Valcin wanted to assert how he was Principal and Thallium was not by having his son sit in the smaller chair across the desk from his own.

TWENTY-SIX YEARS EARLIER

Valcin sat behind the desk, hands folded neatly on its surface. The fireplace behind him was sparklingly clean because he never used it—the smell of the smoke bothered him. Everything in the room was in a place from which it never moved. Empty shelves lined the walls. They should be filled with books. Thallium would fill them when this room was his.

"It's not surprising that we've arrived here," Valcin said, hollow cheeks pulling farther into his face as he spoke. "I've been waiting for it like a sneeze tickling at the top of my nose. Frankly, it's a relief to get it out of the way."

Thallium stood across from him, having refused to sit when asked to even though he knew how long this discussion might take. "Waiting for what?"

"For you to give up," his father said. "You've always been more suited to a simpler lifestyle. Occupations that would allow you to nurture your simplistic mindset. Eat, sleep, drink, and the like. Sleep in particular—with anything that moves."

"I was born to rule this city. You've hounded me with that burden since birth. Marked it on my body." He shoved his left sleeve back and slammed his hand down on the desk. "Loving a woman doesn't change that."

Valcin looked positively bored, more of a robot than his favorite toy, Eydis. "It absolutely does. We don't marry. It's a distraction and, in fact, a liability when you're in our position. You need sexual satisfaction? Find it wherever you like. Progeny? Hire a woman for that need. Compensate her for her services and be done with it."

Thallium took a clove cigarette out from under the crisp collar of his burgundy shirt. "Like you did?" He lit his smoke with a silver lighter engraved with his family crest.

"Precisely as I did. That woman was well taken care of for the rest of her days." The smoke bothered him enough to rouse his hands from their resting place to wave through it. "Put that out."

Thallium released a chest full of smoke with his neck craned upward.

Valcin ignored his rebellion. To do otherwise would incite a fistfight with Thallium, one Valcin couldn't finish. Not like he used to. "Take what you need from women. But marriage? I forbid it."

Thallium was far from finished with his smoke, but he put it out on his father's desk all the same. "I wonder how you plan on stopping me?"

"That's simple enough even for you to comprehend." Valcin brushed aside the ash mark Thallium had left on the desk. "You may have this woman or your inheritance. Not both."

Thallium shoved the desk toward his father with both hands and spat at him. "You're a sadist! Patron saint of shit fathers spreading their seed around this waste of a world. Die and burn!"

"You're emotional. Weaknesses upon weaknesses. You collect them like you collect those pointless books—so many that you've lost count. Calm down. Think, *then* react. That should give you ample time to realize that this woman? She's not worth it."

PRESENT DAY

Thallium squeezed his left hand to make the scars on his arm dance. He dropped his glass, and what was left of the Sangre del Sol came spinning out in a circle as the glass tumbled end over end and landed with a dull thump on the red shag rug.

He felt like vomiting. The realization that he had not only adopted his father's office but also his mindset overwhelmed him. Valcin hadn't died—he was still alive in Thallium. He'd become his father, and the shock of that kicked him in the chest and took his breath. He slid out of the chair onto the floor. The pain in his side as he landed on his drinking glass was little more than a vague stinging. He'd left his body again, and this time, he wasn't sure he'd find his way back into it. Wasn't sure he cared either way.

Then he was on his back. Eydis rested on her knees next to him as she picked pieces of glass from between his ribs with tweezers, dropping them into a metal bowl. She'd pushed back the sleeves of her gold robe to reveal her graceful arms.

"You're really quite beautiful," he said with a slight slur. "Have I told you that?"

She paused. Those eyes of hers, gold like her robe, flicked to his and then away. There was something vulnerable about the motion. "Thank you."

The plink of glass on metal filled the silence between them, as did an occasional pop from the last of the embers in the fire. Bursts of dying.

"I'm losing him," he said. "Again."

She dropped the tweezers in the bowl and felt around the wound gently, checking for any remaining pieces she'd missed. "He's living under your roof. Closer than he's been in years."

"Doesn't trust me. Doesn't love me. Worst of all, thinks I don't love him."

"You do."

"I want him to see Wren," he said slowly, enunciating past the alcohol.

She wiped at her forehead with the back of her arm. "You know we can't do that. I've just gotten through to her. She's nearly a new creation at this point. The woman he cared about is gone. Do you think he'll forgive you when he sees how she's changed?"

"I took her from him."

"You did your duty to your people. I've told you how important she is."

He tried to sit up, but she put a hand on his shoulder to encourage him to stay put. The fibers of the rug tickled the backs of his ears. "Another instrument of death. Do you think people will ever stop dying? It feels...unnatural, doesn't it? If it's so natural, why does it disturb us the way it does? Why are people terrified of even speaking about it? It's not natural. We're not meant to die—born, die. Born, die. Over and over."

"If we finish our work with Wren, we'll be able to slow that pattern. Perhaps even break it someday."

"I don't understand! What the hell is going on?" he shouted. To his surprise, it startled her. The pieces of glass rattled in the bowl she held.

She stood quickly and bowed to him. "Be still another moment. When you feel able, get to bed." With a swish of gold, she left like a poker player who'd realized her tell was out of control.

He stayed put, threading the rug through his fingers as he had played with Eydis' hair. In his periphery, he could see Reina sitting next to him in front of the fire.

"It's not just our son lying to you. You've been stuck inside the bottle, T," she said, stretching her neck back as she luxuriated in the heat. "Time to crawl out so that you can read the label."

As she faded like a spot of light in his vision, he wished that she would stay. She had loved him, then despised him, but she had always been truthful. Ascribing that same virtue to those closest to him had been his mistake. His alone.

He wouldn't continue to make that mistake.

CHAPTER NINE

Towering rock draperies framed the room in which Survivor sat chained to the cave wall. Long stalactites hung above, forming a ceiling of knives. And across from her, the Holy Tree—a towering stalagmite covered in a crust of draperies, glittering with gypsum in the bit of light from the handful of candles the Marauders had lit in that room of the cave. Survivor's entire underside was damp, and she knew her hair had swollen with the moisture in the air. She laughed to herself, a dry laugh that came back to her as if she wasn't alone. That made her laugh harder. She slipped all the way onto her back, closed her eyes, and tried to catch her breath.

It struck her as more humorous than she expected to be a prisoner. Again. From The Gentleman's hand to a captive of her fear of him after she'd escaped, then Thallium's prisoner, and now back to where she'd started. She was an animal bouncing from snare to snare and doing whatever it took to get free each time. Gnaw off her own foot, lie, or, better yet, kill the hunter. Scratching, tearing, ripping—always fighting. Her whole life had been one long cycle of endurance and resistance.

Except when she was with Alma.

With Alma and the kids, she'd been something other than herself, which was a crooked, gooey, dark thing. She'd become more when she took on the role of co-provider and protector of the kids with Alma. Back then, she'd nearly felt whole, almost like there was a reason to stay alive beyond being too stubborn to die.

It had taken months of being together, hunting and watching over the children in the forest, before Survivor had let Alma near her. Survivor thought about the first time, when she'd been struggling with a burr stuck near her scalp. Until that point, she'd either ignored burrs completely or ripped them out, even if chunks of hair went with them. But this one had worked itself farther in than any other, partially burying itself in the back of her head where she couldn't see it.

After she'd eaten dinner, Survivor sat just outside the light of the fire, not wanting the children to see what she was about to do and get any ideas of emulating it. She took the knife she used to field dress her kills and started digging around where the burr was. The pain was worse than she'd anticipated, and she cried silently, tears escaping against her will because the stinging was so severe.

"Stop," Alma's voice had hailed her.

Survivor paused, squinted past the tears to see Alma walk toward her from where the children laughed and ate around the fire.

Survivor brushed her off. "Go watch them."

"Wren already is. They're fine. Give me the knife."

Survivor hesitated.

Alma gave Survivor her back and dropped to her knees. "I'm not here to hurt you," she said as she held out her arms. "If you really believe I am, use the knife on me instead of yourself."

There was a frankness to everything Alma did. If one of the

children refused to put on shoes, she'd say something like, "Well, that's too bad. Because if you don't put on shoes, something could hurt your feet. A sharp rock or an Apache brown spider. I don't want you to get hurt. Do *you* want to get hurt?"

The Gentleman's words always had a poetry to them, but running underneath was a stink of decay that Survivor had caught only in brief whiffs at first, then choked on in subsequent years. There was no poetry to Alma. There was just truth. And, Survivor had started to suspect, genuine affection.

Survivor put the knife in Alma's outstretched hand.

"I'll be right back." Alma headed for the pine tree stump where she often prepared their food. The children were finishing their dinner nearby—she ruffled their hair and rubbed their backs as she passed them. Alma found what she was after in the bag at the base of the stump then returned to Survivor in the half-shadows. A glass bottle of sunflower oil was in her hand.

"Don't waste that on me," Survivor said.

"Hush. I won't need much. Be still."

Alma set to work. A big drip of the oil, warmed by the heat of Alma's hands, seeped through to Survivor's scalp around the burr. Then there was tugging at the back of Survivor's head, a firm but gentle pulling starting at the end of her hair in the back. Alma worked her way up until she reached the burr.

"You made a bald spot," Alma said.

"Doesn't matter."

Alma coaxed the burr out slowly until it separated from Survivor's scalp and slid down and out through the detangled stretch of her hair. Her muscles unwound with relief.

"Have you ever cared for your hair before?" Alma asked, just a touch of sarcasm to her tone. Survivor liked it.

She thought about how her hair used to shine, used to smell of lavender or thyme, depending on the day. She'd come to hate its perfection after the façade of her easy life fell to pieces with the staining of a white sheet.

"Not in a long time," Survivor finally replied.

Without asking, Alma set to work on the rest of her hair. She started with the worst of the tangles at the ends, tugging through them gently with her comb when she could, then resorting to picking up individual clumps and working through them with her fingers. It felt so good that Survivor nearly fell asleep. Alma took a break to put the children down to bed, then got back at it. For hours, she worked to save as much of Survivor's hair as she could, to undo the damage that had been done.

"Do both of us a favor," Alma said when she'd finally finished. "Run a comb through it occasionally. Just occasionally, that's all I ask. Because next time, I'm shaving the lot off." She'd kissed her on the head before going to bed herself.

Something had stirred in Survivor in that moment, and although she'd still refused to fully acknowledge its existence, it was there: hope.

Now, again a prisoner of the same clan but with a different Master, she knew that tiny bit of hope was what made it seem like the effort of escaping might possibly be worthwhile. She was fighting for her remaining family—she was fighting for Wren. And though she loved her sister inasmuch as she was capable of it, her need to protect her went beyond Wren herself. She'd made Alma a promise to do so, and she was damn sure keeping it.

Survivor must have nodded off because suddenly, someone was with her, touching her, making her arm sting. She sat up more slowly than she'd intended because of the weight of the chains on her wrists but quick enough to knock over an oil lamp nearby. In the dying flickers of the flame before it was smoth-ered by the oil, she wrapped one of the chains around her visitor's neck, but before she could pull tight, the person whispered, "It's just me."

Amelie. Survivor let her go.

"Hold on," Amelie said in the darkness. Glass gently clinked against the stone, the strike of a match, and then the wick of the lamp glowed again.

Amelie was still as beautiful as she had always been, almost cherubic. Tons of dark hair, big eyes. But unlike her sister's manic eyes, hers were big with innocence, with timidness. And they were reluctant to meet Survivor's.

"You ripped my stitches," Amelie said softly. She reached into the front of her leather smock and pulled out a strand of thread.

Survivor's arm burned, and she realized a line of thread loops was keeping the gash in her bicep closed. Half of them were now busted. Survivor pulled her knees up and propped her elbow on one, exposing the injury to Amelie.

After holding her needle in the lamp's flame, Amelie managed to rethread it to continue her work. She held the gash closed with one hand and tugged the thread through with the other. Survivor watched her progress.

"You've gotten good. Didn't even wake me right away," said Survivor. The corner of her mouth was swollen where Genny had torn it, and a crusty wound there throbbed when she spoke.

"That's more to do with your pain tolerance than my skill. But I've had lots of practice. A little with you. Before you left, I mean." She tore off a fresh stitch and went in to begin another.

"How have you been holding up?"

"I'm still here. He's not anymore, thanks to you. I'm better now."

"Good."

Amelie chewed her lip a little, then said, "I missed you."

Survivor fell quiet.

"I'm not trying to make you feel bad for leaving. I would have done the same thing. It's just, I thought you might like knowing that you were missed. Beo missed you too, but he could never talk about it with me. Or anyone. He kind of stopped talking altogether for a long time."

"He talks now. Won't shut up."

Amelie met Survivor's gaze. "He's with you?"

Survivor held her finger to her lips.

"Good." She returned her attention to her work. "I'm glad. But I have to ask—why did you come back? Why attack us during the Dig-in? You had time to disappear."

"Maybe I couldn't help but come back to brag about killing him. You believe me?"

Amelie chuckled. "Seems plausible."

Survivor returned her laugh, then asked, "How long have the messengers been gone?"

"Since yesterday. They left right after Genevieve brought you inside. It took so long to convince her that the Masters would rather see you cleaned up that I was afraid it would be too late for stitches. But we caught it just in time."

Survivor calculated quickly in her head. "That means a couple of days until they arrive. Good. That should be enough time."

"Enough time for what?"

Survivor didn't answer, and when Amelie glanced up again, Survivor just gave her a tired wink.

Amelie pursed her lips and nodded. "Better I don't know. We could hope for more time, anyway. They're close this time of year, all down south, but it takes a lot of effort to move the clans. Maybe they'll be slow, and you and I can have another day together."

The winter move was a massive production. As nomadic as Marauders were, that time of year was still difficult for even the most experienced. With the trial, they would all be moving *again* after settling in for the cold season. Showed how gross her offense had been that she was worth all the effort.

"Something tells me they'll make it here pretty quick," said Survivor. "The fanfare of a trial is pretty motivating."

"Should be the biggest reunion we've ever had, at least since I've been with the clan. All for you." Amelie tied off the last stitch and then held the lamp closer to critique her work. "I was waiting for you to wake up before setting your nose. Genny wouldn't let me give you any painkillers. You ready?"

Survivor set the back of her head firmly against the rock wall. "Do it."

Amelie set the lamp back down and felt around Survivor's twisted nose with her thumbs before pressing hard near the top. The bone crunched as it slid back into place. Survivor cursed but quickly calmed her breathing. Once she'd stilled, Amelie spoke.

"Why did you come back? You were free."

Survivor felt her nose—Amelie had done well. "You know I wasn't. Not once everyone heard what I did, what my sister did."

"Wren, right?"

Survivor stared at her.

"Fen told us her name. When he got back last time, I mean. It's pretty."

That meant the whole of the clans knew Wren's identity as well as where she was. It didn't matter that they knew Survivor had been the one to kill The Gentleman—Wren would be a target anyway after how many of them she'd killed. The urgency of Survivor's plan had just reached new heights, and the consequences of failure were greater than she'd realized.

"I imagine she's pretty like her name," Amelie said. "And strong, like you."

Survivor stretched her arms up. The weight of the chains on her wrists made her stretch fall short. She dropped her hands into her lap. "Yeah, she is. She's also in trouble like me. Like you, Mel. She needs our help."

"*Our* help?"

"Have you heard Genny talking about the trial? Do they plan on sharing my blood before they kill me?"

Amelie hesitated but finally nodded.

"Full spectacle," said Survivor. "Good. Blood will have blood, that's what they taught us, eh?"

Those big eyes grew bigger. "Blood will have blood," Amelie repeated.

"I need you to do something for me, and if you do it, I can get you out. I can get everyone out."

Amelie shook her head fast. "Genny, she'll—I can't."

"Genny's nothing. She's The Gentleman's overeager shadow, and, with him dead, his shadow will follow. The one good thing about her is how she underestimates you. But *I* know you, Mel. I *was* you for years. I know that, when he was still alive, you'd feel the urge to let your hand slip when you were shaving his neck. I know that whenever you lie down to sleep at a new camp, you calculate how far it is to the nearest settlement, if you could make it there before you died of thirst or before they found you."

Amelie chewed on her lip again, then said, "I always wondered how many of the younger kids I could carry. One in each arm, one on my front and another on my back. Could I fit a fifth on my shoulders? And how could I keep them quiet? Maybe we could make it into a game."

Survivor nodded.

"On the way here, they took two whole families," said Amelie. "Just scooped them up and divided them like pieces of a butchered animal. Maybe the kids are young enough to forget. If they get to leave soon."

"With your help, they will."

She narrowed her big eyes at Survivor. "What do you need me to do?"

Before Survivor could answer, footsteps carried from the corridor toward them. Whoever it was would be close enough to hear anything else they said. Mel busied herself cleaning the last of Survivor's wounds.

Genevieve and two lackeys came around the bend, men Survivor didn't recognize, and she had a feeling that was intentional.

"You should have finished already," Genny said to her sister. "Time to eat. Let's go." She turned to leave.

"You smell like him," Survivor called out. "You know that?" She sniffed the air for emphasis, and it came out more like a snort from the swollen cartilage of her nose. "Sandalwood. That's the oil he wore when he was feeling saucy. Probably the one he wore around you most of the time, huh?"

Genny turned back and dropped to her heels across from Survivor. "You don't know anything about what he and I had."

"No, not directly I don't. He never liked me that way, never liked any clan member that way. But from the way you're reacting, I'd say he got lonely in his old age. And you were convenient." She jutted her chin out when she spoke, gave Genny a big smile.

That was all it took to push her over the edge. Genny struck the closest thing she could reach—Survivor's cheek. To her credit, it was a fair hit. But not hard enough.

"I mean, look at you!" Survivor cackled. "Your head looks like a testicle older than his, puckered and dried up. Did you think those scars made you beautiful? Did you get them for him?"

Genny stood for leverage and then hit the other side of Survivor's face, but too high.

Survivor rose to her feet and shimmied. "Come on, I'm more woman than you! He would have had a better ride with me. I guess in the end, I sent him on his final ride, didn't I? Straight to hell."

Genny struck her square on her already-bruised jaw this time, and Survivor fell flat on her back. Amidst the pain filling her mouth, she located her tooth, finally knocked free. With extreme caution, she moved the tooth to the front of her mouth. She sat up and launched bloody spit dramatically toward Amelie, and her tooth went with it. "Blood will have blood, right Genny?" she said, glancing pointedly at Amelie and then back to her sister.

"Blood will have blood," growled Genny. "Can't wait to taste yours."

"Why share it with the others? You could take it all now."

Genevieve groaned. "Oh no, it'll be sweeter for the waiting." She blew a kiss before sweeping out of the room, followed by her flunkies. From the stone passageway, she shouted, "Hurry up, Mel!"

Survivor pointed at the tooth emphatically, and Amelie grabbed it and put it in the pocket of her smock. "Coming!" she called.

"Psst," Survivor hissed, and Amelie got close. "Get someone else to bear the cup. You can't be at the trial."

"Mel! I'm hungry!" Genny's voice rumbled against the rocks.

Amelie scrambled to her feet.

Theo was a good kid. Quiet, always followed orders. Most amusing to Thallium was how terrified Theo was of him. When Thallium entered the surveillance room, Theo was already standing at attention. The semicircular wall of screens fluttered with motion and shifting lights that, when taken in all at once, produced nausea in the Principal.

"Welcome, sir," said Theo.

"Saw me coming, Operator?" Thallium asked after the reinforced steel door had sealed shut behind him.

"Yes, sir. Oh—was that a test?" asked Theo. Seventeen, but he could have passed for at least two years younger with his build, all soft around the edges. He had a tattoo on his neck, another on the back of his hand. Overly bold designs—an eye and a skull—probably intended to make him look older. They didn't, especially since they were simple lines that Theo could have done himself in the mirror.

"I don't need to test you, Theo, do I?" Thallium took a step toward him, and the oversized eyeball on the middle of Theo's neck slid up and down. Hilarious.

"Of course not, sir."

"How about a break?" Thallium asked. "I'd like to check in on my people—no better place to get an overall view than here. Don't you think?"

"No better place, sir." Theo started for the door but caught himself leaving his jacket and spun around to grab it from the back of the chair. He nearly slammed into Thallium as he did so, and the kid let out an actual squeal.

Thallium barely held his laugh in until Theo closed the security door on his way out. The Principal wiped a tear from his eye as he dropped into the chair, the plastic-covered cushion of which had formed to the shape of Theo's backside.

How the Operator could stand to look at these screens all day, Thallium hadn't a clue. The unnatural light and constant motion continued to make his stomach turn. In truth, it wasn't the cameras he'd come to check. Not before he'd checked something else.

The ID bracelets worn by those who served Thallium were alarmingly limited in how accurately they could track their wearers. That wasn't what the wearers believed, of course. They thought that they could be located wherever they were in the city at any time. Not true. They could be called via the bracelets, but tracking was another matter. The ID tags inside the bracelets were read only when they passed a scanner location in the city. All government buildings had scanners hidden at their entrances, as did the major intersections of popular walking paths. Any time a bracelet went past one of these scanners, its location was recorded and kept here at the central databank. What resulted was a convenient, yet vague, map of where the wearer had gone.

Thallium tapped at the keys on the console to pull up the list of bracelets. His typing was slow and awkward, only two fingers at a time. He much preferred pen and paper.

He entered "V" and there, in the top spot, was "Valcin, Caster."

A record of Caster's scans came up. Today, he'd left the Main House at 8:46am, which had been shortly after they'd sat down to coffee and breakfast together. Then he'd gone into the med ward. Not unusual—he often lent his assistance there. Far from suspicious.

He hadn't stayed there too long, as the next record was from one of the neighborhood scanners. He'd been in the southern family housing district. Visiting his friends, most likely. The most recent scan was, surprisingly, at the Water Treatment Plant. According to the record, he was still there.

Thallium reluctantly looked to the wall of screens. They were divided into sections by neighborhood. He found the plant's section and glanced through the four screens there. One of them was posted above the treatment facility, overlooking the glass platform and the workers near the tanks below. While all of the cameras had audio recording capability, they were individually silenced most of the time. When the Operator had cause to listen in or use the PA system, he would take a particular camera off silent and use it as needed.

The water facility workers were little red blips, nearly indistinguishable from one another from this view. But there were three men closer to the camera on the platform. Well, two men and one nearly man—Caster, Oliver, and the Grunt from Caster's Body. His name was of Greek origin. Thallium recalled it was ironic, though he couldn't remember it specifically. Ollie shook the Grunt's hand.

Thallium turned the camera's audio up and listened in over the rushing hum of the water's motion below.

"—know this likely isn't your idea of an exciting assignment," Ollie was saying to the boy, "but you'll learn valuable skills here."

"If it's where my boss wants me, then it's where I need to be," said the boy, the barest hint of disappointment in his tone.

"Thank you, Ollie," Caster said. He appeared distinctly different from how he was around Thallium. Difficult to say how exactly, but there was something in his bearing. A warmth and openness in how he stood. With Thallium, he always kept one foot back like he was prepared for an attack or considering attacking himself. Now, he stood wide and at ease, and the difference stung. "I think, together, we'll be able to make positive changes."

Oliver put his hands out before him. "Please, join me in my office. I know how much Caster likes tea these days. You too, Adonis?"

They walked out of view of the camera toward the path

behind the platform that would lead them to stairs going below and subsequently to Ollie's office, which was not wired. He'd made that request for privacy long ago, a request that Valcin had happily honored.

"Of course you think they'll be talking about you. Narcissists always do." Reina's voice seemed to come through the facility camera. "Why don't you just speak to your son?"

Thallium pushed Theo's chair back and stood. "I was planning to."

There was no night or day inside the High Cave, just one long stretch of time measured by how Survivor's heart continued to beat. Her wounds were more severe than she was willing to admit, but she'd put her energy toward healing and rest. Since Amelie had stitched her up, she'd done nothing but sleep, eat the meager porridge Amelie was allowed to offer, and drink the familiar, salty water of her youth. She would need her strength for what was to come, and the drums that had been sounding off and on to welcome arriving clans for hours now told her that time had just about arrived.

The drumbeats traveled through the corridors of the cave, swam in waves through the rock under and around her, made her chest rumble with their song. But then they fell silent, and they stayed silent. That was when Amelie came to see Survivor, and this time, it wasn't food or drink she brought.

The same two Marauders who had carried Survivor to the Holy Tree initially, who she suspected also rotated guard duty outside this chamber of the cave to keep Survivor from manipulating them, accompanied Amelie. They stopped near the far wall, just close enough to serve as witnesses to what Amelie was about to do.

Amelie set a tray on the ground near Survivor's feet before sitting herself. She looked mournfully at the supplies—small bottle of alcohol, stretch of cord, huge syringe, and an ornate silver bowl that caught the light of the lantern Amelie had set beside it.

"I see Genny made you polish the silver. Always hated that job."

"Special occasion," Amelie muttered.

Survivor leaned toward Amelie. The chains pulled her arms back, but Survivor was able to nudge Amelie's shoulder with her head and get close to her ear.

"Are you ready for this?" asked Survivor.

In a rush, Amelie uncorked the alcohol and took a swig. Her face puckered, and she exhaled like her tongue was melting. "Are *you?*"

Survivor nodded at the bottle. "Share?"

Amelie lifted the bottle to Survivor's mouth. As it burned its way past her lips, she was thankful that the wound near her mouth had scabbed over. "That's even worse than I remember," she coughed.

"Like licking sweat."

"From between the folds."

Amelie chuckled, then fell quiet. The drippings of the cave filled the silence as Amelie hesitated to begin her task.

"It's time." Survivor offered the inside of her arm.

With a deep breath, Amelie set to work. She wiped the skin near Survivor's elbow clean with the alcohol—a step that really should have been skipped since this "trial" wasn't a process to determine guilt. Then she tied the bit of cord above Survivor's elbow before taking up the syringe. She stuck the needle into Survivor's arm. Blood rushed into the syringe.

Amelie called out to the guards behind her, "You witness this blood taken?"

"We witness," they said together.

"Blood repaid," Amelie finished the ritual halfheartedly. Her hands shook as she drew back the plunger slowly. Once it was full, she untied the cord, pulled out the needle, and put pressure on the wound with a piece of fabric.

With Amelie close, Survivor whispered, "This repayment I'm giving will come with a little extra, right?"

Amelie released Survivor's arm and patted her smock near her chest pocket. She nodded. As she expelled the blood into the bowl, it swirled around the surface, making the shiny interior slick and dull.

"Remember—don't attend the trial," said Survivor. "Have Genevieve present the bowl. Stay here."

"Genny won't allow that."

"Feign illness, then."

"I'll have to go," Amelie said. "Everyone has to. You know that."

Boom, boom-boom. Boom, boom-boom. Boom-boom-boom.

The drums had started. Not a rhythm of greeting, but of ceremony. Of trial. Amelie cringed at their song.

Survivor spoke quickly, "As soon as your job is done, get to the back of the clan. Understand?"

Amelie took a breath, then exhaled slowly and silently. "I understand."

Survivor looked past her to the guards. "It's time. Why are you just standing there?" She got to her knees, pulled against her chains as if she'd simply grown tired of them. "Let's go."

Survivor had attended Marauder trials before, and it was her intimate knowledge of them that gave her the confidence to accept the risk of being at the center of one. But even though this trial was following the same beats as always, it felt different. Not simply because Survivor was the accused, but also because of the sheer spectacle. The seven clans gathered only for the rarest of occasions, most often for the Masters to discuss issues that affected all of them. Marauders were territorial creatures. Like coyotes, they shared a way of life, but that was where their family ties ended. They were loyal to their own family above their species.

The clans were the closest they'd ever come to being united thanks only to what The Gentleman had accomplished in his lifetime, the lengths to which he'd gone to join them together. Everyone knew who he was. The other Masters had respected him enough not to murder him for his efforts, and that was a high compliment.

Which meant that the person who killed him was wanted by all. Her crime was against every clan, and they were eager and entitled to share in justice.

She braced against the growing light as she was led up the slope to the ladder at the cave entrance. As she climbed the ladder, her feet kept slipping on the moist rungs and the filthy shreds of what was left of her dress and the pants beneath. Finally, she emerged into crisp air and sunlight.

There had never been a Marauder crowd like the one gathered at the base of the trail leading up to the High Cave. As she descended, she tried to get a head count but only reached two hundred before she gave up. Maybe twice that number was gathered, and at least half of them were slaves. Easy enough to tell the difference by their clothing—white and tan working clothes. The attire of the full clan members was more varied and colorful, as were the scar patterns along the faces and limbs of the soldiers. Honor marks. The soldiers stood toward the middle of those gathered in a great half circle of clans, and behind them, their masses of slaves. On a rise above and in front of all the others were the leaders—two Commanders from each clan and their Masters.

The two guards stopped Survivor at the top of the rise upon

a signal from Genevieve, who spoke with such authority that it almost sounded as though she'd been running a clan for years rather than playing at it for mere weeks.

Genny's voice carried through the canyon: "You've been called here because we no longer have to wait until the warm season to hunt down the traitor who sent my former Master from his body. She's come for further bloodshed, but what she's found is that the only blood left to spill is her own. And so it has been."

At that, Amelie stepped from between the two Commanders of Genevieve's clan and brought the silver bowl filled with Survivor's blood to Genevieve. Below, a drummer from each clan started the slow, soft beat of trial, and in time with their rhythm, the seven Masters stepped forward to form a circle around Survivor.

"Angel," Genevieve continued, "you abandoned your clan and hid in the desert like a coward. You have admitted to murdering your father, our former beloved Master, The Gentleman. Is all of this true?"

Survivor smiled. "It is."

"Then by your own admission, I condemn you—"

Survivor held up a finger. "But that's no longer my name."

Genevieve's eyes twitched around the edges as she bellowed, "You dare speak more?"

"As someone condemned, I have the right. Before you drink, before you kill me with seventy cuts, I have the right."

Genevieve looked ready to pop Survivor's head off, but the other six Masters stood patiently and waited for what Survivor had to say. They knew this was a done deal, and she'd piqued their curiosity.

The drummers continued softly.

"Angel was what he called me when I was a child," Survivor continued, louder now. Her voice carried against the rocks, and she hoped it reached as far as the slaves watching. "When I was treated with kindness. When I didn't know the measures to which my clan went for food, water, luxuries. And then The Gentleman took that name from me. I wore white like you do now, and they made me stain it with blood. I became Death's Daughter.

"And doing that? Killing for them? I *liked* it." She thumped her chest. "Because it was the only time I got release! When I did their bidding, I could let the rage, the pain, and the fear out to wreak the havoc I dreamed of releasing on them. Night dreams, daydreams, dreams every waking second of what I wanted to do and how I was incapable of doing it."

She held The Gentleman's mark on her hand up high. "I did not choose this life, but I lived it well. And now that same life is finally going to kill me. It will do the same to you." She paused, braced herself to project as loudly as she could. "If you have the chance to leave as I did, grab hold with both fists and take it!"

A restless shuffling among the slaves set the soldiers at the front of the crowd on edge.

Survivor turned her attention to the Masters and Genevieve, met their eyes as she spoke, "My name is Survivor. Drink my blood and be filled—I'm ready for death."

The drummers took their cue at that and picked up the beat, louder now.

Boom, boom-boom. Boom, boom-boom. Boom-boom-boom.

Amelie held out the bowl to Genevieve as if it were a thing with fangs, and Genny took it. With all eyes on Survivor and the Masters, Amelie was able to slink back past the soldiers and into the midst of the slaves. Survivor was relieved to see her go.

Genevieve raised the bowl to Survivor in a one-sided toast. "Blood will have blood." She sipped from it, greedy and deep, and made a show of swallowing before passing it to the Master on her right. Her teeth were pink, and she flashed them at Survivor as she took a knife from her belt, ready to take the first cut once the last Master had finished drinking. It was the same as the knives of the other Masters—a knife of authority. Beo had used The Gentleman's to make his first kill, initiating him as a full member of the clan. They were reserved for only special occasions.

Each Master sipped from the bowl in turn, passed it along, and readied their knives. The drums beat faster, faster.

The bowl reached the last Master on Genevieve's left, and he emptied it. As he took out his knife to join the others, Genevieve struck out at Survivor and slashed her along the inside of her forearm. The cut was hardly lethal, but that was the point—to punish and to play, and eventually, all of the cuts together would end the accused's life.

Another Master struck out at Survivor's side, right along her hip bone, before another sliced the back of her shoulder. When one went for the fleshy part of her thigh, she could tell the cuts would turn deeper soon. Deeper and faster with the rhythm of the drums.

But just before Survivor's gut could become a target, a new movement began around the circle, starting with Genevieve. She collapsed, writhing like a pinned snake and kicking up dirt. Then the Master on her right did the same, then the next and the next, until the circle was complete.

The Master at the end, who had drunk even more deeply than Genevieve, writhed less and died faster than the rest next to the bowl he'd sipped from moments before. Not long after the chain reaction started, they all fell still, and the dust they'd tossed about tickled Survivor's nose in the sudden quiet. She looked up through it at the pure blue of the sky.

As loud as she could muster, she screamed at the heavens, "Blood will have blood!"

An answering rifle shot cracked in the distance, starting a clock ticking in her mind, counting up, urging her to move. But for several seconds, she savored stillness, her own laughter, and the thunderous echo of the shot through the canyon.

The fourteen Commanders roused themselves from their shock and ran at her, but she'd counted to ten and had already turned and started sprinting back up the trail. At the end of the rise where the trail turned on itself, she kept running right off the edge and landed on her backside to slide down the hill. She'd known this was going to be the hardest part—outrunning the Masters' highest-ranking soldiers with her injuries when they were all fueled by outrage and adrenaline. But she hadn't anticipated her own excitement, the way she felt ready to burst with energy even as the ache of her wounds from a few days ago reminded her of what her body still hadn't recovered from. The rush of air as she ran kissed the Masters' fresh cuts on her skin, and she counted them as her own honor scars. What she was running toward would likely kill her, but in that moment, it didn't matter.

She'd counted to forty-five, but still hadn't reached the marker. Too slow. Finally, at fifty seconds, she spotted a white X on a rock off to her left and heard a faint hissing. The higher-ups were maybe ten seconds behind, close enough that she could hear their gear rattling and the evenness of their breath. She sprinted to the right and dove into the two-foot trench Beo had dug, just big enough for her to fit inside. She heard the feet behind her turn in the same direction before she pressed her hands hard against her ears.

BOOM.

The earth shook with the force of the blast. Despite plugging her ears, they still rang, but she couldn't wait for them to stop. She clambered out of the trench and into pure carnage. Beo had no choice but to make do with the rocks of the landscape rather than the metal shrapnel they'd wanted, but they'd done the job well enough, slicing and tearing into the flesh of her pursuers. Of the fourteen higher-ups, those closest to the blast had taken the bulk of the damage and were unrecognizable as human. Out from there, others gasped for breath, but they wouldn't for much longer. The three that had been the closest to Survivor were still standing, cradling their heads, and staring mystified at the scene around them.

One turned, a man who had concentrated his honor scars on his chest, and regarded Survivor as an evil apparition. Fear warred with fury across his features, but before he could choose which one to give into, his gaze went up and behind Survivor. A shot that should have been much louder in Survivor's ears rang out, and a bullet sank through the Marauder's scars into his chest. Beo ran past her right side and, for good measure, slammed the butt of his rifle into the man's face. Once he was on the ground, Beo moved on to the second one who still lived. Beo didn't waste a bullet on him; he took the shovel from its strap across his back. The striking of metal against bone broke the otherwise eerie stillness of the canyon. After he'd finished with all three, he returned to Survivor and began looking over her injuries.

"Were you hit?" he asked, and it came to her throbbing ears as though spoken from the far end of a tunnel.

She shook her head and realized she still hadn't caught her breath.

A dull crunching and the shifting of the light off to her left made Survivor turn. Marauders and slaves approached, an intermingled mass of hundreds of wide eyes coming from where she'd left the dead Masters. Most of the Marauders were men, most of the slaves women. Children were scattered throughout the crowd, generally holding onto adults who looked nothing like them but, as Survivor knew, were the family they had made in the midst of an eternal nightmare. At the front of all stood Amelie. Where the crowd stopped, afraid to come any closer, she continued on, straight up to Survivor.

For all the destruction and gore surrounding her, Amelie didn't recoil. She stood taller, lighter on her feet as she took Survivor's damaged, swollen face in her hands.

"Thank you," she mouthed.

Survivor wrapped an arm around Amelie's neck and disappeared into the mass of her hair. Then Amelie backed up, and with more volume than she'd ever used in her life, shouted to the crowd, "Show respect to the one who has set you free!" Amelie fell to one knee.

The slaves present joined Amelie in her bow immediately. Those soldiers who had just watched their superiors die in a way they didn't fully comprehend only had to take in the shift in the air around them, the energy pulsing between the slaves, before following suit. For now, they would let this play out.

Beo moved near Amelie, and she looked happy to see him. He lifted his rifle above his head and shouted, "Loyalty!"

Half the crowd echoed back, "Loyalty!"

"Unity!" cried Beo.

"Unity!" the crowd returned, more enthusiastically now.

Beo shook his rifle and yelled with deep resonance from his chest, "No mercy!"

"No mercy!"

Then Beo whooped, drawing out the sound low and slow. Amelie joined into the call, then it rippled through from the front of the crowd to the back. It sped up and increased in pitch. Their voices grew until Survivor could no longer hear the pounding in her ears, just the power of their cries, the pain they released more and more with each repetition of the call.

And in the wake of that pain, allegiance to the one who had taken it away.

CHAPTER TEN

"Really? This doesn't seem excessive to you when you have a perfectly good gym?" Caster asked through a grunt as he and his father worked together to finagle a metal stand through the door of his office. The stand was still warm—Caster suspected Thallium had been working on it all night and his weld points hadn't entirely cooled yet. The sweat and grime on the front of Thallium's black tank top supported this theory.

"When you possess more power and resources than anyone else, son, isn't everything you do more or less 'excessive'? Convenience itself is excessive." He grunted. "No, to *my* left more, not yours."

After a great deal of struggling and myriad expletives, they had the stand in the office. Thallium backpedaled all the way to the far side where one of his bookcases sat curiously empty. They set the stand down.

"When you invited me to have lunch with you, I didn't imagine I'd have to do manual labor in exchange," said Caster.

"We all have to work for our food, isn't that right?" said Thallium. He stood beneath the crossbeam of the stand, grabbed it, and did a quick set of showy pull-ups, shifting his weight first to one side and then to the other on alternating reps. "It'll do," he said as he dropped down. He couldn't seem to stay still, which wasn't entirely unusual. But the redness in his eyes was new.

"Are you feeling okay, Dad?" Caster asked.

Thallium wiped his hand on his pants. "I am. Miss you, though. You've been working so hard lately that I feel like we only see each other at mealtimes, and those only occasionally."

"I've been busy. Sorry." Caster nodded at the empty bookcase. "Tell me you didn't get rid of them."

Thallium shook his head. "Of course not. Packed them away to keep them safe."

"From your explosive pull-ups?"

Thallium thumped his son on the back. "Can't be too careful around books." He waved Caster back the way they'd come, through his office and his bedroom. At the bedroom door, Thallium stopped with his hand nearly on the handle. "Before we go out there, any updates for me regarding our trusted Keepers?"

"Nothing concrete," replied Caster. Which was true, more or less. Caster reached to open the door, but Thallium put his hand to the wood.

"No updates at all? We have privacy here. You can tell me anything, son." The honest plea in his voice was so surprising that Caster nearly asked Thallium to repeat himself to make sure he'd heard him correctly. It reminded Caster of when he'd been a kid asking Thallium if he could stop working and come play kings and dragons.

Caster tried to relax his muscles, but Thallium's sincerity forced them into knots. "I know, Dad. Just have nothing to tell you at the moment." He went for the handle again, and this time, Thallium put his back against the door.

"I have something to tell you, nonetheless," said Thallium. "I've been thinking a lot lately. That's most of what I've been doing, in fact. Your mother has been...present...in my thoughts. I truly believe she would be proud of everything you're doing. Before things get too out of hand, I wanted you to know that." Without warning, he put his arms around Caster and hugged him more tightly than he had since Caster was a teenager.

"Things are going to get out of hand at lunch?" Caster asked as he wrestled out of his father's grip. For a second, Caster would have sworn Thallium's bloodshot eyes were wet.

"Absolutely. The most dangerous cheese board you've ever seen. Let's be off!" Thallium threw his bedroom door open with such gusto that it slammed into the wall, then strode into the hallway without so much as a glance back.

As Caster slowly followed behind him, taking in the power of his steps, he wondered if his father slept at all anymore. And if not, what was he lying awake thinking about?

Survivor had a lot of shit to say about Marauders, but one of the things she could never fault them for was their efficiency. A day after she had wiped out their leaders, the clans had arranged—under the advisement of Beo and Amelie—a new hierarchy of authority with Survivor at the top.

Marauders understood power more than any other language, and Survivor had taken it with a bowl of cyanide-laced blood and a well-placed explosion. Nobody could deny her gall, and with it, she'd earned their respect. Earning their loyalty would take more time, but as long as she continued speaking their language and rewarding their service, keeping the family together, it would come.

The temporary encampments set up by the visiting clans

were buzzing with excitement, most of it coming from the slaves' quarters. Each clan had one Senior Slave that served as their representative when pleas had to be made to the Masters, such as for new clothes, extra blankets, or medicine. Survivor had asked for a meeting with all of them. From the looks on the faces of the seven Senior Slaves gathered in her tent—an impressive canvas monstrosity that had previously belonged to the wealthiest of the clan leaders she'd just killed—there was as much trepidation among the slaves as there was hope.

Five women and two men stood in a line of white, baggy clothes before Survivor, hands behind their backs in deference. Among them was Amelie, who had long held a place of respect among the slaves, and now that Genevieve was dead, she apparently carried a great deal of clout. Survivor would need that clout for what was ahead. Amelie held her head higher than Survivor had ever seen before; knowing that she was responsible for her joy meant more to Survivor than she had anticipated.

Survivor stood behind a table she'd set up between herself and the Seniors. The spoils of that morning's hunt were laid out before her: a couple of bottom-feeders—one rabbit and a prairie dog—as well as three snakes. All rattlers, one impressively large, almost six feet long. He would serve a variety of purposes; as his head had already been removed, Survivor would start her work with his skin.

"Relax," Survivor said to the whole of them as she made a small slit on the underside of the snake, near the belly. "I'm not here to hurt you."

Amelie relaxed her posture, but she was alone in doing so. One slave in particular stood stiff and formal, her hands tight behind her back. "Why are you doing that?" she asked. Her head was nearly clean-shaven, and she had a purple bruise edged in yellow on her right cheek that was likely the doing of a soldier who would now face dire consequences if he repeated his abuse.

"Doing what?" Survivor asked as she began pulling the skin off in one great length toward where the snake's head had been.

The slave gestured at the table. "That. Work."

The skin came off in an unbroken strip. Survivor beamed with satisfaction as she set it aside. "You want to eat, don't you? These will spoil if I don't clean them soon."

"But that work is beneath a Master."

"That's the confusion then." Survivor slapped the snake carcass down. "Let's clear this up—I'm not your Master."

The woman tilted her shaved head and eyed Survivor. "Then what are you?"

"Nothing to you if you have somewhere you'd rather be. I need you to pass along a message to your clans: all slaves, prisoners, and anyone else who didn't ask to be here are immediately released. I'll provide up to a week's worth of supplies to those who choose to return to wherever home was before they were forced into service. But for those who have no home to return to, they're welcome to stay here—no longer as slaves, but as members of a clan in which everyone is autonomous and provided for."

Survivor could pretty well see their minds working through her words. What she'd proposed was a foreign concept to them all.

"And how will you be providing for them?" the shaved woman asked. "Through the same methods as the leaders you just murdered?"

"No." Survivor's reply came out with more anger than she'd intended. She tempered her tone—something she'd have to get better at if she wanted these people to see that she was different from their former Masters. She hoped she *was* different enough from them. "Which means life will be harder than it was before. But no harder than it is for anyone else living in the Open."

"What do you demand in return?" the man at the end of the line asked, voice soft but sure.

"If you stay, you are loyal to me, and I to you. I won't keep you prisoner, but you will still answer to my authority."

Amelie's sweet face turned all the sweeter, as if she were in the presence of a heavenly spirit rather than a recent conqueror drenched in sweat and the fluids of a dead reptile. "What would you have us do?" she asked.

"I'm going to organize us as one clan, one people, with the goal of taking down the man who would take the Open from us if we let him."

"Thallium?" asked the man at the end of the line. "We can't attack The Disc, not even the Border Valley around it. We have a truce."

"That truce died with The Gentleman," Survivor replied as she set her knife aside. She put her hands down on the table and gathered her wits. "Thallium has my sister. Because all of us here are family, that makes her your sister." She raised her head. "And we will take her back together."

Nobody argued. Instead, they all bowed before turning to leave. It was a better reaction than she'd expected. After the way she'd disrupted their lives, she'd counted on subsets of them reacting violently. Instead, everyone had been peaceful, accommodating. Most likely, that meant the displeased minority were just biding their time. She'd take that risk on happily if it meant having the resources she needed to get Wren safe.

After they were gone, Survivor turned her attention back to her chore. She took a break from the reptiles and worked on a rabbit. She really should have started with the rodents, but it was cold enough out that they would last a little while longer before souring. She made a slit into the skin near the back of the rabbit's neck, then slid her fingers back and forth in the opening to separate it from the meat. As she tugged with both hands to remove the pelt in two pieces, she thought about how Wren never had gotten over her reluctance to eat something she found to be endearing. Survivor wondered if she were similarly naïve today or if her time in The Disc had relieved her of that burden. Part of her hoped it hadn't.

"You again," Beo said outside the tent, just on the other side of the door flap where he'd taken it upon himself to stand guard. "Get out of here."

"Hey, big man! *She* sent for *me*." Gray. Survivor walked around the table to get better lighting on her work from a window slat in the tent. This could go on for a while. She sliced into the belly of the rabbit and moved her blade upward as Gray added, "Don't want to disappoint her, right?"

"You're the disappointment," Beo replied.

"I'm hurt. After you put a small fortune on my tab in Ranlock, I thought I'd earned better."

"My respect means nothing. Hers does."

"And 'her' is tired of listening to you two argue," Survivor called. Men were idiots.

The fabric of the door flap rustled. Two sets of footsteps entered.

"We'll be fine, Beo. Leave us," said Survivor, attention on removing the innards of the rabbit with one firm pull.

No footsteps retreated in response. "You sure?" Beo asked.

She inspected the nearly spotless cavity of her subject. "Am I ever not?"

"In this case, I wish you weren't," muttered Beo.

Survivor looked over her shoulder to see Gray saluting Beo with a couple of fingers as he passed toward the tent opening. Beo grunted and went out of his way to bump Gray with his shoulder hard enough to knock him back a step before he left.

"Such a lovely guy," said Gray. He wore more practical clothes than he had within Ranlock's warm clutches, including a brown wool sweater—undyed and lush-looking—that Survivor couldn't help but think about stealing. His gaze traveled around the tent, taking in the size of it, and he whistled. "Impressive place you have here."

She turned to face him full on. "Guess you got my message."

His eyes widened at the site of her, focused not on the mess along her knife and hands but on her face. She'd forgotten about the lesser injuries, but the colorful bruising across her jaw and under her eyes was hard to ignore. Apparently, they were still bold enough to knock someone back at the sight of them. He took two quick steps forward. "Damn. You okay?"

She waved him off and turned her attention to the prairie dog. "I'm fine."

He opened his mouth like he wanted to ask more, but smartly didn't, and settled for clearing his throat. "When you said you could get Marauders to join the fight against Thallium, I didn't realize you meant *all* of them. Under *your* authority."

"It was an all or nothing situation. Die or take over. I never was easy to kill."

"Your legend won't be, either." He folded his arms over his chest and grinned at her. "Everyone in the area's talking about it. Won't be long before word gets back to The Disc. Glad you reached out."

"We had a deal."

He sighed. "Yeah. Sure did." He dropped his arms and paced around the tent fiddling with the furnishings, particularly drawn to the blankets and other textiles that called to his knowing touch.

"When are you heading for The Disc?" she asked as she finished with the prairie dog.

A blue curtain concealed a separate eating area, and he rubbed at its fringe. "Depending on my numbers, as soon as possible."

She dropped her knife on the table near a bucket of fresh water. She took the two mammal carcasses to the bucket and cleaned them thoroughly. "I can give you one hundred soldiers."

"By soldiers, you mean Marauder murderers?"

"Current Marauders, former murderers."

"Old habits die hard and all that."

"And sometimes those habits never die. But these soldiers are what I have to offer, with restored slaves among them who have chosen to fight in service to me rather than resume their former duties." She set the fresh meat on the table near the unfinished snakes, which would keep for now, and started cleaning her hands in a stone washbasin with a bar of yucca soap behind her work area.

"Seems you've had quite the effect on everyone around here," Gray said to her back.

"People who've lived through the same hell learn to recognize each other, share a shorthand."

"Your hell was something different from theirs, though." She stopped scrubbing, and Gray must have sensed her tension. "Amelie let me in on a couple family secrets when I was waiting outside," he said at last.

She finished washing. "She shouldn't have."

"I asked her. I can be pretty persuasive."

Survivor turned and took fast steps toward Gray. "Why are you asking about me?" she spat.

"While you're forthright—sometimes painfully forthright—

you're far from transparent. And you," he looked her up and down, "fascinate me."

She rolled her eyes as if that could cover the flush that climbed up her neck and cheeks. "Stop it."

"Tell me if I get something wrong, then I'll stop. Because I'm pretty sure you and I?" He pointed between them. "We also share that shorthand. Being someone's target—their plaything—would hurt badly enough. But when that person was supposed to protect you, supposed to love you according to the basic laws of human decency, those scars throb. Keep throbbing. Here especially." He poked at his forehead. "I swear my uncles are still alive in there. Tearing me down, nagging. The Gentleman still talk to you?"

She squinted at him, then said guardedly, "So what if he does? That doesn't make us the same."

His nimble steps meandered toward her. "Oh no. Not the same. It does help me understand you, though. You're powerful, but you're more than that. You're unpredictable, fueled by whatever impulse suits you at the time. A visionary who sees a fight worth starting and charges into it with glee. Who feels so deeply that she wants everyone to think she doesn't feel at all. A woman who won't be used—never again." He reached out and gently tipped her chin up. "How'd I do, Hyena Mother? That's what they're calling you out there. I kind of like it." He stretched down and put his lips near hers.

She closed her eyes, felt her body pull toward him, but then smacked his hand down. "We had a couple of fun nights. Don't ruin it."

"Not trying to. I know that time meant nothing to you. But even then, you knew it was different for me."

"That's your burden to bear." She turned away and busied herself with organizing her clean knives on the table.

"It's no burden at all." There was a rustling as he withdrew something from his pocket. "Thanks for the troops," he said, barely brushing against her back as he put something near her elbow on the table. She resisted the urge to look. "I'll have one of my men work out the details with Beo in the morning." Dirt crunched underfoot as he turned to leave.

She finally looked down to see he'd left a sprig of fresh rosemary, somehow dotted with blue flowers this late in the season. As she crushed one of the leaves between her fingers, its aroma filled her, loosening her muscles. "You weren't lying," she said, turning to face him.

He stopped just inside the tent flap and leaned lightly against the pole there. "You'll find I'm annoyingly truthful."

"Or plain annoying." She set the rosemary near her tools, then made a show of slowly taking off her smock and letting it drop to the ground.

"That too." He watched as she started on the ties at the front of her dress with nervous fingers. It was far too long until he finally came closer, stopping just out of reach, watching.

She let her dress fall and stood there feeling like an idiot for several seconds before he spoke.

"Whether you like it or not, you mean something to me." He took two big strides, and then she was in his arms, her legs wrapped around his waist, his hands in her hair. The bed was separated from the great room by heavy ivory curtains, and they brushed against her as he carried her between them.

Waking up in a nylon sleeve that would have been generous to refer to as a "two-person tent" was a humbling experience for Asha. The way her back ached in areas she'd forgotten were part of her made her feel significantly older than her age, as did the pain in her feet and calves after only one day on the road.

She'd made this journey before but never at this pace. In her dark moments, she'd notice bits of gray hair or how her hands no longer looked like her own, but this? A new level of awareness of her mortal body had been discovered. As a doctor, she should have been fascinated.

Gray hadn't been in Dearborn when they'd arrived the previous day, and his people remaining there weren't eager to share his whereabouts with two known citizens of The Disc who, upon their last visit to their lovely town, had nearly destroyed it. If they did have sick people among them, they lied about it, thereby refusing the help Asha had come to offer. Asha and Gavel had spent all of yesterday pushing themselves as fast as possible to get there, and all Asha had to show for it today was the pain. Everything hurt.

The next logical place to go was Ranlock. Gray had spent time there in his youth, along with Caster, and if someone was looking to hire experienced soldiers, they would have to stop there. But Gray was well-connected all over the Open and could be anywhere. Like the people of Dearborn, nobody would be eager to say if they'd seen him when it was Asha and Gavel asking. This was all starting to feel like one long, pointless death march.

They were behind their desired pace by almost four hours already, and although Gavel had been kind enough not to mention it, Asha was watching the sun's position in the sky as well as theirs on her father's old map of the Open. Gavel walked next to her, shortening his gait, she noticed. He was just as ancient as she, but he'd been doing this for years when the most trudging she'd done had been up and down the length of the med ward.

He had been unusually quiet since breakfast. However, he wasn't used to snuggling with his freezing wife all night when out on a mission like this. She assumed he hadn't slept well.

"I could use a break. You?" Gavel said, breath so even that Asha wanted to kick him.

She wedged her thumbs under her pack straps to take some of the weight from her shoulders. "Screw you."

He raised an eyebrow at her. "Did I really deserve that?"

"No. You also don't need a break," she said past the burning in her throat and sides. "Don't patronize me."

"That's not my intention, as you know."

"I do. I'm sorry." She reached out for his hand, and as she did, a spine from a dead prickly pear cactus, all smashed and covered up by dirt, found a weak spot in her boot and stabbed into the arch of her foot. "Motherfucker!" she hollered to the desert.

Gavel threw his pack on the ground. "Sit."

She did.

He unlaced her boot until it loosened enough to slide off. With it went her long sock and the cactus spine. Asha chewed on her curses and opened her own pack for first aid supplies. Tucked next to her bag of bandages and sheathed pair of trauma shears, wrapped in an inconspicuous length of tan cloth, was the silver canister Bug had given them. Asha hoped they'd get to use its contents to do some good out here. Save lives, if not prevent a war.

"I'm so stupid," she said as her foot throbbed deep in the muscle tissue.

Gavel plucked the spine from her boot and tossed it aside, then held up her foot up to inspect it. "Came out clean. Try not to react when I tell you—we're being followed."

She went still but managed to keep most of her surprise from her expression. "Why do you say that?" she asked as she tipped a glug of her homemade ethanol onto a square of fabric and blotted her wound.

"I heard someone this morning just before dawn, walking. They were far away, didn't get any closer, so I stayed put."

"What were they doing?"

He blew into his hands to warm them, then replied, "Based on the rhythm of what I could hear, they were pacing."

"Pacing?"

"Waiting for us to get up, I believe."

"That's wonderfully disturbing, hon. Perfect, in fact." She wrapped her foot with a bandage, using as little length as possible, and tied it off. If they ran out, nobody was likely to trade with them to replenish her stock. "Is it just one person?"

Gavel nodded as Asha pulled her sock back on. He guided her foot back into her boot and began lacing it up.

"Why haven't they attacked us already?" she asked.

"I was wondering that myself. They had the opportunity and didn't take it, which means they want something else."

"What else?" she asked, but as it left her mouth, she saw the answer in Gavel's tense shoulders. "Oh. Something that your presence makes it difficult for them to try for."

He nodded again.

Asha set her foot down. She was too sore for this shit. "Then maybe it's time you gave us a little privacy so he can take his shot?"

"Are you up for that?" he asked as he helped her to her feet.

"With this stupid injury, we have another night out here before we reach Ranlock. I want to sleep, not lie awake listening."

"All right. Try to walk, baby. With a limp, if you can. Maybe whimper a bit."

She took a step with her injured foot, and though it did throb, it was hardly immobilizing. But that was exactly how it would look to a bystander by how she yelped in pain.

Gavel guided her back down to sit on his pack as if she

couldn't support her own weight. "It's okay," he said, a touch louder than necessary. "Rest for a while. I'll head back to Dearborn. They'll have rosemary oil."

They had that exact oil—good for inflammation and pain relief—in her bag, but she would never waste it on an injury like this. "Only if you're sure," she replied.

"I'll be back before nightfall." He unhooked a blanket from where it was rolled up and attached to the bottom of his pack and wrapped it around her shoulders.

"I'm so sorry I did this. It's my fault," she said.

"No. Rest up. I'll be back as soon as I can." He kissed her on the head and took only his bow, quiver, and canteen as he ran back through the brush the way they'd come.

She sat there for what felt like an age, the cold taking over her muscles a little more every minute she didn't move. Nothing happened for at least half an hour until, finally, there was the faintest scuff of shoes against the ground in the distance. Easily missed if she hadn't been listening as hard as her ears would stretch, frigid as they were even under her beanie.

Then a voice, not far away, but directly behind her. "Hello, Asha."

A fresh trail of coldness went down her neck like the caress of a skeletal finger. That voice didn't belong to a thief or someone wanting a stranger's body, but to a murderer hunting the woman who got away—Quin.

He walked around so that he was standing in front of her. He carried almost no gear, just a large water bladder slung over his shoulder and a cinch sack tied near the front of his belt. Then of course, the weapons he had plastered to himself: a hatchet in hand, boot knife, and whatever he had concealed under his thick duffle coat. "After the way you slipped out of my apartment with that boy, I didn't feel we'd had a proper goodbye."

Asha shivered harder, fully aware that it wasn't due to the cold. "You followed us out here and stalked me for two days to say 'goodbye'?"

"You're right," he said as he rolled his shoulders like a recent prisoner basking in his newfound freedom. "I did that part for fun. Couldn't help myself."

He knelt on the ground to study her, and suddenly, Asha was back in that damn cage. Even if he'd struck out at her, she wouldn't have moved; she was paralyzed under her blanket by repressed fear. She remembered how the piece of his lip had felt rubbery in her mouth before she spat it out. He reached toward her.

Before he could touch her, an arrow struck his left side, above his heart and lungs, knocking him onto his back. Gavel came out from the brush, another arrow already nocked. Asha knew he was only waiting for Quin to sit up to draw his bow.

PART 4

TRUST

CHAPTER ELEVEN

Survivor had never been held the way Gray held her. Reskin had held her, but it hadn't been for romance. It was for heat, for keeping her from danger. And to keep her from leaving.

It wasn't cold here, not with the amount of blankets on the bed and the insulation of the tent. If anything, *he* was in danger here—on her turf, in her bed, where she could end him with the blade she kept hidden on the right side of the bedframe under the edge of the mattress. She did still feel the urge to leave, but the reason was entirely different than it had been during her years with Reskin. The danger here was that she was a *willing* captive, and Gray's touch made it difficult to fight that danger.

Gray traced his fingers around her back, making shapes maybe. Or letters. He hummed softly against her ear, and the way her chin fit in the crook of his neck was oddly comfortable.

He stopped humming. "These curtains make it feel like we're inside a cloud. You do that on purpose? Take me to heaven?"

"No such thing."

He gave her a playful squeeze. "Come on. That's pessimistic."

She rolled away from him onto her back. "You sound like my sister. She believes in God too."

"And you don't."

"If he does exist, all he's ever done is take from me."

"Hmm. It's people who do the taking, I think. Like Thallium. Tell me—is your sister worth all of this trouble?"

She thought he was joking, but there was genuine curiosity in his expression. "Yes," she said at last.

He tucked his hand between his face and pillow. "It was an impossible thing you did. Your reputation here in the Open is about to rival hers. You're on the map now."

She'd known the risk of notoriety when she went down this path. Beo had expressed the same concern. "I'll be one of Thallium's targets either way. Hiding in a hole wasn't an option anymore. Wren will like having a community around her."

"But it's not your preference."

"Even this," she smacked his chest, "whatever 'this' is that we have, makes me uncomfortable." She kissed him, then nibbled at his neck before sliding away. He groaned and tried to pull her back, but there was a rustle behind the curtains framing the end of the bed.

"I've been waiting outside," said an exasperated voice.

There was something familiar about that voice, but still, Survivor dove over Gray to grab the knife hidden under the edge of the mattress.

He sighed and pulled his pants on. "I asked you to wait."

"I have been waiting. For longer than you know," the voice said with an edge of sadness.

Survivor's heart jumped to her throat when she finally realized who was on the other side of the curtains. She bounded toward the sound of the movement, not taking time to dress, and yanked the curtains back. Then promptly dropped the knife.

Alma stood there. Alma.

Silver hair tied back in the same braid as always, deeper wrinkles around her eyes and across her forehead. Just standing there as if she'd only stepped out for a minute, not died horribly in fire along with almost everyone else Survivor had ever cared about.

"I'm sorry to interrupt," Alma said, slightly annoyed, as if Survivor had kept her waiting all these years rather than the other way around.

"It's fine," said Survivor, naked and in shock. In the presence of a dead woman, she couldn't think of anything better to say.

"I told you I would come get you," Gray said to Alma. He scooched across the bed, pants and sweater back on. He pulled the top blanket from the bed and draped it across Survivor's shoulders.

She shrugged out of it immediately. "*You* know her?"

"She's a friend, yes." He picked up the blanket and again covered Survivor with it, and this time, she let him. He spoke as he stepped away from the bed and closed the curtains behind the three of them. "I know her as Jane. She sometimes spends the cold season with us in Dearborn. My people directed her to our camp here, and she told me she knew you. I was going to bring her in to see you earlier, but then you took off your clothes, and I got, uh, sidetracked. She is a friend of yours, right?"

She kept studying Alma's face and responded to Gray automatically, distracted as she was. "Her name's not Jane. It's Alma. She's my mother. *Was* my mother."

Alma pushed the hair back from Survivor's face with

rough, callused hands. "Still your mother. That's not a title you lose, even in death."

At her words, Survivor felt like a wayward adolescent again. The first time she'd met Alma, her voice had enveloped Survivor's listless existence and the weight of her guilt at leaving Beo like a worn blanket. It was simple, curt, yet effective in easing the cold ache deep in Survivor's heart and bones. Alma's voice wrapped around Survivor again, and defenses she'd never consciously erected—fearlessness, drive, anger— sank into its fabric and realized for the first time in a long time just how tired they were.

"Ma? It's really you?"

"It's really me, child."

Survivor dropped to her knees, and Alma went down with her. As her tears fell, Survivor became vaguely aware that Gray had left the tent. Her crying turned to deep sobs that shook her body and reached into her gut. Alma held her silently, tried to run her fingers through the tangles in her hair.

Was it really possible that, for just once, God had given something back?

The tingling of Eydis' arms woke her, but the accosting light of the room against her eyelids made her hesitate to open them. Last she remembered, she had been falling asleep in Thallium's bed to the sound of him snoring. It was clear that she was no longer horizontal but vertical. Sweat pasted her cotton night-dress to her front. She resisted the urge to open her eyes until she'd calmed herself.

"You've been twitching for a while now. I know you're awake," said Thallium as if from across the room.

She squinted against the oppressive heat and light of the fire that Thallium had built so large that it was spilling out onto the hearth, threatening to ignite the rug.

He sat atop his desk, cross-legged and shirtless, cigarette dangling from his lips as he casually turned a page in her red lab notebook. Her heart took to hammering. How much had he read?

Finally, he tossed the notebook aside on his desk. The heat from the fire had to be scorching on his skin. "Seems you really loved Liam. Shame what happened." He took his cigarette between two fingers and blew smoke. "You know, I think a part of me loved you. Did you ever feel something real with me? I'm genuinely curious."

Eydis tried to lower her arms to no avail. Her wrists were tied high above her head, the rope looped over a metal cross-beam. The tingling in her arms had progressed to loss of feeling. She tried to think past the dizziness of her head and the shock of what was happening. "What's going on, sir?"

"I have to apologize—I raided your medication shelf in the lab. Mid...mida..." He picked up a brown glass vial next to him on the desk and started to read it, then tossed it over his shoulder instead. It shattered against the mantle. "Something I've seen you use on Wren a time or two, back when *she* was the most interesting experiment around. Had to use an entire bottle on you! Barely had time to string you up before you started to rouse. Impressive."

"You drugged me?" she said.

He flicked his cigarette into the fire behind him and hopped down from the desk. "Drug an android? Well, that would be impossible, wouldn't it?"

It would be. Which meant, somehow, he knew. She had been more distracted lately, caught up in the feelings of her past. In what it felt like to be human and whole, then remade into something strong but hollow. Reliving it had cost her somewhere—details in her behavior, which she'd controlled successfully since she'd met Thallium's father, must have given her away.

"What are you implying?" she asked, delaying the inevitable.

"Again, I apologize. Allow me to be clear." Three silver knives sat near the edge of the desk in a perfect line. She'd seen the set before, his favorite for target practice in the private yard of the Main House. He took the knife closest to the front of the desk and crossed the room to her, where he rested the flat side of the metal against her chest. It was warm from the fire, nearly hot. "I assert—not imply—that you are human and that you have been lying to me since before I could form words."

She kept quiet. He would keep talking if she did, and she needed to know what he knew.

He pulled the knife away and started pacing. Sweat gleamed all along his back, which had turned a fiery pink. "At first, I thought that meant that my father had been lying to me too—he must have known about you. That was until I realized that, if he had known, he would have dissected you. Which spiraled into the rude awareness that, most likely, that's what you think *I'd* do to you if I found out. You weren't wholly wrong in that assumption. Of late, I've been disgusting myself with how much I've emulated my father, though I never made the conscious decision to." He kept talking indistinctly to himself. A quiet rant as he gestured emphatically.

She chose her words with caution. "You wouldn't want to tear apart someone who—"

His knife whooshed past her left cheek, slicing the inside of her arm stretched above her head. The knife thwacked into the empty bookcase behind her. The tingling on that side dissipated as pain took its place for but a moment before the cut closed, leaving a delicate smear of red where it had been.

He leaned in close and gently, almost seductively, ran his hand along her arm. "Huh. For all my suspicions, I did not expect that." He looked her up and down as if seeing her for the first time, then returned to the desk where his other two knives waited. "I may have to continue experimenting to see if there's any damage I can make stick." He picked up another knife. "However, as educated as I am—highly self-educated if I might be so brash to say—I don't possess the knowledge to figure out why you're still young. And apparently invulnerable to an unknown degree. Strong too if our adult activities are any indication. After me, the next best candidate to pick you apart would be our little Bug. But she'd likely not tolerate putting her own mentor under her knife, eh?

"So not only do I have nobody capable of figuring out what exactly you are and why, but I don't have the time to investigate it. Caster is coming for me, and I don't believe he's the only one —someone has corrupted my own men. They'll stick a knife in my back any day now." He stabbed the air enthusiastically with his blade. "Therefore, I don't want to cut you up. Instead, I'd like to ask you a couple of simple questions. If you answer them, I'll untie those ropes."

She fidgeted. If he was correct—and not merely paranoid— that there were multiple conspirators against him, then she had to get out of here as quickly as possible. This had not been her plan. When Wren returned to The Disc after killing those Marauders in the Open, Eydis' need for Thallium's resources and influence to find Wren's siblings had begun its slow death. Survivor had been a tool she'd used to enrage those in the Open that Thallium had wronged. She'd meant for him to die as a result of his own sins. His lockdown had postponed that, but it was inevitable. When the war started, Eydis and Wren were going to disappear.

But now, it was apparent that the war had already begun. She'd been so caught up in Wren that she hadn't seen the danger within the city. There were too many unknowns. She had to get out of The Disc with Wren. But first, she had to get out of this room. "I have answers to give."

He held his arms open wide. "Excellent!" In a flash, he threw the second knife at her other side, cutting her right arm the same as her left. It healed quickly. "Fair warning, if you lie to me even once more, I will aim two more inches inward to see what happens. As much as your body might heal itself, I'm betting a knife through your eye would still hurt." He picked up his final blade.

She waited for his questions. He waited to ask them.

"Are you human?" he said at last.

"Yes. Mostly."

He paced in front of the desk. "What does that mean?"

She swallowed stickily against the dry air in the study. "When I was human, before The Fall, I was part of a research team charged with making humans better."

"Oh? I feel we're already quite sufficient." He waved along his own body as if it were evidence of the power of humanity.

"For this world, in most ways, we are."

His eyebrows shot up. "But not for another world?"

"To travel to and settle new worlds, we needed to be sturdier. To live longer. My team made that possible."

"Let's see, by my rudimentary math," he tapped his blade against his fingertips, "you're at least two centuries old. As a long-term case study, I'd say you were successful. Congratulations. Seems like a lonely life, though."

She needed to get his focus off of her. Tied up here, she couldn't protect Wren. Especially now that her longtime dreams were becoming reality, she couldn't let Thallium interfere. "It has been lonely. Until recently." She hesitated, anxious about how he would respond to what she was about to admit to.

He gestured for her to continue.

"Caster did not recover from the poison on his own when he brought Wren and her sister here from the Open," she said at last.

The array of emotions that fluttered across his face was astonishing. He settled on cold indignation. "You did something to my son?"

"He was dying. I saved his life."

He took to pacing again. "Then the people you do this to, they need to be dying first?"

"No. But the change it causes can kill them. With Caster already dying, it was a risk worth taking. For him, for you. For Wren."

"My, my. You are quite the giver." He twitched as if someone had interrupted him. "I know! If you're going to be here, please do be quieter," he snapped, gaze cutting sideways toward something Eydis couldn't see. He looked to Eydis again. "Does Wren know about all this? Is she like you?"

"She knows. But she's not like me." Eydis chose her words carefully. "She's something else entirely."

"My secret weapon," he said fondly. His attention went elsewhere, listening to something off to his side, then his face grew contrite. "Yes, my dear. I apologize." He reached out awkwardly with his free hand like he was waiting for someone to take it, then dropped it. "But it *was* her intended role. One she may yet assume if she so chooses."

Even though she felt like she was interrupting a private conversation, Eydis said delicately, "Sir? You now intend to give Wren a choice?" On the surface, it didn't seem like a radical idea. But compared to everything she knew of Thallium up until now, it was profound. Revelatory change that was nothing short of miraculous.

He shook his head at Eydis' voice as though he'd forgotten she was there. "Ah, well, I've recently had it pointed out to me that I'm a woeful hypocrite for viewing the woman my son loves as less than human. Isn't that how you put it?" he asked the invisible participant in the conversation. An indulgent smile lit his face, and if Eydis hadn't thought it so unbelievable, she would have sworn he cleared his throat against the emotion trying to sneak into his voice.

Her wrists started to scream under the tightness of the ropes, and her shoulders burned nearly as powerfully as the fire across the room. "What do you want from me, sir? Now that you know what I am, how can I serve you better?"

He tossed the knife up and caught it by its point before reaching over his shoulder to use the handle to scratch his back. "For a genius, that was an exceptionally dumb question. We obviously both have a problem here with the traitors in our midst. I'm willing and able to solve that problem for us. Just need a little help from Wren and you. Wren as my first line of defense, of course. You as my contingency."

"Contingency? I don't—"

"I need you to change me like you changed my son. I need to be like you."

Eydis fell silent. His request made her feel even heavier against the pull of the ropes.

He spun the hilt of the knife in his hand and caught it as he spoke. "Before you bring it up, I understand that this attempt may kill me. But you can try and you will. I have enemies within my own staff and home—should I be overpowered, they will not take my life. I won't be assassinated. No knife in the back. At least, none that I can't recover from. Not to mention that eternal life doesn't seem like a bad side effect." He crossed the room to her. With a hot hand on her cheek, his tone turned genuine, all drama and posturing dropped as if they were close friends who didn't have need for either anymore. "I suppose there are lots of things you'd like to say right now. How I'm evil and allowing me to live forever would be a terrible mistake. How whatever you're really up to with Wren will be undermined by my infinite existence. I understand your concerns. But I think, even though our time today has been brief, it's been illuminating on both our parts. It's clear you're not the affable android I once took you to be, and perhaps I'm not the stock villain you've believed me to be. In light of all this, we may find we can be real allies to one another. That's what I would like."

He drew closer, and their lips nearly touched when he reached high above, and the ropes holding Eydis' hands snapped. He tucked the knife into the waist of his pants as she hugged her arms around herself in relief.

She cleared her throat and tried to focus, still dizzy from the heat and the whirring of her own mind. "Sir, I have to make the risk clear. Caster was the first test subject in a long time. I don't know what could happen to you."

His head pitched to the side, listening to something unseen again. "Oh, all right. I will," he whispered. Then he threw his arms around Eydis in a massive, sweaty hug. "Thank you for your honesty at last. I'll get my affairs in order. Tomorrow, I'll come by the lab, and we'll fix our problem together. Starting with releasing Wren so we can make these traitors rethink their actions. Good night for now!" With a slap on her behind, he vaulted over the desk and sank into the chair by the roaring fire. He took a sheet of paper from the tray on his desk.

Eydis passed back into the cool retreat of his bedroom to the sound of his pen scratching away as he whistled a jaunty tune. The marks on her wrists were already gone, but even so, she felt as if the ropes were still there binding her like her limited options bound her now. She needed to leave with Wren into the Open, but that would take preparation. A couple of days, at least. To buy time, she would have to honor Thallium's request tomorrow. The idea of giving him what he wanted made bile rise up her throat, and the only comfort she could find in that moment was in Wren herself. Eydis would give her the chance to intervene—she hoped Wren was capable of doing so.

Survivor and Alma sat next to each other on pillows at the low table in Survivor's tent, sharing breakfast the morning after Alma's unexpected arrival. Last night, the why and how of Alma's reappearance mattered little compared to the importance of her remaining now that she was back. They'd slept close to one another, Survivor's arms around Alma as if to continually verify that she was not only real, but not going to disappear again.

They had finished warm bowls of creamy grits and now picked at a shared plate of dried fruit as they listened to the sounds of dawn outside—the metallic *shink* of blades being sharpened several tents down, indistinct conversation from the clan's dining area, and the shuffling of people passing by on their way to assigned tasks. Survivor pushed her side up against Alma's, convinced that if she didn't keep touching her, the woman would reveal herself to be a hallucination after all.

Survivor tossed a half-eaten slice of apple back onto the plate. "You were dead," she said at last. "I believed you were dead."

Alma patted her knee and spoke around the fruit she slowly chewed. "I meant for you to. Otherwise you would have come after me."

Survivor stared at her, watching her eat as if entranced. "Wren was right. She never believed it. Not like I did."

After a large swallow and a sip of water, Alma turned her attention fully on Survivor. "Her intuition is rarely wrong. She was right about you, after all. When you scared the rest of us."

"I scared you?" There was no reason for Survivor to feel hurt, but she did all the same. She'd thought she'd made it clear that the kids had no need to fear her. Only those who tried to hurt them needed to fear her.

"Hmm. It was more that I was scared of what you were capable of. Never afraid you might do something to me or the kids. Wouldn't have let you in the family if I were."

Survivor steeled herself and asked the inevitable question they both knew was coming. "What the hell happened to you, Ma?"

In her time with the kids, Alma hadn't seemed to get any older. She'd been constant, a landmark on the horizon around which the sun and moon rose but took no effect. Looking at her now, waiting for the answer to her question, Survivor was overwhelmed by how much she had aged. Not just physically, but there was a heaviness to her presence. Her head hung forward as if too much for her shoulders, which were likewise hunched. "The same thing that happened to the rest of us—I lost my home to the fire. Nearly took all of our lives."

The hope of another miracle ached in Survivor's chest, and she was so unused to the feeling that she didn't recognize it until words were spilling from her. "Are you saying that others survived?"

Alma nodded as she reached over and squeezed Survivor's knee. "After I sent you away with Wren, I went back into the glade. I gathered who I could—four alive and two dead."

"Who died?" Survivor asked quickly. Delaying the answer wouldn't make it any easier.

Alma sniffed and wiped under her eyes, which Survivor politely ignored. "Gully from a fallen tree, Mack in the fire. The four remaining I helped through the blazing end of the forest away from the men who'd come to take us. We hid in the canyon until they left, then climbed out. I spent time putting them in permanent homes, homes of people I could trust. I check in with them every six months. It's safer if we're not all together."

"And you know Gray?"

Alma waggled her wiry eyebrows and chuckled a wheezy chuckle. "Not as well as you, clearly."

"Ma. Answer the question."

"I go to Dearborn for seasonal work. It's better if I make my living on the move. I have various identities—helps keep me concealed. And I always listen for news of anything unusual in the Open. When I checked in at Dearborn as usual, they told me Gray had sent word of an alliance with Marauders. They were united under a new leader, someone who betrayed The Gentleman. Not hard to figure out it was you, child. Of course, everyone's been hearing about Wren, but they call her 'Thallium's weapon.'"

Survivor picked up a prune and rolled it between two fingers absently. Her mind whirred with questions. It was unusual for it to be so active and uncertain. The only way to make it stop was to get answers. "How did you know it was her they were talking about? And why do you need to stay hidden? From who?"

Alma hunched forward farther. "When it was just us in the forest, did you really believe we were hiding from typical evil?"

"I knew *I* wasn't—I was hiding from the devil. You all wanted to keep to yourselves too, which worked out just fine for me. I never thought about it beyond that."

"We were doing more than merely keeping to ourselves.

Before you came, they'd send bounty hunters. Occasionally, they would get lucky. A pair actually hiked down into the canyon once, caught a glimpse of our fire. Never should have happened, but I guess they were getting desperate. I imagine the bounty was significant."

Impatience gnawed at Survivor and set her feet tapping. "Ma! Who were 'they?' Who was after you?"

"Eventually, the hunters stopped coming," Alma continued, clear she would get to her point on her own time. "Until the fire. It wasn't an act of nature. I came across a soldier as I left with the children. He'd tripped and hit his head on a rock. Common accident at night in the Open. Cost him his life. He had a little black bracelet engraved with a small V slashed through on one side."

Realization hit Survivor like a thousand shards of glass sliding back into place all at once. "You're from The Disc."

Alma sipped from her water slowly, then finally answered, "Yes. When I lived there, Thallium's father, Valcin, was Principal. I served in his house, primarily assisting Eydis. Gray told me you spent some time in The Disc—did you meet her?"

The beautiful woman in white who spoke in riddles. "Yes. Wasn't a fan."

Alma chewed on the inside of her cheek before asking, "What did she say to you?"

Survivor bit through the prune she'd been playing with. "Drivel, mostly. About how Wren's restored, Thallium's evil. Tried to get into my head by pretending we were connected somehow. Like she knew me." She spat the pit from the prune across the tent.

"She always did like to wax poetic." Alma cleared her throat. "Anyway, Valcin wanted to use the technology we recovered. They were just pieces and parts of machines, bits of metal, but they had once been put together in such a way that humans relied on them to live. And live well.

"Literal tons of technology were lost in an instant during the gate accident," she continued. "The machines man had made were vulnerable, and their destruction pressed the reset button for humanity. Valcin wanted to protect what we pulled from the dirt. Eydis helped him do it. She's absolutely brilliant. I asked her where she came from once, and she said she was made hundreds of years ago. Strange as she is, she's not just any android off the assembly line. She's unique.

"She pointed out that the most resilient things in the world are humans. They survived The Fall, radioactive fallout, earthquakes, diseases. What if they could combine the two—humans and technology? *Really* combine them. We tried and failed, initially." She paused, as if considering how much more to say.

"They did something to Wren," Survivor prompted.

Alma shook her head slowly. "They didn't *do* something to her. They *made* her. Then all of her siblings after the initial promise she showed. They were able to embed aspects of technology that existed before The Fall into human DNA so that they could be carried down through inheritance. Humans with machines in their genetic code. They called them 'Carriers' because they carried the hope of a better future in their bodies."

"How do you know all of this? You had to be more than just an 'assistant' to that android."

Alma turned toward her. "I was a scientist. However, when the Carriers' abilities weren't manifesting fast enough as they grew from infancy, Eydis retasked me. I was to take care of the children, bond with them, give them someone they could trust and love. It worked, and they started to show their abilities. But one thing Eydis didn't account for." She closed her eyes as if letting the memories wash over her. "I started to love them back."

Survivor stood, no longer able to contain the energy pulsing through her—these pieces of the puzzle made all the bullshit they'd gone through in The Disc make sense. Wren's connection to it all, why they wanted her so badly. "You took them, didn't you?"

Alma started to push off of the table to stand, and Survivor jumped to help her up. "I did. Eydis never stopped looking." She smacked Survivor's cheek lightly. "And then you two! You just walked right in, didn't you?"

All because of that idiot prince boy and his friend's good boots. How had Survivor been so stupid? "It was my fault."

Alma shrugged her bent shoulder. "Doesn't matter now. I'd hoped that by keeping away from you that it would make the two of you less recognizable. Eydis knows what I look like well enough, but not you two. Wren was a child when I took her, and you..." She trailed off. "You were a stranger to them. I thought it would keep you safe," she whispered hoarsely like her throat was stuck together. She reached for her water on the table, but Survivor beat her to it.

"You could have told us you were alive at least!" Survivor protested.

Alma paused in her drinking. "Could I have? Would you have let me leave if you knew that? Would Wren?" The woman had her there, and from the way she returned to guzzling water instead of waiting for an answer, she knew it.

"Then why are you back now?" Survivor asked.

"With all the commotion you two have been causing, it appears that the time for hiding is over." She set the empty cup on the table with a clatter. "Wren is still in The Disc?"

"Not because she wants to be. Last message I got from Thallium's son, she was still locked up in the Main House. That's all he knew—don't think Wren likes him for his brains. Must be that Goldilocks hair. I don't know."

"Thallium's son?" Alma said suspiciously. "He's with you?"

"We have the same end goal—get Wren out of that city. Hide her. Like you wanted, like you did successfully for years."

Alma attempted to tuck Survivor's hair behind her ears, all in vain. "You kept her safe for a long time."

"No, no I fucked up Ma. It was my fault we ended up in The Disc in the first place."

Alma didn't argue with her. She kissed her on the forehead and said simply, "We can fix it."

"That's what I've been trying to do out in this scrotum of a desert." She took in the sight of her luxurious dwelling, the thick fabric, and the warmth of it all. Yes, she'd gone down this path initially for Wren, but standing here in the midst of her triumph, she had to admit that part of her motivation had been far more selfish. It was time to refocus. "I'm going to take her back, Ma. I swear to you, I'm going to get her back."

Alma put her arms around her and thumped her between the shoulders. "I'll help you do it."

Alma used to dwarf Survivor by a full head of height, but now, they were nearly even. "How?" Survivor asked.

"I worked in that lab for years. Valcin always planned for emergencies, backups upon backups. He insisted that every secure facility have more than one way out. The lab does too. The same way I got Wren and the children out last time. Underground."

Excitement sent Survivor's fingers twitching. "You know how to get to her."

"Unless they destroyed the tunnel, yes. I doubt it though. Their mistake wasn't building the exit but telling me about it. I'm sure they didn't repeat that mistake. It's most likely still there, just well-concealed. But I can't get into The Disc itself."

Survivor pulled the keycard from her shirt, held it aloft,

feeling proud for the first time since the start of this conversation. "I've got that taken care of."

Alma smiled. She put her hands on her hips and stretched her back. When she came back up, she asked, "When can we leave?"

CHAPTER TWELVE

Wren had dozed off. For how long, she didn't know, but she woke slowly. While her vision was still hazy, she saw the outline of a face across from hers. Tall forehead, blond hair pulled back. Her body jerked ungracefully, both startled and thrilled by Caster's arrival. Finally. The last bit of sleep left her eyes as they shot open. Instead of Caster, Thallium stood there, and Wren's heart sank. He raised his arms as if to embrace her through the glass.

Ever since Wren had arrived in The Disc, Thallium had treated her as "other." "Special." But there was something different in the way he viewed her through the glass today. It was as if he saw her as a person for the first time. He let his arms fall and drew closer. The lines at the outsides of his eyes deepened as he gave her a tired smile, and for a moment, he appeared shockingly human.

"I'm sorry to wake you," he said finally. "But I'm afraid we need to talk."

Wren crossed her arms, more an act of modesty than of defiance, and waited for him to speak.

"Eydis and I have been chatting," he said with a quick look over his shoulder. Eydis stood behind him, next to the recliner Caster had sat in when he went into Wren's dream with her weeks ago. She wore a beautiful white dress trimmed around the waist and long sleeves in gold. From the way her posture sagged, it looked like she was about to bury someone. Perhaps herself. "It seems that all of our time here in the Main House will be coming to an end soon," announced Thallium.

Wren's confusion must have shown on her face.

Thallium popped his lips and wagged a finger at her. "I suppose you wouldn't know what's going on outside. I'll catch you up. Our enemies are recruiting my Keepers. Caster is not on my side. That second bit probably doesn't surprise you much."

The first real smile Wren had felt in weeks tugged at her mouth.

"I didn't think so." He grabbed the rolling chair from the console near the isolation unit and sat before her, hands clasped together between his open knees. "Because someone is coming after—or through—those closest to me, it implies they aren't planning an outward assault, but an infiltration. They want to take The Disc without a fight, or at least, not much of one.

"Which should be easy since they've been turning my people against me, making them believe I'm sending my Keepers after their women and children. All that I'm left with, the only hope of freedom *you* are left with," he held his hands open as if to receive a gift, "is your ability to defend us."

Wren had known this was coming ever since Eydis had put her in the box. Thallium's intentions for her had not been nearly as mysterious as those of Eydis. Even though she expected this, she couldn't help but open her mouth to laugh at the absurdity of the situation. Though she made no sound in the fluid, the tensing of her belly and the rippling chuckles coming through the BCI were fairly satisfying. Thallium watched her patiently as if her reaction didn't surprise him. Once she'd gathered her composure, she said over the BCI, "After everything, why would I defend you?"

He stood to sit backward in the chair, arms crossed on top of it. "I suppose, in the end, you might not," he replied. "I'll leave it to you to decide. If it's Caster who unseats me, I expect you'll help him. The thought of him being the one, demanding his birthright from the man who taught him to take what he wanted, makes me proud. It hurts, but I understand his drive and respect it. In that case, I wish you both well, and I'll figure out what's next for me in this life.

"If, however, it's not Caster who comes for me, but someone else," Thallium continued, "I hope you'll fight. With me, you know the brand of evil you're getting. No surprises here. Additionally, I will promise your freedom. A new ruler? They'll see you as a weapon only, as I once did. They'll take you to war and, in between battles, stick you back in your case." He made a rectangle shape with his finger in the air. "But if you come out now, we can make a show of your power that will scare these scorpions back into their burrows until I can cut their heads off for good."

Eydis went up to the control console. "It's time to come out, little one. You're ready." She started typing.

"No, I'm not," Wren replied firmly.

Eydis left a hand on the keyboard but turned to hold Wren's gaze over Thallium's shoulder. "Yes, you are. You have to do this now." She then looked pointedly at Thallium's back, then to Wren again, a hard and determined edge to her expression.

So that was it. Eydis wanted Wren to kill Thallium.

Wren looked at the Principal, his face that was so much like Caster's, then back to Eydis. "I can't do it," she said

quietly in her mind, careful of the words she directed to
the BCI.

"You can," Eydis urged Wren on as if she needed her out of
the box right that moment. She pointed boldly at Thallium,
whose focus remained on the box. "I believe you can handle
this, Wren. You've come to accept this part of yourself." Her
tone turned deeper as she added, "We can't stay here any
longer."

Wren had been desperate for this moment. For weeks, she'd
wanted nothing more than to be let out. She'd bloodied her
knuckles demanding freedom as she felt her sense of self slipping through her fingers like the sand of the Open.

She'd decided to unleash this force inside her, to finally
accept it if that meant getting out of here. Going to the stars.
Being free of the pain of resisting. This moment, here, it was
the time to just let go of it all.

But instead of feeling relief at this moment's arrival, she
panicked for the world above her. Not one person would be
safe once the seal of the isolation unit was broken. Thallium
wouldn't be the only one to die. It would be Caster. It would be
men and women shopping in the market. Children who had
nightmares of sharp-toothed, hunched things would die
instantly from something far more frightening if she lost
control. It would only take seconds.

Wren pressed her hands against the front of the unit as if
she could retreat farther inside, and her words came out via the
BCI in a rush. "If I come out, there's no going back. People will
die."

"Well, here's hoping, anyway." Thallium crossed his fingers
and kissed them. He stood and came close to the box. "I'm sure
you'll be unsteady on your feet at first. Don't worry—I'll catch
you."

Wren shook her head and spoke to Eydis, ignoring Thallium entirely. "Good people will die. Whole families. They have a chance at living out their lives simply and with joy. That chance was taken from me; I won't take it from them."

"Then you plan on staying here?" Thallium asked, mimicking how she held herself in the box with his arms across his chest. "How long do you think you can stand that? Another month? A year? A lifetime?"

An image came to Wren's mind of her still in the box, red hair turned white, eyes just as white, like she had turned into something beyond this world and any place she had in it. It might be easier that way—fully given over to a new identity outside of the real world. "Until I know I can save people rather than kill them, I will stay here."

Eydis let her hand fall from the keyboard. "I see."

Thallium held out his hand to the box as if Wren could take it. "Wren, I'm offering your freedom. Please accept it."

"Get out!" Wren screamed. "Leave me here. Leave me out of your war and out of your lives. Leave me and don't come—" Painful feedback, high and warbling, came through the speakers before they cut out. She settled for screaming "back" into the liquid.

The three of them stood in the echo of Wren's pain. Then Thallium turned toward Eydis, shoulders squared. "I'll take that contingency now."

Eydis pursed her lips, then spoke as if disciplining a student. "No, sir."

Thallium took leisurely steps toward her. "We had an agreement."

The same woman Wren had seen when Eydis lost her temper over Liam's untimely death emerged—she held herself more loosely, limbs and posture relaxed as if her mask had been heavy, and she was relieved to have it off. "I believed your son deserved eternal life. I don't believe you do."

Thallium got close to her and brought her chin up with a gentle push of his open hand. "It's up to you then? To decide whether to give life or withhold it?"

"As someone who has toyed with the lives of others since adolescence, surely you understand the impulse." She kissed him once on the lips. "You can't kill me."

He put his arms around her. "There's more than one way to die." He slapped her on the back and then leapt away.

Eydis fell to the ground in a fit of seizing. Wren had no idea what was going on until she spotted the small black circle between her shoulder blades—a shock tablet. After seconds that felt far longer, the seizing stopped.

Thallium hiked up his pants and dropped down to squat near Eydis, out of her reach. "Got one of the guys in tech to hook this tablet up to my ID bracelet so I can turn it on and off. They've been bored, locked out of the lab and all. Amazing, isn't it?" He pressed a button on his bracelet again, sending another shock through Eydis, then released it. "Say you'll give me what I want, or I will let this go until your heart gives out. When your body heals and you wake up, you'll be bound and gagged. I'll throw you in a dark cell to live out your eternity or until you give me what I asked you for in the first place." He sank back deeper onto his heels. "Just tell me when to stop."

Eydis writhed again, and this time, Thallium didn't let go of the button.

Wren screamed, but no sound came from the BCI this time. Her body shook with rage coming from somewhere deep within her, beyond any conscious choice to feel it. The part of her that Eydis had nurtured and encouraged thrashed—indignant and furious. Wren's body glowed, but before the light could shift to the deep purple at which point the power peaked, Eydis screamed through the tremors, "Stop!"

Eydis fell still as the shock tablet went quiet. Wren's body mimicked Eydis' stillness, the light coming from her pausing in its growth, desperate for Eydis to move.

And move she did. Slowly at first, but she managed to stand. "I'll do it," she said through tight lips.

"I'd hoped you might!" said Thallium with a clap. "Let's go fetch whatever you need, then." He held his arm out to usher her ahead, and after straightening her dress, she headed for the stairs. Plodding at first, but her steps turned more and more sure as she went.

Alone in the lab, Wren felt the urge to sleep as the adrenaline finally passed. Eydis and Thallium returned, and because they ignored her and no longer argued, she found it easier to breathe and sink into the cool comfort of the fluid.

Thallium walked to the same chair in which Wren had sat when she and Caster went into her dreams. As he sat and reclined in the chair, Eydis took a small plastic case from the pocket of her skirt. She took a pair of tweezers from her other pocket and removed something from the case—a Biorg. Out of Wren's forced memories and into the present.

"You will feel a slight pinch," Eydis said to Thallium, "on the inside of your wrist."

He flipped his arm over to expose its underside. "Anything else I should know?"

"You may die," she said, and the way she said it made it sound as if she was hopeful for that outcome.

Thallium held his arm up off the chair. "Just like any other day."

This man, who had hurt everyone Wren loved, was going to live forever.

Wren wearily mouthed "no" over and over, but still no sound came from the BCI. She watched as Eydis touched the seed to Thallium's skin. It awoke, that same little silverfish from Eydis' memories, and disappeared into his wrist with a quick slither that Wren would have missed if she'd blinked. She expected the messy, painful spectacle of Liam's change, even that of Eydis' which had ended successfully. But nothing happened.

Thallium opened and closed his hand as if expecting to feel something. "Did it not work?"

Eydis bent over and examined his eyes. "It worked."

"Hmm. May I borrow those?" He held his hand out for Eydis' tweezers.

She dropped them on his palm, and without hesitation, he stabbed them into his opposite shoulder.

Wren flinched, sending a wave through the fluid of the isolation unit.

He tore out the tweezers and tossed them onto the floor, where their impact left little red specks on the tile. He yanked his black shirt collar aside and raised his head to peek under the fabric. Then he grinned and pulled Eydis down by the front of her dress to kiss him.

Eydis pushed him away—the first time Wren had seen her do so. Thallium ignored her, and the recliner slammed upright with the force of him leaping out of it. He stretched his arms out and rolled his neck as if he'd woken up in a new body which, Wren realized, he had.

The last thing in the world that Asha wanted to be doing was treating a wound on Quin. But God was funny that way. She rebandaged the puncture wound Gavel's arrow had made on the left side of Quin's upper chest. It was healing nicely. Gavel's draw was so strong that the arrow had gone nearly through Quin's back, so removing it had been easy enough. Now it was just a matter of keeping it uninfected. Although if

God wanted to be even funnier, that would be a great way to do it—allow this warrior to die because his wound wasn't clean enough. But that wouldn't happen because Asha was, damn it all, an excellent doctor.

They were nearly to Ranlock, would be in a few more hours after they broke from having their midday rest. Gavel had eaten his lunch quickly and stood with his bow at the ready. Not drawn, but an arrow nocked as he guarded Asha while she finished up with Quin's wound. Asha pulled Quin's shirt back onto his shoulder.

"You aged well," Quin said.

"Shut up," she and Gavel said together.

"It was a compliment." Quin buttoned his shirt with hands secured together with e-binds, apparently unbothered by the cold that ate through all of Asha's clothing layers no matter the time of day. "I wasn't going to hurt you."

"That's what you keep saying. Bizarre that it doesn't sound any more convincing each time you say it." Asha closed up her pack and stood, keeping her weight off of her injured foot that nagged at her with each step. "Might as well bless us all with silence."

"Move," Gavel ordered Quin, gesturing for him to walk first. "Don't act like you don't know the way."

Gavel and Asha walked next to one another with Quin out ahead. Asha's teeth were sore from grinding them against the stabbing pain in her foot, an aching reminder of how out of practice she was out here. The air was so dry that she could have sworn she heard the outer skin of her hands tearing as she made fists and stuffed them into her pockets. Everything around them was likewise parched—leafless ocotillo that would grow leaves in the summer rains, creosote whose evergreen foliage was incomplete without its tiny, yellow flowers.

Nearly every winter, one good, heavy snowfall came to the

Open, bringing relieving moisture that would take them through to spring. In The Disc, they gathered the snow on the outskirts of the city into deep barrels to be added to the water refinery. As Asha imagined snow hugging the rises and falls of the tan hills around her, she wondered if she'd be out here in the Open when it happened this year. Part of her craved the peace of it.

Quin called back, "Ranlock's a nasty place. You're a sweet couple—why would you want to stick your hands in that rat's nest?"

"Better question for you to consider in silence: why did you follow us when you had a perfectly warm little apartment in The Disc?" said Asha.

Quin spoke loudly so they could hear him as he pitched his weight forward to mount a hill. "I told you—I was bored there. And the three of us have unfinished business."

"I could finish it now," said Gavel, even though he'd shouldered his bow to make the ascent.

"I know you could, Beta," Quin replied, then added, "Part of me wants you to."

Before he could elaborate any further, all three of them stopped as a smell wafted down from the top of the hill.

Decay.

They stopped talking and went faster to reach the top. When they did, Asha's eyes burned, in part from the stench, in part from the despair that she felt.

Lying in a shallow trench were five bodies. Three of them older, two middle-aged. They'd been there a while. Even though it was cold out, the sun was still the sun, and it had done a number on their exposed faces already—faces covered in the dried, black remnants of rubedo.

"This is why we're out here, Quin. To stop this," Gavel said. "You will not keep us from our mission."

"I don't intend to," replied Quin as he knelt and tossed dirt into the trench as a sign of respect.

"What *do* you intend—" Asha started, but Gavel cut her off with a hand signal asking for silence. He cocked his head to listen, but before he could even turn around, four Marauders popped up from behind them, having climbed the hill in stealth while capitalizing on the distraction of the mass grave. They were dressed in white with white face coverings, as if they'd been the ones who had laid these people to rest.

Gavel went for his bow, but too slowly—two Marauders were restraining him before he could get his hands on his weapon. Quin put up his bound hands in surrender. Asha reached for the knife in her pocket, but she'd barely grazed its cool metal with her fingertips before something hit her hard on the side of the head and she passed out.

Asha woke to the worst headache she'd ever had, underneath the highest tent ceiling she'd ever seen. She rolled onto her stomach and pushed up onto her knees so quickly that everything started to go dark again.

"Take it easy, Ash," said someone nearby. A hand went to her back. "Your men are in the tent next door. Perfectly fine."

As Asha's vision came into focus, she raised her head to see Gray helping her into a sitting position. "You. I'm here to find you."

"Well, you found me!" Gray said. He gave a faux punch to her chin and pushed his stupid splinter to the side of his mouth before saying, "But before we can chat about why, someone else would like to ask you a few questions. Friendly questions, I've been promised." He moved away. Behind him on an ottoman, sitting like a queen in a deep blue cotton dress, was Survivor.

Asha pinched the bridge of her nose. "You've got to be fucking kidding me."

Survivor hadn't allowed her party to stop to eat until nightfall, and now, she was starving. She recognized the irony of that. She'd spent years eating bits and pieces of nearly anything to sustain herself, and now only after a couple of cushy days of eating her fill, her stomach had already grown weak.

With her and Alma, she'd brought the third highest ranking soldiers from three of the clans. Any more and they would no longer be able to maintain the stealth their mission required. She still had doubts about the loyalty of the second ranking soldiers who had watched helplessly as she killed their Masters and Commanders. But the third ranking soldiers she had met with individually. They were particularly eager for a promotion, and as for the deaths of those above them, Survivor hadn't seen any tears streaming down their scarred faces over the loss. In fact, they had been among those chanting the loudest after Survivor's ascension. They would do to assist in infiltrating The Disc. Beo and Amelie would keep the tender new arrangements they'd set in place with the clans from falling apart in her absence. She trusted nobody else to do so.

One of the soldiers was cooking two large snakes, hunted just before sundown, over a large fire he'd built earlier. The two other soldiers patrolled outside the light of the fire, on guard. They paced a wide circle around their camp, shadows blending into more shadow. Survivor sat with her back against a wall of rock, which stretched over her and a sleeping Alma in a low overhang. They faced the fire and the open span of black desert beyond it. It was bizarre having an above-ground fire like this at night. But then, Survivor and her clansmen were what people would be hiding *from* out in the Open now. She had nobody to fear in this darkness anymore.

The soldier who'd hunted the snakes—Cowan, he'd called

himself—had been smart enough to bottle the serpents' blood. The bottle sat on the ground near the fire. Survivor would give it to Alma when she woke up; it would ease the pain in her hands and knees.

Alma would never admit it, but she was old and tired. Hardly her fault. It was a lucky person who came to be so out here in the Open. A strong person. Rocking back and forth, teeth knocking together in the seat of a Marauder dune buggy all day, stopping only to empty your bladder or bowels, was rough enough if you were young.

Survivor turned her attention from dinner to Alma lying next to her, face to the rock wall. Her silver braid had grown frayed and chaotic from the speed of the buggy, and her back rose and fell with the heaviness of finally being still.

The snake smelled ready, and Survivor wasn't willing to wait any longer. With a snap, she ordered the food be brought. She reached over and shook Alma's calf gently as Cowan brought two portions of nicely cut meat on tin plates.

"Ma, food," said Survivor.

Alma pushed herself up and turned to face the fire. She refused the plate. "That's too much. I'm not that hungry."

"Try to eat? Please?"

Alma shook her head.

"Here." Survivor picked up the little bottle of blood and took the tiny cork out of it. "I made sure he didn't puncture the venom sacks when he harvested it. Drink."

Alma didn't argue with that. She upturned the bottle and drained it, licking the bit that escaped her mouth off of her lips. She shuddered once.

Survivor wolfed down her dinner in two mouthfuls while Alma slowly got through a piece of hers, chewing thoroughly. Survivor pushed herself to her knees and shuffled on the ground until she was behind Alma. She sat and put her legs around Alma, taking her fingers to her braid and undoing it. She worked the tangles out until the hair was smooth down Alma's back. With difficulty, she separated it into three sections and began to braid.

"Wren's better at this," Survivor mumbled. "She even did my hair that one time when I was sick. Remember how I yelled at her when I realized what she was doing?"

Alma didn't answer. Survivor caught the edge of her profile as her jaw went up and down, still chewing.

"Ma?"

"I remember."

Survivor finished the braid. It was uneven, with sections already falling out, but it was the best she could do. She tied it off at the bottom with a short length of cord.

"You're worried," said Survivor to Alma's back.

"Yes."

"The doctor could be wrong. It may not be as bad in the city as she says. How could it be? They have everything there. Food, water, shelters that you have to see to believe."

"I'm not worried about what we'll be walking into, child. I'm worried about how Wren's doctor hasn't been allowed near her for weeks. Nobody has. We need to get there as fast as possible."

Survivor stood and walked around to face Alma; the fire warmed her back. "If the doctor is telling the truth, it just means that Wren is still in the lab like you thought she'd be. That's a good thing. Easier to hit a target when it's not moving."

Alma's tone lost the exhaustion of minutes prior, and her words came out with the irritation of stress Survivor knew intimately. "It's not that easy. None of this will be easy."

"Sure it is. We'll use the card to sneak into the city at night, break into the lab from the tunnel you used to get her out before, and leave the way we came."

Alma stretched her legs out, bending one at the knee, then the other, alternating. The snake blood should be starting to help her pain by now. "You always did undersell the strengths of your enemies," she said, and there was an edge of frustration in her tone. "You'd be smart to remember that confidence is often madness wearing a more attractive mask. It got you your current position, but it could just as easily have gotten you killed."

Survivor turned away from Alma toward the fire. She let the power of the flames take her attention as she said, "I don't know why you're so angry with me. I'm doing my best to fix my mistake of getting Wren captured."

Alma reached over to kiss her roughly on the side of the head. "It's not that. It's not you at all. I apologize. I'm just tired."

Survivor bit at her nails, spitting out the grit from underneath each one after scraping it out with her teeth. "Something's on your mind. Can't hide that from me."

"I guess not." Alma smacked Survivor's hand away from her mouth. "Stop that, please."

Survivor lowered her hand. "We'll get her out. There is no other option."

Alma licked her thumb and ran it over a particularly stubborn smudge on Survivor's cheek. "No, there isn't." She reached for her bedroll, clearly thinking their conversation was over.

"When we do get her out, will you come with us?" Survivor asked quickly. "You don't need to hide from Thallium's people anymore. I can protect you."

Alma pulled her braid over her shoulder and examined it while she thought. "You've worked hard to become the force you are today. Done things I can't imagine," she said sadly. Then she tugged a couple of the sections of the braid into order. "You're right. Wren's better." She leaned over and kissed Survivor on the newly cleaned spot on her cheek. "Sleep, child."

Alma's breathing turned deep as soon as her head hit her bedroll. She had always known how to take care of things. Now, it was Survivor's turn to take care of her.

TEN YEARS EARLIER

Survivor had never experienced excruciating hunger like she did the day after she'd run from The Gentleman. One thing about him, the only thing she missed, was that he kept her and all of her fellow slaves well-fed. His men liked the girls and boys fit and spunky with firm muscles. And she had always been spunkier than the rest. Reskin had loved her for it. After she watched him die, she ran. As she ran, darting between cacti and bounding over boulders, she thought about how she hadn't taken anything with her. No food, no weapons, not even a blanket. There hadn't been time, and even if there had been, the instinct to get away was so strong it likely would have overtaken her before she could so much as steal a scarf.

She reached the canyon in the dark that same night so exhausted that she almost stepped off the edge to her death before she stopped herself. She climbed down to a thin ledge in the dark, feeling blind and dumb, and rested below the rim of the canyon. As tired as she was, she couldn't sleep. She knew they would have found Reskin dead by now and that they'd punish the others since they couldn't hurt her.

None of the slaves were supposed to use their names, but she knew their faces. Braid girl with her dark face and round lips, the one-eyed woman, the skinny girl. But Beo had been special. He was her family, her single source of hope, and she'd watched The Gentleman begin to twist him into something without light. Lifeless, yet alive. That night in the canyon, visions of what Beo might be going through tortured Survivor. Was he to be punished? Would he miss her? Would he be tasked to retrieve her?

In the pit of her stomach, she knew that the answers to those questions were irrelevant. She had left him, and she didn't deserve his forgiveness for that. If the hunger and the elements didn't kill her out here, the astonishing pain of her guilt would. Fitting since her death was long overdue.

The climb down into the canyon was difficult, and it took two full days. By the time she got to the forest, she thought for certain she was about to die. The lack of water and food was a new sort of pain, one that she tried to remedy. But her hunting tactics were sloppy, impeded by her desperation and lack of energy. The birds and small rodents she stalked seemed to hear even her mouth filling with saliva before she pounced.

Three days after she'd left the clan, she sat hunched over against the trunk of a tree, perched on one of its thick branches. That's when she saw her—Alma, her then salt and pepper hair in a short braid, holding a bow at her side. She walked beneath Survivor's tree and drew an arrow from the quiver on her back, listened intently, and then in one quick motion drew her bow and let loose her shot. Under a canopy of bunchgrass below, a quail squawked once and then fell dead. Alma retrieved the kill. She swished her white coat back to reveal two more birds lashed to her belt. Survivor's stomach lurched.

She carefully followed Alma to camp, moving behind the cover of three young piñon pines, peeking through their greenery toward the middle of a glade. It was growing dark, and the shade of the trees made it darker still.

Alma lit a fire with a bundle of tinder. She wasn't alone—a

young redhead sat on a tree stump, humming as she plucked the quails' feathers. She was lanky and her hair swirled like fire as if she were a lit match. Gathered around her stump on little sleeping nests were still more children—three that were maybe seven or eight years old and three more that were younger still. The littlest ones were stacking stones. A girl accidentally knocked down a boy's tower with her elbow, and he got angry. Before he could pinch the girl, the redheaded girl reached out to tap him on the knee with her foot. He grumbled as he started putting the tower back together.

The older kids watched Wren pluck the birds with rapt attention, and she let the boy hold a small sack for the feathers she removed. He held the sack with care and an open mouth as if them eating dinner depended upon how well he did his job. The little girl from earlier started to cry. Alma, apparently content that her fire was established, went over to the group and enveloped her in a hug before tickling her stomach.

The whole scene was outrageous—a woman and seven children in the Open. Alone, somehow still breathing. Survivor hoped her exhaustion and hunger hadn't progressed to hallucinations yet, but that was more likely than this spectacle being possible.

Alma skewered the three quail on whittled sticks and propped them over the fire. As they all sat around the fire, watching the birds turn from pink flesh to browned meat, the smell hit Survivor like a heat wave, soaking into her skin and driving her mad. They were children and one woman—what could they do to stop her?

No longer able to control herself, Survivor sprinted out from behind the cluster of pines and leapt over the nearest children, intent on nothing but the stick holding the crispy birds, all in a line like soldiers waiting to be devoured. The children yelped and scattered. Survivor groped for the birds, but before she could even graze one with her fingers, something hard caught her around the neck. She fell backward with a heavy thump, knocking the wind out of her. As she gasped, she fumbled to feel what had her around the neck—the curved wood of the woman's bow was pressed to her windpipe.

She looked up and back, eyes rolling toward her forehead to see Alma calmly holding the bow and looking down at Survivor's face. Alma hushed them, maintaining perfect control of her bow and Survivor, who was far too exhausted to fight back.

Alma tilted her head to the side, eyes running over Survivor's hair and features like a hunter studying tracks. Then, as abruptly as she'd subdued Survivor, she let her go. Survivor rolled onto her hands and knees. She kept her eyes to the ground—the pine needles and dirt—listening to the whimpers of the nearest kids as she waited for Alma to put an arrow in her as she had the quail.

"Look at me," said Alma.

"Just kill me," said Survivor.

"I said look at me, child."

Survivor did. She sat back on her heels, raising her chin to meet Alma's gaze.

"All alone. And alive," said Alma, shouldering her bow and relaxing her stance. She smiled. "You're quite the survivor."

Wren knelt next to the fire, ripped a tiny leg from one of the quail, and handed it to her. "What's your name?"

The children looked on, not whimpering anymore, but instead fascinated by the new girl covered in dirt in the middle of their circle.

She hated all of her names from before—they weren't who she was and never had been. Somehow, Alma had known the heart of who she was before she'd even asked her name. "Survivor," she answered, and then promptly wolfed the quail leg, nearly swallowing the bone with the meat.

"Welcome," said Alma. She held a hand out. Survivor took it and rose to her feet.

PRESENT DAY

Survivor looked at Alma's sleeping form facing the wall of their shelter. Alma's body may have been tired, but her mind and her will were far from it. She was still the same woman who'd horse-collared Survivor that first night, who'd set her to work and nurtured her mind. Who'd welcomed her.

Survivor got to her knees and crawled to Alma, laying on her side and tucking herself around her back under the blankets. Alma roused for only a second, long enough to take Survivor's hand in hers and rest them against her stomach. Within minutes, Survivor was asleep, her breathing synchronized with Alma's, strong and steady as her resolve to get Wren back tomorrow and fade into the desert together again.

CHAPTER THIRTEEN

Adonis hadn't realized he would ever be able to hate water. After spending so much of his life with too little of it, despising the sight and sound of it flowing en mass had been inconceivable. But that was before he'd spent four days stuck in Ollie's treatment facility. Quitting time was over two hours past, but Ollie had kept Adonis late. Only Adonis. It was just the two of them in the artificial light of the water plant, and Adonis was fairly certain as he pulled on a fresh set of latex gloves that he'd never been more bored in his life.

He began testing the water. The tank edge came up to his chest, so he had to use a stool to get high enough above it to lean over. He removed the cap of a plastic bottle and handed it to Ollie before stretching over the water toward the point at which it flowed the fastest. The bottle filled quickly, and he settled back on the stool to cap it.

Ollie stood next to him, watching everything he was doing. When Adonis reached out to get the second sample, Ollie shook his head and got close so he could hear him. "A little farther out—right in the middle of the stream like you did with the first one."

Adonis adjusted. He brought the sample back in and set it on the edge of the pool. Ollie slid two labels toward him, and as Adonis wrote the date, time, and every other bit of miscellaneous information about the samples, he died a little inside.

Ollie slid back the top on a red cooler of thick plastic to receive the samples. Inside was ice formed into neat cubes, something few people would ever see. Frozen pipe in the middle of winter? Sure. Icicles hanging from a roof as the singular good snowfall The Disc got on more fortunate years melted? Yeah. But this was different. Intentionally formed, perfect squares that energy had gone into producing. Luxury at its most extreme. Or, in this case, luxury converted to science. Water formed specifically to protect the integrity of the samples so that they could be tested, leading to the refinement of more water. A beautiful cycle, or so Ollie had declared it. Adonis had settled on "admirable, but still soul-crushing."

He should be two hands into a card game with his buddies by now. The meeting of Tyr's Army scheduled for tomorrow afternoon would be the highlight of Adonis' week. He knew that Caster meant well, and he had a suspicion that Sans had been the main one behind this reassignment, but that didn't mean he had to like it.

Ollie closed the cooler and rested his arms on the edge of the pool. He peered out across the water. There was something dark in his eyes. Over the last few days, Adonis had been his shadow—cleaning equipment, checking gauges. Every day, Ollie had become more withdrawn. When his men had come up to speak with him, Ollie had left Adonis to his task alone. As confident as that made Adonis feel in his ability to do this job, it struck him as odd. Leave this kid to do a task solo that he learned to perform minutes prior? Made the whole thing feel like a charade, somehow. Like everyone here was playing pretend.

Ollie leaned back and stuck his hands in the pockets of his jumpsuit. "Well, I think we're about finished for today," he said over the whirling of the water.

Adonis tried to hide his excitement at being released, getting to take the evening to himself and see Sans. Hell, even Six. He had a bunk in the water facility now, and he'd been staying there. Sharing a one-bedroom with Sans had been luxury compared to a room with three other workers who all smelled like chemicals.

"Would it be okay if I took a little ice with me?" Adonis asked as they headed for Ollie's office to store their samples and equipment for the overnight crew when they took over the careful watch of the facility. "I don't think Sans has ever had any before. I want to watch his face when the shock of it gives him a headache."

Ollie let out a tired chuckle. "Maybe tomorrow." He patted the yellow pipe painted with a blue smiley face stretching horizontally overhead—a superstitious habit shared by all who worked in the facility. Adonis followed suit and hopped up to reach it.

They got the gear settled in Ollie's office—a cramped space that had definitely contributed to the slight hunch of the man's shoulders over the decades. Then he turned to Adonis and just...looked at him.

"Um, can I go now?" Adonis asked.

"Hmm." Ollie shook himself free of whatever he'd been thinking. "Yeah. It's past that time, isn't it?" He gave Adonis' shoulder a squeeze. "You've been doing so well here. I know it's not where you want to be, but I've enjoyed working with you anyway. Wanted you to know."

"Thanks, Ollie." Adonis shrugged. "It's not so bad."

"Aw, come on. It's boring."

Adonis shuffled on his feet. "Maybe a little," he said sheepishly.

Ollie smiled and pointed at him. "You would rather be doing Thief training." He crossed his arms. "Why that specialty, if I can ask?"

"Oh. Sure, you can ask. Sans is a Thief and he...saved me. A long time ago. Sounds stupid, but I want to be like him."

"Doesn't sound stupid." He stepped back and ushered Adonis ahead of him, down the corridor leading out of his office. As they walked, he said to Adonis' back, "I hate to presume, but are you nervous at all about the procedures they do? How they make Thieves?"

"Not really," Adonis replied, and his voice came back as a hollow echo down the metal corridor. "I want them, even if they do hurt."

"You want to be different?"

Adonis hesitated, but then answered honestly. "I *need* to be different." He started to veer left, toward the stairs that led up toward the main exit checkpoint of the facility.

Ollie stopped him with a question. "As a thank you for your help, would you like to see the mod room?"

Adonis turned so fast he made himself dizzy. "Really?"

"If you'd like. My pal there owes me a favor. Or two." He jerked his head down the right path. "It's near The Pits. You mind the walk?" He didn't wait for an answer, just started plodding down the hall.

"No! I don't mind." Adonis jogged to keep up with him.

The area of The Disc near the southwestern arc of the wall was quiet. Heat that the interior bricks of the wall had been soaking up in the sun all day radiated toward them from the left, making it almost pleasant to walk in the cold of the early evening. The silence with Ollie was comfortable, easy. Adonis recognized the outbuilding as they approached—he'd eyed it often during training sessions in The Pits. Having a literal goal in mind made Six and Sans' beatdowns seem worthwhile.

Ollie opened the door and held it for Adonis.

"Second room on your left," Ollie said after him. The main door closed behind them with a squeal of metal that irked the ears.

The hall stretched long into the dark, but the second door was open, the light on and inviting. Someone was inside like they'd been waiting.

"My cousin, Simon," said Ollie. "Simon, this is the young man I told you about."

Simon was only a little taller than Adonis, with skin so smooth, it made him look nearly as young as Adonis too. But from the way he carried himself, it was clear he was much older. "Future Thief, correct?" he asked as he shook Adonis' hand.

Adonis swallowed hard and nodded.

"I'm just finishing up today's work. Feel free to look around," said Simon kindly. He headed to a counter and started putting bottles and tools away in drawers.

The room was rectangular with a U-shaped counter and cabinets wrapping around its edge. A reclined chair stood in the middle of the open space of floor. Something about the room set Adonis on edge. It was clean enough. Well, compared to the majority of The Disc, it was near spotless. No, there was something else. There was a smell that was camouflaging another smell, like something had burned and then they cleaned the surfaces nearby with ammonia. It felt like a crime covered up by a lie.

He tried to explain away the haunting feeling. After all, he knew what they did here—they cut into people, changed their senses and physical features to meet the needs of their occupations. They even tweaked their minds if needed. It was brutal, so of course it would feel brutal in here.

Scouts like Caster were operated on to improve their vision and hearing. Sometimes the operations were enough, sometimes they weren't, and they'd receive implants or other mechanical modifications that made them good enough to hang in with the rest of the Bodies, whose job was to defend The Disc and predict future threats. The modifications might as well be magic as far as Adonis was concerned, but everyone who received them was informed that this kind of technology had been considered rudimentary before The Fall. Really, compared to Wren and whatever was going on in Caster's body, it was basic stuff. Still, Adonis wanted it more than anything.

It would finally make him special, give him an edge that few others had. And those that did? They would be his new comrades. He would be an asset rather than a burden. Accepted by his peers. Good enough. Finally.

The reclined chair shot upright, startling him. There was a hand crank and a couple of levers on the pedestal under it— ways to manipulate it and its occupant during various procedures.

"Would you like to sit?" Ollie asked as he patted the seat of the chair. "See what it will feel like the day you get your mods?"

"Oh. No, no I'm fine."

"Come on." Ollie went over and elbowed him playfully. "Just for fun?"

Adonis thought about it. "Guess it wouldn't hurt." He headed for the chair. Too big for him by far, but he managed to settle on the seat. The plastic squeaked as he adjusted his weight.

"Comfortable?" asked Ollie.

"Not really."

Ollie laughed. "Not supposed to be, after all. As a Thief, you'll get enhanced senses and a fair bit of work done on your appearance. Have you considered what you might want to look like?"

"As long as I don't look like me, I'll be happy."

Ollie put his hands on his hips. "Now that's no way to think, is it?"

Adonis pondered for a second, then said timidly, "If I get to choose, I'd like to look older."

Simon click-clacked on a keyboard, and binds came out of the chair across all of Adonis' major joints—elbows, wrists, knees, ankles. One wider, more flexible band slipped out of the headrest and across his forehead, clicking into place. On a screen atop the counter near Simon, numbers shot up higher, and Adonis realized they represented his own heartbeat that now hammered in his ears.

Ollie's face remained impassive, which made Adonis question the terror climbing up his restrained limbs. "Um, Ollie?" said Adonis. He swallowed hard to get the words out. "I want to get up now, please."

Ollie's cousin kept clacking at the keyboard, and the clatter of the smacking plastic was the only sound other than Adonis' own heartbeat, which he swore was audible through the walls now. Then, without looking from the screen and still typing with one hand, Ollie's cousin gave a thumbs-up.

Adonis started to struggle. "I didn't mean I wanted to change today. Let me up!"

Ollie put a cool hand on Adonis' forehead, and there in his eyes was the darkness Adonis had seen creeping in for the past few days. "I'm not a cruel man, even though I'm sure that from where you're sitting, it seems that way. I'm not. What I am is tired. A lot like you—undervalued, overlooked. It really does wear on you, even if you aren't a proud person. It's been wearing on me for decades."

Adonis spoke when Ollie paused for breath. "I don't want this." He helplessly flexed his arms against the binds and scratched at the metal clasps around his wrists with his fingernails.

Ollie just pulled up a rolling chair and sat down. "Here, hold my hand." He loosely gripped Adonis' sweaty, frantic fingers. "It's getting harder to keep my mouth closed around Valcin Jr. You don't know this—few do now—but there was more than one of us in those formative years of The Disc. He certainly didn't raise the walls and wire the grid by himself. *We* founded this city, and he had the audacity to claim it as his and pass it along as an inheritance."

Adonis strained his neck forward as hard as he could to try to free his head, grunting and then screaming with the effort. All for nothing. He started to sob softly.

Ollie rubbed his forearm as if to give him credit for trying. "I've had to watch Thallium turn this promising city into a rock on which he scrapes the junk from his boots. I'm the last of the founders left. Now I have to act before I'm dead like the rest of them, understand? I'm running out of time. It's forced me to resort to recruiting Thallium's own Keepers. Forced me to encourage them to do whatever they want to my citizens just for the sake of turning hearts against Thallium. And toward that same purpose of convincing others of Thallium's evil, I'm forced to do this to you." The chair rose higher, and Ollie stood with it, cold hand still on Adonis. "I want you to know that it won't hurt. When the time comes, you won't feel anything. You shouldn't even be present enough to be afraid—plenty of painkillers to help you through. For now, you'll just take a long nap."

Something went into the back of Adonis' neck with a

pinch, right near the top of his spine. He fought it, tried to keep his eyes open, but they got to be so heavy so fast.

Adonis stared at the ceiling. "I don't want this," he managed to choke out.

Ollie and Simon spoke softly to each other, or maybe it wasn't soft and Adonis' ears just interpreted it as if their voices were coming through wads of fabric, all quiet and indistinct. The last thing he saw before his eyes closed was Simon taking a tiny knife from a drawer and Ollie nodding.

The leadership of Tyr's Army appeared to be shrinking. Gathered in Vee's tent for a status meeting were Sans quietly blending into the fixtures; Six lying down from boredom; a sluggish but healthy Frederick nursing a burnt-smelling cup of coffee; and Caster periodically peeking out of the tent to check the changing position of the sun.

"Donnie's late," said Six from the floor of the tent. He was on his back with his knees up, tossing up a hunk of dark rock and catching it.

"Stop doing that!" Vee shouted as she entered the back of the tent via the entrance near the alley. She held a stick of roasted grasshoppers in one hand. "That's valuable!"

Six tossed the rock up again. "It's space garbage, Vee. Boring rock spat from space to land here until it weathers into nothing. And as I already purchased this space garbage from you to be a conversation starter in my home, I'd say you can no longer tell me what to do with it."

Vee started to speak but then stopped and dug into her dinner instead. "You boys are supposed to be done with my tent by now," she said mid-chew.

Six caught the rock and sat up. "He didn't come to hang out

with us last night, either. You sure you told him when we were meeting today?" he asked Caster. Again.

"He'll be here," replied Caster. But the truth was that Adonis should have been there already. Not only was he never late, but he was also excited about this meeting. Caster feared that he was feeling ostracized in his new job with Ollie. When Caster had told him that they needed to show their support to Ollie in order to deserve his in return, that it was a long-term investment toward an easier leadership transition when Thallium was gone, Adonis perked up at the importance of his new role. Still, the kid probably felt cooped up there. When the traffic outside the tent picked up as they neared the peak dinner hour just before sundown, Caster began to worry that Adonis hadn't simply worked late at the water plant. Something was wrong.

"I can go look for the boy. The sooner the better. I'll miss out on prime selling hours if this takes much longer," Frederick said as he pulled his fox scarf farther up his neck. He'd dressed up tonight, all texture and color, clearly eager to reenter the world of the healthy.

Before Caster could reply, he heard something in the distance. At the open space near the far end of the market, something heavy was being dragged. The rhythm of the evening shoppers was suddenly disrupted as they stopped to watch whatever was happening.

Sans broke his frozen stance. His hands and feet started twitching, every bit of him suddenly uneasy.

"Let's go," Caster said simply.

The four of them filed out of the tent and were swallowed up in a river of pedestrians following each other, all asking what was going on. The flow came to an abrupt stop just outside the main market aisle. Above the heads of the crowd, on a cobbled-together stage of large packing crates, were six Keepers. All wore their striped robes and had their faces covered. In their midst was a criminal with hands bound at the front and a sack over their head. Above them, two drones hovered, taking it all in.

Caster tried to shove his way closer, but the thick crowd didn't oblige his efforts. The Keeper in the center of the stage spoke, his face concealed by the mask coming up just below his eyes.

"Our Principal is a noble man who has grown tired of the ungratefulness of his people," the Keeper projected stiffly, as if he were trying to remember every word of the script he'd been given. His voice was familiar, but Caster couldn't put his finger on who it belonged to. He held his spear in his left hand with the mysterious prisoner on his right. The drama, the theater of it, stank of Thallium.

Sans fidgeted next to Caster, and his eyes were veined with pink. "Do you smell that?" he asked.

Caster inhaled deeply. He smelled, well, everything around. Body odor, smoke, cheap vendor food. Too much to take in at once. But then, just barely, a hint of someone he recognized.

"Donnie," he said softly.

Sans' changing eyes focused on the criminal being held by the Keepers.

The Keeper holding the prisoner proclaimed, "This is what happens to people who join Tyr's Army or any other force prideful and foolish enough to go against Thallium Valcin." He yanked the hood from the prisoner's head. The crowd gathered gasped as if they shared a set of lungs.

Dear God.

It was Adonis. Or it had been up until recently. The boy standing there now, barely thirteen, had been mutilated. Beyond the degree that Marauders went to in their modifications. His lips had been cut through at the corners, eyes swollen mostly shut from blunt force. The curls on his head were shaved off, leaving scraggly chunks of hair on an otherwise bald head. Both of his arms hung grotesquely forward, dangling, making the ropes around his wrists superfluous since it was clear he couldn't move anything from his shoulders down.

Sans bellowed in rage as his Harbinger took over, eyes shrouded completely in red, veins bulging along his forehead and neck. There was hardly room to even turn sideways in the crowd, but Sans still managed to draw his massive club from under his long cloak.

Before he could shove through the mass, the Keeper swept his spear up at an angle. The metal head went through Adonis' chin and out through the top of his head with a wet crunch. Adonis' eyes widened for just a second, and there was brief joy there as he spotted Caster and Sans. Then the light went out as his weight sank forward onto the spear. Getting the spear back out was more challenging, and it took the Keeper two firm tugs before it released. Adonis slumped forward off of the stage, on top of the closest members of the crowd who retreated immediately and let him fall to the ground.

Those nearby were too stunned to speak. The Keepers just stood there as if to engrain it on everyone's memories who was responsible for this atrocity—their ruler.

Then a swath of people started to flee against the force of the Harbinger pushing past them. The Keepers spotted Sans, and they stood still no longer. They started to retreat through the back of the crowd toward the Main House. The one who had killed Donnie ran faster than the rest.

Sans charged toward the stage. The two drones overhead released shock tablets; they fired with a dull *thwip* through the air. Two of them landed on Sans' back. Those in the crowd unlucky enough to be touching him fell unconscious, and Sans fought past their dead weights. He reached back and ripped one of the tablets out of his skin, and the other alone wasn't enough to take him down. More tablets started to fall, and he batted them with his kanabō, sending them flying high and away.

While Sans kept the drones back and the people scattered, Caster and Six went to Donnie. Caster put pressure on the top of Adonis' head like a fool. Six pushed Caster's hand away. He turned Adonis over and held his head in his lap. The boy was long gone, swollen eyes closed the rest of the way and his heart still.

Six started to hyperventilate as he stared at Adonis' face. But he soon took control of his breath, and the effort shook his body and Adonis' shoulders lying against his legs. Six looked up at Caster, eyes wet and narrowed in anger. "We did this to him."

The truth of his words hung heavy in the evening air. Somehow, Thallium had found out their identities. Caster's mind whirred with theories as to how. Had they screwed up concealing their ID bracelets and Thallium tracked them somewhere damning? Or had they been too careless when speaking in public and the Operator had picked up the audio? Or had one of their own betrayed them?

In the end, Caster didn't care how Thallium had found them out. Thallium had done this to Adonis—a kid—to make an example. Six believed they'd been rash, but Thallium's brutality showed that they could no longer afford to wait. Not for one more person, resource, or for any assurance that what they were doing was free from risk. As the sun dropped behind the west wall of The Disc, casting the scene in an eerie yellow-gray, Caster took out his knife and leapt onto the impromptu stage.

"Keeper!" he yelled so loudly that his throat hurt. In the

distance, at the base of the hill that led to the Main House, the masked Keeper that had killed Adonis turned and waved. A handful of people in the midst of the fleeing crowd paused, boulders in the flash flood of panic. Caster knew their faces— men and women who had sworn their loyalty to him in Vee's tent not long before. All of them glanced between him and the bowie knife in his hand that reflected the last of the sun before it dipped behind the western wall. Recognition was in their eyes, and it wiped away any trace of fear.

Trevor, the recruit that was about Adonis' age, stood next to his big brother in front of a clothing booth as people blew past them. All gawky limbs and excitement, he looked up to Javen, who simply drew his club. Trevor took the dagger that Caster had given him from his belt. In a voice that cracked only slightly, Trevor shouted, "For Tyr!"

More members of Tyr's Army—twenty strong—stopped amidst the market booths and turned toward Trevor's call. A mere moment was all it took before one of them hollered in response to the call, and they all set off in pursuit of the Keepers that had run. Just then, another ten Keepers drawn by the commotion emerged from the market and nearby streets to cut them off, quickly escalating the situation into a brawl.

Frederick still stood near the stage. He was taking quick breaths as if to give himself courage as he watched the chaos. From his coat pocket, he took a metal cylinder. With a push of a button, it extended into a rod that sparked with electricity. Freddy saluted Caster with a pointed raise of his chin, then charged into the fray with his weapon buzzing as his high-pitched scream trailed behind him with the tail of his purple overcoat.

Overhead, one of the drones sent out a shower of sparks as Sans beaned it with one of its own shock tablets. It fell out of the sky and spun on the ground in a wonky circle until

Sans turned it into shards of scrap with one overhead swing of his kanabō. The second drone, finally empty of ammunition, rose higher and quickly retreated toward the Main House.

Sans—a sweating, furious mass of pulsing veins—dropped his weapon. He bent to take Adonis' limp form from Six, lifting him as if he weighed nothing. Groans came from his heaving chest, and as he slowly returned to himself, the groans were replaced with sobs. He placed Adonis gently on the stage and straightened his limbs as if to make him more comfortable. He kissed the kid on the forehead, then looked up to Caster with eyes still ringed in deep pink. "If you don't go kill your father now, I will."

The anger Caster had been holding on to tightly for so long bloomed along his limbs. He wanted to be done with this insanity—no more lying to his father, hoping he'd changed while also praying he hadn't, because Thallium being evil would make betraying him that much easier. And it would make it possible to kill him after what had happened tonight. But had Thallium *really* done this to Adonis? Was he even capable?

Caster had to know.

He addressed Sans, and this time, he was the one to expose his neck in respect. "Lead them here, brother." He leapt from the stage and sprinted for a side street amidst the shouts of his men answering the call to fight.

Eydis had yet to return to the main floor of the inner chamber since Wren's outburst. Bug was the only one Wren wanted anywhere near her. She refused to consider leaving the isolation unit, and as much as Eydis wanted to release her, she knew the risk of doing it against Wren's timing. Even Thallium seemed to understand the risk involved now.

She and Thallium sat in the observation booth. Eydis looked down at Wren, whose eyes were closed, and Thallium scribbled notes on personnel files splayed out on the console.

She had debated the best way to remove him. No, he couldn't be killed by typical means now, but her odds of killing him before he'd received the Biorg had been poor anyway. He'd trapped her, and placating him with the Biorg had given her time to think. Her intention all along had been for his own actions to be his undoing—he'd made a slew of enemies. What she needed was for the strongest of them to confront him while she took Wren. But Wren would have to decide to come out of the box for that plan to work. Eydis had held her prisoner, and now, whether knowingly or not, Wren was doing the same to her.

Thallium spread his stack of files out farther and began turning each to the photos of the individuals detailed within: bespectacled Head of Agriculture, Charles Indigo; solar lead Tess, with her spiky hair in full glory; and finally, Oliver, Head of Agua, who was on the verge of retirement.

Thallium waved his hand over the photos. "My top suspects. Which one looks like a traitor to you?" He clicked his pen open and closed rapidly. "Perhaps it takes one to know one?"

No longer having to put up a respectful façade, Eydis met his gaze and rested her chin on her hand. "I don't know—do you recognize despots on sight?"

He laughed heartily, then slapped his knees. "You really are incredible! Successfully pretending to be a subservient android for decades! I'm sure I'll never know all you've been up to, unless you're feeling like sharing suddenly? Taking credit?"

Eydis said nothing.

"Fine, fine. But tell me this at least," he begged. "All these years, was the idea to use my family's resources until your research here was complete? And what would that mean, exactly? What's your endgame?"

Eydis rolled her chair closer to his. "Let me be clear. The only thing you and I have in common now is that we both want Wren to come out of the isolation unit. As for what I want after that, it's beyond your fathoming." She caressed his throat. "The little black disc you have shoved into my back is the only thing keeping me from wrapping my hands around your neck right now."

With a low growl, he ran his hand through his blond hair and squirmed in his seat. "Which would do little good, except for the pleasure factor. There's something special about what we had, don't you think? Or perhaps we could still have it?" He draped a hand on her thigh.

His hand fell as she rolled her chair away, hiding her knees under the desk.

Thallium groaned. "Shame. I think we would have had even more fun now that we've dropped all pretenses. And share similar physical capabilities." The desk creaked as he leaned on it to get near her and whispered, "I have to know—is it different after the Biorg?"

A laugh rippled through her chest and came flowing out. When she'd finally composed herself, she said with a sigh, "After living hundreds of years, let me assure you—*everything* is different after the Biorg." She added seriously, "And it never ends."

Thallium opened his mouth to speak, but Theo's voice came through his ID bracelet. "Sir, we have footage coming in from two drones. There's commotion in the streets."

Thallium sat up straighter. "Send it to the screen in the inner chamber, Operator."

"Yes, sir. One—"

Loud banging on Theo's end of the line cut him off. Another man's voice yelled something indistinct.

"Hold on!" Theo shouted. He spoke more quietly, "Sir, I can see Keepers outside the security room. There's six of them. Why are there so many?"

Thallium cursed, and he looked at Eydis as he spoke. "It's happening." He held his bracelet closer to his mouth. "Theo, they're traitors. Do not open that door. They're looking for me."

More thumps from Theo's side. "I understand, sir. B-but you need to know," Theo hesitated, "Caster is coming. I checked his tracker when the drones started sending footage. Shall I call his ID bracelet and warn him away?"

The recording started to play on the oversized screen in the lab behind Wren. No audio, as if the drone had taken damage, but the video was clear—Caster stood in a crowd of people near the drones, stepping past a dead body onto a stage and drawing his bowie. Wren stirred even though the audio of the footage was silent. She turned in the box and watched the footage, head angled to the side as though she wasn't sure if it was real or if she was dreaming.

"His recent scans show he's headed toward the Main House, sir. We need to warn him," Theo said quietly, as if the men on the other side of the security door could hear him over the clamor of their efforts to break in.

Thallium's eyes—speckled gold like Eydis' now—narrowed in thought. "I believe there's no place he'd rather be right now than here, Theo. Let him come." He finally stood and looked down at Wren, then at Eydis. "Open the box."

Eydis rose from her chair to face him. "No." He turned and made a move to throttle her, but she held up a hand and said, "If Caster's coming home in this mess—enemy or not—he's coming to protect her. Let him this time."

He hesitated. "You believe she'll leave the box for him?"

Eydis chose her words carefully. "At this point, I believe he's our best chance. With her out and her power freed, this coup can end swiftly. Theo can get you to safety. I'll greet Caster when he arrives and bring him down here."

The furrow in his brow smoothed out as he realized what she was proposing. He searched the console for the PA button and pressed it. "Bug."

From below, she turned up to face him.

"We're under attack. Stay with Wren."

Thallium held the door of the booth open for Eydis, and they sprinted down the walkway, footsteps clanging, as Bug stammered out an inaudible response from below. They passed through the main lab and when Eydis opened the door with her code, she was about to head outside when Thallium stopped her.

He listened at the doorframe, then leapt out. He grabbed Prady by the front of his robes. The two men stared at each other for a moment until, finally, Thallium released him. Eydis stood between them at a distance. The air was heavy with the tenseness of rage before a fight.

"We're under attack," Thallium said at last.

Prady straightened his uniform but didn't salute nor stand at attention. He studied Thallium, staff raised and at the ready. "I've long been loyal to you," the Keeper said at last, leaving his words to hang there.

Thallium, unarmed, widened his stance. "No doubt. And to my son."

"Especially to your son," Prady said. "But what you've done to that young lady in there," he jerked his head toward the lab, and there was a hitch in his weathered voice, "must end tonight." He moved as if to attack, but Thallium threw up his hands.

"We agree on that as well, old friend," Thallium said quickly. "Will you help my son when he arrives? He's coming here, but I'm afraid I have to leave. If you'll allow it."

Prady blinked past the fog of anger clouding over his features. He relaxed and drew his staff upright. With a stiff nod, he turned his attention from Thallium as if he doubted his ability to restrain himself if he looked at him for one second more.

Thallium and Eydis headed for the stairs leading up to the ground floor. At the landing near the entryway of the Main House, he grabbed her waist in a tight little hug. "If Theo tells me you left the Main House, I will press my magic button. I'd rather not hurt you, so don't leave. Please." His "please" almost sounded genuine. He kissed her cheek once. "Theo, lead the way," he said toward his wrist, and then he continued up the stairs, hugging the outside railing as he went.

Once he was out of sight, Eydis went not through to the entrance of the Main House to greet Caster, but instead took a quick left toward the access tunnel that would lead her to Theo's security shack where six Keepers out for Thallium's life waited. The enemies—the distraction—Eydis had been waiting for had finally arrived, and she intended to personally let them into the lab where Caster would no doubt be shortly. Wren *would* come out of that box if properly motivated. Eydis was just sorry she wouldn't be able to personally guide Wren to her new destination.

For a group that had been shirking its duties for weeks, the Keepers were currently out in the streets in more force than Caster had ever seen. There was a Keeper fighting with one or more citizens on every street he turned down. There was no way they had mobilized *after* Adonis' public execution—there hadn't been enough time for that. They had been organized and put in place before the execution. Why? To maintain order? Make a statement on the Principal's behalf? After the time Caster had spent working with his father, he had believed he understood his way of thinking. But something felt off about this whole night. Caster tried to shake the strange tingling sensation from the back of his neck as he took the long route around the Keeper's apartment buildings on his way to find Thallium.

As for how Caster intended to get into the Main House, he was praying that none of the Keepers manning the door had seen men shout out their support for Tyr right after Caster showed himself in front of the mass of people. He was Tyr. Now, everyone would know it before long. Hopefully, a little longer than the time required for Caster to enter the Main House as Thallium's loyal son one final time.

He came about the far side of the Keepers' quarters and started the ascent to the Main House. Night was fully settled over The Disc, but the dull solar pathway lights were more than enough to guide Caster's steps. He reached the top of the walkway. Four Keepers stood outside the main door—double the normal guard—and spotted him right away. The security net hummed, crisscrossed over the threshold. Caster jogged forward with all the confidence he could muster, knowing that they could easily subdue him if they suspected something was amiss.

"Sir!" one of them shouted. The other three stood at attention, and Caster continued to move forward despite the alarms ringing in his head.

When he reached them, the one who had hailed him spoke. The white stripes of his robe took on the pale blue of the security net's light. "Sir, there's disorder in the streets. Please, get inside."

"Where's the Principal?" Caster asked.

The Keeper hesitated, then replied, "We're trying to locate him now, sir. He's not in his quarters, and his ID bracelet is unresponsive. But we'll find him. I swear it."

Caster only nodded, then barreled past the net, which opened at his approach. He slammed the main door shut behind him with the Keepers on the other side.

Thallium had gone dark. If he'd just put on that macabre display in the market, why was he hiding? His disappearance created a bigger problem: if even his loyal Keepers had no idea where he was, then Caster was unlikely to find him. How much time did Caster have before the Keepers in the Main House realized his role in the chaos outside? Would he be able to find Thallium during that time?

Or should he instead do what he'd wanted to do for weeks —bust into the lab and take Wren when he had the chance?

The city was turning to anarchy, and he was out of time. He ran to the staircase near the entryway of the Main House and raced downward. If he was quick enough, maybe he could get Wren *and* find his father. But if he had to choose just one, it would be Wren.

As he jumped the last five stairs to the next landing, he realized his choice would always be her.

CHAPTER FOURTEEN

THE LAST TIME SURVIVOR HAD GONE THROUGH THE REAR exit of The Disc, she'd been driving an open-topped SUV out of it with a sniveling prisoner in the front seat. Quite the opposite now as she, Alma, and three Marauder soldiers approached it in silence. Unlike the front entrance, which would be lit up after nightfall, this one was left dark. Undetectable from the smooth metal surrounding it. Impossible to spot, and few knew it existed.

Even fewer had a key that would open it.

Survivor signaled to her men to take position against the wall on either side of the large door. They obeyed, blending comfortably into the darkness in which they'd done their most praiseworthy deeds as clan members. Survivor felt around for the keypad near the door's edge with only the dim white light of a tiny flashlight to guide her.

"Here," Alma said, her hand above where Survivor had been looking. Alma flipped up a panel that blended in with the silver surface around it.

Survivor pulled the key from around her neck and, after

discerning the direction of the slot with her fingertips, slid it in horizontally.

The door moved upward, surprisingly quiet for such a large piece of machinery. As it rose, Survivor turned to Alma. "You really think you'll be able to find the lab tunnel?"

Alma gazed into the yawning, cool blackness of the passage that angled down as if she were about to enter her past, a place she'd run from for years. Yet, standing on its edge, her bearing lost at least a decade of age with the way she bounced eagerly on the balls of her feet. She'd been waiting for this. "I followed it in the dark when I last used it to take my children from here." She glanced at Survivor, eyes sharp in the glow of Survivor's light. "Yes, I can find it."

"Good enough for me." Survivor turned off her light and pocketed it before waving a hand at her Marauders. As they crossed into the city, the familiar sounds of violence came dully through the ground down to them.

The little thrill that went down Survivor's back urged her join in.

When Caster emerged from the stairwell, he found Prady standing in front of the door to the lab, staff at the ready, waiting to be attacked.

"Sir," Prady lowered his staff, "are you all right?"

As Caster approached him, he said, "Is my father inside?"

"No, sir. Neither is Eydis. They both left not long ago. I reluctantly let them. Thallium said you were coming."

How in the hell would Thallium know Caster was coming? Had the drones followed Caster here? Was his father expecting immediate retaliation for Adonis? Is that why he'd done it? Caster pushed back the damp hair that had fallen forward onto his face and cursed. "This isn't right. He wouldn't assert his authority like that and then disappear. And why would Eydis leave the lab when there's fighting in the streets?"

"I don't—"

The lab door opened, and standing there was Bug looking as confused as Caster felt. When she saw Caster, she exhaled so loudly that her hair near her face fluttered in the breeze. "You're here! I was coming to get you. Took me ten minutes of working myself up to it. I don't want to go out there. But since you're here, and Wren's..." She straightened up, pushed forward. "Wren needs to leave while she has the chance. We won't get a better one." With a sad smile at Prady, she turned and left the door open behind her.

Caster nearly sprinted after her but stopped himself. "Can you help me find my father?" he asked Prady.

"Sir, I just allowed him to leave. If he's running, why not let him?" Prady asked. "Could this not be the nonviolent answer you were looking for?"

Caster shook his head, and the sweat running down it turned cool. "I don't think it's that easy. Something is wrong here, and I think my father knows more about it than I do. Will you help me locate him?"

"He was in a hurry, and if he's managed to turn off his ID bracelet, it won't be easy to find him. But I can try the cameras in the surveillance room. With what's going on, I believe Theo will gladly let me in. I'm sure other Keepers will be looking for Thallium shortly—they'll head to surveillance too." Prady bowed and turned to leave.

"Not all of those Keepers will be on our side," Caster said. "Watch your back." He put a hand on Prady's shoulder.

Prady lowered his gaze, ever the humble servant who had always taken Caster's bullshit while offering nothing but his respect in return. Then he raised his gray head and ordered,

"You get that girl out of here. Hurry." He jogged to the stairs, staff tapping fast, and disappeared into the stairwell.

A completely non-stealthy "psst!" came from inside the lab. Bug was waiting at the door of the inner chamber on the far side, waving at him rapidly and close to her chest as if she were a spy giving a discrete signal.

Caster ran to her, and the main lab door closed behind him. She put a hand on his chest before he could cross the threshold into the inner chamber.

"What you're about to see, I don't..." she said, voice breathy. "I'm sorry."

He pushed her hand away, stomped into the chamber, and took it all in from the upper landing.

In the center of the deep white and silver room was a green blotch standing out like a sick soul. In the isolation unit, Wren was a blur of white fabric strips and long hair floating around her top half and face, the red turned dark in the green of the fluid. Her toes barely scraped against the platform, one leg pulled up higher than the other, slack and strange.

Caster bounded down the steps a half-flight at a time and approached the box. Wren was asleep. He stood in front of the unit like a moron, frozen.

He shattered on the inside.

He took two steps away and bent over before he vomited. He was a broken vessel, a sham of a protector. God knew what Wren had gone through, living the life of a sample in a beaker. God, Eydis, and Thallium. And Bug.

"I'm so sorry," Bug whispered behind him.

He fought the urge to take her by the throat. Instead, he focused on calming his breath, keeping his head low by his knees. "Can she hear me in there?" he said, eyes fixated on the white tile of the floor. Spotless, smelling faintly of bleach tainted by the bare contents of his stomach. He dared not look at Bug for fear of losing his temper at the sight of her.

"Yes," she said simply. "I'll get the box open, but you can wake her now. Probably better that way." The faint clacking of keys started up as Bug worked at the nearby computer.

Caster gathered his bearings, spit on the floor to clear the sick from his mouth, and returned to the unit. The movement of Wren's hair was mesmerizing, looking as though an intangible wind continually licked through it gently. He rapped his knuckles on the glass.

Wren's whole body twitched once, and she slowly took control of her limbs. With a wide sweep of her arm, she moved her hair from her face. Her eyes were hazy, tired, and he wondered if she realized she was actually awake. Even when she met his gaze, the only hint of recognition in her expression was the slightest of sad smiles, the smile of someone looking at a picture of memories long past. Not Wren's eyes.

"I'm here," he tried to say, but it stuck in his throat. He cleared it and tried again. "I'm here." He put his hand against the cool glass. The amethyst tied to his wrist popped out of his coat sleeve.

She spotted the stone and perked up a little. She pointed to him, then to her head.

He chuckled as he wiped at his nose. "Are you kidding? Of course I remembered. Been holding onto it for you."

She groggily put her own hand up to his on her side of the glass, letting it curl instead of pressing it flat.

Bug typed furiously. "Come on. Come on!"

"Why isn't it opening?" Caster said.

"I'm trying." A dissonant tone sounded from the computer, and Bug sank into her shoulders as if she might pass out. "Oh no."

Caster reluctantly left Wren and put an arm around Bug's shoulders to steady her. "What's wrong?"

"I don't have clearance to open the unit. She never did trust me after all."

"Who?" Caster asked.

Bug began to cry. "Eydis."

As soon as she said it, the squawking of the alarm system went off. It was faint here below the Main House, but Caster felt it reverberating through the walls of the chamber. They'd been found out. Or something else was wrong upstairs. Either way, they were out of time.

"Bug, get her out. Now!" he said.

"I can't," she moaned.

Caster went back to Wren and started examining the box. It was smooth with no visible hinges, but he knew that there was an invisible seal along the front right edge of the box from the last time they'd been in the lab together. A time that felt like a thousand years ago.

Her eyes cleared as she watched him, and panic sent her limbs flailing before she braced her hands against the sides of the box. She shook her head at him and crossed her arms over her chest as she moved to the back of the unit.

"We have to go," he said, voice thick at the sight of her recoiling from him. "I'm sorry it took me so long. I'm sorry for everything." Her face pinched, and if she hadn't been surrounded by liquid, Caster suspected he could have seen her tears. "Let's get you out of here," he begged. "Far away from this box and this city. Please?"

She hesitated.

"We can do this together," he said tenderly. "We can do anything together. Don't you think?"

She didn't move, and he thought she might not respond at all, but then she kicked at the seam of the box he'd been picking at. Her effort was half-hearted, but he nodded at her encouragingly nonetheless.

"We can do this," he said again. Her kicks gained more power. He pried at the edge, but his nails couldn't find any hold. He started hitting up and down it with his fists. The skin on his knuckles split, smearing blood on the glass before the wounds quickly closed. He tucked his shoulder and rammed into the box, heaving his weight against it to try to separate it from the platform and knock the whole thing over, but it stood firm.

He continued to push on the unit as he spoke to Bug. "They'll know you betrayed them. Get out."

There was a tap on his shoulder—Bug was holding out a small pry bar, something far better suited to opening packing crates than advanced tech. He tried to wedge it in the corner seam of the box over and over, desperate to find purchase, but the tool simply slipped off. Bug joined his efforts with a metal folding chair. She smacked it against the glass. The alarm continued sounding up above in the Main House.

"Someone will be down here any minute," Bug said as she wiped sweat from under her glasses. "We can't open it."

He shouted in frustration and threw down the pry bar. Bug put down her chair, and he snatched it. He took massive swings at the broad face of the glass. Wren moved again to the back side of the box while he hit its front. The barest of cracks appeared, but still it held. Caster heard the thumping of boots through the floor of the lab above.

Wren put both of her hands against the glass. "Go," she mouthed.

He breathed hard, a million options going through his head. Thousands of plans, all shot to nothing with one simple, inaudible word from her and the desperation in her eyes to see him get away safe.

"No," he said. He dropped the chair, put a hand over one of hers, and pressed his forehead against the glass.

She closed her eyes and rested her forehead against the inside of the box. They didn't move as the main door slammed open above and the clamor of boots made its way down the stairs behind him. Bullets racked into chambers and arrows nocked to bowstrings. The lab fell quiet, but Caster stayed still.

"I'm not angry, Bug. I know how much you care for her," said Eydis. Her heels tapped against the metal steps, descending gracefully.

"I couldn't do it anymore," Bug said almost to herself. Then her voice gained strength. "What are we doing down here? This is madness!"

"This is something beyond your comprehension, beyond even Thallium's. But it is not madness," Eydis replied, on the bottom level now. Caster heard her brush past the Keepers' robes. "These men belong to our new Principal. They're here to take over Wren's care."

Caster finally tore himself from Wren and turned to face Eydis and the others. Dal stood at the front of four Keepers, looking as happy as Caster had ever seen him—a big, ugly kid finally getting the present he'd always wanted. He held his spear at his shoulder, itching to throw it.

Caster knew that spear, still tainted with blood. It had just killed Adonis. He clenched his fists.

"Bug, come with me," said Eydis. "Things are going to get violent here momentarily."

Bug looked over at Caster, unsure.

Dal's stance and the tension in the room like a low hum had him convinced Eydis wasn't bluffing. "It's okay. Go," he said.

After a shaky adjustment of her glasses, Bug started walking toward Eydis. Bug stopped halfway to her and turned to Wren, but only opened and closed her mouth as if words were meaningless now. She reached Eydis, who put an arm around her. Eydis looked to Wren and spoke like they were the only two in the room. "You *can* control it, little one. Then, when it suits you, you can also let that control go. And now, you *need* to let go." She started up the stairs with Bug under her arm, who was unsteady on her feet.

The Keepers tightened their grips on their weapons.

Eydis and Bug ascended the second flight of stairs, and the android called down, "Kill Caster, by order of our new Principal."

The Keepers hesitated, possibly having second thoughts about their allegiance. All except Dal. "Yes, ma'am," he said.

Dal threw his spear, starting a chain reaction through the others, whose shots were erratic from the shock of what was happening. Caster dodged the spear mostly, but it caught the outside of his arm. Arrows followed, one in his outer thigh, another in his shoulder. A 12-gauge slug took his left arm off in pieces at the elbow just before a torrent of bird shot tore up his right side, making a mess of flesh and bone. The assault stopped, and a hushed silence fell as Caster dropped to his knees, fighting for breath amidst the pain.

"This wasn't necessary," one of them said.

"He's a dry branch on a dead family tree," Dal declared, the stiff words of a man echoing someone above him. "I'll finish it."

But before he could take more than a couple of steps, arrows and slugs fell to the floor en masse from Caster. His arm lay next to him, discarded like a forgotten toy, and he grimaced as he reached for it. It wobbled, awkward and heavy, before he held it still against what was left of his elbow. It knit itself neatly back together. Shreds of muscle and bits of bone regrew enough to fill in the gaps between what was left. Fresh skin covered it all. Multiple Keepers offered fearful prayers aloud.

Caster cursed under his breath when he felt the last wound seal over and stood to address his attackers, who looked on with dumb expressions that were admittedly understandable.

"Wren and I are leaving," said Caster. "I don't know or care who you're following, Dal—*I* have authority here, even if you don't like it. Stand down, all of you."

Everyone but Dal obeyed. "Always knew you were a freak."

"You have no idea how badly I want to kill you where you stand," Caster replied. "But if you don't leave, I'll never get the chance." He inclined his head back toward Wren. "She'll kill you first, and I don't want that burden for her. Take your men and go."

Dal peered around Caster at Wren and laughed. "Some secret weapon," he scoffed.

"Your new ruler wants this done," Eydis' voice came through the speakers of the room. Caster spotted her in the observation booth above. Bug stood next to her, pale and miserable.

Dal held his hand out to the Keeper on his right, who relinquished his shotgun to his superior.

"Kill Caster now," Eydis said, enunciating every word precisely. Caster realized she wasn't looking at the Keepers—she was watching for Wren's reaction to her words.

Caster followed Eydis' gaze. Caster started at the sight of Wren's eyes—they were a pure white with the barest purple halo in their centers, and in them was a rage that mirrored Caster's own at Eydis, Thallium, the world.

"Let's see if your *head* grows back," said Dal. He racked the shotgun.

Wren moved her hands over the hairline fracture in the glass that Caster had made with the chair earlier, and they began to glow. The liquid in the box undulated from an unseen tide.

"Everyone, get out! Get out now!" Caster shouted. But nobody moved, transfixed as they were by the Principal's mysterious weapon. Caster looked up—Eydis' smile was proud.

Bubbles rose from Wren's feet to the top of the box as if the liquid were boiling, and her white eyes stared. Purple light came from her hands and the smallest trace snuck through the crack in the glass. Her whole body was consumed by the light, which turned white. The heat of the tiny portion escaping the box was incredible.

"Get out!" Caster called again, this time charging at the Keepers.

They finally fumbled toward the stairs, Dal shoving ahead of the others, but it was too late. The isolation unit shattered, not breaking to pieces as much as evaporating, and the green liquid splashed to the floor. Wren continued to float like the liquid was still all around her. The woman Caster knew was completely gone, replaced by a creature of light and pain. Once she returned to herself, she would have to carry the weight of the lives she took tonight. That weight could crush her.

Caster changed direction and ran toward her. "Stop! Wren, no!"

Her head shot back, and she released a wet, grating cry that wasn't entirely human. Ribbons of white heat snapped out from her. They whipped past Caster and struck the Keepers, who disintegrated into nothingness with the sound of a sharp exhale that shook the air. The space they'd once occupied was replaced by a vacuum; not even their ashes remained. Dal's eyes widened in horror as he watched two of his men fall before a ribbon ran through him at the spine, and after just a half-second's worth of tremendous pain twisted his face, he vanished, reduced to a fading shimmer in the air.

When the Keepers were all gone, the light faded back into Wren, looking much like a creature both separate from and tied to her. It returned to her, grabbing hold of her core and pulling itself back inside while she floated above the isolation unit's platform. Once the light had receded, she collapsed. Her knees slammed against the edge of the platform as she fell forward to slide around on the green fluid covering the smooth floor.

One of Caster's feet slid on the fluid as he dove for her, but he caught his balance before he could fall flat out. He gently turned her onto her back and put his ear near her mouth—no breath. But before he could give her a breath of his own, she stirred, turned her head to the side, and heaved up a green stream.

"It's all right. Great job, just breathe," he said as she coughed raggedly. He pulled her into his lap and held her tightly.

She finally stopped coughing and took a couple of awkward breaths like this was the first time she'd tasted air. Caster swept her hair from her face, and she looked up at him groggily. She whispered, "You're really here?"

He put his forehead against hers, nothing between them now. "I'm here."

They rested in each other's presence, and a peace filled Caster that finally made the painful anger of the past month fade to a dull ache. He could stay like this forever.

"Caster," came Eydis' voice through the speaker system.

He looked up at her peering down from the observation booth. Bug wept beside her, and Caster couldn't tell if it was out of relief or horror.

"More are coming," Eydis said, all android calmness. "Behind you is a tunnel. It's hidden beneath the fifth tile from the left against the far wall. It's your only way out now. When you reach the surface, cut a block over. Take the south evacuation exit—you have clearance."

A hundred questions ricocheted in his head, but none of

them mattered. There was no time to doubt Eydis' motives or her truthfulness. He thought only of getting Wren out.

"When she wakes, tell her something for me," Eydis said. Her voice sounded tinny in the giant space. "The stars are waiting—northwest of here where Queen Cassiopeia dips beneath the horizon. I wanted to take her myself, but she'll have to go on her own now. The Cleaner will know her. It's the only safe place for her now."

Not one word of what Eydis had said made sense, but the stomping in the lab overhead—more boots running—didn't allow him time to question any of it. Caster supported Wren's back with one arm as he shrugged out of his black coat, which he then tucked around her shoulders before taking her in his arms as he stood. She felt heavier than he'd expected, weighed down by something unseen. Something he could never understand. He didn't look back at the observation booth as he carefully stepped through the remnants of the liquid toward the back of the lab and broke into a run.

The hidden hatch came up easy enough, and Caster prepared to drop down with Wren bundled securely in his grip. The light from the lab spilled into the tunnel entrance and showed it wasn't too far of a fall. He braced himself, tucked Wren closer, and jumped.

The hatch fell back into place above, leaving them in total darkness. His breath sounded painfully loud in the tunnel. It was just tall enough for him to stand without hitting the top of his head, but Wren's feet brushed against the tunnel's edge as he ran with her. Had he not been a Scout, he wouldn't have been able to see a thing. Since he was, he saw dark gray nothingness rather than black nothingness. Not much better.

He had absolutely no plan beyond this—put one foot after the next. Repeat. They had no supplies, no weapon except his bowie. Wren didn't even have clothes. He'd have to hide her until he could reunite with his men and regroup. With Asha and Gavel gone, Adonis dead, and his other men MIA, it was difficult to know where to start. He could take Wren to Asha and Gavel's place—Asha had probably left clothes behind that would work for Wren, and their place was as safe as anywhere else. Which was to say, not very. But he couldn't just leave The Disc, abandoning his men to fight the battle he'd dragged them into. He would help them as soon as he found someone he trusted to take Wren far from here.

Wren had barely enough energy to hold her head against Caster's chest. She was awake, though, and that seemed as good a sign as any. Just as he was about to tell her his scrap of a plan, noise up ahead in the tunnel stopped him.

He froze and dropped to a crouch, holding Wren atop his knees as he listened and watched. There were vague shapes of people moving in formation up ahead. Silent, focused. From here, he couldn't make out their faces.

Whoever it was must have heard him too because their footsteps—multiple sets of them—ceased.

He tried to put Wren down, but she clung to him when he did. His coat began to slide off of her, and he tugged it back on. He couldn't fight with her in his arms but refused to drop her. With no other option, he resorted to something his father had taught him—even when you're powerless, don't let anyone else know *you know* you are.

"Who's there?" he called ahead, hoping he sounded confident. "Reveal yourself by order of the Principal."

The high, rolling laughter that came back at him brought a familiar foul taste to his mouth, but with it came relief. "That you, prince boy?" asked Survivor. The person at the front of the group continued toward him, and he could make out a few of her features—short stature, wild hair darker than their surroundings. She smelled better than she used to.

She took a sniff of her own. "Oh yeah, that's you. Why are you on the floor?" She bent down and felt Wren in his arms. "You're not as useless as I thought, blond one. Give her to me." Survivor reached for Wren as Caster stood, but Wren whimpered when she did.

"She needs to rest," he said.

Survivor's spittle hit his face as she argued. "She can rest when we're out of this oozing cyst of a city and safe in the Open."

"She won't be *safe* anywhere," he said slowly, hoping she would hear the certainty in his tone. He'd seen what they'd done to Wren—Survivor had no idea.

Survivor returned his intensity, confidently declaring, "She'll be safe with me."

He thought about that and decided she was right—Survivor would defend her sister to the death. He'd watched her do it before. If *he* couldn't take Wren from this place, Survivor was the next best choice. "You have everything you need to take care of her?"

"I have more than you could imagine."

Caster resisted the urge to ask how that was possible when, last he'd heard, she was in hiding in the Open with little more than the clothes on her back. "Good. I'll escort you to the back gate." He started to walk.

Survivor stood in his path. "We know the way." She reached underneath Wren as if to scoop her from his grip.

Wren's hands clasped tight at Caster's neck, and Survivor shook her head disgustedly.

"We're on the same side," said Caster. "Let me help you leave."

Survivor hesitated, and Caster suspected it wasn't because she didn't trust him, but because she hated him. Hated him not only for who he was related to, but also because *Wren* cared for *him*.

"Wren? Can you hear me?" Another voice spoke. A second figure with stooped shoulders came closer and reached down to touch the top of Wren's head. Caster couldn't make out the details of her face, but he still recognized her from when he'd shared Wren's dreams with her in the lab—Alma.

When Wren heard her, she loosened her grip on Caster and turned toward the sound. "Ma?"

"We've got to go," Alma said gently. "Caster's going to take you out of here so we can leave the city."

"It's a dream," Wren said as she relaxed in Caster's arms. "Good. Nobody can get hurt in a dream. Not really," she babbled.

Survivor cursed but smacked Caster's arm companionably. "Keep up, prince. If you can."

As Caster adjusted her weight in his arms, Wren realized that the burning in her lungs and how weak she felt likely meant that this was not, in fact, a dream. As much as she wished it were for the safety of everyone huddled in the dark with her.

"After you," Caster said to Survivor.

Then they were running. Wren couldn't see any of them, but she could sense them, just as she had felt Caster's energy above her in the lab after she'd woken from a nightmare. Each of them hummed uniquely, and she recognized both Survivor and Alma just from the way it felt to be near them. Survivor burned, putting out excited pulses that felt like a steady drumbeat. Alma felt more like a rhyming poem with a rhythm practiced and perfected over time. There were three other people with them, but all Wren felt when she sensed them was cold order.

"Almost there," Survivor whispered.

But then they slid to a stop—a pool of moonlight appeared in the tunnel just ahead as the scraping of metal came their way. Someone had opened a hatch in the top of the tunnel. A shadow blocked out a section of the moonlight. Caster and Survivor, who were at the front of the group, dropped back against the walls of the tunnel. Gently, Caster set Wren on the ground and helped her sit against the wall. He took out his knife and waited.

A blue beam of light illuminated the ladder and floor, searching. Across from Wren, Survivor tensed and soundlessly withdrew a machete from her waist like a scorpion angling to strike.

"Caster? You down there?" came a man's voice.

Caster exhaled and put his weapon away. He waved at Survivor to lower hers. "A friend," he said. He stepped into the light and shielded his eyes against it as he looked up. "Ollie. How'd you find me?"

Ollie gave a creaky groan up above. "Ah, it's you, kid. Been checking every manhole, dumpster, and alleyway. Figure you've stepped full on into the light after what happened in the market today. They'll be after you. Keepers are everywhere— hurry." He gave a tired wave upward.

Caster returned to Wren. "Can you hold onto my back?"

She wasn't actually sure if she could, but she nodded anyway. He reluctantly took his coat from her and held it open. The cold shocked her skin, almost took her breath. Her muscles should have been too tired to shiver, but they did anyway. After he'd buttoned the coat all the way down to her knees, he crouched as low as he could. She wrapped her arms and legs around his back before he stood, though her hold on him was shoddy.

Survivor stopped him and whispered. "Who is this guy?"

"An ally. Wants Thallium out of power as much as we do." He hiked Wren's weight up a little higher.

Survivor dug her fingers into Caster's forearm and hissed, "Enough to stick his neck out for you in the middle of anarchy in your streets? And how the hell did he find you?"

Caster hesitated, then said, "Alma, you first."

The look Alma gave Survivor was all too familiar—it was the same one they used to exchange when danger was near but they didn't want to scare the kids. Line between her brow, cutting focus in her eyes, but a tight smile that disarmed anyone not in the know. Survivor nodded in response, affirming her concern, then helped Alma begin her ascent up the ladder.

Survivor's three other companions were still in the dark— Wren could barely make out the toes of their boots. Survivor put a hand up, signaling for them to wait. The edges of their boots retreated farther.

Survivor followed after Alma as if there were a cord tying them together. It made Wren smile to see the closeness between them just as it had been before the fire. Before everything had changed. Now that they were together again, maybe not everything from before was lost. Hope for that roused her enough to tighten her grip against Caster as he climbed rung by rung up the ladder.

Heat flowed from his back to her front. She'd dreamed of feeling his closeness again, and now that she did, she'd do anything not to be separated from it. From the way he grabbed hold of her waist immediately after she got off his back above ground, she thought that he might feel the same.

Wren couldn't tell where they were, exactly. Outside of the Main House grounds, somewhere behind it, she supposed.

Ollie waved in the direction of an awning to their left, and all five of them went as fast as they were able to its cover. Parts of buggies and Quick Carts with no engines lay all around, towers of packing crates, metal sheets. A storage place.

Ollie gave a low whistle—four men emerged from behind boxes and parts and converged on them.

"My men have been helping me look for you ever since the tragedy at the market," said Ollie. He had a kind face, and he wore a red jumpsuit that looked brown in the dark. "You're slipperier than you look." He gave Caster a friendly nudge.

Caster got Wren settled on a plastic rain barrel. Survivor and Alma stood at her sides, each with an arm around her back. Caster pushed Wren's wet hair behind her ears, then turned to face Ollie. "Do you remember what you said? That you wished I would just walk away from my cause?"

"I do," Ollie said after a pause.

"I still don't intend to. But I have to help Wren get out of here first."

Ollie waggled his fingers at Wren like he'd been dying to meet her. It made her stomach turn. "Well, I can appreciate that, Caster. I truly can. But from the sound of things out here, I'd say it'd be risky to try. Don't you think? I can help you hide her here in the city." His presence had hummed, steady as a stream, flowing out of him and back like a loop. But it turned choppy now. Tension disrupted it. All of his men behind him put out similar energy—jagged and anxious, like shards of glass waiting for a foot. Their gazes flicked to her as if they were having a hard time not staring.

Wren tugged at Caster's sleeve. He bent down and she whispered through her shivers, "We need to go. He's not safe."

Caster gave a slow nod and kissed her forehead. When he faced Ollie again, he kept his back so close to Wren that it pressed against her knees. "Thanks for the hand in the tunnel. I left my men fighting in the market—can you join up with them? My Body's Assassin and Thief will be able to tell you how to best deploy your men. We need to get civilians safely in their homes until this fight is over, and it won't last just one night. I'll find you after I get Wren out."

Ollie's men all took quarter steps forward, but stopped themselves when Ollie asked, "Where are you planning on going with her?"

"None of your damn business, jumpsuit," said Survivor, dropping her arm from Wren to stand with Caster.

"Unfortunately, she's right," said Caster. "Better nobody knows where they're going, not even me. We just need to get to the evac tunnel without my father's men spotting us."

"Men? I don't have men anymore." Thallium's voice startled them all. He stepped out from behind a wheelless Quick Cart near the edge of the storage area. Nobody had heard him approach. He was armed with a rifle which he aimed not at Caster, but past him at Ollie and his guards. "Not after that stunt you pulled today, old friend."

Ollie's men pulled out weapons Wren hadn't noticed at first, tucked as they were beneath coats and behind their backs. Two rifles like Thallium's and two batons. The men clung to them as if it were a relief to finally have them on display.

"Thallium," said Ollie with a bow. "Surprised you're not sheltering in your silver tower after what you did to young Adonis in the street."

"Too busy beating down your fellow traitors on the way here." Thallium didn't take his eyes off of Ollie and the others, but it was clear he was speaking to Caster. "I didn't have that boy killed. Even if you think I'm pure evil, you know that I don't resort to such extreme measures unless there's something to gain by doing so. Hallund was a test of a weapon I thought would bring the Open under control. Wren was a project—"

"She's not your *project!*" Caster roared, and it sounded like he'd been holding in those exact words for a long time.

Thallium groaned and adjusted his grip on his rifle. "Yes, something I've come to realize was an overly simplistic view, but shut up and let me finish. Wren *was* a project to the same end—giving our city, and myself as its ruler, an advantage. What would killing your friend give me? Your hatred. The anger of everyone in this city. What's the question you always need to ask yourself in these situations where you don't know who to trust?"

Caster shuffled around and widened his stance. "Who stands to gain?" he replied as if from a lesson learned long ago.

Thallium touched his own nose with his finger before resting it near the trigger again. "That's it. Who gains from making me look like a monster?"

Survivor snorted.

"Fine. *More* of a monster, if that makes you happy, you Marauder brat," said Thallium.

"I'll be happy when you're hanging by your guts from the main post of my tent," said Survivor.

"Ooh, vivid image. I love it." He looked her up and down. "Nice to finally see you in the flesh, banged up as you are. Lovely new clothes, by the way. Blue almost makes you pass as human."

She took out her machete and leapt onto the back of an old buggy. "I can fix this complex political power struggle right now." She pointed her blade at Thallium. "Seems like nobody wants you around, Principal. Unlike these schemers, I have the balls to say it to your face—I want you dead. Have for a long time. Can we stop being bitches here and get down to it?"

Thallium's eyes widened, and he nodded approvingly. "Of everyone left in this world, who would have thought that you,

The Gentleman's daughter, would earn my respect. You really have."

She mock curtsied to him, then a smile lit her face like Wren hadn't seen since she'd torn through the guards when she'd broken out of prison the last time she was in The Disc—absolute bliss coupled with absolute rage. Both were so loud that they rattled Wren's bones. Emotions that powerful should have combusted when they collided, but somehow, within Survivor, they were in perfect harmony. She'd been looking forward to this.

"While I would love to shoot that smirk off of your dirt-smeared face," Thallium continued, "this isn't about the hatred you harbor for me—join the club. It's hardly exclusive. There's only one person's love I care about, and he's standing behind you at this very moment with a woman I harmed pressed against his back and a pack of traitors around him in the form of our noble Head of Agua's men. Perhaps, just for now, you could help me get him and your sister out of here? I promise to kill you another day."

The way they communicated was odd, as though they spoke a language that the others were only vaguely familiar with. One thing was clear—as much as these two people despised each other, there shared a mutual respect of power. Because that's what they were both made of at their core, what they embodied more than any of the rest of those present —power.

"I left Adonis with you, Ollie," Caster said, clearly and calmly above any threats flying between Wren's sister and his father. "With him so well insulated by your men, how could my father have grabbed him to then put him up for public execution? And at the hand of Dal, who I know was against the Valcins."

Ollie stared at Caster for a moment, considering how to

answer. "He wasn't my prisoner, Caster. Adonis came and went as he pleased. Thallium's men must have taken him when he was away."

Caster shook his head. "No. He wasn't taken last night because, if he had been, you would have told me he was missing this morning. Either he was taken today, or he wasn't allowed to leave the plant last night." He spoke as if he was working out the details in the moment, and he grew angrier with each revelation. "I gave him an assignment; he would have followed it. Every detail, every request. I asked him to stay near you. To assist you, learn what he could so that he could reach his goals faster."

Ollie watched him silently, waiting for the hammer to hit the final nail.

"That's exactly what he did, isn't it?" Caster shouted. "And you fucking killed him!" Wren felt his rage passing from his body to hers, even pulsing through the ground on which he stood. She felt it as though it were a tangible, living thing. Maybe it was.

Ollie's expression dropped, revealing his prior friendliness as a mask. "I told you back in my office that people you cared about would die for your cause. You knew the cost of your actions. You should know that the boy didn't suffer. He served a purpose that was grander than anything he could have accomplished on his own—inspiring change that this city has needed ever since your father was born and a rotting legacy began. Why couldn't you reject that legacy like I begged you to?"

Caster turned and lifted Wren off the rain barrel as if she weighed no more than a toddler. He set her on the ground and encouraged Alma to sit with her, tight and tucked between barrels and boxes.

He stood, took his knife from his belt, and nodded to Survivor, then to his father. "Together?"

Thallium's grin spread from ear to ear. He returned the nod.

Survivor rolled her eyes. "Let's get this over with."

The three of them ran at Ollie's men.

Ollie shouted out above the excitement, "Get the weapon!"

Seeing Survivor, Caster, and Thallium fight was like watching a dust storm converge on a structure—total chaos bent on destroying everything in its path. Caster had never seemed so angry, and it was clear in the way he hardly tried to defend himself that he'd given over trust of his body to Eydis' meddling. The changes she'd made did their job—he was cut and restitched, hit and recovered, over and again by the biggest of Ollie's men that tried to get around him to Wren. Caster's next strike sent his knife up under the man's ribs, and he finally dropped. Caster kept trying to get past his attackers to Ollie, who had stepped back and higher up onto a tiered stack of metal beams to give orders rather than join the fight.

Any rust Thallium might have felt as a long-time ruler and long-gone fighter he shook off within the first couple of blows he landed against Ollie's best and brightest—he tore through the two men rushing at him with perfect shots of blue energy from his rifle at their chest and heads. Two to the heart, one to the forehead, and they dropped immediately, surrendering to the dirt. He too had eyes only for Ollie.

Survivor—she was just having fun. It was as if she'd been craving this almost as much as getting Wren out of confine-ment. Wren knew that, after love, she dreamed of death. Her own and those of others who didn't deserve to keep living. Always had, and she was looking for it this evening. She ripped through a man with machete swings into bone and muscle, intent on leaving smears rather than a corpse.

Ollie whistled twice, and if it hadn't been clear before, it was completely clear now—he was out for blood. Another wave of men and women came from alleyways and the shadowy sides of buildings. Some wore the striped robes of Keepers, others wore jumpsuits like Ollie's, and there were at least ten of them.

Caster shouted in frustration from the midst of his own fight when two men in jumpsuits headed for Alma and Wren. Survivor spotted them too, and in the minds of her fight, sang out a starling call Wren recognized. The men reached Wren and Alma. One of them managed to grip Wren's arm for just a second before a scarred Marauder appeared at her side and put the man and his friend down without mercy, slashing one across the chest. He elbowed the other in the head near his temple, and when the man stumbled, the Marauder removed his head entirely with multiple swift swings.

Two more Marauders emerged onto the scene and into battle, leaving the first to defend Wren and Alma. Within seconds, they had joined the fight near Survivor and taken out a man each, stabbing rapidly and without mercy. But the sheer number of Ollie's fighters stood out plainly, and there was no way Survivor's men would be enough to win this fight. As talented as Caster and his father were, as ruthless as Survivor was, quantity would trump quality here.

They weren't going to make it.

Before Wren realized what was happening, her hands started to glow purple. She felt it as a stretch of overtired muscles, and the effort made her limbs turn cold and her vision go dark.

Alma smacked her cheek lightly. "Absolutely not, child. Not now. If you kill these people, the effort could kill *you*."

Another man in a red jumpsuit separated from the fighting to run toward Alma and Wren, bellowing when he confronted the Marauder waiting for him. The Marauder took him out easily, but neither he nor Wren saw the Keeper coming up from behind. A burst of light left a hole through the Marauder's chest. The smell of cooked flesh rose into the air as he collapsed.

The Keeper with the rifle went to yank Wren up by her elbow. Alma bit his arm, and he grunted but didn't let go until a strike from a staff to the back of his head knocked him unconscious.

Prady stood there, and seeing him made Wren want to cry. He fought to catch his breath and ushered the women back against the barrier of the barrels and bins. He took the Marauder's position at their front. "Are you all right?" he asked Wren without looking back.

"It's good to see you," she said. Everything in her wanted to stand to embrace Prady, but Alma kept her hold tight around her waist.

Prady took his gaze from Ollie's men just long enough to give her a smile over his shoulder. "Made you a promise, didn't I?"

He pivoted as the swing of a baton came in from one of Ollie's men, and Prady shoved him back with the end of his staff. The man faltered, and Prady's blow to the side of his face sent him sprawling. Prady swayed on his feet. He wouldn't last much longer at this pace.

Wren's hands began to glow faintly. This time, she would push past her body's protests.

When Caster saw Prady, he debated for just a split second before turning his attention back on Ollie and trusting Prady to protect Wren. He and Thallium headed for Ollie on his stack of beams. Thallium raised the sight of his rifle to his eye as he ran. Caster saw what he was going to do and dove for a man coming at Thallium from behind. Thallium took the moment to stop running and exhale, then fire at Ollie. It was a sure shot, headed square for Ollie's chest, but one of his men stepped in the burst's path and took it instead. When Thallium fired again, the gun clicked. Out of charge.

Ollie looked unsurprised by everything. He stood above like all this had been inevitable and he was simply watching it finally unfold. He'd killed Adonis—mutilated him—and he just stood up there as if he hadn't had a choice in the matter and the burden of sin wasn't his to bear.

While they tried to regroup, Caster fought against his father's back, a position he hadn't been in since before his mother had died. A position he never thought he'd be in again. Thallium used his rifle as a blunt instrument. Caster sank his bowie behind the collarbone of a Keeper. He recognized her; she'd started in her post in the Main House right before Caster left it at eighteen. One of countless others who agreed with Ollie that the time of the Valcin dynasty was over. Most of Ollie's fighters left standing weren't water workers, but Keepers. Ollie had gathered more to his side than Caster would have ever imagined. And he'd completely missed it.

Caster glanced back in Ollie's direction—two more Keepers had taken up position next to him as he smugly watched this shit show.

"We can't get to him," Caster said.

"No. But it looks like Wren thinks she can," said Thallium. He tugged at Caster's elbow to urge him to turn around.

Caster's heart dropped.

Wren was floating with her feet off the ground, standing casually on nothing at all, radiating purple light. It poured out from beneath his long black coat. When that light turned white, he knew that not only would Ollie die, but they all could, including Wren. Her body couldn't take another outburst like the one in the lab.

"I have to get her out of here," said Caster.

Thallium withdrew a knife from under his coat and threw it across Caster's chest at a Keeper heading for them. Once the Keeper dropped, Thallium grabbed the back of his son's neck and yanked him close. Sweat poured from him, plastering strands of hair to his face that had fallen out of the tie. "I need you to know—I did love your mother. As much as I'm capable of it, I love you too." He kissed him roughly on the forehead. "Go get Wren."

He shoved Caster in Wren's direction, then sprinted all out toward Ollie with a jubilant cry. Nearby Keepers turned their attention to him. Caster hesitated only long enough for the shock of what his father was doing to sink in before running toward Wren.

He passed Survivor, whose Marauders lay dead amidst a slew of bodies. Survivor sat atop the shoulders of a man easily a foot and a half taller than her with her legs wrapped around his neck. A wide spot of her dress near her shoulder was singed through, and blood poured down her sleeve as she held that arm limply. Another rifle wound marred her left knee. She saw where Caster was headed and snapped the man's neck with a hand on either side of his jaw. She was up and running with a limp before the dead man had time to slump to the ground.

"Just let Wren take them all out!" she yelled as she came up alongside Caster.

"No. She can't handle that right now. Trust me."

She didn't argue, and with Survivor, that meant something. "We have transport outside. South gate."

They reached Wren just as the light changed from purple to white.

One of Prady's fellow Keepers slid under his strike and swept his leg. Prady fell to the ground. The Keeper hesitated as if he didn't want to kill the man at his feet but was urged by duty nonetheless. Then the man saw Wren floating higher and higher, the light within her turning pale.

He ran.

"Child, listen to me!" Alma shouted. "We're done here. You need to stop this before you do damage that can't be taken back. These are *people*. You will regret taking their lives."

Wren looked down at her. Alma had no idea what she'd already done, nor what she was feeling at that moment. Through tears that dried in the heat before they could fall from her face, Wren said, "But I *want* to."

Alma's look from her nightmare, her retreating in shock, became reality. She was back, finally back, and Wren horrified her. Wren would do anything to make that horror go away.

She willed the power to stop, pulling it in as if she were tugging on a hundred ropes stretched in all directions. It fought back, but she persisted. Her raw lungs burned as she held her breath and strained under the effort. Then, it felt like the ropes snapped, and the light went out. Caster caught her as she fell in an exhausted heap of limbs. She was so very tired.

After a quick check to make sure Wren was breathing, Caster said to Alma and Survivor. "Take her and go. Prady and I will guard your escape." He passed her carefully to Survivor, who heaved Wren onto her good shoulder. But when she tried to stand, her wounded leg buckled, and she nearly fell over.

She grimaced, tried again, and did fall that time. Caster guided her and Wren to the ground.

Survivor sat up and looked down at Wren with both frustration and love, hair wild as ever. "Get up and walk, you tall freak. My hurt ass isn't up for carrying you."

Wren started to sit up, but her vision grew fuzzy. The faces of those above her—four people she truly loved—faded to black. The next thing she knew, Caster was standing with her in his arms once more.

He looked to Prady. "I have to get her out. Come with me—we'll come back when she's safe."

Prady tried to cover up how hard he was breathing and nodded.

The five of them started running, Survivor and Prady pulling up the rear, both limping. Alma kept ahead of them, silver braid thumping against her back. Wren's vision went in and out, but around Caster's back, she managed to spot Thallium on his knees next to Ollie in the distance. Two Keepers had him by the arms. She tugged at Caster's shirt until he turned to see Ollie bash his father's head in with a baton. Thallium went slack between the Keepers' hold. Caster gripped Wren tighter. She felt the sorrow rise in his chest, thick and heavy.

But then, the dent on the side of Thallium's skull snapped back out, and Wren swore that, even from this far away, she could hear the bone fragments crunching as they ground against one another and into their proper places. Thallium looked up at Ollie and laughed like a madman.

Caster was shocked, but he didn't have long to take in what had happened before two Keepers were nearly on them. Prady saw them coming and stopped. "I'll cover your exit, sir." He stood unsteadily, and he'd barely been able to get the words out.

Caster stopped, and his attention went to Prady's deep limp. "You can make it. We're nearly there."

Prady put his hand to his heart. "My duty is to protect you. Both of you." He bowed to Wren, showing her the top of his gray head. "Take care, miss." He smiled warmly, then faced the oncoming Keepers, giving Caster and Wren a view of his striped back straightening for one final fight.

Caster ran, while all Wren could do was watch helplessly as the image of Prady swinging his staff faded into the distance. She saw him go down. He didn't get back up. Someone was screaming, and it took Wren a moment to realize it was her.

The city lights faded, as did the clamor of battle. They passed through a tunnel after Survivor swiped some kind of key in the wall. Caster put Wren down on the back seat of a buggy and fastened her in. He sat next to her, wrapped his arm tight around her shoulders, and then they were speeding away. The Disc grew smaller like a shrinking bowl of light in the haze of dust trailing behind the buggy. Up above, a cloud passed in front of the moon. In the renewed darkness of the sky, the stars had never felt so close.

We've emerged from the Open once again! Thank you for going on this adventure with me. Glasses of Incendio all around!

Do you know how much your review of *Blood for Blood* would mean to me? More than I can say! As an indie author, I value every single review. I sure hope you loved this book, but regardless, would you please leave a review online wherever you purchased it? It only takes a quick minute for you to make a real difference in the life of this author.

I can't tell you how much I appreciate your readership. I would LOVE to hear from you! Have questions or thoughts about The Disc Chronicles? My contact info is at the end of this book. Let's chat!

Best,

Madeleine

CREDITS

The wonderful people listed below helped bring this book to life. Madeleine would like to thank...

David Mozley: Husband, best friend, and ultimate encourager. You're the real hero of this story.

Josiah Davis: Editor extraordinaire who helped convince me that this series might just be worth reading.

James Schlavin: Cover artist and designer, who possesses more visual prowess than I can say.

Sheri Coen: Eager beta reader and the very best mom. It's from you that I learned perseverance, and I used every ounce of it working on this book. Thank you!

Melissa Burnham: Sister and proofreader. If I missed a typo, it's your fault. Also, I love you.

Rachelle Clifford: Proofreader with an extraordinary gift for storytelling that I aspire to emulate...and am only a little jealous of.

Tracy Jones: Awesome friend and design expert. Thank goodness for your talented eyes!

Killian Coen: Brother whose combat expertise helps keep the action rolling.

Ben Clifford: PA whose dedication to medical accuracy in fiction keeps us writers honest.

ACKNOWLEDGMENTS

The writing life is a strange one. Thankfully, there are a bunch of people who keep Madeleine grounded. She'd like to thank...

The Author of Life. Thank You for allowing this hobby of mine to appear in my life's story. I hope I can show just a sliver of Your astounding grace in my writing.

David...again. And always.

My beautiful children. Some day, a long time from now, I hope you'll read this series and get even one ounce of the entertainment and joy you give me.

Thomas Umstattd Jr. and James L. Rubart, the OGs of publishing who continue to inspire and challenge me.

Dan Smith, Kat Caldwell, and so many other awesome authors I've met along this publishing journey who prove we don't have to live this crazy writer's life alone.

You, my dear reader. You breathe life into these characters with the power of your mind. I hope they bless you as you have blessed me by picking up this book.

ABOUT THE AUTHOR

Madeleine Mozley is a desert-dwelling word fiend. She lives in New Mexico with her husband, kiddos, and fur babies. Her desire to put green chile into everything she cooks can't be contained.

If you'd like to connect with Madeleine, you may:
- Visit her website MadeleineMozley.com.
- Email her at MadeleineMozley@gmail.com.
- Find her on Instagram, Goodreads, and YouTube.